Praise for The

"If you enjoy a rollicking good romance story, you'll love Best Dating Rules as much as I did."
Carol Marrs Phipps, Author
The Heart of the Staff Series

"The line between smut and puritanism has rarely been tweaked so enchantingly, with just the right amount of yearning and heat applied in all the right places that makes the Best Girls books suitable for young-hearted romantics of any age."
Jan Hawke, Author
Milele Safari: An Eternal Journey

"Dearen elicits laughter, gasps and even tears. The emotion which she imbues to her characters is enchanting."
Scotty Shepherd

Books by Tamie Dearen

Sweet Romance

The Best Girls Series:
The Best is Yet to Come
Her Best Match
Best Dating Rules
Best Foot Forward
Best Laid Plans
Best Intentions

Sweet Romance

A Rose in Bloom

Christian Romance

Noelle's Golden Christmas
Haley's Hangdog Holiday

The Alora Series
YA/Fantasy

Alora: The Wander-Jewel
Alora: The Portal
Alora: The Maladorn Scroll

Her Best Match

Her Best Match
by Tamie Dearen

Copyright © 2013 Tamie Dearen

ISBN-13: 978-1975846206

ISBN-10: 1975846206

Her Best Match

The Best Girls Series
Book One

By

Tamie Dearen

To Ann Vassallo, my third grade teacher, who taught me to love writing.

Acknowledgements

Undying thanks to all my early readers: Nancy, Heidi, Alyssa, Emily, Wesley, Kay, Mom, Courtney, Sarah, and Carol. Your encouragement kept me going, and some of you even took the time to mark mistakes for me. I'm also indebted to Avery, who edited and formatted and worked to put this book online for her computer-challenged mother. And most of all, I need to thank my sweet husband, Bruce, who calls himself a writer's widow. He inspired me with romance, acted as primary reader and consultant, and battled jealousy as I spent endless hours, late into the night, in an intimate affair… with my computer.

Special Thanks

God gives us unexpected gifts that keep on giving. My pot-luck (heavy on the luck) college roommate, Katherine Dinsdale is one of those gifts. She's talented and funny, and she's an amazing author. When I started writing, Katherine not only encouraged me, but also did some point-by-point editing, with corrections and suggestions for improvement. I've learned so much from Katherine, and not just about writing. She's one of the kindest, most giving people I know. Thanks, Katherine! You're the best!

Chapter One - Interview

ANNE TRIED VAINLY to stop her knees from trembling, pushing on her legs with her hands. But her hands were shaking, too. Was it because the reception area was too cold? Or was it because her rivals were too intimidating? She shivered in her short-sleeved beige cotton blouse and straight brown linen skirt as she glanced around, sizing up the competition. What was she thinking when she agreed to this interview? She didn't really stand a chance of landing this job. The room was filled with twenty-somethings. Nine other women and two men were vying for the same executive assistant position. Without exception, the other applicants were impeccably dressed in smart business attire and carrying leather attachés that stored their MacBooks, iPads, and iPhones. Somehow each one looked beautiful and confident, as if stepping out of the pages of some style magazine.

She attempted to smooth her skirt, hopelessly creased from the long cab ride across Manhattan. Why had she chosen to wear linen, knowing how badly it wrinkled? But she knew the answer. When the recruiter called about an interview in two days' time, she'd packed hurriedly, throwing in every skirt she owned—a total of three. Only after arriving at the hotel in New York, two hours before her appointment did she realize that only one skirt still fit her. And that one only barely.

For the fifteen years since her husband died in an accident with a drunk driver, Anne Best had thrown herself into raising her two daughters. But once both daughters were out of the house and independent, she discovered she'd lost interest in ordinary activities. Activities like eating and shopping. So she had no alternative but to wear the linen skirt, which hung loosely on her hips and fell to an unflattering length just below her knees.

She tried to look nonchalant while grabbing the yellow legal pad that was slipping from her lap. But when the pencil slipped from the pages of the pad and rolled across the floor, she cringed at the disdainful glances directed her way. Why didn't she have some sort of briefcase like the others? To one particularly haughty glare, she returned a scalding look like she would give a misbehaving child in public. The girl gasped and quickly averted her eyes.

At two o'clock on the dot, a pair of large carved wooden double-doors swung open and a secretary invited the first candidate to enter the inner sanctum. The beautiful blonde's three-inch heels clicked on the marble as she strode confidently into the interview. From her manicured nails to her elegantly stylish coif and vogue skirt suit, she looked flawless, and Anne hated her. Well, maybe she didn't exactly hate her, but she hated how old and frumpy she felt in comparison. Children! They were all just children! Of course they looked beautiful and perfect and firm everywhere. It wasn't fair—they didn't even have to try. Just wait until they'd been through real life for another twenty years. It was disheartening to realize her age, forty-five, made her old enough to have parented all the other candidates.

Anne pushed a stray hair behind her ear. She knew there were a few grays peeking through, but she'd never been bothered enough to start coloring the brown unruly masses that fell just past her shoulders when not confined to their usual barrette. She'd always thought her hair was one of her best features, but she felt outclassed as she compared her ten-dollar Supercut to the fashionable hairstyles that graced her challengers.

Yet again, she inwardly berated herself for even applying for this job. She had a home and a job in the small Texas town where she and Tom had settled after graduating from college. Granted, her job of fifteen years at the small travel agency provided little challenge. But she'd been happy enough working part-time while raising two daughters. Though now Tom was gone and both daughters had moved away from home permanently, there was little to hold her in Weatherford.

Since the girls left, she'd gone through the motions of life like a robot, not caring much about anything. Then recently, her old college roommate started bugging her to try something new, change jobs, make a move. Anne realized she could do something different with her life. And different sounded really good to her. So when the recruiter called at the last minute about this job interview in New York City, she decided she had nothing to lose. In the face of her competitors, however, she determined she'd lost something after all—her courage.

She startled as the wooden doors opened and Miss Clickety-Stilettos exited the room with her still self-assured smile. Another applicant was called into the office, leaving Anne in nervous contemplation. What was her potential boss like? Was he younger than she was? Would he scoff at the idea of hiring someone her age? What kind of questions would he ask? She wished fervently she'd studied the information in the email links she'd received from the recruiter. She'd assumed she didn't have a real chance of being hired, only coming on the interview as a lark. A chance to visit New York City! Now she regretted putting so little effort into preparation. She stared at her ragged fingernails to avoid the sight of the other too-perfect interviewees sitting across the reception area. Time dragged as one Barbie or Ken after another marched in to their meetings.

Finally, she was alone in the room. The previous interview had been over for a full ten minutes. Had they forgotten about her? Maybe her name wasn't even on their list. Maybe they didn't even realize she was out here. Had they already given the job to one of the others? Should she go and knock on the door? Or should she simply leave quietly? She considered herself a confident person, but this whole New York City interview experience was way out of her comfort zone. She'd even practiced speaking without a Texas accent, but her determined efforts had only produced snickers from her older neighbor, Minnie. That hadn't stopped her from encouraging Anne to go to New York City.

"Oh honey," she'd said. "This could be a once-in-a-lifetime opportunity. You've got to go!"

Suddenly the doors opened, and a deep stern voice spoke her name.

"Ms. Best!"

The voice resounded in her head. She stood up quickly and gathered her mettle. She maintained her composure despite a racing heart as she quietly entered through the foreboding doors. Ah, at least she wouldn't be alone for the interview. She noted a petite young woman pouring coffee for the man bending over the contents of the file on his desk in intense concentration. She could only see the top of his head since he didn't bother to look up when she entered. She waited quietly, studying his thick dark hair, peppered with grey. Anne threw a questioning look to the woman when the man continued to ignore her presence.

She offered a kind smile and indicated a chair opposite the desk.

"May I offer you some refreshments, Ms. Best? Coffee? Tea? Water?"

Anne was about to politely refuse and meekly take her seat, when the gentleman behind the desk spoke sternly.

"That won't be necessary, Ms. Carson. Please, leave us alone."

"Yes, Mr. Gherring," she murmured, heading for the door.

Anne felt the blood pounding in her head. She might not have any chance of being hired for this job in the face of her young, sleek competitors, but she would be treated with respect. She turned to stop the woman who was leaving the room.

"Wait… Ms. Carson? Please, wait. *Yes*, thank you, I would *love* some water."

Anne stared fixedly at the startled woman, who froze in place, and glanced hesitantly from her boss to Anne and back to her boss again. Silence hung like ice in the room. She felt his eyes boring into the back of her head.

"Well, Ms. Carson, what are you waiting for?" asked the man in a sarcastic voice. "Please retrieve some water at once for our honored patron, Ms. Pest."

Anne swirled around to face the man behind the desk, who now gave her his full attention.

"My name is Anne *Best*, and I can see this interview is a waste of my time and a waste of your resources. Sorry to have inconvenienced you!"

Anne shook with fury as she glared at Gherring, but it wasn't rage that took her breath away. The man was striking! He wasn't cute or handsome like a young, smooth-faced jock. His face seemed chiseled, and his jaw was strong. He had dimples that appeared as he flexed his jaw, without a hint of a smile on his face. He was the kind of guy whose looks only improved with age, and he'd obviously started off really well. How old was he? Maybe late forties or early fifties? He regarded her quietly with his intensely blue eyes. She kicked herself inwardly. How could she be attracted to this boorish, obnoxious man? He obviously felt his position of power gave him the right to treat others any way he pleased. Yet she felt tingly all over as he slowly perused her from head to toe.

Suddenly acutely aware of her rumpled, sub-standard appearance, her strange combination of vehemence and attraction was quickly replaced with acute embarrassment. She dropped her eyes and fumbled with her purse and legal pad as she began to slink out of the room, blinking back tears.

"I'm sorry, sir," she mumbled. "It was a mistake to come—"

"Wait!" demanded Gherring as she attempted to push past the assistant who was still frozen in shock. "I said, *wait*!" commanded the voice.

Anne hesitated a moment and glanced over her shoulder.

"Please!" he said, somehow having arrived right behind her. "I meant to say… *please wait*." He lowered his voice and spoke soothingly. "Please, Ms. Best, would you come back and sit down? I've obviously started off on the wrong foot with you. I've given you a bad impression."

He gently guided her to the interview chair, and motioned for the assistant to bring the water. He wore a satisfied smile as he sat back down, noticeably more comfortable as he gained control of the situation. "And you've given me an *interesting* impression as well."

Anne felt anything but in control. Abruptly dry-eyed, she noticed a tingle where he'd touched her elbow. Experiencing a bit of light-headedness, she smiled gratefully as Ms. Carson handed her a glass of water. She took a sip and tried to control her shaking hands.

"Shall we begin again?" he inquired in a polite voice, clearly a bit bemused at the situation. "Do you know who I am, Ms. Best? Let me introduce myself. I'm Steven Gherring. I'll be interviewing you today for the position of my personal executive assistant."

He was staring at her, waiting. What did he expect? How was she supposed to react to his revelation? She forced a grim smile and stuck out her hand.

"Pleased to meet you, Mr. Gherring. My name is Anne Best."

He seemed disappointed in her response.

"Perhaps you've heard my name before."

She shook her head. It sounded familiar. Where had she heard the name before?

"Well, I'm sure you know of my company, Gherring Inc.?"

"Do y'all make car parts?" she asked hopefully.

He sighed. "No, I'm afraid not. We're an international trade company with holdings... You mean you really have no idea who I am? No idea at all?"

"Well, no. I'm sorry. The recruiter just said y'all were in the Town Center Economic Tower, on the top floor."

"Yes," he said, shaking his head with obvious exasperation. "That's because we, or I, *own* the tower. I'm the chairman of Gherring Inc." He sat back as if waiting for the information to sink in.

She wondered how she should respond. He was obviously waiting for her to fawn on him. He must be accustomed to the attention and adulation that came with his position. Strangely, she felt more in control when she realized he wanted something she could choose to give or withhold.

"Nice to meet you, again, Mr. Gherring." She gave him her best sarcastic smile. "You've probably heard of me as well. Anne Best? Sole owner of a twenty-five hundred square foot home in Weatherford, Texas?"

Gherring's eyes opened wide as he considered her.

"You're not what I expected, Ms. Best."

"Neither are you, Mr. Gherring!" She clapped her hand over her mouth. What was wrong with her today? She'd lost control twice. Something about this man rubbed her the wrong way.

She remembered the advice she'd gotten about speaking when you're nervous—imagine your audience in their underwear. She gave it a try. Ohmygosh! Bad idea! This man would look amazing clad solely in underwear. The image filled her mind and refused to go away. Immediately, Anne felt flushed. She grabbed the water glass and gulped rapidly, causing a coughing fit.

Gherring's stern expression changed to concern. "Are you alright, Ms. Best?"

She nodded furiously, regaining her composure. She tried to think of Steven Gherring in an Eskimo suit, so the underwear image wouldn't sneak back into her head.

"Let's talk about your qualifications for this job. You have a B.A. in Chemistry, and you worked part time as a travel agent. Hmmm...." He stared at her resume. Then he flipped the single page over to see the blank backside. "You don't seem to have any actual experience as a personal executive assistant. Am I missing something, Ms. Best?"

Again, her temper flared, and she glared at Gherring.

"Well, if a personal executive assistant is someone who organizes someone's life and work, acquires all the needed tools and supplies, keeps the person's schedule, finds calm in the midst of chaos, and works countless hours in a thankless job... What you really need is a mother, and I have twenty-three years of experience!"

A painful silence fell on the room. She attempted to maintain her fiercely confident expression, but her eyes quickly fell away from his surprised scrutiny. She thought of all the things she could have said—should have said. Why hadn't she pointed out that her research work demonstrated her independent thinking and aptitude for learning? Why hadn't she explained how her education and work experience made her more than qualified to be an executive assistant? But once again, she'd let her temper rule over her common sense. This was not like her. She was always calm, always a rock. No one and nothing got her flustered. There was no emergency she couldn't handle. Why was she losing her composure now?

Finally, Gherring broke the silence.

"Well, Ms. Best," he spoke in a deliberate voice, but the corners of his mouth hinted at a smile. "You make an interesting argument. Perhaps you're just what I need. It might be an absolute disaster. But somehow, I think I'd always wonder what would've happened if I didn't give you a try. You'll begin in two weeks on Monday at eight a.m. sharp. There will be a three-month trial period. Please talk to Ms. Carson about the details. Thank you."

Gherring immediately turned his attention to his laptop as he began to read and answer emails. Anne stood up, staring at him in shocked muteness. After several moments, Gherring looked up, his eyes locked with hers in a powerful gaze. He stood up unhurriedly, moving almost in slow motion. He leaned across the desk and reached out to touch her hand.

"Did you want to say something else, Ms. Best?"

Anne's heart fluttered in response, and she jerked her hand away as if it'd been burned. "No... just... thank you. You won't regret it!" she said as she fled from the room.

Steven Gherring chuckled as she fled the room. She barely registered his last words.

"I hope you're right."

Chapter Two - Weatherford

"GANDALF!" YELLED A DELIGHTED VOICE amid the noise of a slamming door, falling backpack, loud barks, and strangled giggles. "Hey, boy!" gasped the girl, who tussled on the floor with a huge, grey wolfhound. "Hey, did you miss me? I missed you, too."

"What about me? Did you miss me?" Anne asked the girl who was still hugging the dog enthusiastically.

"Of course I missed you, Mom," she laughed from the floor, "but you were too slow. Gandalf got to me first."

"No fair," exclaimed Anne. "He's got better hearing than I do. And somehow, I think he knew you were coming. He's been excited all day." She gave the girl a hand up and pulled her into a bear hug. "Oh Charlotte, I've missed you so much. And I've got so much to tell you."

"It's 'Charlie', Mom. You know everyone calls me Charlie." Charlotte had changed her name to the more masculine form during high school. Now at twenty-two years of age, she still preferred Charlie as her moniker.

"Sorry, sorry—it's just so hard for me to remember. Although you look more like a 'Charlie' than a 'Charlotte' with your curls stuffed up into that baseball cap." Anne snatched the cap from her head and playfully held it up over her head, while Charlie pushed back the loose brown curls that fell past her shoulders.

"That won't work, Mom," giggled Charlie as she quickly retrieved her cap, while her mother struggled to keep it out of her reach. "You know I'm taller than you are, now." She wound her hair back up and tucked it in her cap with practiced ease.

"Are you sure?" Anne pouted. "I'm five foot eight! I know your sister is five foot nine, but I thought you were still a little shorter than me…"

"No Mom." Charlie smiled indulgently. "I'm five eight and a half, and you're definitely the shortest one in the family! But don't worry—you're still a little taller than Gandalf."

Charlie swung an arm over her mother's shoulder to emphasize her "smaller stature" as they walked together into the den and collapsed onto the soft couch. Gandalf followed closely and lay down on the plush rug next to the couch, resting his head on Charlie's legs to command her attention. She absently rubbed his ears while she gave a tired sigh.

"How was the flight from Denver? I thought Emily was picking you up from the airport on her way here an hour from now," Anne queried.

"That was the original plan, but I caught a ride with Ellie and her boyfriend. She decided to book a ticket to see him when she found out I was coming. She was having withdrawal—she hadn't seen him for a whole three months, except for Skyping," Charlie quipped sarcastically. "I don't know how any self-respecting girl could be so dependent on a boy. I guarantee that'll never happen to me. Anyway... I decided to surprise you by showing up early. Plus, I get you to myself for a few hours before Emily comes home."

"I bought you some Cheetos."

"Oh—the puffy kind?" exclaimed Charlie as she ran to the kitchen to retrieve her prize.

"Of course I bought the puffy kind," Anne said indignantly. "What other kind is there?"

"Yummmm!" Charlie popped a Cheeto in her mouth and licked her already orange fingers as she fell back onto the couch. "Okay, Mom... What's the big news you wouldn't tell me on the phone?"

"Well, I was planning to tell you and Emily at the same time so I wouldn't have to repeat the story."

"Yes. But you could tell me now, and then I'll tell Emily for you. That way you still only have to tell the story once." Charlie's huge gold eyes flashed with devilment.

"Your sister would have a fit if I told you first," admonished Anne.

"No, she wouldn't..."

"Yes, I would!" exclaimed a voice from the doorway.

Chaos broke out as Gandalf ran to greet the newcomer. He jumped up and put his front feet on her chest, knocking her against the wall, her bags crashing to the floor. She stood pinned against the wall in a joyful embrace, her stylish glasses knocked askew and a few stray hairs escaping from her long, neat braid of glossy, dark brown hair. The twenty-three year old Emily was neat and tidy, always organized and in control. Only when she was with her family did she let down her guard.

"Get down, Gandalf!" yelled Anne as she ran to the rescue.

"Sister!" shouted Charlie in greeting from the couch with a mouth full of Cheetos.

Emily laughed as she freed herself from Gandalf and rubbed his ears while kissing his nose. She turned to embrace her mom, but sneered at her sister.

"I'm not speaking to you—traitor. Trying to worm the story out of Mom before I got here. It's a good thing I got off work early so I caught you red-handed."

"Orange-handed," corrected Charlie, wiggling her Cheetos-covered fingers at her sister.

"Oh, you started eating treats without me, too," huffed Emily.

"That's because I'm the favorite," claimed Charlie.

"I know I'm the favorite," corrected Emily, "because I brought Mom a new book to read—the latest of the Kate and Curran series." She pulled a book out of her bag and waved it in the air.

"Oh great." Anne snatched the book from her hand, hugging it to her chest. "I've been waiting forever."

Emily laughed. "You could buy your own copy, Mom."

"Yeah Mom," Charlie agreed. "I bought it last month on Kindle."

"Oh I know. But I never can keep up with what's coming out when. I just wait until y'all give me a book or tell me what to buy. It's so much easier, and that's what daughters are for."

"So I *am* the favorite?" Emily questioned her mom, with a wry smile at her sister. "What did you bring to Mom?" she asked her sister.

"I brought the best gift of all—something you can never bring—me."

Emily rolled her blue, almond-shaped eyes and opened her mouth to respond.

"Stop," laughed Anne as the girls began the familiar argument. "You know that both of you are my favorites… except for Gandalf who's always number one." She smiled with contentment to see her girls at home together, but her breath caught in her throat as she realized this might be one of the last opportunities for them to be together in the home where the girls had grown up.

"So, I may be selling the house. Well, that is, I might sell it in three months. But only if I decide to stay… Or if he decides I can stay… If I stay in New York."

"What?" shouted both girls simultaneously. Charlie appeared gleeful, while Emily looked shocked.

"Tell us, Mom, tell us." Charlie danced in circles, prompting Gandalf to join the frolicking with excited barks.

"Yes," said Emily with a stern frown and crossed arms. "Tell us what on earth you're talking about."

"Wait." Charlie pushed her mother back to the comfy couch. "Come sit down and tell us the whole story—don't leave anything out." Grinning, she grabbed her sister's hand and pulled her along. "I'll share my Cheetos."

Anne sat down and looked at her daughters, sitting on either side of her with intent expressions. Suddenly, she felt nervous about explaining her wild plan to them. She'd never thought it would actually happen, so she never worried about having to explain the decision to leave their home in Texas and move across the country to New York City where she didn't know a single soul. Tears sprang to her eyes, and both girls exclaimed and cried in sympathy, giving her hugs and begging her not to cry.

"You know we always cry if you cry," sniffed Emily.

"Yeah, Mom, no fair." Charlie snuffled in agreement.

"I'm sorry," Anne said, breathing deeply and blinking her eyes dry. "It's just very emotional, now that it's actually happening. When I first talked to the recruiter—"

"You called a recruiter?" interrupted Emily.

"Let her finish a sentence," Charlie scolded.

"No, actually, this recruiter called me. I didn't even know what a recruiter was, and I thought it was some kind of scam," Anne admitted wryly. "I guess she got my name from Alice—you know, my old college roommate. She's been encouraging me to get a new job and move into Fort Worth. So I put together a resume and sent it to her. She must have given my resume to that recruiter."

She looked at Emily. "I thought it would be fun to be closer to you, and I thought it would be a nice change to live in the city, maybe get an apartment or one of those cute little Victorian houses they've restored."

Charlie scowled. "What about me? Don't you want to live closer to me?"

"Well, even though you've lived in Colorado for a whole year now, I'm not totally convinced you'll be staying there for long. You do have a record of changing your mind frequently."

"But New York?" interrupted Emily. "Now you won't be close to either one of us. How did you end up interviewing in New York?"

"Well, it's funny, really..." Anne said thoughtfully. "When the recruiter called, she said it was unusual, but they'd offered to pay all expenses for the interview trip. I thought she said someone named Margaret made all the arrangements. But it was actually Katie who set up the interviews. And when I got there, the room was filled with job applicants, all for this same position, and everyone else was in their twenties."

"That's so weird," Charlie mused. "I wonder why they contacted you, if all the others were so young?"

"That's what I asked Katie after the interview."

"Who's Katie? Is that your new boss?" queried Emily.

"No. Katie's the current personal executive assistant for my new boss. She's been working there for four years, but she's getting married and moving in a few months. She said this was the third round of interviews she'd been through with her boss, and he wouldn't consider any of them, even though there were lots of qualified applicants. She didn't explain why I was in the interview group. She was just so relieved he'd finally hired someone. She said her boss kept muttering about how she couldn't just desert him and run off to get married, even though she got engaged almost a year ago. She warned me he could be a little demanding."

"So, anyway, you got the job? For sure?" asked Charlie.

"Yeah, you said something about 'if you decide or he decides' or something." Emily looked at her mom closely.

"Well, I got the job on a three-month trial. Who knows? I might decide I hate it and quit just to save him the trouble of firing me."

"Mom," Emily said shaking her head. "You can't just go live in New York for three months. It's very expensive, and they'll make you sign a yearlong lease. This just isn't practical. I don't think you've thought this through."

"Emily, you're such a wet rag," Charlie fussed at her sister. "She can figure something out. I think you should go for it. It's so exciting."

"No, actually Emily's right. I'd never be able to find a place I could afford to stay for three months." Emily stuck out her tongue at her sister, who stuck out hers in return. "But this company evidently owns an apartment building or two in New York, and Katie said part of the package would include my apartment during the trial period. If I keep the job, Katie said the company would sign some kind of guarantee that's needed to rent an apartment in New York. It's evidently a big deal to find a place to lease there. You've got to get a real estate agent and fill out all kinds of papers and jump through a bunch of hoops."

"Wait, Mom," Emily said earnestly. "Did you say the company owns an apartment building or two in New York? What kind of company is this? Who is it? Have we ever heard of them?"

"I don't think so," Anne said. "I'd never heard of them before. Some sort of international investment company—Gherring Inc."

"Gherring Inc.!" shouted the two girls with disbelief.

"Mom," Charlie said. "Surely even *you* have heard of Gherring Inc. Don't you ever watch the news or get on the Internet? They're *huge*!"

"Wow, Mom, that's really impressive—Gherring Inc. So what does your boss do? What'll your job be? Will you have an opportunity to move up? Will you get to travel?" Emily asked, now expressing real excitement.

"Well, Emily, if I'd known that's what it took to win you over, I'd have mentioned the name of the company first," laughed Anne. "My boss is actually... Steven Gherring. I think he kind of runs the company or owns it or something..." Anne trailed off at the stunned expressions on her daughters' faces. Both seemed to have momentarily lost the ability to speak. "He seemed okay, a little full of himself and not very polite to Katie." Anne caught herself nervously adjusting her hair in its clip, and put her hands in her lap and began to study her nails.

After a few moments of astonished silence, Charlie clarified, "You actually met Steven Gherring? You had an interview with Steven Gherring? *The* Steven Gherring? And you didn't even know who he was?"

"Well, to be honest, the recruiter sent me an email with a link where I could read all about the company, but I never got past the name and address. I thought it was just a secretary job for some low-level guy. Plus," she paused, struggling with her embarrassment, "I think I didn't want to really try hard because I thought I was going to fail. I figured I'd have an excuse for why I didn't get the job."

"So you interviewed with Steven Gherring, and you were totally clueless? I can't wait to hear this story," Emily grimaced.

"Well, there really isn't much story to tell. I just told him why I was qualified for the position, and he offered me the job—on a trial basis." Anne's fingernails were suddenly even more interesting. She couldn't tell them Steven Gherring had made her lose control. She didn't even understand what it was about him that got her so flustered.

"That's it? That's the whole story?" Charlie asked doubtfully.

"Well... it's possible I lost my temper when he was so incredibly rude, and then I stormed out of his office. Well actually, I didn't quite make it out the door, but I was going to leave before he apologized. Hmmm, now that I think about it, he never actually apologized. He sort of took control and led me back into the room."

"And then the rest of the interview went really well?" Emily inquired.

"It was okay, I guess."

"Well you must have really impressed him with your qualifications, since you got the job. What did you say?"

Anne studied her nails again and stammered a bit. "I don't exactly remember, but he was definitely impressed, alright."

"What're you hiding?" demanded Charlie. "You're always good at recounting details. Why're you suddenly so forgetful?"

Emily broke in. "Mom, you're blushing. Ohmygosh! You're actually really red. What did you say? What did you do?"

"Did you flirt with him?" asked Charlie. "I've seen his picture. He's pretty hot for an old guy. Come on—fess up."

"No, no, no. That's not it at all. I didn't flirt with him. I promise. And I really didn't notice if he was good-looking, because he was so arrogant. I swear, I don't even like the guy." Anne fidgeted with her hair again and tried not to look directly at her daughters. She was a terrible liar. She couldn't let them know how attracted she felt to her new boss, especially in light of how rude and narcissistic he was.

"Then why're you even interested in working for him if he was so awful and rude?" Charlie smirked.

"Because of the chance to experience New York, of course." Anne stated reasonably. "I figure I can stand anything or anyone for three months. But it's the chance of a lifetime to actually live in New York City, even for three months. And the company pays for all the moving costs, too. Meanwhile, maybe I can find another job up there. Or I guess I can always come back to Weatherford after he fires me."

Emily studied her mother doubtfully. "Something tells me you're not being entirely truthful. You still haven't told us about the rest of the interview—after you almost stormed out of the office. Did you apologize for losing your temper? I mean, not that you aren't efficient and smart. And not that you're not the best candidate for the job. But I know that because I know you. What did you say to convince him to hire you when he'd passed on all those others?"

Charlie added, "Yeah, Mom. I don't actually believe you flirted with him, even if he was on the *Most Eligible Bachelor List* five years in a row." Her eyes flashed with merriment.

Anne thought back to the fateful interview as she had so many times for the past three days. She felt butterflies in her stomach as she recalled his piercing gaze. Unconsciously, she rubbed the back of her hand, remembering his searing touch. Determined to control his physical effect on her, she forced herself to consider his egotistical attitude.

"He was just so self-absorbed and conceited and full of himself. I really didn't notice his looks. And I may have lost my temper again—just a little."

"Then why on earth did he hire you, Mom?" Charlie asked.

"To tell you the truth… I really don't know."

Chapter Three - New York, New York

ANNE WRESTLED WITH HER BAGS as she shuffled through the airport with her cell phone propped on her shoulder. "Yes, I'm safely here and all my luggage made it. Y'all sent me with way too many clothes."

"You're upset Charlie and I lent you some clothes? We couldn't let you go to New York with your old wardrobe, and you refused to let us take you shopping."

"No, no. It's not that I'm not grateful you both lent me so much stuff. Lord knows my wardrobe was pretty sad. But I had to pay for extra luggage, and now I can barely handle everything. Ahhhhkkk!" Anne screamed as her phone fell from its perch, and she dropped her purse. She scrambled to pick up her phone.

"Emily? Are you still there? Sorry, I dropped the phone. Oh, excuse me sir, let me just get this stuff out of the way." Anne rolled and pushed her gear next to a pillar. "So Emily, thanks for taking care of Gandalf this weekend. Have you heard from Grandpa?"

"Yep, he called this morning when he was on the road. But Mom, why is Grandpa coming to take care of Gandalf? Doesn't Ms. Minnie usually keep him? She loves that dog."

"Yes, she does love Gandalf. You know, she really encouraged me to go to this interview, and she was so excited when I got the job. But right now she's on her honeymoon."

"Honeymoon? Ms. Minnie got married? Isn't she like ninety years old? Who did she marry?"

"No." Anne chuckled. "She's only seventy two, and she married Mr. Greenly. You remember—that sweet old man who works in the garden department at Wal-Mart. I think I told you about him. He always saves me some of the best perennials when they go on sale."

"So how did this happen, Mom? Did you have something to do with this? Have you been matchmaking again?"

"No, I didn't do anything. Mr. Greenly just happened to come by to give me some advice about my roses when I had invited Ms. Minnie over for tea."

"Really?" Emily arched her brows. "Since when did you need advice on your roses? You've got the greenest thumb I know."

"Well, my Simplicity roses got black spot disease, so I asked him to drop by that morning."

"Ah-ha! So you admit you set them up to meet each other."

"I might've subconsciously asked them to come at the same time, but I knew they were perfect for each other. They're so sweet; they both love gardening. And they were both widows, and they were both lonely."

"Mom, you're incorrigible," laughed Emily. "But why haven't you found a match for me? You must be responsible for at least fifteen weddings already."

"You're so particular—I have to find just the right guy. You've refused to even consider the guys I've suggested so far."

"Really, Mom, I'm just kidding. I'm perfectly happy alone, and I'm not sure there's anyone out there that's worth the trouble. Why don't you make a match for yourself instead?"

"Oh, no! I had a wonderful husband already and two great daughters. I'm really not interested in romance for myself."

"Whatever, Mom. I'm just saying while you're looking for everyone else, you ought to look for yourself as well. There're a lot of men in New York."

"Oh stop, Emily—don't tease me. Anyway, I've got to get going. I miss you already. Be sure to come visit as soon as you can. I'm so lonely already. Maybe this was a mistake."

"Mom, are you getting cold feet again? You know everything will be fine. This is the chance of a lifetime. You'll be great. You'll probably get promoted to president of the company."

"Ha! I'm sure secretaries get promoted to president all the time." She chuckled. "I'm just nervous, I guess. But I'll call as soon as I get to the apartment. Bye, sweetie. Love you."

When the taxi dropped her at the apartment building with all her gear, a sharply dressed doorman whisked the door open and quickly relieved her of most of her baggage, leading the way to a comfy reception area.

"I'm Antonio. Are you moving in? Miss…?"

"Hi, I'm Anne. Nice to meet you, Antonio. Yes, I just flew in today, and I'm moving in. At least for a while."

"That's great. I'm on duty most of the time, and Randall is the other doorman. It'll be great having you here. We're always happy when a beautiful woman moves in."

"Oh!" Anne exclaimed, blushing. "You're so sweet. Do you always say things like that to women who are old enough to be your mother?"

Antonio laughed. "I only speak the truth. You couldn't possibly be old enough to be my mother, but I've got a thing for older women anyway."

When Anne stood speechless and crimson, he had compassion on her. "I'm sorry. Please don't be mad—I've got a terrible flirting habit. In fact, I'm going to the FA meeting tonight." He laughed again.

Suddenly, a door opened behind the desk and a woman emerged, moving quickly and efficiently to greet Anne and begin her check-in process. Anne noticed Antonio was suddenly silent as he watched every move the woman made.

"Hi Rayna. Nice weather today. I like your new shoes."

Rayna was quickly engrossed in her work, typing Anne's information into the computer, oblivious to Antonio's words. He backed away awkwardly and returned to the door, glancing over his shoulder. Rayna continued to process Anne's paperwork, scanning Anne's license and credit card before handing her a key card.

"Your room's on the tenth floor, with a window on the front of the building," explained Rayna. "It's one of our nicest efficiency suites."

"Thanks so much, Rayna. You've been so nice. In fact, everyone has been very nice. Antonio was especially nice. Do y'all usually work at the same time?"

"Hmmm?" asked Rayna with her eyes glued to her computer.

"Antonio," she repeated. "I asked if y'all usually work together. I mean, do y'all work on the same time schedule?"

"Antonio?" Rayna looked up and blinked in confusion.

"Yes. You know, Antonio—that incredibly handsome guard at the door. He was so nice and so nice-looking. Wow, if I was only your age, I'd be really interested in him. Oh, but you probably already have a relationship with someone..."

Rayna stared at Antonio as if she'd never seen him before. "No, I don't have a relationship. I *had* a relationship, but that was six months ago. You know, men are such pigs."

"Oh, I know. That's why I was so surprised at what a nice young man Antonio is. I just wanted you to know, so you could pass it on to the management."

"The management," muttered Rayna, tilting her head as Antonio opened the door and helped an elderly man with an awkward box. She turned back to Anne. "Yes, I'll certainly tell the management about, uhmm, Antonio."

"You know, if you ever need someone to talk to, my door is always open." Anne winked.

"Thanks, Anne. I just might take you up on that offer."

Anne ferried her way up the elevator to her room. Once inside with her bags, she moved quickly to the window and opened the blinds. She peered down at the street, slightly off of a main drag, but busy nonetheless. Directly across the street was a beautiful ornate building with the words "The Economist" carved into it. The street sounds were muffled, but she could still see the teaming traffic on the main street, and marveled once again at the hectic pace of the city. Turning from the window, she surveyed her small apartment. The floors were all wood—well it looked like wood, but it was probably a high-end laminate—with nice area rugs. There was a small kitchen area near the door separated from the living area by a bar and three stools. Every surface in the cooking area was gleaming—stainless steel, glass tile, and granite.

Walking through a door she discovered a small, but beautiful bathroom with a marble shower, dark wood vanity topped with granite, and modern fixtures. Another door led to a large walk-in closet, complete with shelves, drawers and hanging racks. Back in the living area, the bed was covered with a fluffy, white, down comforter and throw pillows in a plethora of colors and textures. Bookshelves housed a few classics, decorative pieces and a flat-screen TV. Situated by the window on a beautiful oriental rug were two chairs and a small loveseat anchored by a round tufted ottoman.

Anne used the next hour to unpack her suitcases and check out the kitchen. The cooking area was supplied with basic pots and pans. She found all the necessary basics for cooking in the pantry, and the refrigerator was stocked with eggs, low-fat milk, various cheeses, vanilla Greek yogurt, and blueberries. She realized Katie must have had the groceries purchased specifically for her, recalling some seemingly casual phone conversations discussing her food preferences.

This attention to detail would soon be her responsibility, and Anne suddenly worried whether she could fill those efficient shoes. Her job at the travel agency had required attention to detail, and her clients relied on her to arrange every facet of their travel. She was accustomed to working out problems and planning for contingencies, but she really didn't know anything about New York. Could she really manage all the issues she'd be facing in a city that was so foreign to all she knew? A simple grocery-shopping trip would be an adventure in this city. She began to pace and fret, when her cell phone suddenly rang out with the rock riff that signaled Charlie's call.

"Hi sweetie." Anne smiled as she spoke.

"Hey, Mom. Are you in your apartment? I want to hear all about it. Emily said you hadn't called since the airport."

"Oh, I forgot to call her back. She'll probably be ticked, but I'll call her when we hang up. Yep, I'm here, and it's actually great."

"Okay, great. Let's Skype so you can show me your apartment."

"You know I haven't figured out the Internet around here yet. Knowing me, I'll need some help. But we can Skype as soon as I work it out. Katie lives in this same building, so she'll help me out this weekend, I'm sure."

"Fine, Mom. Just send me some pictures. What does it look like?"

"It's small, but beautiful. Nicely decorated. Tenth floor. There's a front door guy—like a guard—so I feel pretty safe. His name is Antonio, and he's very polite."

"Ooooo! He sounds handsome and mysterious. Perhaps you can introduce us."

"You seem to think my sole purpose here in New York is to find a boyfriend for you."

"Well really, Mom, what else could be more important?" quipped Charlie.

"I'm afraid matchmaking may be the only thing I *can* accomplish here," moaned Anne. "I don't know why I thought I could work here in the city, or work for a big company, or work for someone important. I think I'm going to freak out just trying to use the subway."

"Oh, Mom. Do you need another pep talk? You know we've already done this about twenty times. You impressed Steven Gherring enough to land this job. That man knows how to spot a winner. Everything he touches turns to gold. If he thinks you can do this job, you can do it."

"Yes, but he didn't sound really sure when he hired me. He's giving me a three-month trial."

"But you told me Katie said you'd really have to mess up badly to get fired, because she's leaving for good in three months. If he fires you, he won't have anyone at all. She said he'd interviewed over forty people before he chose you."

"I know, I know. You're right. I think I'll feel better after my first week at work. Actually, I probably just need some dinner. I'm starving."

"Yes, Mom. We all know how cranky you get when you're hungry. And be sure to have some chocolate for dessert. You'll feel better for sure."

"You've got no room to talk, you know."

"That's true, but I inherited it from you."

"Okay, I'm going to eat dinner and chocolate, take a long, hot shower, and climb in bed with a good book. Tomorrow, I'll conquer New York City."

"You go, girl! I almost feel sorry for New York."

Anne laughed as she hung up the phone. Four o'clock. Too early for dinner. She sat down and glanced through the pamphlet Rayna had given her. She spotted an exercise facility on the amenities. Great. She would check out the gym before eating. She ate a piece of candy for some quick energy and changed into shorts and a tank top. Her kids had vetoed her old exercise clothes as too dated for New

York, so she surveyed the more fashionable shorts in the mirror. Wow, these were a little shorter than she would usually wear. Her legs were probably her best feature, and these shorts showed them off—a little too much. The tank top was kind of tight, but it covered everything important. Anyway, she had no other option right now, and knew she wouldn't have to leave the building. Besides, the gym would likely be empty at four o'clock on a Friday afternoon.

She pulled her hair into a ponytail, grabbed a small bag and stuffed in her phone, key, and IPod. The pamphlet said the gym was on floor eighteen. She headed out the door and found the elevator and pressed the button, while admiring the huge crown moldings and ornate furnishings that graced the waiting area. She was still studying the beautiful fresh flower arrangement when the elevator doors opened behind her.

"Ah-hem… Are you getting on?" asked a voice from the elevator.

Embarrassed, Anne swirled quickly around and rushed through the doorway, her bag swinging out to bump against the lone elevator occupant… Steven Gherring.

His eyes opened wide, and he rubbed his arm. "Ms. Best, are you attempting to injure me?"

"I'm so sorry Mr. Gherring. I was just startled, and I didn't realize my bag would hit you. I didn't even really see you there. Are you okay…?"

She stopped in mid-sentence when she realized he was laughing at her. "Oh! You're not even hurt are you? Although you do seem a bit fragile. Perhaps it's reasonable to think even a very small thing could cause you immense pain."

"Ouch!" he said in mock horror. "Now you've really cut me to the quick."

He laughed again, and she joined in this time. Then she realized he was dressed in a suit and tie, while she was in shorts. As his eyes strayed to her legs, she was acutely aware of how short those shorts were. She felt her face flush and fought to gain control of the situation.

"I'm surprised to see you here, Mr. Gherring. Are you checking on your property?"

"No, Ms. Best. In fact, I live here."

"Here? Wow, I bet your apartment's bigger than mine." She blushed scarlet as he raised his eyebrows. Why couldn't she learn not to speak around this man?

"Is there something wrong with your apartment? Is it too small for your liking?"

"No, not at all. That's not what I meant. I only meant I expected you'd live some place really big and fancy since you're so rich." She paused, trying to think of something more diplomatic to say, but she failed completely.

The corners of his mouth twitched up slightly, and his dimples peeked out. "I'm so glad I ran into you, Ms. Best. I need you to make some travel arrangements for me. It really can't wait until Monday."

"Oh, I thought Katie would be handling things until Monday." She was suddenly terrified to be given an assignment so early without Katie's help.

"Yes, I could call Ms. Carson, if that's what you prefer, Ms. Best. I simply thought not to trouble her on the weekend since she's so busy planning the wedding. But if you want, I'll call her and ask her to come over tonight."

"Oh no. I don't want you to bother Katie, I mean, Ms. Carson. I can do it. Do you have the information with you in your briefcase? I'll just take it, now. I can exercise later."

"No, I don't have the information here. I'll have to get it from my computer."

The elevator had stopped on the eighteenth floor, and she was standing in the doorway as the elevator doors tried repeatedly to close.

"I think the elevator is getting angry. I'll get off here and wait for an elevator to go back down to my apartment. I just need to figure out how to login on the wireless. Do you know the password offhand? Never mind," she rambled. "I'll figure it out."

She turned and stepped out of the elevator to let the doors close and felt a shock as he touched her elbow. She jumped and twirled to see him standing, braced against the agitated elevator door.

"Ms. Best, I think it would be easier if you came up so I could explain to you exactly what I need."

"Up? To your place?" Did her voice sound squeaky?

"Yes, Ms. Best. My computer's in my apartment—in my 'big, fancy' apartment."

She froze. Go up to his apartment? Of course it didn't mean anything. Surely Katie went to his apartment all the time to get work assignments or deliver things or whatever. After all, she was his *personal* executive assistant.

"Ms. Best? Are you coming? I think this elevator may have progressed from angry to furious."

"Oh. Yes, of course. I'm sorry. I was just thinking,"

She felt herself blush again as she stepped back into the elevator. She was being silly, worrying about his intentions. She was simply naïve. Anyway, Steven Gherring would never be interested in someone like her. There were actresses and supermodels who'd be thrilled to be with him. Her face was radiating heat. How could she think he'd ever be attracted to her?

She tugged down on the hem of her shorts, willing them to cover a bit more leg. She inspected her legs while pretending to tighten a shoelace. She was certainly glad she'd shaved that morning. Her legs, usually pasty white, had a nice healthy glow thanks to a few sessions of spray tan. Then she spotted a spray streak on her left inner thigh. She adjusted her right leg forward and clamped her legs together to hide the brown stain. This precarious position caused her to lose her balance, and she let out a little gasp.

"Ms. Best? Are you okay? Are you in pain?" He reached out to steady her. She pulled back so quickly she stumbled the other direction, her bag swinging up and striking his chin.

"Ouch!"

"Oh! Oh, Mr. Gherring, I'm sorry!"

He rubbed his chin. "Ms. Best, I believe you *are* trying to injure me."

Anne followed Gherring through the ornate double doors of the penthouse apartment. He disappeared into a back room, muttering instructions to Anne that unfortunately didn't filter from her ears into her brain. She gazed around at the stately opulence that surrounded her on all sides. Colors were sophisticated and subdued, but every finish appeared to be beautiful and expensive, from the granite inlayed wood floors, to the chocolate Italian leather furniture, highlighted by impressive chandeliers suspended from twenty-foot ceilings. French doors led onto an expansive balcony, visible through enormous picture windows flanking the doorway. Anne perched on the edge of the sofa, staring at the marble coffee table that probably cost more than her car, wondering what instructions Gherring had given her before vanishing.

"Did you find it?" He entered the room having shed his coat and tie and, *ohmygod*, his shirt. Anne tried valiantly not to stare and pretended not to notice his muscles rippling as he pulled on a sport shirt. Even from the corner of her eye she could tell there was no flab anywhere. She wondered what he did to look like that. Did he have a personal trainer? She felt warm all over. What was she doing? This man was her boss and miles out of her league.

She forced her eyes up to his. What had he asked? "Did I find what?"

"The laptop. Did you look in the study?" He walked into another room and opened the door to reveal an office with rich walnut paneling extending to cover the coved ceiling. She followed him through the door and found him leaning intently over his desk, presenting her with a nice view of a firm backside. She did like a guy with a fine bottom. Suddenly, she realized he had turned around to face her. Had he noticed her perusal?

"You have a very nice… uhmm… apartment." Heat flooded her face.

"Why thank you, Ms. Best. I do like to know my assets are appreciated."

She squirmed, attempting to extract herself from his amused inspection. She pointed behind him to the computer. "Is that the information you wanted me to see?"

He turned back to the screen. "Yes, you see this is my current itinerary, but the timing of the flights won't work with the meeting that has been changed from Tuesday morning to Monday afternoon. Here's the new meeting schedule. You'll also need to arrange limousine service to coordinate with the earlier flight. Fortunately all the presentation material is ready to go, so no changes are needed there."

She felt a growing confidence. This was all about travel arrangements. She could do this job in her sleep. She leaned in to study the information and email a copy to herself. As she worked she became aware of his presence, her skin prickly where her shoulder touched him. Her fingers began to tremble, and she stumbled as she keyed in the information.

"You're shivering. Are you cold? I should've realized with your... eh-hem... shorts on, you'd be cold in here. Should I turn up the heat?"

"No, I'll be fine. Just let me..." She glanced at him, mortified he'd noticed her shaking. He wore a satisfied smirk—he knew. He was enjoying her discomfort. Her blood boiled. "Actually, Mr. Gherring, I do find it to be quite cold in here. But I seriously doubt there's anything *you* could ever do to warm me up."

She pressed the send button on the email and with determination marched out of the room to retrieve her bag. When she headed for the door, she found Gherring barring her exit.

"Ms. Best." He stepped sideways to intercept her as she tried to go around him, eyes firmly fixed on the floor. She refused to answer and attempted to pass him on the other side, until he finally leaned against the door handle and crossed his arms. "Please, will you look at me?"

"No, I won't. You're not very professional, and you're obnoxious. And if you want to fire me now, then just go ahead." At this, she glared at him and lifted her chin in defiance.

"Please, Ms. Best, I didn't mean to offend you. You're different from my other acquaintances—more sensitive." She started to retort, but he held out a hand to stop her. "Wait, I didn't mean sensitive in a bad way. I simply mean I'm used to dealing with *insensitive* people. I can be sensitive. I used to be sensitive..." His words died off and, for a moment, he looked sad, distant, and lonely.

Her anger melted away as she considered this man who had everything money could buy, but perhaps none of the happiness and joy that couldn't be bought. She thought of her family, her friends, all the people who loved her. He surely must not have this type of love in his life, or she wouldn't have glimpsed that lost look in his eyes.

"Oh Mr. Gherring, I'm fine. No worries. I know I can be very difficult to deal with—or so my daughters tell me." She decided to probe for a bit of information. "So, your current girlfriend isn't very sensitive?"

"No, Ms. Best. There's currently not anyone who falls in the category of girlfriend. I can't say I have had much time or need for dating or patience to deal with the consequences. And to be honest, no one has really seemed worth the effort." He looked surprised at his own candidness.

"Yes, of course. You're a very busy and important man. And I should be getting out of your way so you can be about your business. I'll see you Monday morning, Mr. Gherring." Anne slipped around him and out the door.

She escaped to the elevator, glad to be free of Gherring's forceful presence. Why did she have such a difficult time controlling herself around him? One minute she felt drawn to him, and the next she was furious. He was so arrogant. But then he had accidentally revealed a part of himself he tried so hard to hide. He was actually lonely. She knew what she had to do. Steven Gherring needed a mate, a life-long companion, true love, a match. And she, Anne Best, was just the woman to find that perfect match for him!

Chapter Four - Working Order

"Hey Anne. Ready for your first day at work? Are you nervous?" Rayna came out from behind her desk to greet Anne as she emerged from the elevator.

"Yes, extremely nervous—I feel like I'm fixin' to pass out. But not as bad as I would've been, since I realized Mr. Gherring will be out of town for three days." Anne smiled affectionately at Rayna. "You look very chipper today. How was your date with Antonio last night?"

Rayna blushed crimson and glanced carefully over to the door where Antonio stood, apparently attempting to pretend he was not watching Rayna. Unabashed, Anne waved his direction. "Good morning, Antonio. How are you?"

Rayna positioned herself with her back to Antonio and spoke in a low voice. "It was so much fun. He was a real gentleman and opened the doors for me. We went to this fun pizza place, and we talked for hours. He's a really good listener. I don't want to jinx anything, but I think I may be falling for him. I just want to take it slow so I don't get hurt again."

"Good for you. You deserve someone great after dealing with that Eddie. After you told me your story on Saturday, I was ready to punch that guy. He'd better hope I never meet him."

Rayna giggled. "You're so fierce. What would you do? Beat him up with your purse?"

"Well, I just might. I've recently used my bag for just such a purpose." Anne laughed. "Anyway, I'm glad things are going well with Antonio. I just knew he'd be good for you."

"Don't be making wedding plans just yet." Rayna chuckled as she peered over her shoulder at Antonio. "Although, I must admit, he would look great in a tux…"

On her way out the door, Antonio stopped Anne. "Good morning. I hope you have a great first day at work."

"How did you know?"

"Rayna and I talked about you last night, among a lot of other subjects. I know you're the one who told her about me. She never even knew I was alive before. You know I was right." His eyes twinkled.

"Right about what?"

"I told you on Friday it would be great having you here, and my prediction was spot-on. But I don't understand how you knew. How did you know I liked Rayna? I didn't say anything."

"I just have a sixth sense about relationships."

"Really? So you've done this before? Maybe you should charge a big fat fee. Are you working on anyone else right now?"

"Right now I'm just scouting. I'm always looking for my two daughters, and I have one other match I'm working on."

"Well, if your daughters look anything like you, that should be easy."

"Oh Antonio. You're taken now—you shouldn't be flirting. Did you miss your FA meeting?"

Antonio laughed as Anne zipped out the door onto the streets of New York City and headed for her first day on the job.

"Hi Anne," greeted Katie as she entered the office door, hair and bags askew. "How was your first day negotiating the subway?"

"It was a bit crazy." She huffed a stray piece of hair out of her face. "I did meet someone on the subway, a sweet girl named Ellen who works at a bookstore, but wants to be an actress. Of course, I had to walk here from the station, and I was so late by then I started running. While I was running I tripped on the curb and would have fallen down if Spencer hadn't caught me."

"Spencer?"

"Spencer—the nice young man who broke my fall. He works next door at the lunch bistro, Papa's Place. I promised him I'd eat there today out of appreciation for him saving me from being a bloody mess on my first day at work. It would've been nice if the apartment had been closer to work. Not that I'm complaining—it's a nice place to live. Maybe you can show me a better way to get here from our building."

Katie frowned. "I had you all set up to move into a company apartment in my building, but Mr. Gherring vetoed the idea. He said something about planning to remodel that apartment."

"Oh, I thought I was in your building. I figured he wanted his secretary close so he could give you assignments any time, you know, from his apartment."

"No, I'm in a building about a block away from here. It's handy for work."

"Oh, too bad there wasn't an apartment ready in your building. But I guess it was fortunate I was at the place where Mr. Gherring lives, since he was able to explain about the changes he needed in his travel arrangements after we ran into each other in the elevator."

"Really? When he left here early on Friday, he told me he would email me about a possible schedule change. Then later he sent an email that everything was fine. I wonder why he had you do it instead of me. Thanks for taking care of the arrangements."

"You're welcome. He said something about not wanting to bother you, and I was glad to start off with something I already knew how to do. And it was convenient since the information was on his home computer. It only took a second to run up there."

"You went to Mr. Gherring's apartment?" Katie's mouth fell open.

"It wasn't like that. Nothing improper happened. I just… Wait, haven't you been to his apartment? I mean, for work stuff?"

"No." Katie's eyes were still wide. "I've never been there. Mr. Gherring has a strict policy about separating his work and his personal life. No one from work has ever been to his apartment. Not even the board members or the vice presidents, as far as I know."

"Oh. Well I'm sure it was a fluke, and I'm sure it'll never happen again. I don't think he likes dealing with my emotional outbreaks." Anne forced a laugh. Why would Gherring change his policy about keeping his apartment private? Maybe he was starting to realize he needed company after all. "But he does seem very lonely."

"I don't know. He has an active social calendar. I don't see how he has time to be lonely."

"Now you know being busy has nothing to do with finding meaningful relationships. You have Gary. Think how it'd be if you had to make appearances in public all the time, but you didn't have Gary in your life. You'd be very lonely."

"Wow, you're right. I never thought about it that way. You really are great at understanding people, Anne."

"Thanks, Katie. I can't think of a nicer compliment." Anne contemplated her plan to alleviate her boss' desolate state. She took a deep breath and turned to Katie. "Now let's get to work on my training. I have a lot to learn if I want to keep this job longer than three months."

*****

Emily appeared skeptical, even on the Skype screen. "Wow Mom, you seem to have been pretty busy for only five days in New York. That's one couple you've already gotten together, and several more in the making. In fact, you seem to be doing a lot of meddling, but have you done any work?"

"Emily, how can you ask that? You know I don't meddle. I just intervene a bit. These New Yorkers don't seem to be able to find each other without a little help. There are just too many people here—they get confused." Anne felt a pang of homesickness. "It's so good to hear your voice. I really miss you. And I miss hearing a Texas accent. Everyone around here teases me about my accent and acts like they've never heard *y'all* or *fixin' to* in their whole lives."

"Well, don't let them hear you talking to Grandpa. When you two are talking, you sound so countrified, and you say things like *get foundered* and *cattywhomperjawed* and *bust my buttons*." Emily giggled while Anne looked affronted.

"No I don't."

"Mom."

"Okay. Maybe I do that a bit, but it's not that bad, is it?"

"No Mom, I just think your work colleagues may be a bit too sophisticated to handle your Texas country talk in addition to your drawl."

"Well, they'll just have to tough it out. I'm too old to learn to talk a new way. You know what they say about old dogs."

"At least you need to watch how you talk around Steven Gherring. Did you say he'll be in the office tomorrow?"

"Yes, but I don't seem to be very good at holding my tongue around that man. Something about him just makes me lose my temper." Anne felt somewhat guilty she hadn't told her daughters about meeting Mr. Gherring on Friday. But the whole experience had been so awkward she didn't want to explain it. Besides, he would be so much easier to deal with once she found him a perfect match. "I think he's just lonely."

"Why would you think that, Mom?"

"Well, I've been doing some Internet research and asking questions at work. Steven Gherring is extremely driven. He works long hours and travels a lot. He's been photographed with a variety of beautiful women who accompanied him to social events. But the gossip columns only have short-lived rumors about romances.

"He never seems to be seen with any woman more than once, except for his grandmother. And he's totally devoted to her. She's an extraordinary woman, ninety-five years old. She's done interviews and talk shows, and has said she refuses to die until she sees her grandson happily married."

Emily laughed. "She sounds great. Does she live in the city, too?"

"No, that's the sad part. She lives in a small town about four hours from here. She's his only family, as far as I can tell, and he only gets to see her about once a month."

"Okay, I can see where he might be a little lonely. He's never been married?"

"No, but I think he was engaged once, about five years ago. There was talk of a wedding and speculation about where it would take place. But I couldn't find any information about the break-up. Maybe she died. I don't know. He manages to keep his life pretty private. I found out most of my info from the grandmother's interviews."

"Well, maybe you can be a little more understanding since you know all this stuff. You know, maybe you can keep from yelling at him like you did during the interview. I'd like for you to keep this job for at least three weeks so I can come to visit."

"Yay—three weeks. Really just two and a half weeks, now—I can hardly wait. And Charlotte's coming too?"

"Yep, she's flying in from Denver, but we're on the same flight from Dallas to New York."

"Awesome. I have three weeks to find two nice, good-looking, guys for you."

"And don't forget, we want them to be rich and have ripped abs. Mine needs to be a reader, and Charlie wants an adventurer."

"Believe me. I know exactly what you two need."

Anne arrived early to work, anticipating her first day actually working with Steven Gherring. She wore her nicest wool skirt and blouse, silently thanking Emily for lending her some clothes that fit and were appropriate for a business office. She traveled to work in her bright blue running shoes, which looked absolutely ridiculous. But she couldn't walk well in the high-heeled fashion shoes most New York women seemed to sport.

Once she arrived at the office, she stashed away the running shoes and pulled on the uncomfortable three-inch high pumps that put her eye-to-eye with most of the men in the office. She checked her hair in the ladies room, distressed to find the humidity had re-curled the locks she had worked so hard to straighten that morning. Resigned, Anne pulled her hair back into a pearl clip.

She swiped on some mascara, dabbed concealer under her eyes and smoothed some tinted balm on her lips—her only concessions to wearing makeup. She'd always felt inept at applying makeup, thinking any more than these three staples made her look like a clown. She assessed her face. No wrinkles yet, although there were some crinkles that appeared around her eyes when she smiled. But she'd rather have those than frown lines. Her eyes were like large brown saucers. You couldn't even see the pupils. She got compliments on them, but she'd rather have had blue or gold or green. Brown was boring. Boring or not, time to go upstairs.

She checked the time on her cell phone—still thirty minutes early—and squeezed onto the almost full elevator. Why was it crowded at seven-thirty a.m.? Perhaps everyone was arriving early since Mr. Gherring was back in town. Gradually, the elevator emptied until she was the only one left. Her arms were full, balancing her purse, her shoes, and her newly purchased laptop bag, when the doors opened on the top floor to reveal an office already bustling with activity.

Panicking with the knowledge she must somehow be late, Anne rushed off the elevator. But in the doorway, the three-inch spike of her heel caught in the crack. She flew forward, launching the contents of her hands into the air. As she tumbled to the floor, she managed to catch her laptop bag but missed the purse, which flipped upside down and spilled its contents. Almost in slow motion, she watched one of her lightweight running shoes soar through the air to strike a coworker squarely on the back.

He flinched slightly and spoke without turning around. "I assume, Ms. Best, you've arrived, and the intent to cause physical harm is once again confirmed." Steven Gherring smiled as he looked over his shoulder. But his face went pale when he spied Anne's prone figure and the blood on her elbow. In an instant he was kneeling beside her, supporting her as she tried to stand up. "Are you alright? You're bleeding. Let me help you."

But as Gherring's words sunk in, Anne's pain and humiliation was driven away by her fury. She shook his hand away. "Believe me, Mr. Gherring. This was an accident. If I'd meant to hit you, I would have hit you in the head, and I would have used something harder than a shoe so it would have done some damage!"

"I think you've hit your target this time." His mouth was quirked as he bent over to gather her scattered belongings. The other coworkers had hastily dispersed when the scene began, so Anne had no recourse but to accept Gherring's help. "I didn't know you'd been hurt when I spoke."

When Anne turned to face him, he looked like a sad puppy. Her irritation evaporated. "Well, that's almost an apology, so I guess I'll accept it. I was just hurrying because everyone was here, so I thought I was late. But my cell phone said it was only seven-thirty. Don't we start at eight o'clock? Was my cell time wrong? Or did y'all start work early today?"

"Now that's an interesting story. I'll let you in on a little secret." He glanced around before continuing. "Officially, the office used to open at nine. But I noticed everyone made it a point to arrive before I got here at eight fifty, so I started arriving at eight forty or eight forty-five." He smiled broadly. "So, of course, when I started coming in the office at eight thirty, people began to come at eight-fifteen. And so on, and so on. I wanted to see how far the employees would go to try and make a good impression on the boss. So now I usually come in at about seven-twenty." He chuckled a bit. "But I understand the office opens at eight when I'm out of town."

Anne raised her brows a bit. "You're experimenting with your people at their expense? Just for fun? Or do you actually judge people by whether they beat you to the office?"

"Oh no, I've never been impressed by people who go to great lengths trying to impress me," he paused thoughtfully. "Although I guess I do expect it. No it's strictly for entertainment purposes. So, now you know the truth, I guess you won't need to sacrifice your body to get here early."

"No way!" She grinned, dabbing a tissue on her bleeding elbow. "I'm too competitive to let everyone else beat me to the office even if I know it's just a game. What's a little bruising and blood when you're trying to win?"

Anne sat down at her desk and put away her personal things. "Now let's get to work. What do you have for me today? Katie gave me as much instruction as she could, so hopefully I can handle it myself. She's out for a fitting today."

Anne felt herself relaxing as she managed to have a normal conversation with Gherring. He moved behind her desk and reached to grab the mouse, bringing up the day's schedule on the computer. She felt herself shiver as his arm brushed against hers. She pulled away quickly, pretending to organize something in the desk drawer. Feeling Gherring's piercing gaze, Anne glanced up and realized he was waiting for her to respond to something he'd said.

"Oh, I'm sorry, what did you say?"

Gherring spoke with amused deliberation. "I said, I'm scheduled to be in conference all morning, so you and I can meet during lunch."

"Well, actually, I was supposed to have lunch with Sam, from Accounting." She noticed his frown. "But I could cancel, or you could come with us."

"No," he muttered. "That won't be necessary. You can have lunch with *Sam* from Accounting, and we'll meet afterward."

"But you should come. Sam's a lot of fun. We're eating next door at Papa's Place."

40

"I said *no*!" Gherring stalked into his office.

"I guess I'm supposed to work through lunch when Mr. Gherring is in town. He seemed pretty miffed with me," Anne confided across the small, checkered tablecloth. "I hate to think how much I'll miss my lunches here."

Papa's Place was always busy for lunch, but Papa George and his wife, May, now saved a table for Anne. She'd eaten there every day since Monday, when their nephew, Spencer, had saved her from a disastrous fall outside the restaurant. Anne had returned at noon, heralding huge accolades on Spencer when she met the restaurant owners, swearing he'd saved her life. Spencer protested her exaggerations, but George and May were proud of their nephew.

When Anne explained she was new to the city and alone, and admitted George reminded her of her Daddy, they responded by practically adopting her into their family. Papa and May already treated her like a daughter, and Anne was working on a plan to fix Spencer up with one of the receptionists at Gherring Inc.

"I invited him to come and eat with us, but he refused," said Anne.

"I'm glad he didn't come," Sam replied, shaking her blond head for emphasis. "He's just so intimidating."

"Oh, but I think y'all would get along great. I told you I think y'all have a lot in common. Y'all both like scuba diving and snow skiing. He seems to like dating blonds. You're beautiful and smart. Y'all both have grandmothers you're close to. I think y'all would be great together."

Sam choked, "Together? As in dating? Me and Mr. Gherring? You've got to be kidding! He would never... Oh my god! There he is!"

"There who is?" Anne craned her neck around to see the entrance to Papa's.

"There's Mr. Gherring," Sam whispered into her napkin, her eyes wide with terror. "And he's coming this way, and he looks furious."

Anne looked up at the scowling face of Steven Gherring as he approached her table. "I'm sorry to interrupt your lunch." He scanned the restaurant patrons as he spoke. "But something has come up that can't wait."

"Okay, I can come up to the office right now. Or if it's not something too private, you're welcome to join Sam and me."

"You mean Sam and your other friend here?" He glanced over his shoulder.

"Oh, I'm sorry, I thought you'd met before. Mr. Gherring, this is Samantha Lowe."

"Samantha? This is Sam from Accounting?"

Samantha blushed and spoke without quite making eye contact with the imposing man. "Yes, Mr. Gherring. You'd know me as Samantha. I think we've met at the monthly accounting meeting."

"Samantha," His face brightened. "It's so nice to see you Samantha. Yes, I believe now I remember seeing you in those dreadful meetings."

"You know, you and Samantha actually have a lot in common. She's into diving and skiing, just like you, Mr. Gherring."

"Really?" asked Gherring in a slightly distracted voice. "Well, you two enjoy your lunch. I'm going back up to the office to work on a project."

"Okay. Do you want me to come now?"

"Now? No. No hurry." He turned to leave.

"But I thought you had something urgent."

"It can wait," he said over his shoulder as he strode to the door.

Anne and Samantha stared at each other in confused silence. Finally, Anne broke the spell, asserting with an encouraging smile, "So... I think that went really well. Don't you think y'all would make a good couple?"

"Are you kidding me? I thought you were a matchmaker. Surely you can find someone that I have more in common with than Steven Gherring."

She sighed. Back to the drawing board.

Anne wrestled with the steaming cardboard food boxes while holding her purse wedged under her elbow as she tapped on Steven Gherring's office door with her foot. She tottered a bit, leaning against the door to regain her balance when it was suddenly jerked open. She tried to catch herself without flinging the food across the office, but her ankle turned on the three-inch heel. As she began to fall, Steven Gherring reached around and steadied her from behind, and only her purse fell to the floor.

"Oh my goodness! I just can't seem to control myself in these silly shoes." His arms were still around her, and he was pressed up against her back. Both of her hands were still fully occupied with the boxes of food, so she couldn't push him away. At least that was her reasoning.

Why didn't she just step away from him? She almost felt frozen in place. She could smell his after-shave or his soap or something. It was a clean, masculine smell, not one of those strong, sweet cologne scents. She hated those girly scents on men. Steven smelled good— but like a man. For a moment, she almost relaxed and leaned back into his strong arms. She stiffened and jerked away, swirling to face him.

"Thanks. I'm sorry!" Anne spoke rapidly while holding out the boxes. "I brought you, that is, May sent you a sample of their specials today. It's on the house. May says you've never eaten at Papa's, so you just don't know how good their food is. She says once you taste their food, you'll come back."

"I've already eaten a protein bar. I'm fine, thanks."

"A protein bar? That's all you're planning to eat for lunch? That's ridiculous! A grown man needs more for lunch than a protein bar. Just sit down and try a bite of these specials." She ushered him toward his desk. "I'll take it away if you don't like it, but I won't quit trying to make you eat a healthy lunch every day. I think that's part of my job."

She opened the aromatic boxes in front of him. "Today they have a choice of two Italian pastas and Papa's pot roast. The specials always come with salads or fresh steamed veggies."

Without further protest, he sampled each of the pastas and then took a bite of pot roast.

"Wow!" He forked another large bite. "This tastes just like Gram's pot roast!"

Anne chattered about how great the food was at Papa's Place and told Gherring all about George and May and Spencer. She was relieved to have successfully extracted herself from Gherring's arms before she embarrassed herself. She realized she hadn't been held in a man's arms for fifteen years. It had felt wonderful, just for a moment, to have someone strong to lean against.

She was an independent woman, and she'd taken care of herself and her girls for the past fifteen years without the help of a man. But it would be nice, just once, to have someone hold her and love her and take care of her. Maybe while she was looking for someone for Spencer and Mr. Gherring and a few other new friends, she'd find someone for herself. She really hadn't even looked at a man in that way for fifteen years. New York was a big city. Surely there was someone out there for her.

He was staring at her. "A penny for your thoughts."

"What?"

"You stopped talking, and you were obviously thinking about something, because you were smiling."

Anne blushed up to her ears. "Oh, I don't know what I was thinking about. I was probably thinking about my girls coming to visit. They're coming in three weeks."

"Emily and Charlotte, right?"

"How do you know their names?"

"Just part of the background check I had the detective do on you."

Anne's face turned red with wrath. "You had a detective investigate me—"

"Just kidding. Wait, don't hurt me!" he laughed. "You put it on your resume."

"Oh… Sorry."

"Yeah, I thought it was interesting you told about your children on your resume. Most applicants don't put their children's names on their resumes. But most of the applicants didn't have children, at least, they didn't claim to have children."

"My girls are evidence of some of my very best work. I couldn't leave them off my resume. And besides, I think family and children are the most important things in life."

His face suddenly clouded, and he pushed his food away. "Well, we have work to do."

"Of course," said Anne as she quickly gathered up the boxes and cleared the desk. "Let me grab my laptop."

She hurried to her desk, wondering how her words had stirred up the hurt in his eyes. Her heart went out to the man who for just a moment had looked like a small, lost boy.

Katie returned from her fitting that afternoon and pulled Anne away from her PowerPoint project. "I just remembered I haven't explained one of your most important jobs." Katie lowered her voice though no one else was in the room. "You're responsible for arranging for a female escort for Mr. Gherring for every formal event."

"Escort? Do you mean a call girl?"

Katie laughed at Anne. "Call girl... Wow, I forgot you're from the sticks. You're so wonderfully naïve. Of course I'm not talking about a prostitute. We usually arrange for an escort with this publicist."

She handed Anne a business card. "The contact is Charles Cooper. He handles publicity for many up and coming artists, performers, models, actresses, and businesswomen who need name recognition. Being seen at a function with Steven Gherring guarantees a write-up in the social columns and pictures in all the popular social media. In return, Mr. Gherring avoids having any social obligations beyond the event." Katie continued. "Mr. Cooper knows the qualities Mr. Gherring requires in an escort. He likes attractive women in their twenties and thirties, preferably tall, and able to carry on a decent conversation. And he never takes the same woman to another event."

"But why doesn't Mr. Gherring get his own dates for these events? Surely he wouldn't have any trouble finding someone who'd like to go with him, so he wouldn't have to go with a complete stranger."

"Well that's the problem. Lots of girls would like to date Mr. Gherring. In the past, he's had terrible drama after only one date with a girl. They're all desperate to marry him, and he probably thinks they all want him for his money. Sadly, it's probably true. So he makes it a point never to be seen with any woman more than once. That's why he has a reputation as a player, but in reality, he rarely dates anyone."

"But that's terrible. How will he ever find the right girl if he won't even take someone on a real date? There could be someone right here at Gherring Inc. who'd make him really happy, and he'd never know." Anne grabbed Katie's arm. "And not *every* girl out there would only be interested in him because he's rich. Some people don't care about money, and it's not like he's not attractive."

When she didn't respond, Anne noticed Katie standing with her lips pressed together, looking quite pale. She followed Katie's gaze to find Steven Gherring standing a few feet away, obviously intent on the conversation.

"I think I'm old enough to make my own decisions about my *personal life* and *whom* I will date and whether I will date *anyone*." Gherring turned his back on the pair and returned to his private office, closing the door behind him with a soft click.

Anne looked warily at Katie, who let out a low whistle. "Call the number on this card and have Mr. Cooper arrange for Mr. Gherring's date to the International Business Gala next Friday. Dress is formal, as you know. We've been so busy working on all the details of the reception I almost forgot to arrange for his escort."

"But do you think I should go apologize?" Anne asked, inclining her head toward Gherring's office.

Katie shook her head. "No, I think anything we say would make it worse. He'll forget eventually. Just do your job, and try to stay out of his personal life. And," Katie warned with a serious look, "don't ever gossip about Mr. Gherring. You absolutely cannot share any details about anything he says or does, business or personal. It's very important you stay completely out of his personal life."

"Of course," Anne said, wondering how she could find a match for Mr. Gherring while staying out of his personal life. But she would. She'd find a way. Somehow, she had to find a way.

Chapter Five - Monsieur

MONDAY MORNING, ANNE BREATHED A sigh of relief as she made it to her work desk without incident. No slips or falls on the way to work. This time, she wore her running shoes until she made it to her desk to change into her shiny spike-heeled pumps. She had a few strange looks on the elevator because of her footwear, but she knew she was really protecting those critics from imminent disaster by postponing the change to her awkward dress shoes.

Slipping into her heels and stashing her running shoes in her oversized handbag, Anne glanced at the clock on her computer. Only seven fifteen. She was really proud of herself. She started checking messages and emails, knowing she needed to finalize the plans for the gala on Friday night. Her first big event. She was glad Katie was still helping her. She felt the pressure to make everything perfect.

Not only did she have to prepare for the party, but she also had to make travel and hotel arrangements for all the company's internationally stationed executives. The first ones were due to arrive in New York on Monday morning. Steven Gherring would be holding meetings with international clients all week, but the huge formal party would happen on Friday night. Katie was only working Thursday and Friday this week, so Anne had to handle all the crises in the early part of the week by herself.

This would be a hectic week for all the employees at Gherring Inc. In evidence of the impending increase in workload, employees poured out of the elevators, hurrying off to get an early start.

Although she'd only been at Gherring Inc. for a week, Anne was already well liked. Calls of "Morning Anne!", "Hey Anne!", "Hi Anne," kept her looking up to respond.

Anne liked pretty much everyone, unless they were purposefully rude. She'd always been taught to give people the benefit of the doubt and not to take offense unless she was certain the offending person meant to be offensive. Consequently, anyone who met Anne felt she was a friend, and a number of folks who didn't have many friends were especially grateful to be on the receiving end of her smile and encouraging words. There were other elevators that serviced the top floor of Town Center Economic Tower, where Gherring Inc. was located, but most employees took the central elevator in hopes of seeing and being seen by Steven Gherring, unless they were late in arriving.

"Hey Anne," said a timid male voice from the edge of her desk. Anne looked up to see Tanner West, a thirty-something financial consultant who had moved from Dallas six months ago to join Gherring Inc. "Are you and Sam still having lunch next door today?"

Anne had invited Tanner to join her and Sam at Papa's Place after she was forced to admit Mr. Gherring was not going to be Sam's match-made-in-heaven. Tanner was extremely shy and hadn't agreed to join the lunch pair immediately. Obviously, he'd gained courage over the weekend.

"Actually, Tanner, I'm going to be working through lunch every day this week."

Tanner looked disappointed, but nodded and turned to go. Anne stopped him.

"Wait. I was going to ask if you could go with Sam, and y'all could bring something for me when you come back?"

"Um, sure... if you think she would want to go with me... without you... I mean, I don't know if she'll want to go."

"I'll ask her and let you know. I really appreciate it. You'll be doing me a great favor."

"Well, I'll bring you lunch even if she doesn't want to go with me."

"You're so sweet, Tanner! I'll call you later in the morning." She hoped Sam would agree to go to lunch with him. She'd hate to dash his ego now he'd gotten the courage to meet Sam.

Anne returned to her work, so absorbed she didn't notice when a tall brown-haired man with a neatly trimmed goatee walked up to her desk. He stood quietly for several moments, observing her with unabashed interest.

"*Bon jour, Mademoiselle. Tu est tres jolie!*"

She looked up in surprise at the handsome man in the well-tailored suit that emphasized his broad shoulders. Well, handsome was not an adequate word. He was mouth-watering, smokin'-hot, drop-jaw sexy!

"*Merci beaucoup*!" She couldn't help being flattered by the attention.

He flashed a warm smile with even white teeth. "Tu parle francais?"

"*Non*! No! I've just exhausted my memory of college French. Please don't test me anymore."

He leaned closer and declared, "*Charmonte*!" He continued in slightly accented English, "Yes, you are charming. I love your accent."

"Wait." Anne laughed. "Isn't that my line?"

"I am *Henri*," he said, pronouncing it *ahn-ree*, and reaching out to catch her hand. He pressed his lips lightly on her fingers. "You are new, *oui*? Katie is not here?"

"Oh, Katie is out for three days doing wedding planning, but she'll be back on Thursday."

"Wedding! My Katie is with another man?" At Anne's shocked look, Henri laughed aloud, his green eyes sparkling. "No, I am teasing you. She was never mine. But you… maybe you could be mine."

"Monsieur, I have a feeling I'd just be one of many if I were yours. I think you have plenty of women to keep you company."

"*Non*! No! There have been others before, but they are all gone." He blinked puppy-dog eyes. "I am all alone."

"I doubt that seriously. No woman could resist that face, I think."

"And you? Can you resist me?" He lifted her hand again and turned it over to kiss her wrist gently.

Anne pulled her hand away slowly.

"No, I can resist you. At least I hope I can. You seem pretty dangerous to me."

"I am not dangerous. I am a pussy cat."

"I've always been a dog-person," Anne replied. "You can trust your dog. But a cat can be purring in your lap one minute and digging his claws into your leg the next."

"Do not worry," he countered. "This cat has no claws. Very safe."

Anne laughed. "I don't think I believe you!"

"I can show you how safe I am. You will like this cat. Will you give me a chance?"

"I don't know."

"Earlier I was thinking that this week would be boring. A boring week of business, a long boring time. But now I am thinking that a week is too short. I am thinking a week is not enough time to spend with such a beautiful woman."

"Beautiful woman... Now I know I'm getting a line."

Henri's eyes widened. "You do not know? You do not know you are beautiful? Your eyes are so dark that I could get lost in them. I've never seen such eyes."

"Henri, you're a smooth-talker. But I've been warned about French men. I know y'all just lead women on and then break our hearts."

Henri put his hand over his heart. "Never! For you I would give up my wandering ways. For you—"

"*Henri!*" a stern voice spoke from across the room. Steven Gherring was glaring from his office doorway. "I see you've met *my* personal executive assistant. Now if you're ready to get to work..."

Henri turned toward Gherring's office, then leaned back and whispered urgently. "I do not know your name."

"It's Anne," she whispered back, despite her boss' glower.

"Perhaps we could have lunch together," Henri said over his shoulder as he walked away.

Gherring's voice was scolding. "We'll be meeting through lunch today, Henri. If you worked as hard on your business negotiations as you do on your flirtations, you'd probably have a much better report for me." They disappeared behind the heavy wooden doors.

Anne realized her face was warm. She'd enjoyed the playful exchange with the handsome French stranger. He wasn't really her type. But then again, did she even have a type anymore? Anyway, it was a harmless exchange. Like he said, he was only in the country for a week. Nothing serious would ever come of it. But hadn't she come to New York for a bit of adventure?

The morning flew by as Anne wrestled with all the travel plans. Three more men and two women had arrived to join with Gherring in the conference room adjacent to his office. When Anne entered the conference room to set up the PowerPoint, she noticed Henri trying to catch her eye. But Gherring blocked her view as he asked her to review the location of various presentations on the laptop. She repeated the instructions, thinking they'd just discussed those details on Friday.

"And can I get anything else for you? Would you like for me to bring everyone a bottle of water?" she asked Gherring.

"No, they can get their own waters."

"What about lunch? Do you want me to order in for the entire group?"

"Yes, yes... That'll be fine." He attempted to shoo her from the room.

"I'll just ask everyone what they want to order," she started to skirt around Gherring, heading toward the smiling Henri.

Gherring stepped in front of her, effectively blocking her way. "That won't be necessary, Ms. Best. Just order some of the specials from Papa's."

Henri was waving at her behind Gherring, and Anne leaned sideways in an effort to see him, momentarily forgetting how precariously she was balanced in her high heels. She started to topple over, but Gherring caught her arms and held her upright. Blushing furiously, she rushed from the room, her heart pounding in her chest. Why was she so clumsy? Henri probably wouldn't be interested in such a klutz, anyway.

Anne returned to her desk to order lunch from Papa's. May answered the phone and took the lunch orders, arranging delivery at twelve thirty. "So you aren't coming down for lunch today?" May asked with a bit of a pout in her voice.

"No, I'll be working through lunch every day this week, May. Tell Papa I'll stop by on my way home if the door's open." she knew Papa's was only open for breakfast and lunch, except on Fridays and Saturdays.

"But you need to eat," May protested with motherly concern.

"Don't worry. I won't miss my daily Papa's special lunch. Today, my friends are bringing lunch up to me after they eat. You remember my friend, Sam?" She lowered her voice. "Well today, she's eating lunch with a sweet young man from the office, named Tanner. Be sure y'all seat them at a romantic table."

"But I thought you told me you were trying to set Sam up with your boss?"

"Well, I don't think that's going to work out. I have high hopes for this new match, but I need to keep working on my boss." Anne stopped, remembering what Katie had said about gossiping. "But that has to be our secret. You can't tell anyone I'm trying to find a match for Mr. Gherring."

"No worries, honey. My lips are sealed. They couldn't drag that information outta me even if they tortured me. I won't tell a soul… unless someone offers to give me a good neck massage. Then my lips will go all loosey-goosey." May started laughing.

"Now I'm serious. Katie says I'm never supposed to get involved in Mr. Gherring's private life. I could lose my job."

"Really dear, I won't tell anybody."

Lunch arrived at precisely twelve thirty. Anne attempted to help serve the food in the conference room, *to speed things up*, but Gherring took the food bags from the delivery boy and shut the door before she could even peek inside. The smell of the food was mouthwatering, and Anne waited impatiently for her lunch to arrive, drinking water to quiet her growling stomach. Sam appeared at one fifteen with her lunch, chicken smothered in some kind of wonderful mushroom cream sauce.

Anne attacked her food with a vengeance, while interrogating Sam about her lunch date. "Did you like him? Did y'all have anything to talk about? He's so shy—but you've got to admit he's really cute."

Sam chuckled. "Yes, yes and yes. He is so shy I thought we weren't going to be able to carry on a conversation. That is, he *was* so shy, until he found out I like the Beatles. Turns out he's a nut for the Beatles just like me, and he has a great collection of vinyls. He pulled out my chair for me, waited for me to go through every door first, and insisted on buying lunch. So, yes, he's really sweet and we're going Wednesday night to hear a Beatles cover band."

"I knew it!"

"Don't look so smug. We're not engaged. We're just listening to music together. And anyway, last week you were trying to set me up with—"

52

"Shhhh!" warned Anne, glancing toward the conference room. "I admit I messed up on that one, but don't tell anyone. I don't want to get in trouble."

"Okay, I won't tell anyone you tried to set us up. They wouldn't believe it anyway."

"But if things work out with Tanner, I want full credit."

Anne waited until five forty-five for the meeting to end, hoping to have a chance to see Henri. The door opened and Gherring peered out. When he spotted Anne at her desk, he looked decidedly irritated. "You're still here?"

"Yes, I thought you might need me for something before you go home."

"Well, I don't. Wait, I do need something." He closed the conference room door and stepped toward his office. "I need for you to check something on my calendar." She followed him into his office, and he motioned for her to sit behind his desk. "Would you mind pulling up my calendar for the week? I'll be right back."

He stepped out, shutting the door behind him. Anne pulled up his calendar, puzzling over what his problem might be. They'd been working on the week's schedule, squeezing in meetings at every possible moment with little wasted time. Gherring didn't believe in frivolity and only engaged in social functions when absolutely necessary. Hence, the single formal gala at the end of an exhausting week of meeting, planning, and negotiating. Gherring returned, looking happier and relaxed.

"What did you want me to check on your calendar? Do you need to change something? I hope you don't need to add another appointment. Y'all will have to meet at midnight."

"No, I just want to make sure our calendars match."

Anne stared at him in confusion. "Of course they match—they're synced automatically."

"Oh yes, that's right. Well, that's great—you can go now."

Anne walked out of Gherring's office, giving him a wide berth. She noticed the conference room door was open, but as she approached she saw the room was dark and empty. Realizing he'd purposely hidden her until Henri was gone, she fumed inwardly.

She turned to find Gherring smiling from his office door. "Goodnight, Ms. Best. I'll see you in the morning. It's getting rather late. Would you like a lift home?"

"No, but thank you, *sir*." He was treating her like a child, so she would address him like a father.

"I think *sir* is a bit much—I'm not that much older than you." At Anne's silence, he retorted, "That man's not safe; he's not to be trusted."

"Who?" asked Anne, deliberately obtuse, as she tied on her running shoes, pulling a little too vigorously on the strings.

"*Henri*. You can't trust him—he's a scoundrel. He flits from one woman to another. He's a… "

"Player?" Anne offered the term the media often used to describe Gherring.

"Yes, he's a player." He followed her toward the elevator, and she stopped, returning his glare.

"Well, I think that a *player* is simply a *man* who hasn't found the *right woman*." She turned and stepped into the elevator without looking back.

*****

Tuesday morning found Anne at her desk by seven fifteen. Gherring arrived at nine thirty with fifteen international account executives, fresh from a breakfast meeting. Anne scanned the crew as they filed into the conference room, but Henri wasn't among the crowd. Gherring stopped by Anne's desk

"How was your evening, Ms. Best?"

"It was fine, sir. And yours?"

Although her tone was without rancor, Gherring winced at her verbiage. "So I must assume you're still angry with me?"

"I have no idea what you're referring to. Why would you think I was angry? Did you do something I should be angry about?"

"You know very well what I'm talking about. And no, I didn't do anything you should be angry about. All I did was prevent Henri from hurting you. He would just use you. You're too naïve to realize, but I did the right thing."

"Let's see… How did you put it?" She paused as if trying to recall. "I think I'm old enough to make my own decisions about my *personal*

54

life and *whom* I'll date and whether I'll date *anyone*. But I suppose it's impossible for you to believe a man might actually be interested in having a relationship with me. And I'm sure you're right—he probably just wanted to use me. Why else would he talk to someone like me?" Anne wiped furiously at the tears that began to spill from her eyes.

"That's not what I meant."

"It really doesn't matter—it's a moot point, now."

"Well, for what it's worth," Gherring said quietly, "I'm sorry I hurt your feelings. But" he continued quickly, "I still believe I did the right thing."

Anne still refused to make eye contact. "Did you need help with anything else? Perhaps you've forgotten how to log in to your computer or make a phone call," she suggested with a hint of sarcasm.

"Actually, I do need your help today." He hesitated. "We have an important client from Germany, and he brought his wife on the trip. We have a lunch meeting planned, and I thought you might come along so his wife would feel more comfortable. It would really be a great help, and it might help us land a big account."

Anne didn't look up from her computer. "Of course, Mr. Gherring. I'll be glad to help in any way." Gherring was still standing at her desk. "Is there anything else, sir?"

Gherring's lips pressed in a straight line. "No, Ms. Best. That's all for now. Thank you." He disappeared into the conference room.

Anne had never been in a limousine before. She tried to act nonchalant, but she couldn't hide her excitement and curiosity. There was even a bar inside. The others were obviously accustomed to the fancy ride. The four men, including the client, Alexander Klein, were already intently discussing business. Johanna Klein was an attractive blond in her fifties with an engaging smile. She chatted comfortably with Anne, apparently fascinated by her life in Texas.

"I can't believe how well y'all both speak English. I've always wished I was fluent in another language," Anne confessed to Johanna. "How many languages can you speak?"

"I can speak German, English and French fluently. I can speak enough Italian and Spanish to communicate. We start language training at an early age in Germany, and I have traveled extensively."

Johanna glanced at her husband. "Alexander is a wonderful and unusual man—he has always invited me on all his travels. Most businessmen would think having their wives along was a bother."

"Oh, I'm so jealous. I haven't really been anywhere. I've never even been out of the country, except one time across the border to Mexico for an hour. Even New York City is a big adventure for me, although I haven't really done anything but work since I've been here. But I've got my passport—I got one fifteen years ago, just in case I ever got a chance to go somewhere. I even had it renewed." She peered wistfully out the window. "You never know. Maybe someday..."

Johanna glanced at Gherring who was casually eavesdropping. "So Mr. Gherring, however did you find your secretary? She is delightful!" She turned to her husband. "Alexander, can't you get an extra ticket to the musical tonight? Anne needs to experience New York."

"Yes, of course you can bring her along. I acquired two extra tickets in case we needed them. And Mr. Gherring could come also. I'm sure we will still have business to discuss."

"Oh no—I couldn't impose." Anne stole a terrified look at Gherring. She knew he wouldn't want to be seen in public with her. He was only seen in the company of beautiful young women. His escorts had to be intelligent and composed. He'd be mortified to be seen with his secretary, especially an unsophisticated forty-five-year-old woman from Texas.

"I'm sure Mr. Gherring and Mr. Alexander know an account executive who'd be much more helpful." She glanced at Gherring again, but he hid his emotions well.

"Nonsense," Johanna smiled. "I would love to have some female company. It's settled."

"Gherring, will you be joining us?" asked Alexander.

He was quiet for a moment and then opened his mouth to respond. But Anne interrupted. "Mr. Gherring, don't you have an engagement tonight? I can check the calendar when we get back to the office."

She thought he looked relieved. "Yes, I think you're right, Ms. Best. I may have a prior commitment."

Alexander seemed disappointed, but Johanna said, "That's fine, Anne. If Mr. Gherring can't use the ticket, you can bring a date along."

Anne began a frantic search inside her purse for nothing whatsoever in an attempt to hide the flush she felt on her face.

Johanna continued. "Perhaps you could get off early, and we could go shopping."

Gherring was clenching his jaw and Anne thought he might object, but Alexander said, "I'm so glad you are having fun, darling. If we sign a contract today with Gherring Inc., we will probably be coming to New York often."

At this encouraging pronouncement, Gherring smiled broadly and turned the conversation back to business.

Lunch was long, but productive. Alexander Klein appeared to be ready to make a commitment once a few details were ironed out back at Gherring Inc. Johanna Klein returned with her husband to the top floor, once again suggesting Anne be allowed to leave work early for a shopping trip. On the trip up the elevator, Gherring, feeling very generous because of the successful negotiations, agreed Ms. Best should accompany Mrs. Klein.

"Anything to keep our clients happy," Gherring smiled as the group departed the elevator.

Suddenly Johanna gasped, "What beautiful roses—those are gorgeous. Are they yours, Anne?" Gherring's smile turned to a scowl as he eyed the flowers.

"I don't know." Anne stared agape at the enormous bouquet of red roses on her desk. Her body froze in place, as the rest of the group filed past.

Johanna gently moved her toward the desk. "Come, come. We have to see who sent the flowers to you. Look at the card." Johanna peered over Anne's shoulder as she opened the florist's envelope with shaking hands. "Who is Henri?"

Anne felt her face burning as she read the card.

You have captured my heart with your beauty! I await your call. 212-882-8945
Your devoted,
Henri

Johanna smiled. "Why didn't you tell me you had an admirer? Maybe he could come to the play."

At that moment, Gherring emerged from his office, speaking to Alexander in a loud voice. "I have good news. My calendar is open tonight, so I can accompany you to the musical after all. Thanks so much for the invitation."

*****

As they zipped through traffic in the taxi, Johanna quizzed Anne about Henri. She demanded details about his appearance and how they met. She declared the whole thing to be very romantic. Then she told Anne how she'd met her husband.

"Someone introduced us at a party, and when I shook his hand, I felt sparks. I think he felt them, too."

"So it was love at first sight?"

"Not exactly. I was engaged to someone else when I met Alexander. I tried to forget about Alexander and go on with my marriage plans. But I kept running into him, and every time, those sparks were there. I finally started wondering why there were sparks with Alexander and no sparks with my fiancé." Johanna chuckled and shrugged her shoulders.

"And now? Are there still sparks between y'all?"

Johanna answered with a soft smile. "Every time, there are sparks. But sometimes those sparks come from us hitting our heads together. Still, there are always sparks…"

To Anne's surprise, Johanna led her into an upscale resale shop. "I love shopping here. My family did not have a lot of money when I was a child. I still hate wasting money. I love a bargain!"

Johanna was an expert huntress, quickly spotting several dresses for herself, and grabbing potential outfits for Anne as well. In two hours, each woman had acquired a new dress for the musical, and Johanna had talked Anne into purchasing a number of cute casual ensembles. They returned to Gherring Inc. and Anne rushed to tie up the loose ends from her afternoon hiatus. She decided to leave her roses at work rather than wrestle with carrying them home on the subway. She left work on time, hoping to have time for a quick shower before the musical. But noticing the door was unlocked at the diner, she stopped in to visit at Papa's Place.

George came out of the kitchen to sit and chat for a moment with Anne. "We've missed you. Are you sure you're getting enough to eat?"

"Yes, no worries—I never skip a meal. I miss you and May, and I need some advice."

"About work or food?"

"No, I need advice about a man."

George held up a hand. "Speak no more—I'm going to get May. I'm no good for dating advice, and May will kill me if she misses this, anyway." George disappeared through the office door, calling May's name.

May appeared with a clipboard in her hand. "I've been working on inventory. Whew—I need a break. Now, tell me all about your man troubles."

"Well, long-story-short, there's a Frenchman named Henri who's been flirting with me, but Mr. Gherring says he has a reputation for using women. He sent me roses."

"Mr. Gherring sent you roses?"

"No, Henri sent me roses and asked me to call him. But that's not the only problem. Now I'm sort of going to a play with Mr. Gherring. Not really *with* him, but I will be with him and another couple."

"Mr. Gherring asked you to a play?"

"No, Mrs. Klein asked me to go to the play, and Mr. Gherring decided to go. I think he just didn't want me to go with Henri."

"Henri invited you to the play, too?"

Anne sighed at the perplexity. "No, but Mr. Gherring was invited to the play and didn't want to go if I was going, so he said he had a prior engagement. Then he suddenly decided to go to the play when Mrs. Klein suggested I invite Henri."

May shook her head. "I'm a little confused. So the problem is you don't want to go the play with Mr. Gherring? You'd rather go with Henri?"

"It's not that I don't want to go to the play with the Kleins and Mr. Gherring. It's just that I know Mr. Gherring doesn't want to be seen with me in public."

"And why wouldn't he want to be seen in public with you?"

"Well, I'm not his type. I'm not young and beautiful like the women he usually dates. I'm just a hick from Texas. What if people thought we were, you know... together-together?"

"Well I guess that's his problem isn't it? He didn't have to go. He had an excuse already." May snuffed a bit. "And I think he'd be lucky to have you. There's nothing wrong with you."

"Well, I guess it's his own fault. I think he just likes to control people's lives—especially people like me. He doesn't respect me enough to believe I can think for myself."

"Well, dear. You should just go to that play and have a good time. Gherring will just have to deal with the consequences of his attempt to control your life." She smiled and winked. "And you can still call Henri."

"Yes, you're right. I can. Thanks May. Everything sounds better since I've talked to you. I've got to go and get ready for tonight."

"Good luck, dear. What are you going to see?"

"I'm so excited. My first New York City musical—we're going to see *Wicked*."

Charlie assessed her mom's appearance on Skype as she twirled around in her newly acquired dress. "I'm so jealous, Mom—you get to see Wicked. And now you're making friends from all over the world, although it sounds like Henri wants to be more than friends."

"So, do you like the dress?"

"Yes, it's adorable. But maybe you should wear Giselle." Anne had an extremely sexy, black formal dress, with a deep v in the front and a really deep v in the back. Charlie and Emily had pitched in together to buy the expensive dress, which they nicknamed for its designer, and they'd each worn it for very special occasions. Both girls had agreed their mom should take Giselle to New York City.

"No way—I'm not wasting Giselle on this outing. Anyway, I'd look silly wearing a formal."

"I'm just kidding," Charlie said. "Your new dress will be perfect. What shoes are you going to wear?"

"I've got these cute wedge heels." She held up her shoes to the camera."

"Oh yes, those are perfect."

"Yes, and I won't lose my balance in wedges like I do in those spike heels."

"So let's get this straight—my mom is going to see a play in New York with Steven Gherring."

"No," Anne shot back quickly. "I am *not* going with Mr. Gherring. I'm going with Johanna and Alexander Klein, and Mr. Gherring is going also."

"But aren't you going to sit together?"

"No, I've thought about that. I think the Kleins will sit in the middle, and I will sit by Johanna and Mr. Gherring will sit by Alexander. That way the tabloids won't think we're together."

"I don't know, Mom. After what he did, trying to spoil your chances with Henri, trying to control your life, maybe you shouldn't let him off so easy."

"What do you mean?"

"Maybe you should hang all over him and act like his date. If that complicates his life, that's his problem."

"There's no way I could ever do that. Anyway, a stunt like that could cost me my job."

Charlie screwed up her face. "Yep, there is that little job problem. Well, okay. But maybe you should meet Henri for coffee after the play. You haven't called him yet, have you?"

"You know what, Charlie? You're a genius. I'll call him right now. If he agrees, he can meet me at the theater and bring me home. Johanna won't mind—she thinks the whole thing is romantic."

Charlie clapped her hands. "This is better than Downton Abbey!"

Henri sounded ecstatic when Anne called him. He quickly agreed to the late night coffee date, unfazed by the fact he'd be picking her up from an outing that included Gherring. Feeling freshly confident after Henri's charms were lathered upon her, Anne went downstairs to wait for the limousine, which would pick up the Kleins before stopping at their apartment building.

Gherring, who was already waiting downstairs, looked her way when she entered the lobby. At Gherring's perusal, she was suddenly conscious of the side slit in the dress that revealed a bit more thigh than she was quite comfortable with. She quickly donned her leather dress coat before continuing into the room.

She heard a whistle from her left. "Oh baby—you look hot, Anne!" called Antonio. She laughed and walked over to share a hug with Antonio.

"How're things with Rayna?" she asked quietly. "Are y'all still dating?"

He grinned broadly. "It's great. She's great. And I'm forever indebted to you. So, if you ever need a favor, just let me know." He whispered, "What's wrong with Mr. Gherring?"

She glanced over her shoulder at the furrowed brow of Steven Gherring. "Don't pay any attention to him—he just has a bee in his bonnet over having to go to this musical tonight with some clients from Germany. And he's trying to control my life."

Then she giggled and whispered in his ear, "Let's see if he dislikes Italian men as much as French men." She gave Antonio another big hug.

"Oh my god," Antonio whispered. "Here he comes, and I think he might kill me."

"Anne!" Gherring called as he walked toward the couple. "We should wait at the door. The limo will be here any time."

She turned around, with her arm still around Antonio's waist. "Yes, Mr. Gherring. I'll be right there." She turned her back to Gherring and gave Antonio another hug and a big wink, although the young doorman looked rather terrified facing Gherring's glare.

"I'm ready, now," she said to Gherring as she turned and marched past him and out the front door.

Anne stood shivering outside. "I didn't mean we needed to wait outside the door," muttered Gherring. But she stubbornly refused to return inside. Ten minutes passed. Anne was feeling like a Popsicle and finally beginning to regret the pride that kept her standing in the cold.

"Really Anne, we should wait inside. This is ridiculous," Gherring complained.

Just then, the limousine arrived, and she hopped in, hoping to sit next to Johanna. Unfortunately, the couple was seated together on the short side next to the bar, so she sat opposite Johanna. Gherring joined, but left a large space between them, placing his coat in the space on the seat.

62

Johanna chatted excitedly about the play, while Gherring and Alexander began to talk business. After a short ride, the limo pulled in at the curb in front of the theatre. Although limousines were quite common in New York, the crowd still watched to see who might emerge. She jumped out quickly ahead of Alexander, to avoid being seen with Gherring. As she made her way into the theatre, she heard people in the crowd exclaiming as they recognized Gherring.

When the usher led them to their seats, she found her seating strategy was impossible to execute. "I'm sorry," said Johanna, "but we have two pairs of tickets, one directly behind the other. So I have a plan. Anne and I will sit in the front seats for the first half, and then Alexander and Anne can trade after intermission."

As usual, Johanna had her way, so Anne found herself sitting in front of Gherring, relieved she could ignore him for at least half of the play. She noticed people were looking in her direction, but quickly realized the attention was aimed at the man behind her. She was nervous and uncomfortable, but Johanna was talkative enough for the whole group. Then the lights dimmed and the musical began. She soon forgot everyone around her and all her worries as the story progressed. She was completely enthralled—caught up in the music and plot and emotions.

When the lights came up for intermission, Anne realized she was sitting forward in her seat, entranced.

"Hello?" Johanna tapped on Anne's arm. She turned to Johanna who was laughing with the men seated behind her and heard her saying, "She's in another world—"

"Oh, I'm sorry. Did I miss something?"

"No dear. I think you were actually in Oz. I'm so glad you are enjoying the play."

"It's… It's amazing. It's so wonderful—I never imagined how great it could be. I've never seen anything like it. And the actors are so good and their voices are amazing, and the sets, and the costumes…"

Johanna's voice tinkled with laughter. "It's more fun watching you than watching the play. Of course, I've seen it before, but Wicked is wonderful every time." She patted Anne's arm. "Would you like to visit the ladies room before we change seats?"

Anne nodded in agreement, abruptly feeling extremely tense about sitting next to Gherring. As they walked into the lobby, Anne told Johanna that Henri would be picking her up after the play. Johanna was delighted and promised to drop by Gherring Inc. the next day to hear about the first romantic date with her mysterious Frenchman.

As the lights flickered to signal the end of the intermission, Anne returned to the theater to take her place next to Gherring. She continued to talk with Johanna until the lights dimmed and the second half began. At first, she sat stiffly in her chair, but soon she was absorbed in the excitement of the musical production. Occasionally, she sensed Gherring looking at her, but when she glanced his direction, he seemed to be ignoring her presence.

Then the two lead characters began to sing the emotionally tugging duet, *For Good*. Anne couldn't help herself, as tears streamed down her face. She thought of all the people in her life that had loved her and effectively changed her life *for good*. Sniffling, she dug into her purse looking for a tissue, but Gherring handed her his handkerchief. She looked up, gratefully mouthing, "Thank you," and he simply nodded, a slight smile on the face that had looked so grim the entire evening.

When the play ended, she clapped so hard she thought her hands would break. She even threw in a shrill wolf whistle, at which her three companions stared in amazement or perhaps mortification. But she didn't care. She would've thrown flowers at the feet of the actors if she were able. Gherring must have enjoyed the evening despite having to go with her, because he actually smiled and talked pleasantly as they walked out of the theater into the lobby. Suddenly, his expression became a glower.

"Hello, Anne!" exclaimed Henri as he took her hand and raised it to his lips. "You look very beautiful tonight. And who is this lovely friend you have with you?" he asked, indicating Johanna.

"You must be Henri," Johanna addressed the dashing man with twinkling green eyes. "You are just as charming as Anne described. But you are wasting your flattery on me—I am already taken," she said as she took Alexander's arm. For his part, Alexander seemed unfazed by Henri's flirtations.

"Oh, that is sad for me, but lucky for him." Henri smiled teasingly. "But this one beautiful woman is already too much for me." He tucked Anne's hand in the crook of his arm.

Gherring spoke between clenched teeth. "What are you doing here, Henri?"

"I am here to escort the beautiful woman home, with a little detour *en route*." He winked at Anne. "And we should go now. I have so little time with *ma jolie femme*." He led her quickly out the theatre doors. She didn't look back, but she felt Gherring's intense stare. She knew Johanna would report Gherring's reaction when she came by the office the next day. They strolled along the street, teeming with people despite the late hour.

"Henri, maybe this was a bad idea. Mr. Gherring looked really angry. What if he fires you?"

"He cannot fire me. On paper I work for Gherring, but only by agreement, by contract, with our company, La Porte. We have joint ventures with Gherring Inc. *Mon père*, my father is chairman now, and I will be chairman in two years. Monsieur Gherring needs me." He chuckled a bit. "But he does not like me, that is for certain."

Then he stopped and his eyebrows drew together *"Mon dieu*! He could fire *you*. *Je suis désolé*. I am sorry—I was not thinking. I should take you back?"

Anne considered for only a moment. "No. I'm not going back. I can't let him think he can control whom I date. He's only my boss at work. If he fires me, I'll just go back to Texas." She took Henri's arm and started walking again. "Now tell me about Paris... Is it as beautiful as they say?"

Emily's face looked irritated as she Skyped with her mom. It was Wednesday night, and Anne was reporting in to her daughter. Unfortunately, Emily had learned of her mom's date with Henri from her sister, and now she was demanding details. "I can't believe you didn't even call me."

"Well there just wasn't time..."

"But you called Charlie. You even showed her the dress before your date."

"Okay, I'm sorry, I'm sorry. But you're still my favorite."

Emily knew this game well. "But didn't you tell Charlie *she* was your favorite?"

"Yes, but of course I was lying to Charlie. You're the real favorite."

Emily chuckled. "Okay, just give me the details about the big date so I can tell Charlie I heard about it first."

"Well, as you know, first I went to see Wicked with the Kleins and Mr. Gherring."

"How was it?"

"A-ma-zing! I can't even tell you how much fun it was."

"I knew you'd love it. But how did Mr. Gherring act. You know, was he weird about being seen with you, like you thought he would be?"

"No, he wasn't too bad. He was uptight as usual until after the play, when Henri showed up."

"So was he mad you were going somewhere with Henri?"

"Ohhhhh—yeah. He was furious. It turns out he just doesn't like Henri. Evidently that's why he didn't want me to go out with him. But Henri was a perfect gentleman. We walked to a coffee shop, and I got the best hot chocolate I've ever had in my life. And then we walked around a bit. I was getting cold, so he took off his long wool coat and put it over me. I thought he would freeze to death, but he swore he was used to the cold weather.

"He told me all about Paris, and the little town in the countryside where he grew up. Then we took a taxi back to the apartment and he walked me inside. He kept the taxi outside, so I knew he wasn't trying to get invited upstairs."

"So… did he kiss you goodnight?"

"He just said, '*Tu es si parfait*.' And then he hugged me. When he pulled away, he bent down, and I thought he was going to try to kiss me—I was so nervous. But he just bent down and lifted my hand up and kissed it."

"Oh my gosh. That's so romantic." Emily held the back of her hand to her forehead in an exaggerated swoon. "What does that mean—what he said to you?"

"It means 'you are so perfect.' And today, he sent a box of candy to the office—dark chocolates."

"The best. Did it have a note with it?"

"Yes, it said, '*Tu avez capturé mon coeur*!' That's 'You have captured my heart!'"

"Wow, Mom. So do you like him?"

Anne thought for a moment before she spoke. "Yes I do, I like him. No doubt, he's pretty hot. I don't even know why he's interested in me. But he makes me feel very special, like I'm important. He seems to like everything about me, even my lack of sophistication."

"But?"

"But I feel like… It's hard to explain. I feel like he'd have to change for us to have a future together, and I think he knows it. And I feel like he wishes he could change, but he knows it'll never happen."

"That's a lot of feelings, Mom. You know you can't depend on your feelings. Did he actually say any of those things?"

"No, but he said it with his eyes and his actions. I know he's a bit of a player, but he treated me like I was a lady. Like he was protecting me from himself." Anne sighed. "And then there's Mr. Gherring."

"What about Mr. Gherring?"

"Well, Johanna said he barely spoke on the way back to the apartment after I left with Henri. And then today, he literally didn't speak to me. He just avoided me altogether. He must have been at work by six thirty, and he stayed in his office or conference room in meetings all day. There was no opportunity to talk to him."

"So, do you think he's really mad at you? For defying him and going out with Henri?"

"Or maybe because of the picture that came out in the social column."

"What picture?"

"I'll text you the link. Sam showed it to me at work today. It's a picture of me and Gherring sitting together at Wicked. I had no idea anyone was taking pictures. That play was really emotional, and you know how I am. I was watching the play and crying, and Gherring was staring at me. The caption read, 'Steven Gherring breaks another heart!'"

"I can't believe it. They really don't give him a break do they? I never realized how hard it is to be rich and famous." She thought for a moment, and then smiled. "But I'd still like to give it a try."

"I really do feel bad for him. I took my roses home today, so he wouldn't feel like I'm flaunting Henri in his face. From the little I know of Henri, I have a feeling he does things on purpose to irritate Mr. Gherring. Everything is like game for Henri, and Gherring takes everything so seriously. I wonder if he ever relaxes and lets loose."

"So, are you and Henri going out again?"

"He told me he'd call me tonight, but he's in Chicago until Friday."

Emily looked smug. "Okay, I'm going to call Charlie and tell her everything, so don't bother to call her yourself."

"Oh thanks—you're so much help."

"Don't mention it. That's why I'm your favorite."

Thursday, Katie was back at the office. Anne updated her on the plans for the big reception and briefed her on the new contracts she'd sent to the legal department. Then she casually mentioned Henri's name.

"Henri was here? I love him—he's so much fun. A little flirty, but he doesn't mean anything by it. Gherring hates him, though." Katie gave a furtive glance toward Gherring's office doors.

"Why does Gherring dislike Henri?"

Katie kept her voice low. "This is just between us, right? But I think you need to know. About five years ago Gherring was engaged to a Michelle Caravan. She was sweet and beautiful, and very rich—an heiress to the Caravan estate. But she wanted to have a family, have children, and Gherring wouldn't even discuss it. So they broke up very discreetly, kept everything out of the press."

She stopped to check over her shoulder. "A few months later, Henri started dating her. They dated for six months or so, and she was pretty serious about him, but Henri broke it off. This time it was very public. The breakup happened in France, and the paparazzi took some candid pictures with them arguing and her crying. No one really knows what happened, but Gherring was convinced Henri was cheating on her. He's hated Henri ever since, but tolerated him because of business."

"That makes sense now," Anne said.

"What do you mean? Did Gherring have words with Henri?"

"No, Henri just flirted and asked me out and sent me some flowers. Nothing serious. But Mr. Gherring sort of flipped out and told me Henri was a player and he'd just use me."

68

"So what did you do?"

"I sort of went out with him anyway, because it made me mad Gherring was trying to control who I dated."

"I bet that really ticked off Mr. Gherring. Is he giving you the silent treatment?"

"Silence and avoidance," agreed Anne. "I didn't even see him yesterday."

They both looked up when Gherring's office door burst open. He scowled in the direction of Anne's desk. When he spotted Katie, he smiled.

"Good morning, Katie. I've missed you. I have some contract changes to discuss, if you can spare a moment." He gestured toward his office.

Katie rolled her eyes at Anne before turning back to follow Gherring into his office.

Anne murmured under her breath, "I guess I'm still getting the silent treatment."

With Katie back, Anne decided to take her regular lunch at Papa's Place. She tried to make plans with Sam so she could hear about her "Beatles" date with Tanner. But she and Tanner already had lunch plans together, so Anne headed down alone. Just as she was exiting the revolving door in the lobby, she spotted Henri on the other side.

He broke into a happy grin. "I found you just in time. I am here early! You are going to lunch? You can eat with me?"

He grabbed Anne's hand, and she led him next door to her favorite lunch spot. May inspected Anne's companion with unbridled curiosity as she led them back to Anne's regular table. They both ordered one of the day's lunch specials. Then, to Anne's astonishment, Henri pulled a package from his coat pocket and handed it to her. "I have a surprise for you."

She opened the package to discover a CD of Wicked, sung by the original cast. "I love it. What made you decide to get this for me?"

Henri studied his napkin in his lap. "I saw the picture—you and Gherring in the theater. And I thought that it was the music that made you cry. Was I right? It was not Gherring? It was the music?"

"That's so sweet. Yes, you were right, it was the music." Anne chewed on her lower lip. "Henri, I have a question. What happened between you and the girl Mr. Gherring used to be engaged to? The girl you dated for a while?"

"What? What are you asking me?"

"I hesitate to ask, but I want to know why Mr. Gherring doesn't like you. You see, Mr. Gherring says you're just a player and you'll hurt me, but... but you don't seem like that kind of man to me." She looked into his green eyes as they peered earnestly at her. "You seem to be thoughtful and kind, and not the sort of guy who would use a girl or hurt someone."

Henri studied the table as he responded. "I cannot tell you what happened, because telling *would* hurt her. I promise you I did not want hurt to her. I loved her. I think she was the only woman I ever loved. But I did not deserve her. I did not deserve anyone that good. But she found someone else, someone better than me."

He pushed his chair back from the table and started to stand. "I do not deserve you either. I flirt too much. I should not be here."

"No," Anne put her hand on Henri's to stop him. "Don't go. I believe you. I think you're a better man than you realize, Henri. Only the good in you can recognize the good in someone else. Give yourself a chance. I don't know what you've done in your past, but you've got to learn to forgive yourself." She squeezed his arm. "Thank you so much for the music. It's the most thoughtful gift I've been given in a long time."

His worried face transformed as his eyes crinkled in a relieved smile.

Anne jumped as Gherring's office door opened. Gherring and Henri had been in private conference for over an hour. As the two men stepped out, Anne looked for signs of a bloody battle. She was caught by surprise as Gherring smiled at Henri, shook his hand firmly, then patted him on the back as he turned to go. Gherring looked pointedly at Anne, and then returned into his office and shut the door.

As Henri approached Anne's desk she asked, "What happened in there? I thought y'all almost hated each other. You almost looked like friends shaking hands just now."

"I just did what I should have done long ago. I talked to Gherring. I told him the whole story, good and bad. I thought, *assurément*, he would be angry, *mais non*—he was less angry. What he thought was worse than the truth. He thought I did not love Michelle. He thought I slept with another woman. Now he knows the truth. We can be friends." He laughed, "No we cannot be friends, because I will always irritate him, always, *toujours.* But we can do business and he will not hate me quite so much."

"Well, I'm proud of you Henri. I think you did the right thing."

"That is good. I want you to be proud of me. And now I want you to do something for me. I want you to say yes. I am going to ask you a question, and I want you to say yes."

"What are you going to ask me?"

"*Mon dieu*! It is not bad. I will not ask you to kill someone!" Henri smirked at Anne's expression.

Laughing, Anne asked, "Okay, but what is it? I'm not saying yes until I know the question."

"*S'il vous plaît*, go to the gala with me. *Veux-tu venir avec moi?* You will go? Tomorrow night?"

Anne stared at Henri, dumbfounded. Henri began to plead. "I will be good. I will not drink too much. If you desire I will not drink at all. You will say yes, and make me happy?"

"Henri, you can't go with me. Surely you know many women in the city who'd love to go."

"Why do you say I should forgive myself and give myself a chance, but you will not give me chance?"

"That's not what I mean. I mean I'd love to go, but you shouldn't go with me. You should go with one of your *sophisticated* friends. Like Mr. Gherring. He's going with a famous model, Margo Milan. I won't fit in with you and your important friends—I'm just a simple Texas girl. I wouldn't even know what to talk about in a party full of international business people."

"I do not care about them. *You* are important. You are important to me. *Tu es tres importante*."

"Why Henri? Why me? You barely know me."

"Because, *mes amis importants*, my *important* friends, they see *à l'extérieur*, the... outside. But you, you see the inside. Your eyes see deep, *dans l'âme*, in the soul. With you, I have hope that I will be a better man. I am better, I am good with you." He paused to let his words sink in, watching for a sign of her relenting. "And also, *tu est tres jolie, non... belle. Et chaude!*"

Anne blushed at being called beautiful and hot, but Henri held her hand and gazed at her seriously, expectantly, waiting for a response.

"What about Gherring?" asked Anne.

"Gherring? You told me he is taking someone else. He has asked you to go with him?"

"No, but up until a few minutes ago, he seemed to dislike you a lot. And he didn't want me to go out with you."

"Is Gherring your father? You must ask permission?"

"No Henri—that's not fair. I just don't want to appear spiteful. It is *his* event, and he's my boss. I'm trying to be respectful, even though I'm not very good at it..."

"*Pardon moi.* You are right to have respect. But he said all is well between us, I promise. He knows now, I am not as bad as my reputation. I think he has had a similar experience with reputation. And we will stay across the room and not even go around him, not near him—the party is big, *énorme, infini, vaste.* Gherring will never know you are there..."

"Okay, okay."

"Okay? That means yes? Okay yes?" His green eyes peered fervently at Anne's.

"Yes, yes I'll go with you."

Chapter Six - A Gala Affair

"WHAT!" EXCLAIMED KATIE. "Are you kidding me? Really? Henri asked you to the gala? I can't believe he never asked me."

"But you're *engaged*."

"Well I am now, but Henri's been coming to the international business gala long before I was engaged."

"And Henri is way too old for you anyway. He's *my* age."

"Well he's been going out with girls younger than me in the past, and I certainly don't think he's too old for me. I'm so jealous. Henri is sooooo hot."

"But Katie—"

"Oh don't worry—I'm just kidding. I'm happily in love, so don't fret. I've just always lusted over Henri a bit."

"Well, he is kind of cute."

"Kind of cute? That's the understatement of the year. You're a lucky dog. All these years I've done the preparation and planning, but I've never gotten to go to the bash. And you get to go after your first two weeks on the job. Plus, you get to go with Henri, who is smokin' hot. But wait… We've got to get you ready for the party."

"What do you mean? It's not until tomorrow night."

"But you need to go to the spa, get your hair done, get your makeup done."

Anne's heart skipped a beat. "Oh I couldn't do that. I've never had my makeup done. I don't even wear much makeup. And I wouldn't know where to go. Anyway, it would cost too much."

"I have a connection, a friend who's just getting started in the business. She's great, but she needs publicity. If she could just post your picture to advertise, she'll give you a great deal, I'm sure of it."

"Well, maybe. But I don't really have time. We've got a lot to do tomorrow—"

"Nope, you're taking a personal leave day tomorrow. I'll wrap up all the details for the event. I've done it by myself before."

"But won't Mr. Gherring be mad?"

"Gherring will be so busy with meetings he probably won't notice. But if he asks, I'll just tell him you had a family emergency."

"But that would be a lie."

"No, it's true. You *are* part of a family—you're the mom. And this is an emergency."

Anne's cell phone sounded a musical refrain of a classic Joe Walsh song about a fast Maserati. Anne struggled to answer the call with her paraffin-dipped hands in plastic bags, trying vainly not to disturb the green mud on her face. "Hey Charlie, I can't talk for long, I'm in the middle of a spa treatment to make me beautiful, although it seems to be doing the opposite. I look quite frightful."

"So you're spending the day getting ready for the big date with the French playboy? And tonight, Emily says, you're wearing Giselle?"

"Yes, Katie came over last night. She took one look at Giselle and insisted I wear her tonight. I thought my red one might be better."

"Ughh, Mom. That dress was outdated twenty years ago, which is probably the last time you wore it."

"Well classics never go out of style."

"I guess that about says it all, because that dress is definitely not a classic. Trust me, Mom. Didn't Emily and I tell you to leave the red one at home? Anyway, you'll look great in Giselle. I'm glad I have your genes, so I'll still look hot when I'm old like you."

"Ah-hem! Old like me?"

"Sorry, you know I don't think you're old." Charlie laughed. "But you do look pretty good for the mom of a twenty three year old."

"I appreciate the sentiment, 'cause right now I feel pretty ugly. But I do feel pampered. I already had a hot rock massage, and my hands and feet have been rubbed and seasoned and dipped in wax, and I have a goopy mask on my face. I feel like a turkey that's getting ready to go in the oven."

Charlie cracked up. "Now I have this picture in my head of a big stuffed turkey with your head on it. Are you getting your hair cut?"

"Evidently I'm getting a total makeover, complete with a haircut and some highlights. Josie says they will 'blend with the gray hairs'. But what I'm really worried about is the shoes for tonight."

"Aren't you wearing those super sexy black strappy sandals Emily gave you? They go perfectly with Giselle, and they are sooooo cute."

"Yes but the heels are sooooo high. And I'm sooooo clumsy."

"Yep, you are a bit clumsy. I forgot what you looked like trying to walk in those heels. But you just need practice—nobody is born with the ability to walk in spike heels."

Anne squinted one eye as she considered practicing. "That might work, or I could just wear my black flats."

"No way. That's the reason Emily and I bought that dress, remember? It's extra long. You have to wear heels or you'll walk all over it. And you're shorter than both of us. Here's what you do... Carry the shoes until you're in the taxi. You can hold on to Henri for balance while you're at the party until you get to a chair."

"Fine, I'll just cling to Henri tonight. I can think of worse things."

"I can't wait for a report. Get someone to take a picture of you and Henri and text it to us."

"I'll do it. I feel like I'm getting ready to go to prom."

"It's more like you're Cinderella going to the ball with the prince."

Anne stared at herself in the mirror, or at least she thought that was her face. The woman in the mirror looked nothing like the woman that got up at five a.m. to run on the treadmill. Her hair was the same soft brown color, but the new highlights gave it a healthy shine. The tresses hung in loose curls, framing her face. Her eyes looked huge and exotic—the wonders of an eyelash curler and mascara, combined with some smoky eye shadow. Her lips looked fuller with a light pink sheer gloss.

The halter-top of the black silky dress was cut deeply in front, but the girls had sent her with a special tape to keep everything securely in place with no gaping. Anne was self-conscious about the plunging neckline, although she was small enough nothing was revealed. The back of the dress dipped low on her spine, her back looking smooth with its recent spray tan. She leaned forward and backward and raised her hands experimentally, making sure nothing important was exposed. The material fell in curve-hugging swaths with a side slit that bared her leg from the knee down. Satisfied with the modesty of the dress, such as it was, she picked up her wrap and headed for the lobby.

She entered the lobby to find Henri chatting and flirting with Rayna. She observed he was even more handsome—if that was possible—in his tuxedo. When he spotted Anne, his mouth fell open. "*Mon dieu*! I am in heaven. *Tu es un ange*. An angel from heaven."

Anne felt her face flush with embarrassment. She walked slowly toward him, attempting to look stately, but actually working to keep her balance. Henri crossed the room to her side, and she gratefully took his proffered arm.

Rayna was practically jumping up and down. "Anne, you look great—like a movie star."

Anne started laughing. "I can't keep up the pretense. I'm so awkward in these shoes. If y'all just knew—" She stuck out a foot to exhibit the spiky heel. "This is not me. I'm so much more comfortable in jeans and a tee shirt with flat sandals."

"But you look amazing. You were just hiding all this in those frumpy clothes," said Rayna.

"And I am happy to stay so close to you so you will not fall. It will be our secret, *notre secret*. This way I can touch you all night." Henri tucked her hand in the crook of his arm. "And no one can steal my angel, *mon bel ange*."

Anne felt the flex of Henri's strong arm and realized she felt secure with him. She wondered at the irony of feeling safe on the arm of a notorious French playboy.

"Rayna, would you take our picture?" Anne held out her phone. "I promised the girls I would text them a picture." Rayna snapped a few photos, and Anne sent the texts to Charlie and Emily.

"Please. Will you send a picture to me? *Moi et mon bel ange*." Henri entered his cell number. "This is a new number. This number will reach me in Paris."

Anne flushed as Rayna silently mouthed, "Oh-my-god."

"Mademoiselle," said Henri. "You are ready?"

Anne took a deep breath and returned a shaky smile. "Let's go."

This time, Henri had ordered a limousine rather than a taxi. There was a small group of society reporters gathered at the hotel entrance, snapping pictures and snagging interviews as guests departed the limos. Anne tried vainly not to be noticed, the task made more difficult because Henri basked in the attention. He stopped to converse with several of the journalists he knew, while Anne attempted to be inconspicuous. Henri unrepentantly told them his date for the evening was "an angel from Texas". When one of the reporters joked he didn't know there were angels in Texas, Henri declared there was only one angel from Texas, and she was in New York with him now. He flashed his white smile, while Anne burned crimson with embarrassment.

Henri talked animatedly as they walked through the lobby toward the Grand Ballroom. But Anne tugged on his arm. "Wait, Henri... I'm not ready. I'm nervous."

"No need to be nervous. I will not leave you, and my arm is yours."

"And we'll avoid Steven Gherring?"

"We will stay far, far from Steven Gherring." Henri smiled and led her into the ballroom.

As they entered the ballroom, Anne was filled with trepidation. Why had she agreed to go to this event with Henri? She would make a fool of herself and Henri as well. Anne knew more than nine hundred people had responded affirmatively for the gala, but she was somehow still overwhelmed by the mass of people, all clad in tuxedos and evening gowns.

The ballroom was large and separated into distinct areas. On one side was a buffet and adjacent to that an open bar. Sixty round bar-height tables with tall chairs were available for guests to utilize. However, the majority of the guests were milling about in the main center area, which provided a multitude of tall tables on which they could stash their refreshments. Waiters filtered through the crowd, offering trays of red and white wines, sparkling waters, and various hors d'oeuvres. In the back of the room a jazz band played on a small stage adjacent to the dance floor, their melodies a soft background in the vast hall.

True to his word, Henri spotted Gherring across the large hall and guided Anne away to the other side. He walked slowly, allowing Anne to navigate smoothly through the room. Henri stopped to talk with friends and associates, always introducing her as Anne, his angel from Texas.

Her nerves gradually dissipated, and soon she was laughing and talking, as a rather large group joined in their banter. The international visitors were curious about Texas and particularly intrigued with her drawl. She gave tourist advice to several couples that were planning to spend time in Texas before leaving the country.

"My favorite places are in the Hill Country. You've *got* to go to the River Walk in San Antonio. Y'all should visit SoCo in Austin." She ticked off the sites on her fingers. "And y'all should go to Fort Worth and see the Botanical Gardens. It's even pretty in the winter." She forgot her earlier worries, enjoying the chance to meet interesting people from New York and around the globe.

As one gentleman was recounting a humorous story, he stopped in mid-sentence, his eyes riveted over Anne's shoulder. She heard a deep voice behind her. "Good evening, Ms. Best, Henri." She turned to see Steven Gherring standing directly behind her. His smile didn't reach his eyes. "Are you enjoying the party?"

Henri voice was stiff. "Your reception is magnificent, as usual."

Anne twisted toward Gherring while frantically clutching Henri's arm, trying to still her shaking hands.

"Ms. Best, I hope your 'family emergency' is much improved?"

Anne was mortified. "I'm sorry Mr. Gherring. I didn't want to lie to you. Katie said she could handle everything, so I took the day to go to the spa. You should fire me. I can't even believe I did it. It's really not like me to lie or skip work. I never even played hooky from school—not one day. I'm sorry—"

"Ms. Best—" Gherring interrupted. But Anne continued in her apology.

"I really am sorry. It was just a waste of time—"

"Anne! You're *not* fired." He continued softly, "And your day at the spa was certainly not a waste of time." His eyes raked up and down appraisingly with a hint of a smile on his lips. "Not a waste at all."

Anne felt the blood rush to her face. He'd called her by her first name. And was he complimenting her? Surely not. He must be teasing her.

She searched her mind for a way to control the conversation. "Where's Ms. Milan?"

Gherring glanced about the room and shrugged. "Oh she's here somewhere, networking and publicizing." He turned to Henri who'd been silently on guard. "Henri, can you spare a moment? I need to speak with you… privately."

Henri caught Anne's eyes with a silent question. "I'll be fine," she said, carefully releasing his arm. She joined back in her former conversation, standing unsupported while watching Gherring and Henri from the corner of her eye. The discussion was earnest, but she was relieved to find neither party seemed agitated. Gherring walked back with Henri who took his place at Anne's side.

Suddenly, Margo Milan materialized beside Gherring, locking arms with him. The arrival of the beautiful model brought murmurs from the group. Men jockeyed for the opportunity to meet her and shake her hand, while their wives and dates stared at the willowy woman with flawless olive skin and black silky hair that fell in a straight edgy cut, just brushing her shoulders. Henri smiled at Margo, but made no move to meet her, remaining next to Anne as promised. However, Margo recognized Henri and coaxed Gherring to make introductions. "Steven, you haven't introduced me to this handsome Frenchman."

Gherring obliged her, with slight irritation edging his voice. "Margo, this is Henri DuBois. Henri… Margo Milan."

Henri moved toward Margo, pulling Anne with him. "So nice to meet you, Ms. Milan." Then in a particularly un-Henri move, he grabbed her hand and gave it a firm shake. "*Je suis enchanté*. Gherring, as always, you find the most beautiful women. Perhaps someday you will learn how to keep them."

Gherring looked daggers at Henri, while his muscles flexed along his jawline.

Henri continued. "And may I present *mon ange* from Texas, Ms. Anne Best?"

Anne held out her hand, but Margo ignored her, addressing Henri again. "Henri, you are from Paris, right? Perhaps I'll run into you next month when we do our shoot in France."

"Perhaps," said Henri with no enthusiasm. "*S'il vous plait*, if you will excuse us, I am suddenly thirsty." Henri led Anne away to a table near the bar and snagged two sparkling waters from the waiter's tray.

"She seemed really interested in you," Anne said.

Henri rolled his eyes. "Those models, they are too skinny."

"Ha! I don't believe you for a moment."

"Yes, they have sharp bones. The bones, they poke you. Who wants a boney woman?"

"Oh, so you must think I'm fat, then." Anne accused playfully.

"No, you are perfect, as I tell you with the chocolates. Hmmm… There is one thing I can think. One thing is wrong with you."

"What's the one thing?"

"You are too far away from me."

Anne's face fell at the mention of the ocean that would soon separate them. "Perhaps you could come back and visit—"

"I mean *now*. You are too far away now. All the way across the table. I like having you stand close to me all night. In fact, I think we should get closer still."

Anne's eyes grew wide.

"I think we should dance," he said.

Anne giggled in relief. "Oh, I don't think I could dance in these shoes."

"This song is slow, and I will hold you up."

Anne glanced at the dance floor near the stage. "There's no one else dancing."

"That is even better. If you fall, you will not hurt anyone." A mischievous smile lit his face. "Come dance, *mon bel ange*."

Anne felt like a million eyes were watching as she danced with Henri, but gradually, a few couples joined them on the dance floor. He held her right hand between them and pressed her close with his other hand on the small her back. She felt the warmth of his hand on her skin. He whispered in her ear, and she felt intoxicated by the power of his persuasive words.

As she turned in a slow circle, her eyes locked with Steven Gherring's. He stared intently. What was the emotion in his eyes? Was he angry she'd lied to him? Was he embarrassed his secretary was at this important event with his business associate? Was he disgusted she was going out with Henri, a man that was a source of irritation for him? Henri turned her further and she lost sight of Gherring. Then Henri began to hum the song. His deep voice resonated in his chest, and she felt the vibrations in her own body. She was lost in relaxed reverie, when Henri stopped abruptly.

She looked up, only to see Steven Gherring standing behind Henri. "May I cut in?"

Henri glowered at Gherring. "I do not think the lady desires to change partners."

Gherring returned the glare and spoke through his clenched teeth. "Well perhaps you should ask the lady in question."

Both men turned their scowling faces to Anne, who felt as if she might pass out right on the dance floor. Gherring softened his expression. "If you'd do me the honor, Ms. Best? Just one dance?"

"Okay," Anne hated the shaky sound of her voice.

Henri surrendered her hand to Gherring. "*Qu'une seule fois.* Only one. *Seulement!*" He backed away, keeping his eyes on Anne.

Gherring took her hand in a gentle clasp and placed his hand on her back. Her skin tingled beneath his fingers. His blue eyes gazed so piercingly Anne closed hers to escape them. He started to move in time to the music when Anne stopped him. "Wait... I forgot. I have to tell you something. Before we can dance—"

Gherring's expression was taut. "What? Tell me."

Anne blushed. "I can barely stand up in these shoes. You have to move slow and help me keep my balance."

Gherring's face broke out in a smile, a rare genuine smile that revealed his deep dimples. "I'll hold you up. You won't fall with me."

He moved her across the dance floor in a slow smooth motion, while she kept her eyes downcast. Anne was intensely aware of his touch. Although he held her firmly, he didn't press her against him. His firm chest brushed lightly across her as they glided around the floor, every contact searing.

Anne felt light-headed and faltered for a moment. But Gherring reacted quickly, bringing her close as he supported her. Anne's heart was racing, and she feared Gherring would notice the thudding against his chest. If he noticed, he said nothing.

Why did he ask her to dance? Was he trying to prove something to Henri? Was he making a fool of her? She drummed up the courage to speak to him, to ask him what he was doing. But when she looked up, his gaze held her captive, her breath catching in her throat. She opened her mouth and her lips moved, but no words emerged.

Gherring spoke. "I want you to know…" He paused, a pained look crossing his face. "That I enjoyed the dance. Very much."

They'd stopped moving, and Anne noticed a lull in the music. She tried to understand Gherring's motivation. "But why—"

Henri deftly stepped between the pair, reclaiming her hand. He gave Anne a warm smile, ignoring Gherring completely. "Would you like to dance more? Or sit for a moment?"

"I think I'd like to sit." Anne took Henri's arm, but glanced up at Gherring. His expression was inscrutable. "Thanks for the dance, Mr. Gherring."

"Yes, thank you, Anne. I'll see you bright and early on Monday." Gherring narrowed his eyes at Henri. "When is your flight back to Paris, Henri? Do you need a lift to the airport?"

Henri stared grimly at Gherring and started to retort, when Anne interrupted. "Actually, Mr. Gherring, I was the person who arranged for Henri's transportation, along with the other international executives. And I'm sure I can make alternate arrangements in case his flight plans change."

Henri cracked a smile at Anne.

"So don't worry about Henri at all, Mr. Gherring. And yes, I'll see you on Monday, bright and early. No more spa days for me, sir." Anne thought she detected a slight wince on Gherring's face at her formal salutation.

Henri led Anne toward the tables. Just as they arrived, Anne looked over her shoulder. Gherring was still standing on the dance floor watching their departure with a sphinxlike expression as other couples swirled around him.

Henri retrieved a glass of wine for himself and a grapefruit soda for Anne. He left her at the table while he went to stand in the buffet line. Anne was contemplating her straw when she heard a familiar voice.

Johanna Klein slipped into a chair beside her. "You must tell me everything. I saw the scene on the dance floor—I must know what has happened."

82

Anne told the whole story, starting with the surprise lunch date with Henri, filling in details as Johanna questioned her. When she was explaining how Gherring asked her to dance, she stopped the story.

"Why do you think he asked me to dance?"

"Why do *you* think he asked you?" Johanna questioned.

"I think Gherring still dislikes Henri, even though he explained himself. He still hasn't forgiven Henri, and I think he was trying to put Henri in his place. He acts like he owns me. Maybe he thinks he's taking the place of my father, withholding approval of my boyfriends."

"Hmmm," Johanna mused. "I believe you may be mistaken. I saw him dancing with you. He did not look at you like a father would."

"What do you mean?" Anne felt the blood rushing to her face.

"I simply think he could be jealous, don't you?"

"Jealous? Of me?" Anne was incredulous. "Believe me, you're wrong. I know the kind of women Gherring likes, and they're nothing like me. He likes women like... like Margo Milan. Young, sophisticated, beautiful, society types. Women who've traveled the world."

"Perhaps, but you are just as beautiful as that model."

"No way! But thank you for boosting my forty-five year old ego. I do think I look a lot better than I usually do, thanks to my day at the spa. It took a whole day to look like this. No wonder my five minute beauty routine isn't very effective."

Johanna chuckled with Anne about the hard work associated with beauty. Then she leaned close and whispered, "But what about Henri? Are there sparks?"

Anne thought of the warm security she felt as Henri held her close. "Maybe, I'm not sure yet. I'm just cautious because it's been fifteen years since I even looked at a man like that." Unbidden, Anne recalled Gherring's searing touch as they danced. She felt the heat rise to her face.

"Oh, you are blushing. I think there may be sparks after all!"

Henri returned bearing a plate laden with delectable finger foods just as Johanna got up to leave.

"I must go rescue my husband from talking business all night. So glad to have seen you again. I have your email address, so I will keep in touch." She leaned in to whisper in Anne's ear. "I have to find out the end of the story."

When Johanna was gone, Anne realized she was famished. "I don't think I've eaten anything all day!" She gobbled down the hors d'oeuvres quickly.

"Henri, I know it may be none of my business, but will you tell me what Gherring said to you when he talked to you alone. I want to know if y'all talked about me."

"He wanted to know what my intentions were. And he told me I cannot hurt you."

"He said that? He actually told you not to hurt me?"

"*Oui*. His words were, 'If you hurt Anne, I will hurt you!' I think he was serious."

"Oh no, I can't believe he said that."

"But he did not say what will happen…" He stopped to gaze into Anne's eyes. "He did not say what will happen if you hurt me."

"If I hurt you? Why would I hurt you?"

"Because, as I told you, you have captured my heart. What will you do now? With my heart?"

Anne hesitated. How was she supposed to respond? This was exactly the kind of pressure she'd hoped to avoid.

Henri sighed. "He is watching us now."

Anne glanced over her shoulder to find Gherring gazing their direction from the edge of the crowd.

"He is watching us to be sure I do not hurt you. I will not hurt you, but you may hurt me. I have decided I will risk letting you hurt my heart, *mon ange*." He bent toward Anne and lightly brushed his lips on hers. She jumped, her eyes wide and startled, her cheeks burning.

"I'm sorry Henri. I haven't kissed anyone in a long time. I mean a really long time. Like fifteen years long time."

"That is a really long time," Henri agreed with a grin. "You have forgotten how? Do you still like to kiss?"

Anne chuckled. "Well, I guess the answer is no—I haven't forgotten how. And yes—I still like to, I think. But I'm pretty rusty and pretty nervous. And I don't want to practice here in front of a bunch of people."

"You do not want to practice in front of the crowd? Or you do not want to practice in front of your boss?"

Anne glanced over her shoulder to where Gherring was glaring. "Honestly? Both."

Henri smiled, his green eyes dancing. "Come. I will take *mon bel ange* to a place where there is no crowd and..." He glanced back at Gherring. "And no boss."

He quickly tucked her arm into his and led her across the ballroom and out the door. As she departed, Anne thought triumphantly she hadn't lost her balance the entire evening. No trips, no falls. But then she recalled she had indeed felt off balance one time—in the arms of Steven Gherring.

*****

Anne left the ballroom with Henri and, to her surprise, he led her into the hotel elevator. She watched him nervously as the elevator rose higher and higher. "Where're we going?"

Henri grinned and raised his eyebrows. He spoke in a sultry voice. "We are going upstairs to my room, of course. There, it will be private. No crowd, no boss."

Anne's face turned ashen, but Henri laughed. "*Non,* no. I am kidding you. We are going to the top. There is a private club, a bar. It is a quiet place. You will like it, I think."

Anne pummeled Henri in the arm playfully until he begged for mercy, even as she sighed in relief. The elevator doors opened on the top floor. They entered a large lounge, and Henri asked to be seated by the windows.

As they took their seats Anne exclaimed breathlessly, "It's Times Square! We can see Times Square from here!"

Henri looked pleased by her response. "You like it?"

"I love it. This is amazing. I've never seen Times Square at night— it's so beautiful."

"Yes, it is beautiful. I love to show you beautiful things." They looked out in silence over the busy scene below them. "Paris is very beautiful—I would like to show Paris to you."

Anne's eyes lit up and then her face fell. "Henri, I'd love to go to Paris. I'd love to see Paris with you, but I don't see how that would work."

"It is simple. You will fly to Paris. I will pay for your ticket, and I will pick you up at the airport. You will stay at my home. My home is very large, *tres grande*. You will have your own room. Everything will be very proper." His green eyes searched her face hopefully. "Will you come to Paris?"

She hesitated, her voice apologetic. "Henri..."

"*Non,* wait! Do not say no. Please, *mon ange,* not yet. Do not say that it is not possible."

"But Henri—"

"Wait! You said to give myself chance. I am giving myself a chance with you. I say we make a bargain."

"What bargain?"

"You cannot say no until we try."

"I don't know. What does that mean?"

"I mean you must come one time to Paris. Then you can say no if you want to. But you may say yes, if you give me a chance."

She opened her mouth to respond, but Henri touched his finger to her lips. "Wait! Please wait. If you come to Paris one time and you still think it will not work between us, I will let you go. I ask only for a chance."

"I just don't know, Henri. I'd like to say yes, but I don't know."

"What do you lose if you try?"

"I don't want to break your heart, Henri."

"It is too late—I have opened my heart to you."

Anne felt like running away. She couldn't handle this kind of pressure. How had she managed to lead Henri on? She thought she'd been so careful.

Henri touched her arm. "It is a good thing, I think, to give my heart to you. I have played and flirted, but I have not given my heart. Because I do not want to hurt again, I have not given my heart. For five years I have protected my heart to keep it safe, so I will not be hurt."

He spoke fervently. "But without hurt, I have no chance for love. *Mon bel ange,* with you I am willing to risk my heart again, so I can feel. *Oui?* No chance for hurt means no chance for love. I am forty-five years old. I want real love in my life. I am glad to risk hurting."

Henri lifted Anne's hand to his lips. "I am glad to feel something again."

Anne felt her heart swell with emotion, and she blinked back tears. Henri lifted her arm and turned her hand over to press a gentle kiss on her wrist. She watched as he moved up to kiss the inside of her elbow. She felt a tingle deep inside as his lips caressed her skin. His hand tilted her chin toward him, and he moved his lips toward hers. He touched his mouth against hers, tenderly at first. Then his hand moved behind her head, and his kiss became more urgent, his tongue probing, insisting. Anne's heart raced as she gave in to her need, so long denied. She returned his kiss with passion, their tongues dancing, her body humming, her heart pounding. When he finally pulled back, releasing their kiss, both of them were breathing rapidly.

"*Mon dieu!* You have not forgotten how to kiss."

Anne fanned her flushed face. "But I forgot how nice it is to be kissed. To be well kissed."

"So you will come to Paris, *mon bel ange?* Just one time? Just one chance?"

"But what about work?"

"In three weeks, you have your holiday, Thanksgiving?"

"Yes... We're off Wednesday through Friday."

"So you can come to Paris on Tuesday night. We will have four days together."

"But... I was planning to see my father during the holidays."

Henri leaned toward Anne and nuzzled her neck below her ear. "You could see your father at Christmas, I think."

Anne felt a shiver go down her spine. "Yes, I think I could see Dad at Christmas after all. I guess I'm going to Paris."

Then she sat up with excitement. "And I get to use my passport—I'll get my first stamp."

The limousine returned them to the front of Anne's apartment. Anne, who'd abandoned her shoes on the trip, jumped out of the door with them in one hand, holding her dress up so she wouldn't trip. She squealed as she dashed across the cold sidewalk in bare feet with Henri chasing behind her. They pushed through the doors into the lobby, laughing. She spied Antonio as she was running past and stopped to give him a hug. His mouth dropped open as he noticed her dress and makeover. Though some of the makeup had worn off, her cheeks were rosy and her face was glowing.

"You look hot, Anne. If I weren't going out with Rayna, I'd be coming after you."

"I am glad you have another girl, so I do not have to hurt you," Henri threatened playfully.

"Thanks, Antonio. But don't get used to it—this is a temporary change."

Henri pulled Anne into his arms. "I fell for you without the fancy dress. You were beautiful already."

Antonio raised his eyebrows. "Anne, you've been keeping secrets. Why haven't I heard about your boyfriend?"

"Antonio, this is Henri. Henri this is Antonio—he keeps me safe in my home here."

Henri bowed to Antonio. "I am grateful to you for keeping her safe—*mon bel ange.*"

Anne pulled Henri away to say goodnight. "May I come upstairs? For coffee? That is all, I promise."

"Promise?"

"I do not wish the night to end."

Anne relented, unable to resist his pleading green eyes. "Just coffee. No hanky-panky."

He followed her to the elevator. "What is hanky-panky? It sounds delicious—I might be hungry."

Anne struggled to explain the term until she noticed Henri was suppressing a laugh. "You're teasing me, again. Why am I so gullible?" She punched him playfully. "At least I get to hit your arm and feel your muscles."

Anne dashed ahead of Henri when she opened her apartment door, hurrying in to shut the bathroom door and hide her mess. Henri surveyed the small living area and relaxed onto the comfy sofa. Anne started a pot of decaf coffee before joining Henri on the couch.

"Okay Henri, I said I would come to Paris, and I will. But I just don't see how it would ever work long term. You can't move to New York because of work. I can't move to Paris because of my family."

Henri smirked at Anne. "Do you always worry so much?"

"Yeah, I'm afraid so. I just worry about things."

"But I do not. I do not worry about things."

"Yes, I'm aware. You don't seem to worry about anything."

"You worry too much, and I do not worry enough. *Oui*? So together we are perfect."

Anne rolled her eyes. "I'm fixin' to get our coffee. Do you want cream or sugar?"

"No, just black. You are enough sweet for me."

"Henri, you're so corny." She poured the steaming coffee in mugs. "But it's been a long time since somebody sweet-talked me. I think I like it. And you know it sounds so much better with that sexy French accent."

"*Oui, oui*! I am counting on your inability to resist my accent." He leaned over to nuzzle her neck, but Anne jumped at a knock on the door.

"Who could that be?" She ran to the door and peeped through the hole. "It's Mr. Gherring. Should you hide?"

"No, I will not hide. I have done nothing wrong."

"Sorry, I just panicked. I'm going to open the door." Anne cracked it open and blocked the doorway.

"Hi, Mr. Gherring. Did you need something?"

"No, I just wanted to make sure you were okay." He peered over her shoulder, spying Henri on her couch.

"Why wouldn't I be okay?"

"You know," Gherring stammered. "I wanted to be sure you got home safely."

"Yes, well thank you, Mr. Gherring. I'm home safely."

"I'm glad you're home, safely."

"Okay. Thanks again." Anne started to shut the door, but Gherring stuck his foot in the way.

"Tell Henri my limousine is available now if he'd like a ride to his hotel. I just wanted to offer."

Henri sauntered over to the door, placing a possessive arm around Anne's waist. "Thanks Gherring, but I do not need your limousine tonight. Good night." Henri smiled knowingly at Gherring as he shut the door.

Anne put her hands on her hips. "Henri! You made it sound like you're spending the night."

"I did?" He opened his eyes wide.

"You know good and well what you made him think. I know it seems silly to you, but I'm old fashioned about this. I don't want anyone to think I'm that kind of girl. I want to protect my reputation."

"I am sorry. I was not thinking. I cannot help myself when I have the chance to tease Gherring. But I will tell him the truth tomorrow. I will sacrifice my reputation for your reputation." He plastered his hand over his heart and spoke with such drama in his voice, Anne started laughing.

"Okay, you're forgiven. But only if you let him know the truth."

"Maybe, we should do as he thinks we are doing, instead?" He leaned in close. "Are you listening? Do you hear my sexy accent? *N'est-ce pas*? *Ma jolie femme*? *Mon bel ange*?"

Anne backed away and put her hands over her ears. "Henri, you promised."

"Yes, I promised." He shook his head as his lips formed a pout. "But maybe, a little, I hoped you would change your mind." He smiled and put up his hands to stop her as she began to protest again. "No, I will be good. Do not be mad at me—we will just drink coffee, *oui*?"

"Yes, just coffee."

"And maybe one more kiss? Only one? *Seulement*? A goodbye kiss for three weeks?"

"Only one more. You almost killed me with the first one."

"*Moi aussi*. Me too. But I was thinking... I was thinking that would be a great way to die."

Chapter Seven - Awakenings

ANNE SLEPT IN UNTIL eleven twenty a.m., awakened by romantic piano music emanating from her cell phone. "Good morning, Emily," she said in a groggy voice.

"Mom, were you still asleep? How late did you stay out last night?"

"Oh, I came home before midnight, but Henri didn't leave until almost two a.m."

"Henri was at your apartment? Mom, I got the picture you sent. Henri is yummy. Ohmygosh! You didn't tell me how gorgeous he was. Oh, and you looked great, too. But if you decide you're not interested in Henri, you could introduce him to me."

"Oh no—I'm not letting Henri within five miles of you. He's a bit too hard to resist, and he's downright charming." Anne laughed. "And I mean that in the worst possible way."

"Well I don't know Mom. Maybe I shouldn't let you date a guy like that. Were you able to resist him? And I mean that in the worst possible way."

"The answer is mostly yes, but I did find out he is a *great* kisser."

"Woo hoo, Mom! I never thought we'd have this conversation, but I love it! Do we need to have 'The Talk'?"

"Very funny, Em. Your very existence indicates I don't need to have 'The Talk.'"

"Or maybe my existence means we *do* need to have 'The Talk.' But I'd like to meet this Henri. You know, check him out in person, and see if I approve."

"Ha, ha. I bet you would, but it's too late. By now he's in the air over the Atlantic on his way back to Paris."

"What? He's gone back already? That was a short romance."

"Well, it's not exactly over."

"He's coming back to New York again?"

"No. But I'm going to Paris to see him."

"You're going to Paris? Ohmygosh! Ohmygosh! I can't believe it. When are you going? This is sooooo romantic."

"I know. I can't believe it either. I'm finally going to use my passport. Woo hoo!" Anne laughed. "I'm going during Thanksgiving holidays, so you girls need to make sure Grandpa has someplace to go for Thanksgiving dinner."

"No problem, Mom. We'll take care of Grandpa, if we can pin him down. Hey, maybe Henri has a son who looks like him and you could introduce us."

"Ha! Maybe, but we can talk about it in a week, right? Y'all are coming next Friday?"

"Yep, we're flying in on Friday, and we'll be there by the time you get off work. And we don't have to go back until Monday, so we have two whole days in New York with you."

"I can't wait—I miss y'all so bad."

"I don't know, Mom. It doesn't sound like you've been moping around without us."

"Well, it's been pretty exciting, but I don't like that you're both so far away. And I miss Gandalf, too."

"I would tell you Gandalf misses you, but he seemed perfectly happy last week when I visited him and Grandpa at the house. I think Grandpa just shares his food with him. He's so spoiled, now."

"Oh no, he's gonna get so fat. I need to talk to Dad about that."

"Yeah, good luck with that. You know Grandpa won't listen to anybody."

"Yep, you're right. I might as well give up before I even try."

"But six days and we'll see you in person. It seems like you've been gone for months instead of a couple of weeks."

"I agree. A lot has happened in two weeks. Who knows, by next week I may meet a film director who'll turn me into a movie star. I could be famous by the time you see me."

"Oh my. Will you be willing to associate with us poor Texas folk?"

"Yes, don't worry… I'll always remember the little people in my life."

Anne climbed out of bed and made the decision to head to the gym upstairs and go for a run. She usually went early in the morning or right after work, but she'd been so busy she had only run twice that week. She was tired, but she knew she'd feel better after a quick workout. She loved running on the treadmills that faced the picture windows overlooking the busy street.

She pulled her still-curly hair into a ponytail and stuck her iPod in her pocket. She was surprised to find the gym was busy on a Saturday at one o'clock. Every treadmill was occupied when she walked in, so she walked by trying to peek at the distances to guess if someone might be finishing soon. She found a good prospect, a treadmill on the left end that already had ten miles clocked. The occupant was shirtless and glistening with sweat, but still keeping a nice pace. Surely he wouldn't run much further. She watched him run, admiring the easy stride. He was tanned and well-built, with broad shoulders and a narrow waist. There was no extra fat on his body, so she could see his muscles flexing as he ran.

She glanced down at the other runners, but no one seemed to show signs of cooling down. Finally, the treadmill to her right stopped, and the woman tiredly relinquished her spot to Anne. She quickly climbed on and pressed start for a manual program, wondering if she could match paces with the long distance runner on her left. She casually looked at the man's pace and saw it was set at a six-minute pace. Wow—she could run an eight-minute pace on a good day. Who could run that far at that pace?

She looked at his face. Of course, it was Steven Gherring. Why was she not surprised? The one person she was most embarrassed to see, the one who thought she'd spent the night with Henri. Surely, Henri hadn't called him early in the morning to correct his misconception. Gherring hadn't seen her yet. Maybe she could slip away and run later in the day. She turned the machine off and stepped down.

"Is your treadmill not working?" she heard Gherring's voice ask.

She kept her head down in case he hadn't recognized her and mumbled something about getting a towel.

By now, Gherring had slowed his machine to a walk and he continued the conversation without looking her direction.

"I suppose this means Henri is gone," he said in a flat emotionless voice.

Anne kept her voice calm with great effort. "If you mean 'gone' as in, gone to Paris, he left at ten a.m. If you mean 'gone' as in, left my apartment, that happened last night."

She glared at him. "I know what you think, but you're wrong about me. I'm not that kind of girl. I don't sleep around."

"I don't think you're 'that kind of girl.' I think Henri's 'that kind of man.'"

"But it takes two to tango. You still thought I was easy."

"What was I supposed to think? Henri is… He's… Women can't resist him. And he was there. With you. And you had that dress on."

"Well *I* resisted him. Even though I had on *that dress*," she spit out sarcastically. She turned away from him and started her treadmill again. She ran faster than her normal pace, fueled by her anger and frustration.

Gherring stood watching her silently. He looked like he had more to say, but instead he moved on to the free weights. Anne finished her run and gathered her things to leave. When she stopped for a drink of water, Gherring came beside her.

"I'm sorry."

One look at his sincere face, and her anger melted. "It's okay, I was just embarrassed. I even made Henri promise to tell you the truth."

Gherring nodded. "If it makes you feel any better, I just found a text from him. He said he wants me to know he slept in his own room last night, because he would never take advantage of *his angel*."

"Okay. Let's promise not to talk about it anymore. So embarrassing. But I have a question… You ran like twelve miles at a six minute pace? Are you a marathon runner?"

"No. I do the Iron Man Competition."

"No way. Really?" No wonder he had that amazing body. "Where do you ride? Where do you swim?"

"I have a nice bike trainer up in the apartment, and I swim at a YMCA not far from here. When I have time, I prefer to train outside."

"Have you ever won?"

Gherring chuckled. "No, I've never won. But I do well enough to start with the first group."

Anne shook her head. "I don't see how you find the time to train."

"It's pretty easy when you don't have any obligations outside of work."

Anne felt a pang of sympathy. She'd forgotten how alone Steven Gherring was. She had to find a match for this man. He really was sweet, even if he was a little controlling of her personal life. If he had a wife, he wouldn't worry so much about his secretary. "Well I think it's pretty amazing you do Iron Man competitions," she declared with a smile.

"It's just a hobby," Gherring said, but he looked pleased. And he hadn't bothered to put his shirt back on either, not that Anne was complaining.

Saturday afternoon found Anne down at Binding Books, the small bookstore where she knew Ellen worked. She'd run into the girl two more times since the first day they met on the subway, and she'd seemed starved for the older-sister companionship she found in Anne. They'd agreed to meet for a late lunch on Saturday. Anne found Ellen in the back of the small store, sorting through some used books.

"Anne." Ellen's eyes lit up. "Let me tell my boss I'm taking lunch. I've got so much to tell you."

"I love your store, and Emily will really love this place. I'll have to bring the girls here when they come next weekend. You've even got rare books. Awesome."

"Yep, it's pretty cool. But I'm hoping I won't have to work here forever."

As they walked out of the store and down the street toward a small pizza place, Ellen bubbled with excitement. "I got a part in a play! I have the lead role—I'm Jane and the play is called *Rainbow Junction*. It's way, way, way off Broadway. Really low budget. But it's a start. And if we get noticed and get some publicity, then we could maybe move closer to Broadway. It's a musical, so I get to sing. And the music is great."

"I'm so happy for you. Congratulations. When does it start?"

"We rehearse a lot for the next five weeks, and then we're on. Actually, the rest of the group has been rehearsing already, but their lead got diagnosed with vocal nodes and had to quit suddenly. They didn't have an understudy, so they had new tryouts for the role, and I got it."

"Wow, that's great. I knew you'd make it."

"Ha! You've never even seen me act or heard me sing."

"Yes, but I've been told I can see deep into your soul." Anne laughed. "So I just knew as soon as I met you."

"And who told you that?"

"Henri told me. He's such a flirt."

"Is that the cute French guy you met on Monday?"

"Well yes, but a lot has happened since then. Last night he took me to this big gala Gherring Inc. throws every year. In fact, there were reporters at the party last night. I bet the society page has his picture. You won't believe what a hunk this guy is. I can't even believe he asked me to go."

Ellen took out her iPad and pulled up the society report. "Let's see… Friday night. Okay, it mentions the gala… Let's look at the pictures. What does he look like?"

"Dark hair, green eyes, and hot," said Anne.

"Oh, wow!" cried Ellen. "Here's *your* picture."

"My picture? Me and Henri?"

"Well the first one is you with Steven Gherring. The second one is you with some other hottie—must be Henri. He *is* gorgeous." Ellen licked her lips.

"That picture with Gherring must be from Tuesday night. Why is it in today's report? Let me see…"

Ellen read aloud. "The caption says, 'Desolated by Steven Gherring, Anne—the Angel from Texas—lands in the arms of Henri DuBois.'" She turned to look at Anne. "Honey, you've got some explaining to do."

"Ohmygosh! Is there anything written about us in the article?"

"Hmmm, let's see…" Ellen searched the article. "Yep, here it is. Henri DuBois, one of France's most sought after bachelors, announced his date for the evening was 'Anne, my angel from Texas.' The mystery angel may have fallen from the arms of Steven Gherring, with whom she was seen earlier in the week at the Gershwin Theater."

"Oh no! I can't believe they put that in the report. I hope Mr. Gherring doesn't read the society section. He'll be sooooo ticked."

"So now you're a *player*? Tuesday night with Steven Gherring and Friday night with this Henri guy? I mean, not that I blame you."

"No, no, no! It's not like that at all. I was never with Gherring. We were at the same play but we didn't go *together.* Well, we went together, but we weren't *together* together. We didn't even sit together in the first half. They just took that picture that made it look like we were together."

Anne stopped to take a breath. "I mean, really. You know Steven Gherring wouldn't actually go out with his hick secretary from Texas."

"Well this Henri guy from France didn't seem to mind you were a hick secretary from Texas."

"Yes, well, Henri has less discriminating taste, I think. He's probably dated half of the women in New York."

"Okay, so you didn't actually go out with Steven Gherring?"

"No, I didn't. He really doesn't date much at all. And I think he spends too much time alone. I've decided to find someone for him."

"Oh really? You're going to find a girl for Steven Gherring? Well I volunteer."

"Actually, that's not such a bad idea."

Ellen giggled. "I'll agree to date Steven Gherring as soon as he asks me out or as soon as hell freezes over, whichever one comes first." Anne started to argue, but Ellen stopped her. "My break is almost over. Tell me what happened on your date with Henri La Hottie."

*****

Anne arrived at the office early on Monday, determined to be impressive in her work ethic, just in case Steven Gherring had seen the social column. She'd hate to lose her job over a bit of gossip. Perhaps if she worked really hard, he'd forgive her the embarrassment she'd caused him. He arrived shortly afterward, when she was already engrossed in her work.

"Good morning, Ms. Best," Gherring swept past her desk. Anne returned the greeting, anxious to access his mood, but Gherring disappeared into his office without another word. Anne fretted all morning, but he never reappeared. He hadn't mentioned the first picture from Wednesday's post, so perhaps he wasn't the type who followed social media. Maybe she was worrying about nothing.

"And who are you?"

Anne looked up in surprise at the diminutive, white-haired woman with the piercing blue eyes who stood on the other side of desk, examining her with a stern expression. Anne moved her lips, but no words emerged.

"Speak up, girl! I'm a bit deaf."

"I'm just Anne." She raised her voice a bit. "I'm Mr. Gherring's secr— I mean, his *executive assistant*."

"No need to yell, honey. Do you want to wake the dead?"

"What? No. I mean, no ma'am." Anne felt like she was back in elementary school, being scolded by her teacher. And she felt the same embarrassment and intimidation.

"*Executive assistant?*"

"I'm really just a glorified secretary, but he insists I say executive assistant."

"And do you always do what he says to do?"

"Actually, I have a habit of ignoring some of his orders. But I'm trying to be better. Well, most of the time. But sometimes, he just doesn't know what's good for him."

She stopped herself, but too late. The older woman was staring with wide eyes.

"Oh, Mrs. Gherring." She stood up, pleading words gushing out. "I know who you are. I've seen your picture with Mr. Gherring. Please don't tell him what I just said. He'll fire me for sure. I'm just here on a three-month trial. I really do respect him. I promise I do. I don't know why I said that."

She winced as the office doors opened and Steven Gherring appeared. "Gram!" he exclaimed with more enthusiasm than Anne had ever observed from the prim and proper businessman. "I didn't know you were coming. Why didn't you tell me when we talked last night?"

"It was a last minute decision." She returned the vigorous hug to her grandson who stooped to greet her. "I decided I needed to check up on you."

Gherring's eyes widened, but crinkled in a smile. "Really? You're here on a spy mission?"

"Yes, I am, and I've found my inside source." She glanced at Anne who stood at her desk in terrified silence. "Anne and I are going to lunch."

"But Gram, we always do lunch together when you come to the city."

"I'll be yours for the entire afternoon and evening, Steven dear. But Anne and I have a *lot* to discuss."

With that pronouncement, Mrs. Gherring grabbed Anne's arm and urged her toward the elevator. "Come along, dear. I promise I won't bite."

Inside the elevator, Anne ventured a sidelong glance at the small woman with the commanding presence. Mrs. Gherring gazed up unabashedly. "Well, tell me about yourself. Where are you from? I know that's a southern accent I heard."

Anne took a deep breath to calm her nerves. She had to control herself when talking to Mrs. Gherring. Everything would be reported to her grandson. Her job was on the line. "Mrs. Gherring…"

"Oh no—call me Gram. Mrs. Gherring is the name of my grandson's wife."

"But I thought Mr. Gherring wasn't married. He has a wife?"

"Not yet, but I certainly intend for him to have one. He's been dragging his heels for way too long. He needs a wife."

"Yes, I couldn't agree more."

Gram's eyebrows lifted toward her hair. "Really? And you think…"

"Oh no, I don't mean me." Anne felt the blood rushing to her cheeks. "I mean, I've been trying to find someone for him. It's just he seems so lonely, and I know he'd be so much happier if he shared his life with the right woman. I know, because I had a wonderful, happy marriage myself until I my husband died."

"And you're not the *right* woman?"

"Oh no." Could her face possibly get any redder? "I know what he likes. Young, smart, sophisticated. It can't be me. But he also needs someone who's sensitive and caring and not self-centered."

"And you've found the right woman for Steven?"

"I'm trying, but he's not very cooperative. He seems determined to keep everyone at arms length. I introduced him to one woman with the right traits, but he didn't seem the least bit interested."

"Hmmm," Gram was silent for several thoughtful moments. The elevator opened, and she strode so quickly toward the street doors Anne had trouble keeping up in high heels. Gram led the way to the diner next door where, to Anne's surprise, she exchanged hugs with Papa and May. The two of them were quickly led to a private booth in the back of the restaurant.

As soon as they were seated, Gram fixed Anne with an intense gaze. "I must say we seem to be mostly in agreement about what my grandson needs. Perhaps we can work together to help Steven find his true love."

"Maybe—but I can't let him find out, or I might lose my job."

"It'll be our little secret."

Why did her smile seem so intimidating? Anne noticed her hands were trembling a bit as she took a drink of water.

"You were telling me about your daughters?"

"Did I say I had daughters?"

"Humph! I thought you said that. So you don't have daughters?"

"No, I do."

"So why don't you want to talk about them? Are you ashamed of them?"

"No, I just—"

"Fine, we can start with why you moved to New York City…"

Gram questioned Anne about every aspect of her life. It was like being interviewed for the FBI. She quizzed her about her home and her family in Texas, her marriage, her children, her education, her hobbies, and even her dog.

"You've barely touched your food, dear," Gram noted.

Anne wondered how she could possibly have eaten while answering the barrage of questions, but she simply nodded assent and forked a mouthful of meatloaf into her mouth.

"Do you miss your girls?" Gram asked.

Anne forgot her nerves when she thought about her daughters. "Yes I do, so much. But they're coming on Friday for the whole weekend."

"Oh, that's wonderful dear. The three of you should come to dinner while they're here."

"Will you still be here this weekend? I thought you lived a few hours away from here."

"Yes, but I still keep the home here in the city. I was planning on a short visit, but now I think I may stay for a while. That way you and I can work on getting my grandson together with the perfect woman. You see, I intend to see him happily married before I die, but I don't have much time left."

"Do you have a health problem?"

"No dear, I'm perfectly healthy. But I'm old. I'm ninety-five years old. So I figure I've got one foot in the grave and the other on a banana peel. I've got to work fast."

Anne giggled. "You're so funny."

"Yes, but this is serious business. I've been at this for a while. Steven doesn't have the best judgment when it comes to women. I've tried to encourage him to date more, but he refuses to get close to anyone. And since he broke off his engagement with Michelle, he's been even more withdrawn. It's been more than five years, and he just can't seem to get over it. I'm sure it's because of his past."

"What happened to him?"

"Well his parents put him in a boarding school when he was a young boy. I told my son it was a bad idea, but they traveled a lot and didn't want to be bothered with a child. He was ten when they died in an airplane crash in France. I've always loved him, but that's not the same as having your mom and dad. He inherited his father's flare for business, and Gherring Inc. has grown into a billion dollar company under his guidance." Gram's mouth drooped. "But I'd rather he'd thrown the company away and had a wife who loved him and a family. Believe me, at the end of your life, when you look back at what you've done, you won't care about how much money you have. Family is what really matters."

"You're so right. Didn't you tell him that?"

"I've talked to him 'til I was blue in the face, but he doesn't listen. He just says I'm all the family he needs." Gram leaned in close and put her hand over Anne's. "But someday I'll be gone, and he'll have no one."

Anne's eyes swam with tears for the little boy without a mom and dad, and for the man who was married to his work.

"Don't worry, Gram. We'll work together, and we'll find someone for him. We just have to."

When Anne returned to her desk, Gherring was waiting for her. "How was your lunch?"

"It was great. I had meatloaf. Papa's makes the best meatloaf. That is if you like meatloaf. If you don't like meatloaf, their other special was—"

"That's not what I meant. I wondered... How your lunch was with Gram?"

"Lunch with Gram was great. She's a very interesting lady."

"What did you talk about? You had a rather long lunch."

"A little of this and a little of that. You know. All kinds of stuff. I really can't remember anything exactly. Oh, I remember." Anne forced a smile on her face. "She asked me all about Emily, and Charlie, and Gandalf."

"Who are Charlie and Gandalf?" His brows knotted.

"Well Charlie is Charlotte, and Gandalf is my Irish wolfhound."

His face relaxed. "Ah... Charlie's your daughter. And I didn't know you had a dog."

"Oh Gandalf isn't just a dog. He's a member of the family. I think he may be almost as tall as you."

Gherring smiled and probed a bit more. "That's all you talked about?"

"Are you worried we might have talked about you?"

"The thought has crossed my mind. My Gram can be a bit scheming and meddling at times. I just wanted a little warning to be prepared."

"Hmmm."

"Hmmm? What does that mean? Is she up to something?"

"Well, she did mention she's been shopping for a Christmas present for you. But I'm sorry. I'm sworn to secrecy—you'll never worm it out of me."

"Perhaps you'd rather discuss the pictures I saw in the social column."

"Pictures? What pictures?" Anne began to rifle through her desk drawer, avoiding Gherring's eyes.

"I think you know what I'm talking about."

She was caught. What could she say? She'd throw herself on his mercy. "I'm so sorry about that first picture. I had no idea they were taking a picture. I didn't say anything to them, so I don't know where they got the idea we were together. And I didn't know Henri was going to say anything about me at the gala. I didn't even know there would be reporters there."

She couldn't quite meet his eyes. "I really am naïve about these things. No one in Weatherford ever wanted to take my picture for any reason. You don't think I'd do something like that on purpose, do you?"

Gherring seemed to be struggling to remain stern. "No, I know it wasn't your fault. I shouldn't have even gone to that musical. I knew that might happen."

Her eyes stung. Of course he was embarrassed to be seen with her. He didn't want anyone to think they were together. Well she knew that already, didn't she? This just confirmed what she knew.

"Wait… I didn't mean it that way. I'm glad I went, and I would make the same decision again. I just meant I knew what might happen. So it wasn't your fault. You didn't do anything wrong." His face darkened. "Except for one thing. You did make the decision to associate with a man like Henri."

"I thought y'all had made up. What's so bad about him?"

"He… he… well he just… He's just Henri. He's arrogant and self-centered and disrespectful."

"So maybe he bugs you 'cause he doesn't bow down to you like the rest of the world?" She tried to lighten his mood with a teasing tone.

"Well obviously, his bad habits are rubbing off on my personal executive assistant. And I *don't* expect the whole world to bow down to me. I'm not that kind of person."

"Oh please, I'm just kidding you. I thought you were pretty arrogant when we first met, but now I know better. I think you're all bark and no bite."

"Hey—I do have a bite. My business associates know better than to—"

"Sorry. Sorry. You're so sensitive. First you get mad because I suggest you're too arrogant. Then you get mad because I say you're sweet."

"Sweet? I'm *not* sweet." His hands tightened into fists.

"Don't get me wrong… I still believe you're extremely dangerous. But I've seen how sweet you are with your Gram. You can't fool me anymore." At his stormy look, she broke out in giggles. "Gram told me you didn't take teasing well. I guess she was right."

"Just don't go around saying I'm sweet. That's bad for my reputation. Bad for business."

"I'll take that secret to my grave." She laughed.

He couldn't help himself. A smile broke out on his face. "When did I lose control of this conversation?"

"You know, Henri's not as bad as you think. He admitted to me Michelle was the only woman he ever loved. I don't think he's ever quite gotten over her. You really should give him a chance."

"I *am* giving him a chance, but this is the last time." He heaved a heavy breath. "Well I can see I'm not getting any info from you. I'll just be prepared for anything. Maybe, if I'm really, really *sweet,* I can get my Gram to spill the beans."

He retreated to his office and Anne returned to the work that was stacking up on her desk. At two o'clock, Henri called Anne to set up an Internet conversation. She pulled out her personal laptop and opened up Skype to see his smiling face. Henri had shaved his beard. "I like your new look, sans hair," said Anne. She looked toward Gherring's office. His door was shut. She should have a few moments alone.

Henri gave her a devilish smile. "How much do you like it? Am I totally irresistible now? Maybe I should fly back tonight—"

"You've always been irresistible. But now I can see that cute dimple on your chin."

"If only I had known, I would have shaved off the beard so you would not be able to say 'no' to me."

"Hmmmm… It may be too dangerous for me to come to Paris now. Now I'll have to work even harder to resist you."

"But I have promised to be good and not to tempt you. Do you not trust me?"

"Frankly, I couldn't possibly trust a man with a cleft chin."

"*Je suis desole*! I will grow back the beard at once."

"Ah, but now I know the cleft is there. I still won't be able to trust you."

Henri sighed. "I cannot wait until you come. I feel like I have been dead for years, and I have come back to life. I want you to meet my family. I have told them about you."

"I'd love to meet your family. Do they live in Paris?"

"*Oui.* They live here, in my house. I told you, the house is very big. My sister is here, and my niece and nephew. They will love you."

"I can't wait to meet them. How old are they?"

"My niece, Anna-Laure, is six and my nephew, Jean-Pierre, is eight. You do not mind that my family lives with me?"

"Of course not—they're family. I'd love for you to meet my girls, too."

"This is good. I cannot wait to see you, *mon bel ange*. And I have one more question."

"What's that?"

"Do you think you could ever trust me? Even a little?"

She hesitated, but smiled. "Maybe. At least a little."

"Then perhaps, if you think you can trust me a little... One more kiss? Maybe two?"

"I think that's a strong possibility." She signed off and closed her laptop, still smiling.

"Personally, I don't think you should trust him as far as you can throw him," said a scowling Gherring from his office doorway. Anne gaped at him as he disappeared back into his office. How did he always manage to sneak out of his office at the worst possible time?

When Anne got home, she checked her email and found a note from Johanna.

Dear Anne,
I am anxiously awaiting a report on your night with Henri.
I saw the two of you leaving together. I must know what
happened! I need details. Were there sparks?
Johanna

Anne struggled to decide what she should tell Johanna. Were there sparks? There was definitely some kind of passion burning that night. But she couldn't tell if that blaze had been for Henri, or if it was just because of fifteen years in the cold. He was beautiful to look at, and his attention had done wonders for her sagging ego. Kissing him was certainly exciting, and she was looking forward to a repeat performance. She knew she was playing with fire—she'd teetered on the edge of control. Finally she decided to skirt around the question, but give enough details to satisfy her friend's curiosity.

Dear Johanna,
I can only tell you Henri is a great kisser! I'm sure my long dry spell made me even more appreciative of his skill. I'm determined to limit our physical relationship to kissing for the time being. I know that may seem antiquated, but I won't be satisfied with less than total commitment. Anyway, it would be difficult to do more since an ocean separates us. But the exciting news is Henri has invited me to come to Paris over the Thanksgiving holiday! I'll get to use my passport and see Paris! Mr. Gherring doesn't like Henri, so we've had some strain in our work relationship. He doesn't know I'm going to see Henri in Paris. But his grandmother and I are joining forces to find a potential wife for him. (This is strictly confidential, so don't breath a word about our plan!) I think Mr. Gherring won't be so interested in controlling my personal life when he has a wife to love him. Everyone deserves sparks, right?
Anne

She read over her reply one last time and pressed send. She hoped her new friend would be satisfied with her response. Anne thought about going upstairs for a run, but she finally opted for curling up on the couch with a good book. She would put off her workout until tomorrow. She had leftovers from her lunch she popped in the microwave for a tasty dinner. She chuckled to herself as she remembered her lunch with Gram. Perhaps a better description would be interrogation. Just then her cell phone rang, and she answered the unidentified call.

"So have you made any progress?" Gram's voice demanded.

Anne laughed. "Well not since lunch today. I didn't know it was that much of a crisis."

"Well, my heart is feeling a little weak today. I think we should hurry."

"Did you try talking to him again? Suggesting he should consider dating—really dating?"

"Hon, talking to that boy is like banging your head against a brick wall."

"Okay, well I did have a thought."

"What's that?"

"It just so happens I'm in charge of arranging for Mr. Gherring's escort to a fundraising dinner on Friday. I'm supposed to let the publicist choose someone, but this time I thought I'd pick his escort personally. I'll look at all the available women, and choose the one I think he'd like. I'll make sure she has the qualities we think would be good for a wife."

Gram sounded dubious. "That's a good thing, I guess. Couldn't hurt. But he's so stubborn. We need something to really shake him up."

"Did you have something in mind?"

"No, not yet. But I'll think of something. This time I'm taking the gloves off."

"Gram, I think you're a formidable opponent. Steven won't know what hit him. But you should know he tried to find out from me what we talked about at lunch today. Don't worry though, I didn't give anything away."

"Good job keeping it under the table. Good night, honey. I'll call you tomorrow and check on your progress."

"Good night."

Anne tried to go back to her book, but she was distracted with thoughts of Steven Gherring. This had to be her most challenging match ever. To find a wife for New York's most eligible bachelor! She decided to work on a list of qualities.

Beautiful
Young Kind of young (30-40 years old)
Smart
Educated (must have a college degree)
Sophisticated
Talented

She pondered a bit. These were rather superficial things. But Steven was special. He deserved a wife who would understand him and care about him. He needed someone who loved him for himself and not for his money or power or popularity. How could she put that on a list? Well it was her list. It didn't have to look great. One-word descriptions wouldn't work for this part.

Loves him for himself, not his money
Will take care of him
Will commit for life

She thought further. What else did he need? This girl had to be strong enough to stand up to him a little, or he wouldn't respect her. She couldn't be wimpy. But he wouldn't want someone who irritated him all the time, like she did. She finally decided on the final qualities.

Not a pushover
Not too bossy

Anne folded up the paper and put it in her purse. She could use this as a reference and also show it to Gram. His grandmother might want to add something to the list.

The next morning, Anne got up early to run. She loved running before work, when no one was in the gym. She was a bit of a morning-person, unlike her two daughters—she had learned early on it was best not to speak to them at all for the first few hours of the morning. After three quick miles on the treadmill, Anne hurried for the elevator. She had plenty of time. It was only six a.m.

When the elevator doors opened, Steven Gherring was there, totally dressed for work, with briefcase in hand. Anne stepped in and pressed the button for her floor, self-conscious of her sweaty body and mussed hair.

"Why are you going to work so early?" she asked.

"This is when I usually leave for work." He raised his eyebrows as he observed her condition. "Are you planning to wear that to work?"

"What do you mean? It's only six o'clock in the morning."

"Well, I think I can read the time, but perhaps I'm in error. Why don't you check for me?" He stretched out his arm to show her his Rolex wristwatch. Anne read the dial. She grabbed his arm to look more closely.

"It's five after seven!" she shouted, as the elevator stopped and two more people joined them. "Oh my gosh—I'm an hour off!"

The elevator stopped on her floor and Anne rushed off. She scrambled into her apartment, showered and dressed in record time. She couldn't go out with wet hair because of the cold, so she took the extra ten minutes required to dry her heavy tresses. It was seven thirty-five. She knew she was going to be late. And she couldn't even make up a great excuse because Gherring had caught her red-handed. She hoped this was not a sign of things to come. She hurried down, intending to run all the way to the subway station. She had on her bright blue running shoes anyway. Hopefully her deodorant would hold up to the challenge. When the elevator reached the lobby, she sprinted toward the door.

"Wait! Stop!" she heard Gherring's voice from behind her. "I thought we might ride together today." He pointed to the limo waiting outside.

"You waited for me? I can't believe it—thank you." They climbed into the car and she collapsed into the seat. "I can't believe you waited for me—that was so nice."

He almost looked offended. "Why is it so surprising I waited for you? You don't think I can be nice?"

"Hey, I'm just thanking you. Don't get your panties in a wad."

"Get my... What? What did you say?"

"Nothing. I'm sorry I thanked you."

"It's not that you thanked me. It's that you seemed so incredulous about my display of geniality."

"Well I'm glad you gave me a ride, but I don't want you displaying your *geniality*. Isn't there a law against that?" Anne kept a straight face for a few seconds, and then burst out laughing. When she accidentally snorted, she clapped her hand over her mouth, eyes wide.

He joined the hilarity, and she laughed until she had tears in her eyes. She'd barely gained control over herself when the limousine arrived at work.

"Should I get out after you've gone? What if someone sees us arriving together?"

"I think it'll be fine, as long as I don't display my geniality." She dissolved into helpless giggling while he exited the limo.

It took a full sixty seconds for Anne to regain her composure. She scrambled out of the car and took off, rapidly walking toward the entrance.

"Nope," she said, as Gherring caught up with her and started to make a comment. "Don't you dare say a word. I'm just barely hanging on here. The stress of this morning has fried all my self-control."

"But I just wanted—"

"Nope, not yet. No matter what you say, it's going to crack me up."

"But—"

"Nope. Thanks for the ride. You've proven my point, that you are really sweet, just like I told you yesterday." She smirked at him before she dashed into the ladies room.

Anne's day was as hectic as her start. She had to arrange for Mr. Gherring's trip to Switzerland the next week. He was taking two executives with him for a big presentation the next Friday. One was a thirty year old named Jared, whose wife had recently had a baby girl. The other, a forty-two year old named Jeff, was recently divorced. Jeff made a point of flirting with Anne and, as she'd observed, every other single woman in the office. She tried to do most of her communications with Jeff via phone or email to avoid his constant advances. He was nice enough and a good-looking guy, but she didn't trust him. This time she was grateful when Gherring came out of his office and made some snide comments that encouraged Jeff to retreat rather sheepishly.

At least she didn't have to make flight reservations since Gherring was taking his private jet, but she still had to coordinate for three pilots since it was an overseas flight. She also had to put together the PowerPoint presentation before they flew out next Wednesday, a task complicated by the fact the information to be included was trickling in each day. Anne hated having to make so many changes, but she couldn't possibly get it all done if she waited until next week to start organizing. She wanted to just set an arbitrary deadline for the men to give her their contributions, but she didn't have the authority. Her frustration was making her a little edgy, and she caught herself snapping at Katie when she asked how things were going.

"I'm sorry Katie—this has been a stressful day. I'm really just glad you're still here handling the day-to-day stuff. How did you ever do this job all by yourself?"

"No problem. I know just how you feel; it can be a stressful job. We have all the pressure and none of the power. I don't want to discourage you, because I sure don't want you to quit."

"Well I'm not a quitter. Gherring will have to fire me if he wants me gone. But he might do that if I get any more irritable"

Katie just laughed. "You're not bad at all. One time I actually told Gherring to 'go to hell!'"

"What did he do?"

"He gave me a gift certificate for a day at the spa." Katie leaned in and spoke in a low voice. "He can be so demanding and so infuriating, but then he does something like that... I think he just uses that hard exterior to cover up a soft heart."

"That's just what I think. He's really just a softy."

"Who's a softy," Gherring voice came from his doorway.

Katie stood up, flushing. "Mr. Gherring. I'm sorry."

"We were talking about Gary," declared Anne.

Gherring cocked his head sideways. "I didn't know you'd met Gary."

"She met him at his work one time," Katie lied smoothly.

Anne kept her eyes glued to her desk. Lying was not her forte—at least not getting away with it.

"What did you think of him?" Gherring inquired of Anne, moving toward her desk.

"I thought he was very nice and very handsome." She struggled to remember some detail about Gary from his photograph on Katie's desk. "I love his... uhmm... blue eyes. I think blue eyes are so sexy."

Anne suddenly realized Gherring's eyes were also blue, and felt heated all the way to the roots of her hair.

Gherring's dimples appeared as he enjoyed her awkwardness. "And did you let Gary give you a lesson?"

Anne panicked, unable to remember what Gary actually did. "No, but I plan to let him give me a lesson some other time."

"You wouldn't be afraid to try it?" Gherring asked.

Anne glanced at Katie who looked like she was in great pain. Katie nodded her head slightly. Was she telling Anne to agree she wouldn't be afraid, or to say she would be afraid? Anne decided to try a safe answer. "I just won't know whether I'd be afraid or not until I try."

Gherring smiled, apparently satisfied with her answer. "We should go tonight. Katie, why don't you call Gary and make a reservation for us." He walked back into his office.

Anne glanced at Katie who was rather white. "What does Gary do?"

"He owns a climbing gym."

"Oh... I'm sure it'll be fine." She hoped her words were true. "I've never seen a climbing gym. How high do they climb? Fifteen feet? Twenty?"

"No, it's forty feet to the top. But you don't have to go to the top. That is, if you even try it."

"Of course I'm trying it." Her competitive spirit bubbled to the surface. "And I'm going to make it to the top. But you'd better call Gary and tell him he's supposed to know me already."

"Yeah... Gary's going to be so mad when I ask him to lie to Mr. Gherring."

"Well just blame it on me. I'm the one who took the ball and carried it out of bounds," Anne said, reminding herself to keep a closer watch on Gherring's office door in the future.

Katie and Anne went to lunch at Papa's Place, and Anne invited Gherring to come along. He declined, but agreed to allow Anne to bring him something to eat when she returned.

"I can't believe you're getting him to eat lunch. I've tried telling him skipping lunch isn't healthy, but he wouldn't listen to me."

"That's because I'm a mom," Anne declared. "I know how to speak with authority and how to guilt someone into doing what you want. It's a useful skill."

As they returned with Gherring's daily special, Gram called Anne's cell phone.

"I won't keep you, but I'm picking you up after work. I'll give you a ride home because there's someone I want you to meet."

"That sounds great. See you at five."

She delivered Papa's food to Gherring at his desk. He looked at her curiously when she entered his office. "You know you don't really have to go to the climbing gym tonight."

"Ah-ha. You're afraid I'll beat you, right?"

"Of course not—"

"You should be… I'm gonna beat you like a drum."

"We'll see," Gherring replied with a wry grin.

"Yep, we'll see." Anne was thinking she couldn't wait to see. She couldn't wait to see his muscles rippling as he climbed on that wall. After all, she worked hard. She deserved a little entertainment.

Anne secluded herself at her desk to look through the escort candidates from the publicist, Charles Cooper. There were ten portfolios, complete with pictures. Anne scanned through the files, quickly eliminating three that were in their twenties. Gherring needed someone with more maturity and life experience. Four of the remaining were excluded because the contenders didn't have a college degree. She was disappointed only three met her basic requirements, but all three were strikingly beautiful. One was a model, one was an actress, and one was a news reporter aspiring for a television anchor position.

Anne read all three resumes, but quickly settled on the third, Sharon Landry. She reasoned Sharon would be the most capable of captivating Gherring with interesting dialogue. Anne had no way of knowing whether she would be caring and committed, but at least she had potential. She called Charles, and asked a few more questions about Sharon. He described her as sophisticated and smart, a real go-getter. Anne thought that might be just the ticket.

Once she'd finalized Gherring's escort arrangements for the Friday night fundraiser, she could concentrate on preparing her PowerPoint presentation. She decided to call Jared and Jeff and use her mommy-powers to guilt them into getting their portions of the presentation information to her desk as soon as possible. Both men easily succumbed to her skillful pressure, promising to have the majority finished by Thursday and the final portion by Monday morning. She smiled in self-satisfaction.

When she left the office at five o'clock, Gherring was still secluded in his office. Katie had arranged for a seven o'clock climbing session, so Anne would just have enough time to get home and grab a bite to eat. She found Gram waiting in the back seat of the car as promised. As Anne was climbing in, Gram was already quizzing her about the progress in their matchmaking plan. Anne explained her escort choice, proud of her find, but Gram still seemed skeptical of success.

It still took almost twenty-five minutes to make it back in the heavy traffic, but Gram had the car stop a few block short of the apartment.

"Come with me." Gram nimbly stepped out of the car.

Anne followed her to the door of a shop. The sign read, "Carved Wood Creations." There was a closed sign hanging in the window, but Gram opened the door and marched inside, causing a small bell to ring out their presence. A tall, thin, white-haired man appeared from the back room.

"Mrs. Gherring," he said as his face crinkled into a broad smile. "I didn't know you were in town."

"Good afternoon Mr. Hamilton. I've brought someone by to meet you. This is Anne Best, my Steven's new secretary. Anne, this is Gus Hamilton."

Mr. Hamilton grasped both of Anne's cold hands in his warm ones. His fingers were rough and calloused. "I'm so pleased to meet you, Anne."

Before Anne could respond, Gram continued her introduction. "Anne lives in Steven's apartment building and walks right past your shop almost every day."

"Do you like coffee?" he asked Anne.

"Yes, she does," Gram answered. "And we could both use a cup to warm us up now, if you have a fresh pot."

"Of course I have a fresh pot. Just give me a moment." Gram walked with him behind his work counter and disappeared into the back room.

Anne looked around the shop. It was filled with woodcarvings in a plethora of sizes and designs. The display was dominated by a large number of carved persons, six to eight inches high, that fit together in pairs or groups. The figures were intricate and detailed. So exacting

Anne could detect wrinkles in the clothes. The faces were expressive and poignant. Anne had never seen anything like these creations. Each set fit together exactly, like a puzzle. There was a man, standing while holding a woman in a tender embrace, her head resting against his shoulder. Turning and twisting the female figure slightly while lowering her from the male's arms could separate the two. Another set included a young child, walking between two parents, swinging from their hands. There was a pair laying on their sides, the man supporting his head with his left elbow while his right was draped over the female who nestled against him.

Anne explored the fascinating creations, marveling over the complex fitting of the beautiful sets and touched by the emotions displayed on the tiny faces carved from wood. She picked up a particularly intriguing set, slightly larger than the others, perched behind a small sign that read "Inseparable Love." A male figure was standing with his back slightly arched for balance, his arms around the waist of a female figure who had her legs intertwined around his hips and her fingers locked behind his neck. Their eyes were closed and their lips touched lightly in a lover's kiss. So intricate was the carving, she could detect the stitching in their jeans. But no matter how she rotated the pair, she couldn't find a way to detach them.

"That pair won't come apart," Mr. Hamilton said, emerging from the back with mugs of coffee. "The others were carved from separate pieces of wood, but I carved that set from one single piece of wood."

"It's amazing. They're all amazing, but this one is incredible."

"I'm glad you like it. It's my favorite as well. It took me the better part of four months to carve it, but it was a labor of love. That's why I priced it so high—I don't really want to let it go." He smiled.

Anne glanced at the price tag—seventy-five hundred dollars. Surely he would never have to give up his prized carving. She set it gently back in place, carefully balancing the figures lest they somehow fall and break. She took the proffered cup of coffee, gratefully sipping the piping hot brew. "I love your carvings. Maybe I could come and watch you work sometime."

Mr. Hamilton exchanged a knowing look with Gram. "You're welcome any time. Just stop by and try the door if the light's on downstairs. Come on in, if it isn't locked, even if the sign says 'Closed'. I live upstairs, so I'm almost always here."

"You live upstairs? That's awesome. How long have you been here?"

"Hmmm, let's see…" He looked questioningly at Gram.

"Well," Gram answered for him, "Mr. Hamilton retired twenty years ago. You were seventy when you retired, right?"

"That's right, and I just turned ninety."

Gram explained, "Mr. Hamilton was our family's chauffer for forty years. We gave him this place in lieu of retirement pay. It was his choice."

"And I'm still happy with my choice. It's allowed me to do what I love for the past twenty years. I'm lucky my hands haven't gotten shaky. I have to wear these magnifying glasses to carve now, but I still look forward to my work each day. I'm sure I'd be dead now if I'd simply retired without a purpose."

"Do you sell a lot of these?" Anne asked.

"Enough to pay for my food and buy supplies. That's all I need, anyway. There isn't a huge demand for wood carvings, but I make a few sales every week."

Anne's phone vibrated as a text came in from Gherring. "I need to get back home and change clothes. Tonight I'm going to have a lesson at the climbing gym Katie's fiancé owns."

"Have fun dear," said Gram. "You know the way from here, right?"

"Yes, and thanks for the ride Gram. Nice to meet you Mr. Hamilton." She hurried out the door.

Anne looked back in the shop window to see the two in close conference, looking very serious. She hoped everything was all right. But she knew she needed to hurry if she was going to have any time to eat before going climbing, especially since she needed to shave her legs.

Back in her apartment, Anne downed a bowl of yogurt with fruit, hoping that would hold her hunger at bay. She jumped into the shower to shave, but realized too late the shower diverter was on. Her hair was doused with cold water, and she bit back a curse word at her bad luck. She shaved her legs quickly, regretfully inspecting her white skin. She hadn't had time to get a fresh dose of spray tan. Why was she worried about her legs? No one would see them but Katie,

Gary, and Mr. Gherring. She tried to convince herself she didn't care what Mr. Gherring thought about her legs. Tried and failed. Okay, she wanted her legs to look good for him. It was because he looked so good, and she had always been competitive. It certainly wasn't that she was trying to catch his attention. She just didn't want to embarrass herself.

Satisfied with her explanation, she pulled on tight liner shorts under her regular shorts to ensure complete coverage when climbing. Her cell phone was buzzing again as she put on an exercise tank top and covered up with jeans and a sweatshirt for protection against the cold. She pulled her wet hair into a ponytail and headed downstairs. She'd chosen smooth legs over dry hair. Hopefully, she'd made the right choice.

Gherring was waiting in the lobby to give her a ride to the gym. Anne's heart gave a little lurch. Despite the cold, Gherring had chosen to wear shorts, and his well-muscled legs looked incredible. Anne decided kissing Henri had awoken some urges that had been suppressed for a while. She had to gain control of herself. If the sight of his legs did this too her, what would happen when he took off his coat?

"Ready?" he asked.

"Yep," she said, trying to keep her focus on his face and not look down at his legs. Still, she couldn't help a quick downward glance. She forced her gaze upward and reddened at his amused and knowing expression.

"Still planning to beat me like a drum?"

"Like a big bass drum." She lifted her chin and marched outside to the waiting car.

The gym was a short ride away, and Anne fidgeted while Gherring sat on the opposite side, calmly appraising her.

"Your hair is wet," he remarked.

Anne felt herself blush again. She was not going to admit what a klutz she was. "Yes it is."

"Don't mothers say you'll get sick if you go out in the cold with wet hair?"

"I have a strong constitution."

"Perhaps you need some amendments."

"I *do* have the right to remain silent."

He grinned. "Okay, I won't ask."

Anne fidgeted a little more until she finally broke the silence. "I'm really kind of excited. I've never done anything like this before."

"You like trying new things?"

"Yep, I'll try almost anything. And Charlotte is just like me, or even worse. She's a real daredevil. But Emily is the serious, mature one—always playing it safe. She likes to read about adventure instead of experiencing it."

"They're not married?"

"Oh no, but they're still young, twenty three and twenty one."

"But you were married by then?"

Anne answered defensively, "Yes, I got married when I was twenty, while I was still in college, but I did finish my degree. We were just *so* in love, we couldn't wait two extra years."

"How did your husband die?"

For a brief moment, the memory flashed fresh in her mind, and her stomach tightened.

"I'm sorry. I shouldn't have asked."

"No, it's fine. It's been fifteen years... fifteen years this November. It was the beginning of the Thanksgiving holiday, and he'd driven to pick up his folks in the country. They were driving back on the highway, just after dark, when a drunken teenager in a big truck crossed the centerline and ran head-on into the car. The girls lost their dad and their grandparents that night, and those poor parents lost their son."

"Weren't you angry?"

"Oh sure. Shocked, angry, depressed, worried, sad... You name it, I felt it. But I had two girls to take care of and no time to wallow in self-pity. My faith and family and friends carried me through it." She blinked at her watery eyes. "And I've had a great life. Losing Tom made me realize how precious each day is—every moment with someone you love."

"But fifteen years? And you've never remarried? That's a long time to be alone."

"Well that's the proverbial pot calling the kettle black. How old are you? Forty-five? Fifty? Fifty-five? You've never married at all."

Gherring frowned. "I just turned fifty! Do you think I look fifty-five?"

Anne smirked—she'd known exactly how old he was. Trust an assault to a man's ego to make him forget about his uncomfortable line of questioning.

"Well luckily, the car stopped, so I guess we'll have to postpone this conversation." Her voice was cheery as she climbed out of the limousine. Gherring followed with a grumpy expression.

Anne walked into the climbing gym, staring in amazement at the immense climbing wall, peppered with climbers in various extremely uncomfortable-looking positions, some scaling areas with overhangs, one hanging precariously by one hand some thirty feet above the floor. The single-handed climber suddenly lost his grip and dropped. Anne gasped as he fell, but he only swung harmlessly in his harness before he managed to regain his handhold.

Gherring cocked his head. "You didn't watch the climbers when you came here before?"

"Yes, of course, but no one fell when I was watching." She hoped her lie was reasonable. He seemed to accept her statement, so she relaxed a bit.

Katie approached with Gary in tow.

Gary clapped him on the shoulder. "Hey Steven. What're you planning to climb tonight? Alan laid out a new route that's probably at least a five thirteen."

"That sounds great, but first we want to get the girls on the wall."

"Not me," said Katie. "I'm just here to admire my man." She playfully squeezed Gary's bicep.

"But Anne wants to climb. You remember Anne, right Gary?" asked Gherring.

"Sure thing." Gary frowned at Katie before holding out his hand toward Anne. "Good to see you again."

Anne smiled awkwardly and shook his hand. "Hi Gary."

"Well let's get you in a harness," Gary said. Anne took off her coat and jeans, giving her legs the once over to see if she had missed anything while shaving. She squeezed her feet into the tight climbing shoes she'd been given. Gary handed her a harness and then excused himself to take a phone call. Anne stared bewildered at the tangle of straps and metal, but Gherring took it from her hands and helped her step in. As he tightened the straps his hands brushed against her. She felt a familiar warming inside and held her breath in the attempt to slow her heartbeat.

"Is it too tight?" asked Gherring.

"No, I'm just a little nervous."

He led her over to the wall.

"I'm climbing here?" she asked. "Don't you have a beginner wall? You know, like a green slope?"

"This is the beginner wall. See how it's not quite vertical? And if you use the blue handholds, the route'll be pretty easy." As he spoke, Gherring began threading the belay rope through her harness.

"Are you sure you know what you're doing? Should we get somebody who works here to do this?"

Gherring pinned her with his eyes, the blue glinting. "I assure you I'm more than capable of belaying you on this climb."

"I don't know what that means, but I guess I'm gonna trust you with my life." She looked up at him with wide eyes, and his look softened.

"I'll try to be worthy." His dimples returned.

He began tugging on all the various straps, his hands brushing against her, assaulting her senses. She was all-too-aware of his hard muscles, strong and sinewy. Her head swam, and she tried to catch her breath. Why was her heart beating so rapidly? She must really be nervous about trying the climb. She breathed in and out, slow and steady. He was standing so close she drew his clean scent deep inside. She had to get away from him. The only way was up.

She started her climb. The first few moves were easy, and she felt the comforting tug of the belay supporting her. She started moving up steadily, looking for the next blue hold as she ascended. She made it three fourths of the way up when she noticed her muscles were fatiguing. She felt tremors in her arms. "My arms are shaking," she yelled down.

"Put all your weight on your feet and rest your arms for a minute. You can relax—I've got you."

Anne followed Gherring's instructions, planting her feet firmly and standing tall. She felt the belay rope lifting, easing the strain on her arms. She realized she really could trust him. And somehow, she wanted to rely on him for more than just climbing a wall. She felt a pang in her heart. His feelings for her were more like that of a

120

protective father. But there was no reason why she couldn't fantasize a little, right? He'd never know.

She started climbing again, feeling the strain and ignoring the exhaustion in her limbs. She paused for a moment.

"You're almost there," called Katie.

"You don't have to go any further if you don't want to," teased Gherring. "You can just give up now."

Gherring's words worked like magic on her competitive spirit, sending adrenaline into her system. She scrambled quickly upward and touched the top of the wall.

"I did it!" she yelled. Whoops and hollers came from below. "Now what?"

"Just let go," said Gherring. "I've got you."

"Let go?"

"Let go of the wall. You can hold on to the rope and lean back." He pulled hard on the belay rope and she felt it again—that secure feeling that someone else is protecting you. The knowledge that someone is making sure nothing bad will happen. That you're safe. She let go of the wall and, to her surprise, the rope held her steady. She swung away and then back toward the wall.

"Now I'm going to let you down slowly, and you can just walk down the wall," Gherring's soothing voice rose up from below. The descent was smooth and quick. Anne was shaking from head to toe as she stood on the ground with Gherring loosening her harness.

"Okay—that was a rush!" Her heart was beating rapidly, speeding up with the heady feeling of Gherring's touch. At least he wouldn't detect the effect he had on her.

When Gherring had freed her from the straps, he paused a moment and looked closely at her flushed face. "You really did like it, didn't you?"

She stared back at his piercing blue eyes, so close she could see little glints of gold around the edges. "I did. I liked it."

"You know," he said softly, "I—"

"Hey Steven! Are you ready to climb? I'll belay you." Gary called from across the room.

Gherring sighed, and turned toward Gary. "I'm coming, buddy."

Anne stood next to Katie while Gherring tackled the challenging climb. His muscles flexed and bulged as he pulled himself under an overhang using only handholds. Katie leaned over and whispered in Anne's ear, "He looks pretty good for a fifty year old, don't you think?"

Anne, who'd been thinking he looked pretty good for any age, nodded her head in agreement. She decided climbing was a really great spectator sport, at least when the scenery was this good. "Does he come here a lot?"

"Yeah, he and Gary were friends and climbing buddies before this, and Mr. Gherring encouraged him to start this gym and was one of his initial investors. In fact, that's how I met Gary. Mr. Gherring was pretty mad at Gary when he realized he was going to lose his executive assistant, but I think he's finally accepted it. He didn't really have a choice, and it's helped a lot since you showed up. He was so pouty about the whole thing; he was turning down every single candidate."

"Why do you think he hired me? After turning down all those others?"

"Don't get your feelings hurt, but you made him laugh."

"He laughed at me?"

"No, you're taking it wrong. He laughed because you surprised him. It takes a lot to surprise Mr. Gherring after so many years in this business. He's become pretty cynical, I think. It's more like he laughed at himself, for being caught by surprise."

"Hmmm, that's not really too flattering. But I guess it makes sense. Oh!" she exclaimed as Gherring slipped and caught himself with his fingertips on the hold, while his feet searched for a purchase on the wall. He regained his footing and continued upward, every muscle straining. Anne felt the tension in her neck finally ease when he reached the top and fell back to descend. "So do you usually climb?"

"Me? No way. I've got no desire to climb. But I'm happy to watch Gary and cheer him on. He's opening another gym, and I'm going to help him run the business after we're married."

"Do you think we got away with our little fib about Gary?"

"I don't know, but I guess we just need to quit talking about Mr. Gherring." She smiled. "Or else we need to watch his office door a little more closely."

On the ride home, Anne chatted about the climbing experience and asked questions about climbing technique and the climbing wall construction, attempting to keep the conversation from turning serious as it had on the way there.

"You were a lot more confident on your second climb. The big rookie mistake is relying too much on your arm strength. Your leg muscles are much stronger."

"But you sometimes were climbing with just your arms. You know, when you were under those ledges."

"To be honest, most women don't have the arm strength to do that. Plus, I have years of experience and strength from climbing and weights and swimming."

"Yeah, that's it. I forgot you have *years* and *years* of experience…"

"I said 'years', not 'years and years'."

"Maybe by the time I'm your age, with all those years of experience—"

Suddenly Gherring was tickling her side, and she dissolved into helpless laughter. He didn't relent until she shouted. "I give up! I take it back! You're not old!"

Her cheeks were aching from laughter and burning from her body's response to his touch. Even his tickling started a little fire inside her. She was glad the back of the limo was dark so he couldn't see her flushed face.

"Will you try it again?" he asked. "The climbing?"

She breathed heavily as she caught her breath. "I think so—it was fun. You know what? I should bring the girls to the gym this weekend. I think they'd like it. At least Charlie would."

"They're coming to New York?"

"Oh yeah, didn't I tell you? They're coming on Friday and going back Monday. I'm so excited. In fact, I think we're going to go eat with your Gram one night."

"Gram is staying here through the weekend?"

Too late she realized Gram had been keeping this a secret from her grandson. "Yeah. She said something about having things to do. I'm not sure. I could be wrong."

"Is that so?" Gherring mused. "I think we may need to have a talk."

"Please don't get me in trouble with your Gram."

"It's not like I wouldn't have found out she was staying. I just think she may be up to something."

"Well leave me out of it."

"Sure. If it's possible, I'll leave you out of it." His face grew more earnest. "You know—"

"Oh, we're here. I'm so tired I think I may fall asleep with my clothes on."

"Perhaps you need some help," he suggested, his dimples deepening.

Anne scrambled out of the limo as if she might catch on fire. "Thanks. I mean thanks for the ride. Not… Never mind. See you tomorrow."

She trotted into the building and ran to press the elevator button. To her distress, he sauntered to the elevator just as the door opened and stepped inside with her. She fumbled inside her bag for her keys, effectively eliminating the need for conversation.

"So you don't need any help?" he asked, grinning.

Her cheeks flamed. "No. Stop teasing me, Mr. Gherring."

"I'm sorry. You're so easy to tease. But really Anne, I—"

The elevator doors opened on the tenth floor, and Anne made her escape.

"Good night, Mr. Gherring."

As the doors closed, she looked back to see him beating his forehead with the palm of his hand. She knew he must be frustrated over how sensitive she was. She just had to learn not to take things so seriously. But it was so hard not to be sensitive around Steven Gherring when his very presence made her nerves tingle. Perhaps she could get some acting lessons from Ellen.

Chapter Eight - PowerPoint

AFTER A HECTIC WORK MORNING, Anne headed next door for lunch at Papa's Place. George and May had made her promise to catch them up on things, so she headed down alone. Spencer met her at the door. "Hey Anne! Have you found a match for me yet?"

"No luck so far. None of them are willing to compete with all the girls that are constantly hanging around you, vying for attention," she teased. She started to head back to her table, but stopped dead in her tracks. "How old are you, Spencer?"

"I'm twenty five. Why?"

"And you're in grad school right?"

"Yep, getting my MBA."

"Do you like climbing?"

"Sure. Climbing, bouldering, hiking, mountain biking, skiing—just about anything outdoors."

She pulled her cell phone out of her purse and found a picture of Emily and Charlotte. "Wanna go climbing with me and my girls this weekend at a climbing gym? And do you think you could find another friend to come along? I don't really know any young guys for us to hang out with."

Spencer stared at the picture in his hand, and his mouth dropped open. He looked up with a grin. "I think I could find about twenty friends who'd be willing to go climbing this weekend if I showed them this picture."

Anne laughed. "Great. I'll call you and set up a time."

"Oh, and by the way, search no further for a match for me. I'll take either one. Are they smart, too?" He paused a moment and looked at the picture again. "Never mind. Who cares?"

George came out to get her. "Hey, come eat in the kitchen. We want to talk to you."

Anne followed him into the kitchen where he set her up to eat on a small table in the corner. Things were bustling with the lunch rush, but George and May took turns stopping by to quiz her about the developments over the past week.

May plopped down in a chair opposite Anne. "What about this Henri guy? He's from France right? He seemed really interested in you."

"Yes, we went out a few times and he's flying me to Paris to see him in two weeks."

"Oh, Paris… Romance… That sounds fun." She leaned in close. "And he's enough to make an old girl like me wish I was younger. Don't tell George I said that."

Anne laughed. "It's our secret."

"And now you've hooked up with Mrs. Gherring? She's a lot of fun, but she's always got something up her sleeve."

"Actually, you're right. We've joined forces to find a wife for Mr. Gherring."

George came over to the table. "A wife for Mr. Gherring?"

"Shhhh—keep your voice down. It's a secret." Anne glanced about to be sure no one else was listening.

"Every man needs a good wife, even if they don't realize it." May got up to help one of the cooks.

"If no one's managed to snag that guy in all this time, I don't see how you and Mrs. Gherring are going to pull it off," George said, screwing his lips sideways.

"Well, we think we know just what he needs. It's just convincing him he needs someone."

"Well he dates a lot of women, doesn't he? The tabloids are always full of rumors about his women. He's a real playboy. How will you get him to settle down?"

"Oh, he's not really a playboy. He just tries to keep everyone at arms length. I haven't quite figured out how to get him to let his guard down. I might be able to talk to him about it someday, if I can get him to trust me."

May returned. "You're around him all the time. He might actually listen to you. But I thought he was mad at you about the 'Henri thing.' You said he'd been trying to keep you from dating him."

"Well he doesn't like Henri, and so he doesn't want me—or anyone else, for that matter—to date him. But since Henri's back in Paris, I think Mr. Gherring will just forget about him."

George heard a crash in the next room and went to investigate.

"Oh, and my girls are coming into town this weekend. Spencer's going to find a friend to come along, and we're all going climbing."

"Climbing?" asked May

"Yes, it's a gym Katie's fiancé owns, where you climb up walls. It's all very safe. Ropes to keep you from falling."

"Well, maybe one of your girls will fall for my Spencer."

126

"Maybe. If they're willing to fight off the other girls. He's pretty popular, I think."

"Anne, your lunch is getting cold. I'll let you finish eating." May went to intervene between two waiters fighting about whose order got priority.

After lunch, Anne cornered Katie to get advice on entertaining her girls when they came to town. She told her about their plans to go climbing. Katie suggested the Museum of Modern Arts, and explained how they could get discount tickets to a play. Anne planned to take a tour on a double-decker bus to get an overview and history of the city. She also wanted to see the Empire State Building and the 9/11 Memorial.

"You know, you don't have to see everything on this first trip. Surely they'll come more than once," said Katie.

"But I'm only here on a trial basis. What if this is the only chance we have?"

"Well, he'd better not fire you, because I'm leaving for good when I get married, even if he doesn't have a secretary." Katie glanced at his office door to make sure he was still safe inside. "That is, if he doesn't fire me first when he catches me talking trash about him."

"I think he's gonna fire me for not getting this presentation ready for the Switzerland trip. It's so frustrating knowing I have so much work to do on it, but I can't do any more 'til they get me the information I need. Why do they wait 'til the last minute?"

"They always do that, and Mr. Gherring is the worst one."

"Yes, I'm hoping I've scared Jared and Jeff into turning in their stuff earlier. But I don't think my 'scary mad mom voice' will work on Mr. Gherring."

The office door opened and Gherring looked at the two conspirators with suspicion. Both sent him innocent smiles. "Did you need something, Mr. Gherring?" asked Katie.

"Yes, I need Ms. Best for a moment."

Anne followed him into his private office, wondering whether he'd caught on to her matchmaking efforts already. "Yes sir?"

"You don't need to call me *sir*." He tossed his pen on his desk with more force than necessary. "I have some things ready for the Switzerland group."

"Oh great—I've been stressing about getting that presentation ready."

"Okay, grab your laptop and we'll get started."

"You mean, together? I thought you'd just give me the information, and I'd kind of work on my own."

"Well, the information is in here." He pointed to his head. "So unless I give you my head on a platter, we'll just have to work together."

"Okay. But it'll take a long time."

"Do you have something else to do?"

Anne thought about her daily talk with Henri. She would just have to miss this one. "No, I just figured you had more important things to do."

"Not today."

"Okay..."

"Okay." He smiled at her and lifted his eyebrows while crossing his arms.

Anne swiftly gathered her laptop from her desk. She sent a text to Henri telling him she was tied up that afternoon and then returned to Gherring's office.

Gherring fired off information at a rapid rate, with Anne working furiously to take notes. After an hour of non-stop input, Anne stopped the pacing man. "Wait. I need a break. My brain is fried."

"Let me see what it looks like." Gherring came around to stand behind her.

"Oh, I haven't even begun to put it in the PowerPoint format yet. That takes forever. I need to get it organized first."

"Then show me what you've done from before."

Anne pulled up the saved presentation on her laptop and started going through the slides. Gherring leaned in close, reaching over her shoulder to indicate a bullet point. "There should be more information on this point."

Anne felt that familiar warming that happened whenever Gherring touched her. She shifted a little to the side. "There's a lot more information down below, in the notes section. But we don't want too much writing on the slide. Just summary information."

"Oh, I see," he leaned down further and pressed a few keys. "And this is how we access the notes?" She could swear he purposely leaned against her. She felt her heart rate accelerate and her breathing was shallow.

"Don't you already know how to use PowerPoint? You must've done this a hundred times before." She leaned as far to the side as she could go, but she couldn't escape his presence.

He shrugged, but didn't answer. He was so close, she could sense his intense stare, but she kept her eyes closed, praying for self-control. She couldn't let him know how he affected her. It had been easier to ignore the attraction when she thought he was snobby and obnoxious. But now she knew him better, she found herself wishing for something she knew would never be possible.

Desperate for a reprieve, she stiffened and exclaimed, "Oh no!"

"What's wrong?"

"I need to go to the ladies' room." She slid away from him and disappeared from his office.

In the restroom, she took a moment to calm herself. She had to go back and work with Gherring, but she needed to be in control, in more ways than one. She walked back into his office, and picked up her laptop.

"Okay, let's get back to work. We've got a lot to do," she said in her best *mom* voice. Gherring obeyed, spouting out so many details, she wondered how he could possibly remember that much. When he started to come closer to her, she stopped him.

"No, I need my space to work. Don't crowd me now, I'm on a roll." Gherring kept his distance, though he seemed a bit agitated. Anne was thrilled at the progress, although she knew how much work lay ahead in creating the actual presentation.

She was engrossed in her editing, when Gherring voice pierced her consciousness. "Ms. Best... Anne... it's after five. I think we should call it a day."

Anne stretched, realizing how tired and stiff she felt. "Ughh—I'm not used to staying still for this long. But we got a lot done, and tomorrow I'll be able to put all this into the presentation." She closed her laptop and stood up to leave.

"Anne, you know I've been thinking—"

"Yes, Mr. Gherring?"

He frowned at her. "You know, you could call me Steven."

She felt the heat rising to her face again and quickly turned her face away from him. "Oh no, I couldn't. It wouldn't be proper. Katie still calls you Mr. Gherring and she's been here for five years." Anne knew she needed to keep her perspective with her boss. Calling him by his first name would only make it harder to control her growing attraction. This was all Henri's fault. That man and his kisses had awakened something in her. Now Henri was across the ocean, and she couldn't get that *something* to go back to sleep.

"Yes... well... she's younger than I am."

"And I'm younger than you as well."

"Not *that* much younger."

"Still, it wouldn't be proper."

Gherring followed her out to her desk. "Would you like a lift home? It wouldn't be any problem."

"No thanks, Mr. Gherring," She escaped into the elevator. She saw him watching her as the doors closed, and she let out a breath she must have been holding. Her shoulders were sore and tight. She couldn't handle many more days like this one.

Anne tumbled into her apartment and collapsed on the couch. Her cell rang with the familiar sound of Charlie's theme song. "Hey sweetie."

"Hey Mom. Are you getting excited?"

"Of course I am—I can't wait to see you. Oh, y'all need to pack some workout clothes, too."

"Why? Don't tell me you're gonna make us run on treadmills—"

"No, I've arranged a climbing date for y'all."

"Climbing *date*? What are you talking about?"

"So, last night, I went climbing in this gym Katie's fiancé owns. And I've arranged for us to go while you're here. *With* a couple of good-looking guys."

"I'm not worried about the climbing, 'cause I've done plenty in Colorado. But tell me about these *guys*."

"The one I think you will hit it off with is named Spencer. He's super cute, twenty-five, very outdoorsy and adventurous. I actually haven't met the other one—Spencer's bringing a friend."

"Hopefully we can talk Emily into climbing. Have you told her yet?"

"Not yet, but I thought you could talk her into it. You know you have better luck with her than I do. You just look at her with those puppy dog eyes, and she always gives in."

"Yeah, I usually manage to get my way."

"And bring some casual clothes and at least one nice outfit. Hopefully we'll go see a play, if we can get some discount tickets. And we've been invited to eat dinner with Mr. Gherring's grandma. She's a hoot—you'll love her. And I've got to show you this wood carving shop, and you need to see Ellen's bookstore. It's so cool."

"Mom, we're only gonna be there two days."

"I know, I know. I'm just really excited. And I'm really tired, too. I've got to get to bed early tonight."

"So did you talk to Henri?"

"Not since yesterday, but hopefully I'll talk to him tomorrow. It's too late tonight."

"So just to get this straight, about the climbing date. I'm getting the best-looking guy right? I just want to know so I can tell Emily about it."

"Don't you dare get me in trouble with Em."

"Hmmm… I can be bribed."

"I'll remember this when your birthday comes."

"You win—I surrender. By the way I have some things picked out on my wish list already."

"I know, but everything on that list is about three or four hundred dollars. Don't you want anything small and inexpensive?"

"What can I say? I have expensive taste."

"Good night, sweetie."

"Night Mom. Love you."

"You too."

With her teeth brushed and her mascara scrubbed off, she collapsed on the bed in exhaustion. But the sleep she sought eluded her. She tossed and turned for an hour. Finally she surrendered to her insomnia and got out of bed. She took one Benadryl, considered for a moment, and downed another. She really needed a good night's sleep. She decided to pull on sweatpants and grab a blanket and go for some fresh air on the rooftop patio while waiting for the antihistamines to kick in.

With her feet clad in furry house shoes and a cup of chamomile tea in hand, she wrapped the blanket over her shoulders and headed up the elevator. She'd only discovered the peaceful haven the previous weekend, and had been itching to sit outside ever since. Her home in Weatherford had a big back porch with comfy chairs where she often sat to have tea in the early morning or at night before bed.

She opened the exterior door and peeked outside, assuring herself the retreat was deserted. She settled in on a comfy cushioned couch and sipped on her tea in solitude, enjoying the feeling of being outside with a clear view of the sky. Gradually she became drowsy and slunk down on the couch, snuggled warmly in her blanket and breathing the cool air. She could almost imagine she was camping.

"Anne… Anne…" The voice broke into her consciousness. Woozy from the residual Benadryl, she ignored the voice, refusing to give up her sleep. "Anne!" This time the voice was more urgent, and she felt a gentle shake on her shoulder. "Anne, it's morning. You need to wake up."

Whose voice was that? Was it Tom? She felt someone brush her hair gently off of her face. She peeled open her groggy eyes and tried to decipher her surroundings. Steven Gherring was peering at her, only a few inches away.

He smiled. "Sorry to disturb you, but you were still out like a light. I was afraid to let you sleep past six. That's what time it is now."

She sat up abruptly. "Oymygosh! I fell asleep outside! How did you find me?"

"I sometimes come out here when I can't sleep." He chuckled. "But this time, Goldilocks was asleep on my couch."

"Why didn't you wake me up last night?"

"Believe me, I tried. Are you *on* something? You would *not* wake up." He shook his head and ran his fingers through his hair. "So I decided I had two choices: carry you down to your room or stay out here with you. I was afraid to do the first one. I thought you might be offended."

"You stayed out here with me all night? Where did you sleep? You must have been freezing."

"Well, I left you alone long enough to bring both of us extra blankets. And I slept on that lounge chair. It was comfortable enough."

132

Anne surveyed her surroundings, taking in the fluffy down comforter that surrounded her and the pillow she'd slept on.

"I'm so sorry you had to do all this and sleep outside. I couldn't sleep so I took a couple of Benadryl. But I'm so glad you happened to find me. I would have been frozen solid, and I probably wouldn't have woken up 'til nine or ten o'clock. Unless I froze to death."

She stood up, stretching her stiff muscles, and gathering her things. They walked inside to the elevator. Gherring tried to hide his discomfort from the long night on a lounger, but she could tell his movements were stiff. She felt so guilty.

"I didn't actually say it, but thank you. I really mean it," said Anne.

Gherring smiled, his gaze intense over the pile of pillows and blankets he held. He took a slow breath, as if searching for words. "Anne, I've only known you for a few weeks—"

"Yes, but I hope you won't judge me yet. I know I've been clumsy and sensitive and disrespectful, and I've mixed up the time by an hour. And now I've fallen asleep outside alone on the roof and almost missed work. But I'm usually *very* responsible. I really *can* do this job. And I haven't actually screwed up anything at the office, have I?"

"No, but—"

"You really can't blame me for going up there at night, since you admitted *you* do the same thing. Although I guess it is a little different since I'm a woman and you're a man."

"I don't—"

"I know you probably think it was stupid that I took two Benadryl instead of one, but I was afraid one wouldn't be enough."

"Actually, I—"

"I refuse to take sleeping pills, because I heard they're addictive, so that's why I use Benadryl. Please, give me another chance. You promised me a three-month trial. You wouldn't fire me before the three months is over would you?"

"Anne, I would never—"

"Oh, thank you, Mr. Gherring—you won't regret it!"

She gave him a hug with her arms full of blanket and her tea mug in hand, and rushed off the elevator to her apartment.

Gherring's posture was still rigid when he arrived at the office. Anne felt so responsible for his state she resolved to make it up to him. Somehow. She threw herself into her work, plowing through the PowerPoint Presentation. She added creative graphics and animation, but not so much as to be distracting. Photographs of Bern, Switzerland proved the presentation was personalized for their company. She was working so hard she didn't notice Sam at her desk until she said her name for the third time. "Anne!"

"Oh hey. Sorry, I was just on a roll, and when I'm absorbed in something I'm in another world."

"Impressive powers of concentration. Hey, Tanner and I wanted to take you to lunch today."

"Well, I'd love to if I make enough progress on this presentation. I can't get this one slide to look right. I'm fixin' to pull out my hair. It's got to be really good this time."

"It'll be great, I'm sure. But you're the one who always says you shouldn't skip meals. Right?"

Anne grimaced. "I did say that didn't I? Okay, I'll go. Twelve o'clock? Next door?"

"We'd be glad to take you some place new, but I know you're devoted to Papa's Place." Sam smiled.

"Do y'all have something to tell me?" Anne waggled her eyebrows.

"No, it's only been a few weeks. Don't be silly."

"Hmmm, I notice you didn't deny it was a future possibility."

"You're impossible. Did you know that?"

"So I've been told," Anne laughed. "See ya later."

She went back to work, but shortly after got a call from Gram.

"Hello, dear. I just wanted to ask about this date you've planned for Steven. Who did you say this girl is?"

"She's a news reporter. She hasn't made it big yet, but she's getting a lot of attention. I think she's very intelligent and well informed. She'll be able to carry on a decent conversation."

"But is she the kind of girl who knows the importance of family? She may be totally self-centered. Steven doesn't need a girl like that."

"I have no way of knowing, but it's worth a shot. Mr. Gherring is a wonderful, caring man. Any girl would be lucky to have him. Surely she'll recognize that and be sensitive to his needs."

"But that's just it. These women decide they want Steven, but what they really want is to be 'Mrs. Steven Gherring'. It has nothing to do with caring about him and putting him first."

"Well if she tries to take advantage of him like that, I might just beat her up."

"That's more like it," laughed Gram.

"But we should at least give her a chance, don't you think?"

"I'll reserve my judgment, but do you have a backup plan?"

"I'm evaluating everyone I meet as possible wife candidates. Well, every smart, pretty, sophisticated female between the age of thirty and forty."

"Humph! How did you come up with that age range?"

"First off, Mr. Gherring always goes out with younger women, so that must be what he likes. But personally, I think girls under age thirty just don't have enough life experience to go with Steven. And over forty, they're not pretty enough and too set in their ways to change. You know how it is. Marriage is all about compromise. It'll be hard enough for Mr. Gherring, having been single for so long, without saddling him with a bossy woman who's inflexible."

"It does seem like you've given this a lot of thought, but we may have to re-evaluate along the way. I'm having dinner with Steven tonight. He somehow discovered I'm staying in town, and he's a little suspicious."

"But he can't know we're plotting against him—I mean, plotting *for* him—can he?"

Gram laughed. "Don't worry, dear. I have a feeling this time I'm going to get my way."

"I'm glad I'm on your team and not playing against you."

"We can talk on Sunday night when you bring the girls to dinner. I'll send a car for you."

"Thanks Gram, that'll be great."

"Bye, now. Have fun with your girls."

"Thanks, I will. Bye."

Soon Anne was immersed in the presentation again. Time flew by until Sam and Tanner stopped by her desk. "I figured you wouldn't stop working if we didn't come get you," said Sam.

"Y'all are ready for lunch already?"

"It's after noon, sweetie."

Anne picked up her cell phone. "Oh you're right." She hit save and closed her laptop. "Let's go. I want to hear everything, from the beginning. I am *sooooo* good." She began singing "Matchmaker" from *Fiddler on the Roof*.

Gherring's voice came from his doorway. "I didn't know you could sing."

Anne choked as she twirled to face him. "Mr. Gherring, I didn't know you were there."

"Don't stop on my account; you have a nice voice—"

"We're going to lunch. Would you like to come?"

"No thanks. I think I'm going to take a nap. I didn't sleep very well last night."

Anne felt the blood rush to her face. Sam and Tanner were staring at her. She escaped to the elevator while they trailed behind her.

"Wait up. Why are you so embarrassed? You actually sounded pretty good," said Sam.

As the elevator doors closed, Anne saw Gherring chuckle before giving an exaggerated yawn.

After lunch, Anne called Jared and Jeff to make sure they were on schedule with turning in their PowerPoint data. Both agreed to bring up what they had before five o'clock.

She wondered what it would take to do something more than being a secretary. Perhaps if she went back to school and got an MBA, she could have a job like Jeff's. It would be exciting to have an important job and travel around the world. She didn't regret the decision she'd made to pursue motherhood rather than a career. But what was to stop her from doing something different with her life? With the confidence she gained from taking on this job and moving to New York, something entirely out of her comfort zone, maybe she could do something really interesting. Maybe after she found Mr. Gherring a wife, she would check into night school.

Hoping Gherring wouldn't overhear her conversation, she took her phone and personal laptop and headed to the break room to talk to Henri. When Henri's face appeared on the computer screen, he looked ecstatic to see her. "*Mon bel ange*—I have missed you."

Every time she saw Henri, she couldn't believe a man that handsome would be interested in *her*. "Wow, I love your new scruffy look. I think this is my favorite so far."

"I am glad you like it." He grinned at her. "I have been doing nothing but work, work, work. Anna-Laure had a birthday party yesterday. I bought her a pony."

"A pony? You bought her a *real* pony? I wish you'd been *my* uncle when I was a little girl."

"But I am very glad not to be your uncle. There would be no kissing, if you were my niece." He chuckled. "And I will buy you as many ponies as you want. But perhaps you would prefer diamonds or sapphires…"

"Oh no you don't. You're not buying me anything. This trip to Paris is too much already."

"But the Paris trip is for *me*, so I can see you."

"Well, I'm excited about coming—less than two weeks."

"What have you been doing? You were too busy for me yesterday?" He pouted a little.

"I was working with Mr. Gherring on a presentation all afternoon."

"*Gherring*! He is always interfering between us."

"I'm sure it wasn't on purpose. He pays me to work, you know."

"Yes, and I will forever be grateful that he hired you, because if not, you and I would never have met."

"So maybe you could go easy on him. He's usually pretty nice to me."

"Maybe I do not like him being so nice to you. Maybe he is trying to steal you from me."

"You've got to be kidding. Mr. Gherring would never be interested in me like that."

"Maybe he would just like to steal you so I cannot have you. It is in our history."

"Well let's not waste our time talking about Mr. Gherring. I learned how to climb. On Tuesday night, I went climbing at the gym Katie's fiancé owns. I climbed up to the top twice."

"I think I would have enjoyed that sight. You are not afraid of falling?"

"I was nervous, but it wasn't really dangerous. Do you climb?"

"I do. Would you like to climb in Paris when you come?"

Anne grinned. "Maybe I'd just like to watch you climbing. You know… enjoy the scenery."

"I have a heated swimming pool. We can both enjoy the scenery." He grinned back at her.

"Anne!" called a voice behind her. "Mr. Gherring is coming!"

"Henri, I've got to go. Talk to you tomorrow. Bye."

"But—"

Anne closed the connection, just as Gherring came through the door.

"There you are. Why are you in here?"

"I was looking for a quiet place to work."

"What's wrong with your desk?"

"You're right. I'll just go back to my desk."

She picked up her computer and headed back down the hall with Gherring in tow.

"What did Henri have to say today?"

Anne stopped in midstride.

"I know that's your computer, not the office computer. And I've learned you talk to him in the afternoon."

"I… I'm…"

"It's not like I can stop you. Obviously I've tried to warn you, and you won't listen." He started walking ahead of her. "You don't have to lie to me. If you like him that much, I'll leave you alone." He tried to go into his office and shut the door, but Anne shoved her way in behind him.

"You don't want me to lie to you? Well here's the truth! I don't *know* how much I like Henri. I haven't gotten to spend enough time with him to know. But the little time I have spent with him, he made me feel special and he treated me with respect. I just don't understand why you care so much whether I talk to Henri. You know, you aren't my father! Or my big brother!"

"I don't want to be your father or your big brother either! I want to—"

"I think you want to control me, and it's not happening. You can be my boss about everything *but* my personal life." She pivoted on one foot and stalked from the room, shutting the door behind her.

The rest of the afternoon passed with Gherring secluded in his office and Anne hard at work on the presentation. Jared emailed the bulk of his presentation information to her by three o'clock, but Jeff arrived at her desk with a file in hand at four fifty-five.

"Hey, there's a lot of stuff I need to go over with you. What say we talk about it over dinner?"

Anne cringed inwardly, but managed to keep a civil voice. "I'm really too busy with work to do dinner. And anyway, aren't you dating someone?"

"We've gone out a few times, but we aren't exclusive."

"Well, I'm sort of dating someone."

"You mean that French guy, Henri? The one you went to the gala with?"

Anne nodded.

"He's in France, isn't he? Surely you're not exclusive with him when he's across the Atlantic Ocean!"

"I really don't think that's any of your business."

"Well I say, when the cat's away... I can just scratch that itch for you. It doesn't have to be anything serious."

With a leer on his face, he leaned in close. "You know, you're so hot—I bet you're a real tiger in the sack."

Anne's mouth fell open and she struggled to breathe. She leaned back as far as possible, but he invaded her space. "I have a really good friend in my pocket who'd just *love* to meet you."

"I... You..." Anne's eyes filled with tears. She was mortified. How did she lose control of this conversation and let it get this far? She didn't even know what to say.

"Jeff," said Gherring's voice from his office door.

He quickly straightened up and threw Mr. Gherring a professional smile. "Mr. Gherring, Anne and I were just working out some details about the presentation."

Gherring walked over to stand between Jeff and Anne's desk. Though Jeff was over six feet tall, Gherring still looked downward at him. "I heard you 'working out details.'"

His Adam's apple bobbed up and down. "I'm sorry. She's been giving me signals—"

Anne sprang up from her desk. "I have *not* been giving you signals, except for maybe a great big *stop* sign. And I'd like to say if your 'friend' ever comes out of your pocket when I'm around, I'll cut his head off with a meat cleaver!"

Jeff's face was as white as a sheet. "Look, I didn't mean anything. I just misread you, okay?"

Anne started to retort, but Gherring held up his hand.

"Jeff, we've already had a previous sexual harassment complaint. I'm afraid you're out."

"That was a trumped up charge! She was asking for it and just got jealous when she saw me with someone else."

"We have a no tolerance sexual harassment policy at Gherring Inc. You signed a form when you became employed here indicating you were aware of that policy. One confirmed incident is all we need to terminate you, and this incident was confirmed by me."

"You can't fire me. Especially not before the big Switzerland presentation. There's no one else who can do my part. And I already have the connections with the execs over there."

"On the contrary, I *can* fire you, and I just did. Ms. Best, please call security and have them escort Mr. Murphy out of the building."

He turned back to Jeff. "Your things will be boxed up for you to retrieve on Monday at the security office."

Jeff opened his mouth to reply, his face red and puffed up with fury, veins standing out on his neck, but Gherring silenced him with a glare.

"You'll wait right over there." He indicated the reception area across the room. "And I don't want to hear you speak."

Anne called security with shaking fingers as adrenaline coursed through her body. Gherring watched her carefully.

"Ms. Best, you should sit down. You look a little pale."

A few minutes later, after two security guards had taken Jeff down the elevator, Anne felt tears rising to her eyes. "I'm s-sorry. I've m-messed up Switzerland for you."

"How can you possibly believe that was your fault?" Gherring asked, shaking his head.

"I should have handled it. He's been coming on to me, and I didn't know how to put him off. If I wasn't so naïve—"

"The man is a lecherous jerk, and I'm glad to be rid of him."

"But what will you do about Bern? He's right, there's no one to take his place. He's got all the connections."

140

Gherring sighed as he looked toward the ceiling. "Jeff thinks way too much of himself. I have far more connections than he does. And 'Jeff the Jerk' has offended a good number of people along the way, both male and female. Jared and I can take up the slack, we can work late every night and some on the weekend."

Anne felt her stomach churning. Things were getting worse, and it was her fault. "But Jared and his wife have a new baby at home and he's already leaving them alone for four days."

Gherring grunted. "Fine, I'll do the work myself."

"I'll help. It's the least I can do." She bit her lips, tears shining in her eyes. "You were my white knight today... And last night, too."

"It's not often I get the opportunity to rescue a fair maiden twice in twenty-four hours."

She laughed, choking a bit, but then her hand flew to her mouth. "Oh, I forgot—there's one little problem."

"What's that?" he asked, narrowing his eyes.

"I'll work late tonight and Monday and Tuesday and Wednesday night, but my girls are coming in tomorrow, and I want to spend the whole weekend with them. I know I shouldn't be making demands, but—"

"Of course you don't want to miss any time with your daughters. If I had any sons or daughters I would feel the same." A forlorn look passed through his eyes so quickly, Anne wondered if she imagined it.

"Would you like to meet them?"

To her amazement, his face actually lit up. "I'd love that, but I wouldn't want to intrude."

"It wouldn't be an intrusion. The girls would like to meet you, too. They've heard so much..." Her voice trailed off.

He lifted one eyebrow. "Really? What have they heard?"

"You know, they've seen stuff in newspapers and magazines."

"Ah." He sounded almost disappointed. "So you weren't talking about me."

"No, of course not—that would be unprofessional. We're going climbing again on Saturday morning at nine thirty. Want to come?"

"Nine thirty in the morning? You're starting early."

"I've got a busy day planned. We have breakfast before that, and lunch after, and then we're going to MOMA and trying for tickets to a play Saturday night. Sunday we're going to visit as many sites as possible. You know, Empire State Building, Statue of Liberty, whatever we can fit into the schedule. And Sunday night we're eating with Gram."

"What play are you going to see?"

"Whatever we can get three cheap tickets for at the discount place. We'd love to see *Lion King* or *Phantom* or *Beauty and the Beast*, but anything will do. Except I don't want to see something R-rated. It would be so awkward sitting with my girls watching something raunchy on the stage." Without warning, Anne's stomach made a huge gurgling noise.

"Sounds like you need dinner." Gherring sighed. "Was that a genuine offer to help with Jeff's work? I'll have to pull most of it off his computer, and first I'll have to find it. I'm sure he wouldn't be cooperative and helpful if I called him to ask about it."

"Yes, it was a real offer, and the good news is I've got a lot of the info right here," she pointed to the file folder on her desk.

"Then I guess we should order something to eat and get to it."

At nine forty-five, Anne was sifting through the papers spread out among half-empty Chinese take-out boxes, when Gherring let a moan.

"Ughh! That's enough for tonight. Let's go home and tackle this in the morning."

Anne pushed her disheveled mane out of her face. "Sounds like a good idea. My eyes are starting to cross."

Gherring called for his car as Anne started organizing the mess. "Why don't you leave that? We'll be back here in the morning."

"No, I need to sort these things into organized stacks. Otherwise we won't be able to find anything tomorrow, and we'll waste a lot of time."

By the time they made it to the lobby, the limousine was waiting.

"I noticed this time you didn't argue about riding home with me."

"I'm too tired to argue," she moaned. "And afraid to use the subway alone at night."

"I'm glad you weren't stubborn about it. This time I would've had to put my foot down."

"Well," she said in an exaggerated country drawl, "I'dduh been fine, if'n I'dduh had muh shotgun wit' me!"

Gherring laughed. "I would've liked seeing Jeff's face this afternoon if you'd pulled out a shotgun." He chuckled some more. "Did you see his expression when you told him about using a meat cleaver on him?" He laughed again.

Anne laughed at the memory, covering her mouth to stop a snort that almost came out. Abruptly she sobered up. "Mr. Gherring..." she saw the irritation on his face at the salutation, but ignored it. "Tell me the truth. Do you think I was leading Jeff on? It's so hard to know what to say to guys. I didn't want to be rude. But he always made me feel uncomfortable. Maybe I just need a little thicker skin. I don't know."

Gherring's expression turned dark. "Stop it! I knew you would do this. You're always talking to yourself in your head, trying to reason things out. And you make excuses for people's behaviors because you want to believe the best about them. You've got to realize not everyone deserves that trust you dole out so blindly."

"I know you're probably right, but I think it'll be a sad day when everyone I meet has to earn my trust, instead of a few earning my distrust."

Gherring's gaze was intense. "I never thought of that, but you're right. I'd hate for you to lose that. But it means you need someone to do that for you, to keep you safe."

She contemplated his words. "Maybe. But after fifteen years of getting by on my own..."

"Yeah, I know what you mean. Try fifty years..."

Anne decided this was a good sign. He at least recognized fifty years was a long time to be alone. Maybe he was ready for a change. Maybe tomorrow night when he went to the benefit with Sharon Landry, he would realize how empty he felt. Anne wondered at the knot that formed in her throat when she thought about Gherring and Sharon together. Probably fatigue from such a long day.

The car let them off at the apartment building, and they dragged themselves inside and over to the elevator.

"So promise me not to fall asleep outside anymore. I don't want to have to go up on the roof every night to make sure it's empty."

Anne blushed. "Never again. I promise. I don't want you to have to check on me all the time. You have enough to worry about without me adding to things."

"That's not what I meant. Don't go putting words in my mouth."

"I know you didn't mean that, but I do. I'm sorry I've been a burden to you. And now because of me, you had to fire Jeff and—"

"And get rid of a liability before I had a lawsuit on my hands. It was only a matter of time, you know."

"Oh... I hadn't thought of that... Then I take it all back, and I just promise to sleep in my bed from now on." She nodded her head with satisfaction, and with a wry smile she added, "Alone."

Gherring had to chuckle. "Finally—you've put my mind at ease." The elevator opened on Anne's floor, but he stopped her before she departed. "How about a lift tomorrow morning? Downstairs at six-forty-five?"

Anne thought about how tired she would be the next day. But she owed this to Gherring, so she put a bright expression on her face. "Sounds terrific."

Emily had left several messages on her cell phone, so Anne returned the call.

"Hey sweetie. What's up?"

"Just checking in. What's this I hear about us going climbing with some guys?" Her voice sounded skeptical.

"No big deal, you don't even have to climb if you don't want to. But I think you would like it if you tried."

"You know I don't like doing dangerous things. Charlie got all the adventurous genes."

"It's not dangerous at all. And it's just for an hour, with two cute guys. Oh, and now Mr. Gherring is going also."

"Steven Gherring is going climbing with us? Ohmygosh! Have you told Charlie?"

"Nope, I just found out tonight."

"Great. Don't bother to call her. I'll tell her all about it and save you the trouble."

"Thanks a lot," Anne said sarcastically. "I think this conversation sounds vaguely familiar."

"I know you said he's obnoxious and snobby, but I'm really excited to meet him."

"I didn't say he was obnoxious and snobby, did I?"

"Hmmm, no… I actually think you called him self-absorbed, selfish and conceited."

"I said that?"

"I'm pretty sure."

"I may have been wrong about him."

"May have been? So I take it you've changed your mind about him? Do you like Mr. Gherring now?"

"Of course I *like* him. But I don't *like* like him. You know…"

"I thought you liked Henri—"

"I do like Henri, and I've kissed him too. That counts for something I think."

"And Mr. Gherring—have you kissed him?"

"No—of course not! He would never kiss me. We're not like that. I'm just saying he can be pretty sweet when he wants to be."

"Okay Mom, whatever. You seem a little defensive to me, though."

"I'm just uncomfortable talking with my daughter about kissing men."

"You brought up the kissing, not me."

"Oh, right. How about, let's change the subject."

"Okay fine. So how was your day?"

Anne thought back to her morning—waking up on the roof with Steven Gherring, the phone call with Henri that was cut short, the scene with Jeff, and the evening working with Gherring. Emotionally, it was too much to process. "It was fine." Now she understood why that was always the answer you heard from a teenager.

"Well, I still have to pack. But I'll see you tomorrow. We should be at your apartment before you get home from work, unless our flight is delayed."

"I can't wait to see y'all. Rayna knows to expect y'all, and I left a key so y'all can wait inside. I'm sooooo excited!"

"Love you, Mom."

"You too."

Anne's alarm shrilled in her ear. She reached for it and knocked it off the table. She hadn't slept well, even though she was exhausted. She was afraid to take a Benadryl, even one, since her last experience with antihistamines had resulted in one of her most embarrassing moments. Bleary-eyed, she crawled out of bed and headed for the shower. She'd give herself a blast of cold water at the end to wake herself up.

She made it downstairs right on time, and found Gherring reading the paper with a cup of coffee. "I brought one for you if you want it." He held out an insulated cup with a lid.

"Oh, I love you!" She snatched it from his hand. Only after she'd taken a sip of the still-steaming liquid did she realize what she'd said. Surely he would know it was just an expression. He wouldn't think it was a declaration of devotion, would he? Should she try to explain? Perhaps he didn't notice. He probably didn't pay any attention. She glanced at Gherring. Nope, he noticed. He looked downright smug.

"I always heard the stomach was a way to a *man's* heart, not a *woman's*," he remarked.

"Well, I've heard money can't buy happiness, but it can buy coffee, and that's close enough."

"Yes, but close only counts in horseshoes and hand grenades."

"Well now, that's a horse of a different color."

"Quit horsing around. It's time to go."

"Well, if ya gotta *go*, ya gotta *go*."

Gherring led Anne outside to the waiting car. He opened the door and gestured for her to get in. "Ladies first."

"I give! Uncle! I'm fighting a losing battle here. I should never have tried to go head to head with you. This is a last-ditch effort, but I might as well throw in the towel."

"You win!" Gherring laughed. "It's way too early for my brain to be this competitive. I should've known a country girl could out-cliché me."

This time it was Anne who wore a smug grin, having won the battle of clichés while accomplishing the more important task of distracting him from her little slip-up.

"So what are you doing tonight?"

"Huh?"

"You and the girls, what are you doing tonight? Are you going to see a play?"

"We actually don't have plans for tonight. We were planning a play for Saturday night because I can go get discount tickets in the afternoon. I don't have time for that today. But we may go see Times

Square at night. I was thinking about taking them to that bar in the top of the Marriott on Times Square—the view was amazing from there."

"When did you discover that view?"

Anne realized she had been there with Henri on the night of the gala. Not wanting to bring up Henri, she evaded the question. "I don't remember. I think I went with Rayna and Antonio." She asked a quick prayer of forgiveness for the fib. Luckily, Gherring seemed to accept the answer. She breathed a sigh of relief. Lies always seemed to get her in trouble.

"That's where we had the gala." His face was inscrutable.

"Oh, that's right. I must have gone there when we were planning the gala."

"At night?"

"Yes. I think I went with Katie."

"So you and Katie went at night? Alone? To a bar?"

"Oh no, maybe Gary was there. I don't remember."

"We could ask Gary tomorrow. He'd surely remember."

Anne knew her face was crimson. "Okay I admit it. I went up there with Henri the night of the gala."

"You could have just said that."

"But I know you don't like him, and I didn't want to make you mad."

He frowned. "I don't get mad."

"Call it what you want. You always start yelling at me."

"I've never *yelled* at you. I don't *yell*."

"Well... You used a *yelling* tone of voice." They rode the rest of the way in silence as she swore to herself she would never lie again.

Gherring and Anne worked together in the conference room. The earlier tension was soon forgotten as they immersed themselves in the job at hand. She found she could concentrate around Gherring easily, unless he got too close or brushed up against her. At the slightest contact, she felt her heart rate accelerating. She determined the cause to be her *people-pleaser* personality. She always wanted to make everyone happy, and Gherring was particularly difficult to please. This made perfect sense to her. She couldn't possibly be attracted to him. Well, maybe she could be a little attracted to him… physically. He did look pretty good without a shirt on.

She watched as he leaned over to pick up a paper that had floated to the floor. That was a nice view as well. Hard, tight compact muscles. He turned toward her and flashed a distracted smile, his rugged face, blue eyes, and dimples a winning combination. Of course she was physically attracted to him. Any woman with eyes would be physically attracted. That didn't mean she had feelings for him. She couldn't have feelings for him because that would simply lead to heartache. After fifteen years she wouldn't let herself fall for a guy she could never have. She was much better off with Henri. That relationship was practically impossible and therefore, felt incredibly safe. At least until she went to Paris….

She'd decided to Skype with Henri during her lunch break, so it wouldn't be an issue with Gherring. But as lunchtime approached, Gherring asked, "Should we order in from Papa's?"

She took a big breath. "I'm going to try something new and tell you the truth. I'm Skyping with Henri during lunch. There, I said it. So please don't be mad and don't yell at me." She cringed, waiting for him to vent his anger.

He ran his fingers through his hair. "I'm not mad. I'm… I'm… worried. I just don't want you to get hurt, that's all."

"To tell you the truth, I think you should be more worried about Henri. He seems—I don't know—kind of vulnerable. I'm really taking it slow, you know. After fifteen years, I have pretty tight reins on my heart. I'm not sure I can ever actually fall in love again. I know what true love feels like—I've experienced it before. I'm just not sure that kind of thing could ever happen twice in my life."

He was quiet a few seconds that seemed like an hour. "I sincerely hope that isn't true, Anne. I hope you're able to find love again someday. But not with Henri. I still don't trust him—let's just say I question his motives. And I'm definitely not worried about him."

The conversation was cut short when her cell phone pealed out the Maserati song. "Oh, that's Charlie!" She fumbled for her phone in her sweater pocket.

"Hey Mom, we're on the plane, getting ready to take off. Oops, the stewardess is giving me a dirty look. Gotta go. See you soon."

Anne heart swelled with anticipation. She couldn't believe how much she missed her daughters. It's not like she was used to seeing them all the time when she still lived in Texas. It was just the knowledge they were so far away from her now.

"They're on the plane." She couldn't stop grinning.

"That's an interesting ringtone. Is it for everyone or just for Charlie?"

"That one's just for Charlie. It suit's her personality. The Maserati going one-eighty-five, and losing your driver's license—"

"She's done that?"

"No, but she probably would if she ever got to drive one. I don't think she's ever even seen a Maserati, but she got her fair share of speeding tickets in the little Honda Civic she drove."

"What's Emily's ringtone?"

"Hers is piano music from Pride and Prejudice. That's her favorite book and she loves the movie. She's my ballet dancer and artist. Not one speeding ticket her whole life. She doesn't even like to drive. She wants someone else to drive her everywhere so she can read on the way. She'd love New York. No one has to drive at all."

Gherring chuckled. "And your names? Anne, Emily, Charlotte? Was that a conscious decision or an accident your names match the Bronte sisters?"

"It was on purpose. But I can't believe you noticed that. Nobody ever does."

"What can I say? I'm very observant."

"Not me—I'm kind of absent minded. I get lost all the time and I forget where I parked my car in the parking lot. It's like I don't have room in my brain for those pesky details."

"You mean pesky details like what time it is or where your bed is?"

"You're sooooo funny."

"Well, it's lunch time… Time for you to call your French lover boy."

"He's not my lover boy."

"Sorry if my choice of words offends you." She didn't hear the slightest bit of sincerity in his voice.

"You're using that *yelling* tone I was talking about." Anne scooped up her laptop and headed toward the door.

"I didn't—"

"Yes you did." She let the door slam behind her. For once, she got the last word.

"Henri."

"Hello angel."

"I'm so excited. My girls are in the air right now on their way to New York."

"I am happy for you and jealous that I cannot be there to meet them."

"How are your niece and nephew, and your sister?"

He smiled proudly. "Anna-Laure is riding on her pony. She holds the reins herself. My nephew is taking violin lessons. He is very talented. And my sister has broken up with the no-good boyfriend. I am so glad she will not marry him and take my kids away. They are like my own."

Anne smiled. "I bet you're a good dad to them."

"But we should not talk about them. I want to know about you. What will you do with your daughters when they come?"

"Everything. We are going out to eat, going to a play, going to the Empire State Building. We're even going climbing at the gym."

"Just you and your daughters?"

"Yes, mostly just us. But I have a couple of young boys lined up to go climbing with us." Anne refrained from mentioning Steven Gherring. She wasn't hiding anything or being dishonest. Or was she? No, she just didn't want to upset Henri. Steven Gherring's presence at the climbing gym wasn't really significant.

"Maybe I am jealous of these boys. Are they handsome? Maybe I don't want you to watch these boys climbing. You may forget about me." He winked at her.

"They might be good looking, but they're way too young for me."

"I do not like that I cannot keep an eye on my competition."

"Believe me, those boys are no competition for you."

"And what about Steven Gherring?"

"What about him?"

"Is he my competition? You are with him every day, and I know he does not like me."

"Mr. Gherring's just my boss. He isn't interested in me. He knows just how goofy I can be. You know, Henri, when you get to know me better, you might not be so interested either." Why did she say that? She sounded so needy, begging for compliments. What if it was true? Henri didn't know her that well.

"I know enough. When you come to Paris you will see. You need someone who knows how precious you are. I will show you—I am that man."

Anne felt a little thrill. It was nice to have someone put you on a pedestal, even if you knew you didn't belong there. But maybe she was just being foolish, investing in an impossible relationship. A relationship with Henri was almost as impossible as a relationship with Steven Gherring, but for different reasons.

"But Henri, what happens after Paris? I can't just date you over the computer screen."

"*Non*, I agree. You are nice to look at, but the kissing is not so good on Skype. Please do not look so sad."

"I can't help it, I'm a worrier. I just don't think it'll work, and then you'll regret spending all that money to bring me to Paris—"

"*Non*, I will not. The money is nothing to me." He sighed. "I have something to tell you. I was waiting, but..."

"What? Is it bad? What is it?"

"It is good. I think... I hope it is good. After you come to Paris, one week after, I am coming to New York. Is that good?"

"Really? For how long?"

"I am coming just for the weekend, but I am used to travelling. I come to New York often already. I will just come more often. And you can come back to Paris and bring your daughters." He paused. "That is good? Right?" His green eyes peered earnestly from the computer screen, waiting for her reply.

"Yes, Henri. That's good. That's the weekend of Gherring Inc. Christmas party for all the employees. We could go together."

"Now, I want to know all about your daughters and everything you are going to do in New York..."

After lunch, Anne returned to the conference room to see how much she could accomplish before the girls got to New York. It occurred to her Steven Gherring was going to the benefit with Sharon

Landry that night. She decided to take advantage of the opportunity to help him see her good qualities. He seemed to mostly ignore Margo Milan at the big gala. Her plan would never work if he didn't pay any attention to Sharon.

"So," she said, summoning what she hoped was a casual voice. "You're going to that benefit dinner tonight, right?"

"Hmmm? Yes, I guess so. I'd forgotten, but it's on my calendar."

"And you're going with Sharon Landry, right?"

"Who?"

"Sharon Landry, you're escorting her to the benefit. Remember? I put her file on your desk."

"Oh, you probably did. But I didn't look at it."

"Why not?"

"Because I don't care who she is. She's using me for publicity, and I'm using her to keep my life uncomplicated. And I trust my personal executive assistant to pick someone who won't embarrass me."

"But maybe this girl is different."

"What do you mean, different?"

"She's really smart and informed. She's a television news reporter, and she's beautiful."

"That doesn't change anything."

She tried to hide her frustration. "But how are you ever going to find someone if you won't even look?"

"*Find* someone? *Find* some—"

He furrowed his brows and leaned toward her until she cringed before him.

"Gram!"

"What?"

He stood and paced, flinging his arms about with unbridled fury.

"Gram—you've been talking to Gram. She wants me to get married, and now she's enlisted my executive assistant."

"I... uhmm..."

"That little schemer!"

"She didn't. Not really."

"*You.*" He pinned her with a glare. "You will cease and desist. I don't want a wife. I don't need a wife. You said it yourself. After fifty years alone, no one would be able to live with me."

152

At these words Anne, who'd been cowering, stood up and punched him in the chest with her finger. "I never said that. I didn't say that at all. I was saying I had done everything alone for fifteen years, so it would be hard to find someone."

He stepped back a few paces at her wrath. She continued, punctuating her words with pokes to his chest, forcing him backwards.

"But *you*—you have everything you need to attract someone really great. You're smart and rich and famous and handsome. You're sweet and generous, and you have a great body. There're probably a million women who want you. Any girl would be lucky to have you, and you won't even try."

He backed into a chair and sat down. Anne turned away from him and crossed her arms, breathing heavily.

"You yelled at me."

"I did *not*!" she said over her shoulder.

"You used a yelling tone of voice." He let out a little snicker.

Anne swirled around, determined to stay angry. "And that won't work."

"What won't work?"

"You can't make me laugh so I'll forget I'm mad. It won't work."

"It might work."

"It won't."

"So I should give up?"

"Yes."

"Throw in the towel? Cry uncle? Call it a day? Give up the ghost?"

"Stop it." She stifled a smile. "I'm mad at you."

"Are you fightin' mad? Madder than a wet hen? Do you have a bee in your bonnet? Are you so mad you could spit? Are you mad as a hatter?"

"Yes, I'm mad as a hatter—you're making me crazy."

"What exactly are you mad about?"

"I'm mad because... because you... I don't remember anymore. But that doesn't change anything. I'm still mad." She put her hands on her hips and gave him her best 'you're in trouble with mom' look.

But Gherring grinned. "How can you be mad at me? I'm sweet and generous. And what was that last thing you said... something about my body?"

He stood up and walked closer to her, invading her personal space. Her heart thudded so hard she could hear it in her ears.

She backed away, giving up the fight to keep a straight face. "Okay stop right there. Let's make a deal. I won't be mad anymore, and you promise never to bring up that last thing I said."

He smirked. "But maybe we should discuss it first—"

"No please. Let's forget it. Please?"

"How could I say 'no' when you look at me with those big brown eyes? I promise not to bring it up again."

Anne let out a slow breath, relieved. Why did she say such stupid things around him? He had promised not to tease her about it, but he hadn't promised to forget.

With a temporary truce in place, they once again joined forces to attack the PowerPoint presentation. Gherring had retrieved all the information he felt was relevant, and Anne was busy setting up the slides and the accompanying notes. "Who's going to do Jeff's part of the presentation? You or Jared? Or will you bring someone else from that department?"

"I'll probably do it. Jared's pretty green. I was really bringing him to give him some experience."

"I haven't cancelled the other hotel room yet. Should I do that now?"

"No, just keep it for now. I haven't made up my mind." He stretched and glanced at his watch. "You should head home. Your girls will be in soon."

"That's okay. I can stay until five or even five thirty. I left a key with Rayna, so the girls can let themselves in the apartment. And we don't really have a time deadline tonight."

Reaching into his pocket, he retrieved a small brown envelope. "Actually your play starts at seven."

She opened the envelope and pulled out three tickets to *Beauty and the Beast*. "What? I can't take these. Thanks anyway." She tried to hand them back.

"Don't be ridiculous. Why can't you take them?"

"I don't know. It just seemed like the right thing to say. Isn't there something improper about taking tickets from your boss?"

"Of course not. I give extras to my employees all the time. It's called a perk."

"A perk? Are you sure?" She asked, hopping up and down on her toes.

"Of course. It's not a big deal." He gazed at the ceiling.

"You know, if you keep rolling your eyes like that, they might get stuck up there." A giggle escaped, and then suddenly she hugged him, almost knocking him off balance.

"Thank you, really. Th-thank you s-so much. I..." She swiped at a tear. "N-now I'm s-sorry I used a yelling tone of voice."

"You're welcome. This is actually a much more thorough thank you than I usually get." His tone was teasing, but he seemed quite proud of himself.

"Well, no one ever accused me of being normal."

"And I won't be the first one to do it, either. You guys want to ride together to the gym tomorrow?"

"Yes, sure." Then her eyes grew wide. "Ohmygosh! I'm so excited. The girls are gonna flip. *Beauty and the Beast*—woo hoo!"

"I hope you have a great time."

Anne gathered up her things and rushed out, stopping by the door. "And you... You need to have an open mind tonight. Okay?"

Gherring raised a single eyebrow. "Sure. I'll see you tomorrow."

Chapter Nine - Emily and Charlie

LEAVING EARLY, ANNE DECIDED she had time to stop by the wood shop. She opened the door to find Mr. Hamilton carving at his worktable. "Hey Mr. Hamilton."

"Hello, Anne."

"I'm on my way home. My girls are coming in town today. I wanted to bring them by the shop, but I wasn't sure when you would be around this weekend."

"Hon, I will be here the whole weekend. You can come by any time. If the door's locked, just ring the buzzer. I'd love to meet your girls."

"Have you heard from Gram, I mean, Mrs. Gherring?"

He smiled. "Yes, she came by today."

"I think I got her in trouble with her grandson. He figured out we were plotting to find him a wife."

He chuckled. "Don't worry about Mrs. Gherring. Steven Gherring is no match for that woman. No one is."

"Yes, you're probably right. I haven't known her for long, but she seems to get her way."

"So, I'll see you sometime this weekend."

"Sure thing. See you soon."

Anne beat her girls to the apartment by twenty minutes, just enough time to change clothes and pick up the apartment. She ran downstairs to surprise the girls who thought they would beat her home. She was pacing in the lobby when the taxi pulled up outside. Anne ran outside as the girls spilled out of the car with lots of hugs and laughing. Chaos ensued as bags were hauled from the car and Emily had to go back and pay the taxi driver. Antonio came out to meet them and help with luggage.

Once inside the lobby, Rayna joined the crew.

Anne started the introductions. "This is Emily, this is Charlie, and this is Rayna and this is Antonio."

"Antonio looks just like you described him," said Charlie.

Emily piped in, "I understand my mom has been interfering in your lives. Sorry about that. We just can't control her."

Rayna said, "No it's okay. I was clueless before your mom came."

"Yes, Rayna didn't even know I was alive before Anne started working on her," said Antonio.

"Mom, why are you home early? I thought you had a lot of work to do on that PowerPoint for Switzerland."

Anne looked like she was about to burst. "We've got tickets to see *Beauty and the Beast* tonight. Mr. Gherring got them for us."

All three girls started jumping around, while Rayna and Antonio chuckled.

"Something tells me you're a little excited about this," said Rayna.

Anne explained, "We weren't planning to see anything really popular. We were just going to see what we could get on the cheap tomorrow. But all three of us were dying to see *Beauty*. Mr. Gherring surprised me with the tickets and let me off early."

"Hmmm," said Charlie teasingly. "That was suspiciously nice of him. What did you do for him?"

Everyone laughed but Anne, who felt her cheeks heating. "Charlie—stop it. You're going to make Rayna and Antonio think bad things about me."

"Oh Mom," chuckled Emily. "You still haven't learned to take a joke."

"I can't believe how much you guys look alike—all three of you," said Rayna. "Your hair is different, but your faces..."

"Yes, you obviously inherited your beauty from your mom," said Antonio. "I was trying to get her to go out with me when she got here. That's why she hooked me up with Rayna. She was trying to get rid of me." He winked at Anne.

"I'm hoping I still look that good when I'm Mom's age." Charlie turned to her mom. "Not that you're old or anything—"

"Too late—you already called me old. But we'll see tomorrow who's old when I out-climb you at the gym."

Charlie rolled her eyes. "Mom, I hate to tell you, but you aren't going to out-climb me."

"You guys should go get ready if you're going to a seven o'clock play. It's five fifteen already," said Antonio.

Anne headed up the elevator with the girls and their luggage. The girls exclaimed over the cute apartment and the view from the window. Charlie walked around looking at the photographs.

"Mom, you have seven pictures of Emily and only six of me."

"You can just give me a new framed picture for Christmas to even it out."

"I think the pictures are fine just the way they are. You shouldn't change a thing," Emily declared, surveying the pictures for herself. "Hey, you turned one of mine backwards."

"I was just making it fair."

After downing some tomato soup and grilled cheese sandwiches, the girls got dressed for the play. "Should we dress up?" asked Charlie.

"I've been told you'll see all kinds of clothes at the play—the whole gamut, from jeans to cocktail dresses. I say wear something nice and warm, but not a dress. We'll take the subway, so we'll do some walking."

"Are you sure you know where to go? Which subway to take?" asked Emily.

"None of us can navigate worth a flip, so I vote we just leave early and plan on getting lost," laughed Charlie.

"My plan exactly," Anne agreed.

"I, however, planned ahead," said Emily. "I already downloaded a subway app for my phone."

"Ha!" said Charlie. "You'll probably get us more lost with the app, than without it."

They found the theater easily, stopping strangers to ask for directions and only making one wrong turn. *Beauty and the Beast* did not disappoint.

"Didn't you just *love* the costumes?" asked Anne.

"I liked the teacup," said Emily.

"I liked the carpet," said Charlie.

Anne said, "I liked the part where the beast changed into the prince."

"I don't know," said Emily. "I really liked the beast better."

Charlie quipped, "Of course you would say you liked the beast. You just have to be different."

"No, Emily may be right," argued Anne. "After a while, when you really got to know him and found out how sweet he was, he just got more and more good-looking, even before he turned into a prince."

Emily piped in, "I think it's because the beast was so big and strong and masculine. Then the prince just sort of looked wimpy."

"It doesn't matter. Did you see the playbill picture of the prince? He was hot!" said Charlie.

"Actually," said Emily, "I can't believe we're arguing about this. It isn't real. We're arguing over who was better looking—a make-believe prince or a man in a beast costume."

"I think people were staring at us," said Anne.

"When?" asked Emily.

"Oh, probably when all three of us were sobbing," said Charlie.

"Really," chuckled Emily. "Which time?"

That comment got all three of them laughing, so they took a minute to catch their breaths.

"Okay, where to next?" asked Anne.

"You're the New Yorker. You tell us where to go."

"We should go to Times Square, and then I'll take y'all up to that bar at the top of the Marriot where Henri took me after the gala."

"Okay, but we have to sit at a different table," said Charlie. "I can't sit at the table where some guy kissed my mom."

"Be nice or I'll tell you all the gory details," said Anne.

"Ewww! Yuck! Please, no details," laughed Emily.

A quick cab ride to Times Square and the girls were standing in the middle of the intersection, surrounded by throngs of people, huge digital images, and light shows.

"It's so much cooler than on TV," said Charlie.

"It's almost a sensory overload," said Emily. "I think I'll like it better from above than when we're in the middle of it."

"Still, we need to get our picture." Charlie pulled out her phone and flagged down a friendly bystander to take a snapshot of the three girls together in Times Square. Charlie immediately posted it on the web, and they started walking toward the Marriot. As they approached the hotel, Anne noticed several limousines lined up.

"Oh, I bet we might see someone famous if we wait a minute."

"Mom, you probably wouldn't even recognize someone famous if they came out. You're so clueless. You didn't even recognize Steven Gherring when you interviewed with him," said Emily.

"But I have y'all here for that." Anne argued. "Let's just wait a bit."

"Okay," said Charlie. "I'll keep my phone out and snap a picture if we see someone good."

Two couples came out of the hotel. Charlie swore one of the women looked familiar, but the couples turned and walked past them toward Times Square.

Emily said, "See, they're nobody. Let's go inside," said Emily.

"Fine," said Anne. "You're no fun."

They walked into the lobby, grateful to be warmer.

"I'm going to the restroom." Charlie grabbed Emily's arm. "You have to come with me."

"But I don't need to go—"

"I can't go by myself."

She pulled her sister along beside her. Anne stood leaning against a pillar in the lobby while waiting for the girls. Suddenly, she saw a familiar form at the top of the large padded staircase. It was Steven Gherring. And he was with Sharon Landry.

Anne slipped behind the pillar to hide herself, hoping no one could hear her thundering heart beats. There was one lone reporter at the lobby entrance who snapped a picture of the couple as they descended. Gherring was magnificent in his tux. Sharon looked stunning in a long black evening dress with fish-scale sequins. When she moved, the dress looked shiny and molten. She clung to Gherring's arm as they conversed, his head bent toward hers. At the bottom, Gherring took her coat and helped her put it on before they exited the lobby. Anne couldn't take her eyes off the two of them. At the door, Gherring stopped for a moment and looked over his shoulder in her direction. She slipped behind the pillar, and held her breath. When she peeked around again, they were outside. She felt slightly sick when she saw him put his arm around Sharon as they walked to the waiting limo.

What on earth was wrong with her? Why didn't she just speak to Gherring? But she knew the answer. She didn't want Steven Gherring to see the two of them side by side, to be able to compare them. She could never compete with a woman like Sharon Landry. Hadn't she known that? Hadn't she handpicked Sharon to be a perfect match for Steven? She found herself hoping Sharon had some unseen flaw. Maybe she had bad breath. Maybe her knees creaked like the stepsister in the Cinderella movie. No, Steven deserved to be happy. Anne needed to stop being selfish and hope Sharon would be just the right woman for Steven.

"Hey Mom," said Charlie. "Did you see anybody while we were gone?"

"You look kind of white, Mom. Are you okay?" asked Emily.

"I'm fine. I think I'm a little dehydrated. Let's go on up to the top. No one important is coming down the stairs."

When they entered the top floor bar, the girls were thrilled with the view.

"Oh Mom," said Emily. "This is a romantic spot. I can see why you let Henri kiss you here."

"It wasn't just the ambiance—he said some pretty sweet things. I think my ego needed a little pampering."

"What did he say?" Emily asked.

"I don't remember exactly, but it had to do with me believing in him and him deciding to open up his heart again. He's been hurt before."

"Awww," said Charlie. "And you've always been a sucker for anybody who's been hurt. You're such a bleeding heart."

"And what about you?" asked Anne. "I seem to remember a certain girl crying over a lizard you found with most of his tail broken off."

"Well, how was I supposed to know it would grow back?" Charlie pouted. The waitress approached the table.

"What should we get to drink?" asked Charlie.

Emily asked, "Hey Mom, since we never got to go here with Dad, why don't we drink something he would have ordered?"

"Well, your dad didn't drink much. But when he did, he always ordered scotch."

"Three scotches please," Charlie told the waitress.

"The waitress asked, "With water, on the rocks, or neat?"

The three looked at each other and shrugged.

"Neat," said Charlie. "I don't know what that means, but it sounds 'neat.'"

When the drinks arrived, Anne proposed a toast. "To our memories of Dad and the new memories we make together!"

They all took a sip together.

"Yuk!" yelled Charlie. "Ohmygosh, that burns!"

"That was awful. I'm glad I didn't take a big sip," Emily said.

"I just spit it back into the glass," said Anne. Then all three dissolved into giggles. "People are staring—they probably think we're drunk."

"In this family, who needs alcohol to act embarrassing?" asked Emily.

The girls opted for a quick breakfast in the apartment, not being motivated enough to rise early for a restaurant breakfast before their climb. Gherring was waiting in the lobby when they went down shortly after nine. He was dressed in jeans with a leather jacket, and he carried an athletic bag. Similarly, the girls had brought climbing clothes along—even Emily, who swore she wouldn't climb.

"Mr. Gherring, I'd like you to meet my girls. This is—"

"Wait, let me guess. You must be Charlie and you must be Emily. Am I right?"

"How did you know that?" asked Charlie. "Did Mom show you pictures?"

"No I didn't," Anne answered for him. "How *did* you know? Charlie doesn't have a hat on or anything. Both of you have your hair in ponytails. Emily isn't carrying a book. Did you forget your book?"

"No, it's in the bag."

"How did you know which was which?" asked Anne.

Gherring smiled, looking much like a Cheshire cat, but gave no answer. He led them outside to the waiting limo.

"Wow! We get to ride in a limousine—cool!" said Charlie.

They climbed in and proceeded to investigate every inch of the car.

"I could get used to this," said Charlie.

"Mom, do you get to do this all the time?" asked Emily.

"Yes, probably ten times now, but I still get excited," she answered.

Charlie said to Gherring, "Mom always taught us money wasn't important, but it sure is fun."

"Thank you for the tickets last night. It was amazing, and you were very generous," said Emily.

"Yeah," said Charlie. "We loved it. And we spent all our money to get here, so we weren't going to any cool plays."

"Charlie," scolded Anne. "We don't talk about how much money we have."

"Why not? It's not like I told him how much is in our bank account."

"Quite right," cut in Gherring. "I think your honesty is charming. I'm glad to have given you a fun evening."

"Speaking of fun evenings... How was the benefit dinner last night?" Anne tried to keep her voice casual.

"Fine."

What did that mean? Fine? That's what she had said about an emotionally powerful day. Was it emotional? Was he covering something up?

"What did you think of Sharon?" Anne asked.

"Who?"

"You know, your date? Sharon Landry?"

"Oh, she was fine."

Anne bit her lip to keep from saying, *you looked awfully* cozy *together.* She decided to let the subject drop for now. She hadn't really learned anything. Perhaps Gram could get better answers.

But Emily had been listening. "So you went to some benefit dinner last night with a girl, and you don't even remember her name today?"

"Emily! Don't be rude." Anne cringed, waiting for Gherring's retort.

"No I'm not offended. It does sound pretty awful when you put it like that. I guess it's a fair question."

He contemplated the roof for a moment. "It's like this... Suppose you're expected to do something you don't really want to do, like a benefit dinner, but it's a good thing, so you decide to do it. And then suppose you're expected to go with a date, but the only potential escort you know would take it as a sign you wanted a committed relationship. And suppose you haven't met a person you want to take that risk with. Would you maybe be willing to go on a blind date with someone who promised he'd never expect anything else from you—not a goodnight kiss or another date or even a phone call? Especially if someone you trusted had screened this escort for you?"

"I got lost somewhere on the third 'suppose,'" said Charlie.

Emily chewed on her lower lip before responding. "I *suppose* I might be willing to do that under those *supposed* circumstances." Then she flashed him a grin, and he chuckled.

"So really, how did you know which one of us was which?" asked Charlie.

"Easy—your mom described you a bit, and I made an educated guess. Emily, you carry yourself like a dancer. And Charlie, you just look like you'd drive a Maserati really fast if you got the chance."

The girls laughed and Charlie said, "I thought maybe you were a Facebook stalker."

Anne was sweating, wondering what her girls might say next. "We're here. Let's go before you make me lose my job."

The boys had arrived early. Spencer was watching his friend rappelling down from the top of the wall. When he saw the girls arrive, he deserted his buddy to meet them.

"Hey, I'm Spencer." Towering over the girls at almost six foot four, he was wiry and athletic in build.

His Asian friend came running over when he disconnected. "Hey, I'm Mark." Anne judged him to be just under six feet tall.

"I'm Charlie." She shook their hands firmly and asked Mark, "Are you a swimmer?"

"Yeah, how'd you guess?"

"Shiny hair, swimmer's shoulders..."

"Impressive," Mark replied. But Charlie was already on her way to change into climbing gear, including her well-used climbing shoes.

Spencer asked Emily, "So you are...?"

"I'm Emily, and I'm not climbing."

"We'll see." He grinned at her, but she crossed her arms as if the matter were settled.

"Excuse me, but are you Steven Gherring?" asked Mark

Gherring stepped forward and shook the boys' hands. "Yes, I'm Steven Gherring. Spencer, you look familiar. Do you work at Papa's Place, perhaps?"

"Yes sir. But that's not a permanent job. I'm getting my MBA."

"What's your undergrad degree?"

"Economics."

"You should put in for one of our internships, and put my name down as a reference."

"Thank you, sir. Wow, that'd be a dream to intern at Gherring Inc." Spencer was all smiles.

Charlie was already stepping into her harness when Gherring and Anne went to change clothes. Emily sat down and pulled out her book, without changing clothes. Charlie was starting up the wall when Gherring and Anne came back out.

"Go Charlie!" yelled Emily. She watched her sister work her way efficiently up the vertical climb with far spaced holds.

Gherring sat down next to Emily. "A real book, huh? Not an e-book?"

"I have a Kindle, but I still like real books. I like to hold them in my hands and turn the pages. I like to physically see the progress I'm making."

"What are you reading?"

"Robert Jordan."

"The Wheel of Time series? I got tired of waiting between books, but it was so good. I swore I'd never start a series that wasn't finished again."

"I know, me too. I'm actually re-reading the series."

"So you don't plan to climb?"

"Nope, and you can't talk me into it."

"Well, I won't try. I doubt you can be *talked into* anything."

"What do you mean by that?"

"Just that I think we may be a lot alike."

Emily scoffed. "Right."

"Let's see how close I am. You aren't really afraid of adventure as much as you don't see the value in it. I think you'd climb without any fear whatsoever if there was a good reason to do it."

"Like what?"

"Well, if someone held a gun to your head and told you to climb or else, you'd probably cross your arms and tell them to shoot."

Emily laughed, but she nodded agreement.

"But if someone held a gun to your sister's head, I bet you'd be up that wall before you could blink."

"Okay, you're right. But no one's holding a gun to my sister's head, so... What other good reason can you come up with?"

He drummed his fingers on his leg. "Hmmm. You don't care what anybody thinks, and you're not competitive in that way, so it has to be an internal motivation."

"And believe me, I'm not internally motivated to climb that wall."

"Let me confirm something else. You know, your mom interviewed at Gherring Inc. without doing any research and without the slightest idea of who I was. But I'm betting you've already read everything there is to find about me and Gherring Inc. Am I right?"

"Yes, you are." She lifted her chin a bit.

"Well, don't believe everything you read, okay? But I bet you know in my younger days I dated a lot of different women?"

"Oh yeah. That would be an understatement according to what I read."

"I'm sure the number is exaggerated. But it wouldn't surprise you to know I dated a prima ballerina for a while? That woman could really climb. She couldn't do overhangs, but she could do anything else. Ballerinas have strong leg muscles that don't fatigue easily. That's what you need for climbing. People think you need arm strength, but the key is to use your legs."

"Okay, so what?"

"Your mom said you dance. Do you still do ballet?"

She nodded.

"Then you just might have the ability to be an amazing climber, and if you don't try, you won't ever know."

"You really think I might be good at it? Even my first time?"

"There's a good chance."

"Oh man! I can't believe you did it! Now I *have* to do it so I'll know." She stood up to get her climbing clothes from the bag before turning back to Gherring. "What did you mean about us being alike?"

Gherring sighed. "How old were you when your dad died?"

"Eight... I was eight years old."

"I was ten when I lost my parents. I'm betting you never let yourself be a little girl after that."

Emily was quiet. She nodded before she disappeared in the dressing room.

Anne's eyes were brimming with tears when he looked up at her.

"Yes, I could hear everything," she said.

"I hope that was okay for me to talk to her like that."

Anne sniffed and dabbed at her face with her shirt. "It was good. I mean... She needs... She didn't have any father figure in her life. Just her grandfather when he was visiting. It's good for her to talk to a man like that. She's so... careful... She puts up such a wall around her heart. It's amazing you got her to open up at all. I just don't want her to end up alone like..."

"Like me?"

"No I didn't say—"

"That's okay. I don't want her to end up like me either."

He stood and walked to the wall to gear up.

Gherring was halfway up the wall when Emily came out of the dressing room. Charlie almost knocked her over with a hug.

"Em! You're going to climb—yay!"

"Just this once—to see if I like it."

Charlie looked back toward the guys. "Wow, he's got a nice butt. And those back muscles are incredible."

"Which one?" asked Anne. "Spencer or Mark?"

"Are you blind? I'm talking about Mr. Gherring." Charlie grinned.

"Charlie, that's creepy. He's old enough to be our father." Emily was lacing her shoes.

"Have you looked at him?" Charlie grabbed her sister's face and turned it toward Gherring who was making his way under a ledge.

"Ohmygosh, you're right! No wonder he makes that Most Eligible Bachelor list every year."

"Does he just work out all the time, Mom?" asked Charlie.

"He does Iron Man competitions," Anne replied.

"Of course he does. And he said we were alike. Riii-ight!" Emily rolled her eyes.

Charlie grabbed Emily's hand. "Come climb, sister."

Soon Emily was making her way up the wall. Her brows were furrowed with concentration.

"That's it," called Gherring, having joined the group after his successful climb. "Use your legs."

She climbed slowly and steadily, asking for guidance when she was stuck.

Charlie called up, "Put your right foot on that yellow jug and move over to the right. That's it. Now can you reach that blue crimp with your left foot? You've got it."

The moment she reached out to touch the top, the clan below began to cheer."

"You did it! She did it! Yay, sister!"

Emily rappelled down and stood on the floor with a huge grin on her face.

Gherring asked her, "So, was I right?"

"I have to admit, it was pretty easy."

"And you'll do it again?" Gherring asked.

"Sure, why not?"

"This spring you can come to Colorado, and I'll take you climbing for real, on cliffs. It's so much cooler," said Charlie.

"*That's* why you're so good," complained Spencer. "You're making us guys look bad."

Charlie walked toward Spencer and gave him the once over.

"I don't think you look bad." She grinned and winked at him.

Spencer started laughing and pretended to fan himself.

"Oh, you made him blush," teased Mark.

Charlie grabbed her mom's arm. "Come on, Mom. You're the only one who hasn't gone yet."

"I'm ready," she said. Gherring moved over to help her gear up and set up the belay. With her girls in audience, she was even more self-conscious as Gherring's hands brushed against her while securing the straps. She felt the blood rise to her face, and Emily raised her eyebrows.

Gherring asked, "Ready to try a harder climb?"

Anne swallowed. "Sure."

Gherring set up Anne's belay on a medium level climb, while Spencer set up to try the overhang climb Gherring had completed.

"Race you up," called Spencer.

"You're on," Anne replied.

She started her climb, adrenaline flowing. The holds were farther apart, and the wall was vertical. She struggled to pull her weight up.

"Use your legs, Mom," called Emily.

Anne shifted her weight and concentrated on utilizing her leg strength. Soon she was climbing steadily. She spied Spencer above and to the right. Determined to at least put up a good fight, Anne started climbing faster. Spencer had reached the ledge and was struggling on the overhang. Then Anne's foot slipped on one of the holds, and she almost fell.

Charlie was yelling directions from below. "Put your left foot on that red crimp! You've got it! Just a little further. Keep going."

"I made it! Woo hoo!" yelled Anne as she touched the top. "Do you have me?"

"You can let go. I've got you," said Gherring.

Anne started a quick decent.

"Did I win?"

"You won, Mom. But it wasn't quite fair. Spencer's climb is almost impossible." Emily looked up where Spencer was making a third attempt on the overhang.

"But Steven did that climb twice," whispered Anne.

"Yes, Mom. We already know Mr. Gherring is Superman in disguise." Emily waggled her eyebrows and started laughing.

Charlie giggled, having overheard the exchange. "Yeah Mom. Have you found his kryptonite yet?"

Emily whispered something in Charlie's ear, and she snorted with glee.

"What?" demanded Anne.

Charlie whispered to her mom. "Em says it's you."

A few more climbs, and the group was ready to go. Spencer asked, "Are you guys doing lunch at Papa's today?"

"We're stopping by the bookstore first, but then we're going to lunch. Y'all wanna come?" Anne gave a sweeping glance, casually including Gherring in her invitation.

Spencer and Mark agreed to meet them for lunch.

"Mr. Gherring, are you coming with us to lunch?" Emily asked.

"I've got to go to the office today." Anne remembered he would have to work alone all weekend because of her altercation with Jeff.

She jumped when he put a hand on her arm. "It's not the presentation. I've got other things to attend to that I've been neglecting all week."

"I thought Papa's place was right next door to Gherring Inc. Couldn't you just take a lunch break?" asked Charlie.

"I was actually planning to skip lunch—"

"Mom says you should never skip a meal."

Gherring's dimples deepened. "So I've been told. Sure, I'll come over for a quick lunch. I just can't play around *all* day."

Gherring dropped the girls off at Binding Books. As they walked into the quaint store, Charlie protested. "Mom, we're never going to get Emily out of here!" She pointed to Emily who was already totally absorbed in the book collections. She gravitated quickly to the antique books.

"Come meet Ellen," said Anne, dragging Charlie to the checkout counter. Ellen's straight glossy brown hair was pulled back in a ponytail. Her razor cut bangs emphasized the almond shape of her brown eyes.

"Ellen, you got your hair cut. I like the bangs," said Anne.

"Thanks. Just got it done. It's for my character in the play. This must be your daughter. She looks just like you."

"Hi, I'm Charlie."

"Ellen. Nice to meet you. I met your mom on the subway."

"Yeah, I couldn't get anyone else to talk to me. I kept trying to start conversations, and people just looked at me like I had antlers or something."

"I don't usually talk to people on the subway either. No one does, except for your mom. She's just so friendly."

"Charlie's just like me. When she was a little girl, she would meet people in a store and invite them to our home."

"I bet you had some interesting house guests," said Ellen.

"So, Mom says you're an actress."

"Well, I'm trying to be. I have my first lead role in a small production. We may only be open for a week, but it's a start."

"She's very talented," declared Anne. "She sings and dances, too."

"Your mom's never actually seen me do anything."

"I can tell. I have a sense about these things."

"That's my sister, Emily, over there sitting on the floor."

Ellen looked over to where Emily had plopped down on the floor, surrounded by a pile of old books. "You can tell her there's a seating area in the back."

"She's happy. No use bothering her," said Anne.

"So Emily's your big reader in the family?"

"We all read a lot, but Emily is excessive," laughed Anne.

"Do you have a sci-fi/fantasy section?" Charlie ambled toward the inviting books.

"On the aisle opposite your sister."

"So, how's the play coming along?"

"It's so much fun. We rehearse again this afternoon. But they're having money troubles—one of the big underwriters dropped out. Hopefully the money will last until we open. Nothing's for sure with these small groups. That's why I can't quit this job at the bookstore."

"I hope it all works out."

"Me, too! Especially because of this other actor. She's got a kid who's sick, and she doesn't have insurance. She needs this to turn into a steady gig. I've been trying to get donations to help her with hospital bills. And we've been taking turns at the hospital to give her a break."

"Oh, that's so sweet. You know, maybe Mr. Gherring could help."

"Your boss? Is he that kind of guy? I've just seen the stuff in the news about him being such a big playboy."

"I don't know what his donation policy is, but he's a kind and generous man. Or he might even be willing to sponsor the play. In fact, this might be a good way to get the two of you together."

"What do you mean by *together*?"

"You know. Together as a couple. Didn't you volunteer to date him when we talked about him before?"

She started laughing. "I was only kidding. There's no way Steven Gherring would date me. I'm nobody."

"Well, he goes out all the time with up-and-coming actresses."

"I'm not up-and-coming, I'm more like 'trying to pull myself up and hope to come someday in the future!'"

"You never know until you try."

"Why don't *you* date him?"

"He always dates younger women."

"But you're younger than he is, aren't you?"

"I'm not sophisticated enough for Mr. Gherring."

"Well, I'm not sophisticated either. And if he's that snobby, I wouldn't want to date him anyway."

"But he's not snobby at all. He's really nice, and he doesn't talk down to me or treat me like a secretary. He even bought tickets for us to go see *Beauty and the Beast* last night."

"I just don't believe he'd want to go out with me, anyway. But I think you have a better shot at it."

"Well, I'll introduce you sometime after he comes back from Switzerland. Maybe Gherring Inc. would sponsor your play."

"I'm willing to meet him if you think that could convince him to help us out."

"Just wait. I have a feeling I'm right about y'all. I'm a really good matchmaker."

"Yep, she's got quite a reputation back in Weatherford." Charlie arrived at the checkout counter with Emily in tow.

"Is she trying to set you up with someone?" asked Emily.

"Yes. With Steven Gherring, if you can believe that. Isn't it ridiculous?"

"She's responsible for quite a few marriages, so you never know. By the way, I'm Emily, and I love your store. Mom, aren't you going to buy me something?"

"Put it on your Christmas list. It's time for lunch."

"I'm Ellen, nice to meet you."

"Come on, we'll be late." Charlie hooked arms with her mom and sister, pulling them outside.

Spencer and Mark were waiting when they arrived at Papa's Place.

172

"Aunt May put us in the back room since Mr. Gherring is coming." Spencer led them to their table, already set up with water and menus. Anne and the girls sat down on one side of the table, and the boys sat down opposite the girls. The aroma of home cooking wafted through the room.

"Wow, that smell is making my stomach growl," said Emily.

Charlie grabbed a hot yeast roll from a basket on the table, slathering it with butter. "I can see already why this is your favorite place to eat, Mom. I'm surprised you haven't gained weight."

"I probably would've if I didn't have to walk so much everywhere I go."

Gherring appeared in the doorway. "I'm afraid I'll have to eat quickly and get back to work." He took the empty chair opposite Anne.

Charlie spoke between bites of roll. "So let me ask you a question, Mr. Gherring. Do you love what you do? Do you find fulfillment in your work?"

"Charlie, don't start this with Mr. Gherring." Anne groaned, recognizing a familiar argument.

Gherring raised his eyebrows. "Why do you ask?"

"We have this ongoing debate about whether you should work at a job you hate just because it makes money, or whether you should work at a job that pays less doing what you love to do," explained Charlie.

"For instance, Charlie thinks I sold out by getting an accounting degree. I've already passed my CPA exam, and I'll be certified in another four months," said Emily.

"But she hates it," said Charlie. "Admit it, Em. You dread going to work."

"But the truth is there's not a job where you get paid to read really fun books of your choosing all day," said Emily.

Charlie laughed. "That's why I said your ideal job was to be a princess, like Belle in *Beauty and the Beast* with that huge library."

"And your ideal job?" Gherring asked Charlie.

"I'm doing it. I ski all winter and get paid to teach kids to ski, and in the summer I get paid to take people rafting and rock climbing. What could be better?"

"Maybe a job where you made enough money you didn't spend every cent on food and rent and then live in a crowded apartment all winter and sleep on friends' couches all summer," said Anne.

Gherring laughed. "I'm not getting in the middle of this one."

"But you didn't answer my question," said Charlie.

Gherring thought for a moment. "There's a lot of things I could say to that. But if I'm honest, I'd have to say I've never thought about it. Gherring Inc. was my destiny before I was born. I never had much choice."

"Maybe you should take a year off. Come to Colorado and be a ski bum. Take some time to enjoy life."

He laughed, but his expression was almost wistful. "I'll keep that idea in mind."

The young people started a debate on whether technology had caused a decrease or increase in communication. Anne and Gherring were quietly listening to their banter, when he said, "I can see why you miss them."

"They're really fun, aren't they? Although I wish they were a little more careful of what they say. Things just pop out of their mouths before their brains have engaged."

"It's possible they inherited that trait."

Anne felt a spark of instant anger, quickly abating when she realized he was teasing. Besides, he was probably right.

"There… You did it again," he said.

"Did what?"

"About twenty different emotions just zoomed across your face. It must be your eyes. They're so expressive—I just try to guess what you could possibly be thinking."

"Well, I hope you can't ever figure it out. You know, read my mind. That would be really uncomfortable." She lowered her chin to hide her face.

"Why? What are you thinking that I shouldn't know? Are you saying secret curse words under your breath?"

Anne reddened, unable to think of a decent comeback. It would be terrible if he knew what she thought about him. What if he knew how his touch affected her? What if he knew her heart beat harder when he came close? What if he knew the real reason she wanted him to have a wife was to help her stop thinking about him all the

174

time? No, that wasn't the reason. She wanted someone to take care of him. She didn't want him to be alone. He deserved to have someone to love him, and the worst thing was he didn't even know what he was missing.

He was still studying her face when the plates arrived. They devoured the food and stayed at the table chatting for almost thirty minutes. To Anne's surprise, Gherring no longer seemed to be in a hurry to get back to work.

"I'm not trying to get rid of you or anything, but did you say you had to work some more?"

He stretched and groaned. "I think I'm going to take a break and tackle it tomorrow. I've got plenty of time. In fact, if you guys want a ride back to the apartment I could take you."

"That'd be awesome. I'm not even sure what we're doing this afternoon since we already went to a play. Oh yeah, we're going to do MOMA. Hey girls, Mr. Gherring's going to give us a ride home, and we can rest a bit and then go see the Museum of Modern Arts. They have an Impressionist Exhibit."

"Can we invite the boys?" asked Emily.

"I don't mind, but they may have other plans."

"No ma'am. We have nothin' but time today. We'll study tomorrow."

"Okay, meet you there at, say, three o'clock?"

"Works for us."

Rayna exclaimed the moment she saw the group enter the apartment lobby. "Look! Look what came for you. You got a dozen red roses. And two gift baskets. I didn't read the card."

Anne glanced at Gherring, who was brooding near the elevator. She opened the envelope attached to the roses, but didn't read it out loud.

"It's a welcome to New York present from Henri," she told the girls. "Why don't you grab the gift baskets and we'll take them upstairs to open them?"

With their arms full of flowers and cellophane wrapped packages piled high in decorative baskets, they tromped into the elevator.

"Aren't you going up?" asked Anne when Gherring remained outside the elevator doorway.

"No, I've decided to go back and accomplish something at work." His voice was flat and his eyes stormy.

"Thanks for the ride and for everything else," said Charlie.

"Will we see you again this weekend?" asked Emily.

His glower softened. "I'm not sure. We'll see."

Upstairs, the girls started unpacking the baskets while Anne called Henri on Skype. She turned the laptop toward the girls so he could see them busy exploring their surprises.

"We love the stuff, Henri. You didn't have to do that."

"I am sad I cannot be there, so I will try to bribe them to like me."

"Hi, I'm Charlie. This is awesome. Thank you, thank you! Look Mom—they're full of different New York stuff, mostly food. There's a New York Checker Cab Crunch, Statue of Liberty Lollipop, Hampton Popcorn's White Truffle & Parmesan Popcorn, New York Mints. What's this? New York Traffic Treats. What's in that other one, Em?"

"Sour Puss Pickled Ginger Carrots, McClure's Garlic and Dill Potato Chips, NYC Hot Sauce, Mast Brothers Chocolate Bar, Butter+Love Moustache Cookies. There's some other stuff in the bottom. Oh! McClure's Bloody Mary Mix, Z crackers. Ohmygosh! This is so much fun. Oh, sorry. Hi Henri. Nice to meet you. I'm Emily."

The girls continued to examine the goodies, while Anne turned the computer screen back. "That was so sweet, Henri."

"And did you like the card with the roses?"

Anne blushed. "Shhhh. I didn't let anyone read it."

"Why not?"

"Because," Anne glanced toward the girls to make sure they were not eavesdropping. "Because you said something about wanting to kiss me again."

"Is that bad? They do not want you to kiss me? Perhaps I should talk to them."

"If y'all are going to talk about kissing, y'all should get a room." Emily's teasing resulted in even more heat in Anne's already flushed face.

"Mom you're such a prude. We don't really care. Just don't make kissing noises where we can hear them," said Charlie.

Exasperated, Anne grimaced at Henri. "That's why."

The girls left early for the subway station, so Anne could take them by Carved Wood Creations. Mr. Hamilton was nowhere to be seen, so Anne showed them all the beautiful carvings. Each girl picked out a favorite.

"This one is mine," declared Anne, showing them the Inseparable Love pair. "He carved it from a single piece of wood. That's how he made them where they won't come apart."

"I like this one," Emily picked out a mom reading a bedtime story to a small pajama clad child, nestled in her lap. "Or maybe this one." She spotted a pair of ballet dancers, with the female, gracefully arched backward, and perfectly balanced over the head of the male dancer by one hand.

"These are the best. Look." Charlie found a group of five figures, male and female, with their feet together and their hands clasped, stretched all the way out in a leaning position and held up by the balance of the others. "Look, you can change them around, but they only balance if you put them in just the right order. Otherwise they fall over. It's like a puzzle."

"I secretly call that one 'World Peace.'" Mr. Hamilton emerged from the back. "It's a really delicate balance and if anything is out of order, it topples over. These must be your daughters you were so excited about."

"Yes, Mr. Hamilton. This is Emily and Charlie."

"I'm so glad to meet you both."

"Mom told us about your shop, but I couldn't really picture it. These carvings are incredible." Charlie managed to balance the figures in their original order.

"How on earth did you ever learn to do this? The detail is amazing," said Emily.

"Lots of practice. I was a chauffer for the Gherring family for many years. That's a lot of time sitting around waiting to drive them home. Whittling was how I passed the time. Now I have to use these magnifiers to see what I'm doing, but I still love it."

"See Charlie, it wasn't that he loved his job, but the job made his pastime possible. And he loved his pastime," said Emily.

Charlie crossed her arms. "So if you had your life to do over again, would you do it the same way. Would you choose the same job?"

"Yes dear, no regrets. It's not really the job anyway. It's the people. Wherever you work and whatever you do, whether it's a job or a hobby, it's the people you interact with that really matter. If the Gherring family hadn't been such incredible people, I would've found another job, lickety split."

"Round two for Emily." She sported a smug smile.

"You haven't won yet," said Charlie. "Mr. Gherring hasn't given an answer yet, so round one is still up for grabs."

"Have you met Mrs. Gherring?" he asked.

"Not yet," said Anne. "We're having dinner tomorrow night at her house. I can't wait for them to meet her."

"Yes, she is quite a woman." Mr. Hamilton chatted easily with the girls, and by the time they left for the museum, they were exchanging hugs and regrets.

"He's like a great-grandpa, right?" asked Charlie. "I mean he's old enough to be ours?"

"Yeah, I guess he is. He's ninety."

"Maybe we could just adopt him," Emily suggested. "He's so cute and artistic and talented. That's what I want to be like when I get old."

"Not me," said Charlie. "From what Mom has told me, I want to be like Gram."

The girls arrived fifteen minutes early to MOMA, having effectively traversed through the subway system with Emily's phone app. Spencer and Mark were waiting inside the lobby. Anne trailed behind the other four, who conversed easily about the artwork. Charlie loved a huge picture of a man that was made up of thousands of tiny photographs of other people. Emily loved everything in the Impressionist exhibit.

"I can't believe I'm actually looking at 'Starry Night'," said Emily. "It's a lot smaller than I thought it would be. Look. People are taking pictures of it. I thought you weren't supposed to. They just kind of wait 'til the guard wanders off."

"Maybe it's okay as long as you don't use a flash," suggested Spencer.

"I'll get you next to the painting." Charlie pulled out her phone and took a picture of Emily standing by the famous painting.

"Ma'am," said a guard who happened to pass by. "Picture-taking is not allowed."

"Okay, sorry," said Charlie, giggling.

Emily, totally mortified, gave a scathing look to Charlie. And both boys stifled laughter. Charlie immediately posted it on the Internet. "It's not like they're going to put us in jail."

Anne stood for a long time looking at the Monet paintings. He was her favorite. She loved the colors and the peaceful impact of the artwork. In contrast to the Van Gogh, the Monets were huge, covering entire walls.

As the group moved through the museum, Spencer seemed to be spending more time near Emily, while Mark was talking to Charlie. Anne was surprised that the pairs were reversed from her prediction. But both pairs seemed to enjoy a good bit of verbal sparring, and Anne congratulated herself on a successful matchmaking effort, at least for the span of the day.

Arriving back in the museum lobby, Anne said, "I wanted us to do a tour of some kind, double decker bus, maybe. But it's kind of late, I guess."

"Hey," Spencer said. "We should all go on the Twilight Tour. It's a boat that takes you on the Hudson. I think it costs about thirty bucks. Is that too much?"

"Well, since we got theater tickets for free, we could afford that," said Anne, glancing at the girls to see if the idea was agreeable.

"I'm gonna want a warmer coat and a hat, if we're out on the water at night," said Emily.

Spencer quickly checked out the departure time. "If you hurry, you've just got enough time to go back and change. But you'll need to catch a cab."

Anne and the girls took a cab back to the apartment. Rayna was still at the lobby desk. "Hey, what are you guys up to?"

"We're going on a twilight cruise on the Hudson River. We just came home to change into warmer clothes."

"And we're going with Mark and Spencer," said Charlie. "Mom's really trying hard on this matchmaking thing."

"Charlie, I didn't plan for y'all to be together all day. That just happened."

"Mom," said Emily. "If we didn't like spending time with them, we would've ditched them a long time ago. You know that."

"Yes, it's true. You're both pretty good at ditching guys—much better than you are at keeping them. We've got to hurry. Will we have any trouble getting a cab?" she asked Rayna.

"Probably no trouble. You might have to go around the corner. Or I can call one for you."

"That's a great idea. Fifteen minutes?"

"Done."

Seventeen minutes later, a breathless Anne returned to the lobby. "The girls are almost ready. Is our cab already here?"

"No," said Rayna. "I got you a limo instead. Is that okay?"

Anne's face fell. "Oh Rayna, I don't think we can afford—"

"It's free," said a voice from behind her, "if I can tag along."

Anne turned a big smiling face toward Mr. Gherring. "We'd love it. Well, the girls might not notice since the boys will be with us. You really want to go on a touristy cruise on the Hudson? What if people recognize you? Tourists aren't cool about being around famous people the way New Yorkers are."

Gherring pulled an old beat-up baseball cap out of his pocket and added a pair of glasses. "Voilà!"

Anne was astounded. With the cap and glasses, jeans and a nondescript jacket, no one would suspect his identity. He could easily be a tourist from Weatherford, Texas.

"Now we just need to teach you how to drawl, and people will just think we're a couple from Texas."

"Are *y'all* ready to go?" he stretched out his words.

"That's pretty good, but it's not 'red-dy', it's ray-eh-dy."

Emily and Charlie came running down. Emily asked, "Are we too late? Did the taxi wait for us?"

"Mr. Gherring is taking us," said Anne.

"Oh hey, Mr. Gherring," said Charlie. "Dig the cool glasses—I didn't even recognize you."

"Yeah, love the nerdy look." Emily whispered to her mom, "I think he really is Superman."

Despite the cold evening air, the girls were delighted with the cruise. It was ninety minutes long and included all the sites along the Hudson River, including the Statue of Liberty and Ellis Island, Brooklyn, Manhattan and Williamsburg Bridges, and views of the twinkling lights of the Empire State Building and Chrysler Building on the New York skyline.

"I know this must be boring for you," Anne said to Gherring, when the young people had gone to the outside railing. "You've been so kind. You've really made this weekend great for the girls. It wouldn't have been half as much fun."

"But you had all your gifts from Henri..."

"I'm sorry that happened in front of you. I know you don't like him. I'm really not trying to flaunt him in your face, you know. And it doesn't change how much I appreciate your efforts to make this weekend special for the girls."

"It was nothing."

"No. I know you gave up a lot of work time. And now... coming out here... I don't know how I can ever repay you."

"You don't need to repay me. I just wanted to show you—"

"Hey Mom! Come outside—it's prettier from out here," yelled Charlie.

Anne rolled her eyes at Gherring. "I'm coming."

Gherring walked with her to an empty spot on the railing near the girls.

Emily called, "Isn't it beautiful, Mom?"

Anne noticed both girls had extra protection from the wind using the boys as windshields and a little extra body heat from their arms. As she stood shaking from the cold, Gherring moved beside her and opened his coat to wrap it around her back. Suddenly Anne felt not only protection from the wind, but also the warmth of Gherring's body against her side. Anne felt a little shiver of thrill ripple down her spine.

"Are you still cold?" asked Gherring.

"No, I'm fine," Anne muttered, embarrassed by the quivering of her voice.

"You *are* cold." He opened his coat again, turning her and pulling her against his chest, wrapping his arms around her and enveloping her in his coat. Anne panicked, knowing he must feel her heart thrumming against him. She tried to slow it down, but he moved his arms in a gentle caress on her back, and her blood pumped even faster. She could feel his strong hard muscles pressed against her, and it seemed his heart beat quickly as well. She felt a heat that reached to her very core. Breathing so rapidly she felt a bit faint, she couldn't summon the strength to pull away from him.

The desire she'd been holding back came to the surface. She couldn't let herself feel this way. This was a road that would lead to endless pain. Even these few moments of sheer pleasure would cause incredible suffering when she came crashing back to reality. She didn't dare let her imagination run in the arms of Steven Gherring. She had to keep a hold on her rationality, her practicality, her good judgment. She wasn't the right match for Steven Gherring. She knew that in her head, but not in her heart.

"Your hair smells good," remarked Steven in a slightly strained voice.

"It's eau d' bargain brand shampoo."

Steven started laughing. With her head against his chest, the deep sound resonated in her ear.

"Are you warm now? You've stopped shaking."

"Yes. I'm cozy. Thanks. You must be freezing now, since I sucked all the heat out of you."

"No problem. I've got a lot of heat in here."

"Oh I know. All the tabloids say you're really hot."

"I don't think I've been in the tabloids for quite a few years. And back then the stories were all hyperbole and hype."

"What did you say? You were hypertrophied and ripe?"

Anne started chuckling and felt Gherring's chest shaking as he joined in. She was warm and comfortable. Too comfortable. This was wrong. Why was he standing here hugging her to keep her warm? If he had any idea how he made her wish for things that could never be, surely he would keep his distance. She needed to guard her heart. She'd tried so hard to control her thoughts, but her body betrayed her. She had to bring herself back to reality before her heart got any more ideas.

She pulled her arms back and straightened up. "We shouldn't stand like that. The kids might get ideas." She backed away and stuffed her hands in her pockets, checking to make sure the wind prevented the girls from hearing her comment.

Gherring frowned and spoke in a low voice. "There was nothing wrong with me keeping you warm."

"Yes, I know you often put your arm around women to keep them warm. Like last night with Sharon."

"Who?"

"Sharon Landry—your date last night. I know it's not a big deal for you to help a woman stay warm, just like when you put your arm around Sharon last night on the way to the car."

"What are you talking about? How do you know—"

"Don't get me wrong. I'm glad you're so sweet and thoughtful. It's just that people can get the wrong idea."

"You're not making any sense—"

"It doesn't mean anything to you, but maybe it does to someone else. Don't you see? You led her on. You put your arm around her last night, and today you can't even remember her name. I know you didn't mean to hurt her, but you did."

"Are we talking about Sharon or—"

"We're talking about... about... I can't do this with you."

"Do what with me?"

"I'm your secretary, and I want to keep my job. And I know you've been with thousands of women—"

"I haven't been with thousands—"

"And you probably can't even remember most of them, can you?"

"I... Well that was... I do remember—"

"I'm just saying I've only ever been with one man my entire life. *Nothing* is casual for me. *Nothing*! Not even hugging to stay warm. It... It does something... It means something it shouldn't... Something it can't."

"But did you ever think—"

"That's just it... I never think. I've got to keep my head and keep my heart and to do that I've got to keep my distance."

"You didn't keep your distance with Henri," he muttered.

"Henri is in France. How much more distance can you get? He'll soon tire of this long distance thing. He thinks he won't, but I know better."

"You don't really know him. He can be very persistent. He's like a weed—"

"This is not about Henri. This is about us. I mean it's about there-is-no-us, and I need to remember that. And when you keep me warm it's too hard to remember."

Gherring was quiet for a long minute. Then he turned his unsmiling visage to Anne and said, "I promise... From now on I'll let you freeze to death."

Anne tried to keep her distance from Gherring for the rest of the night. She was mortified. She'd made such a fool of herself over something that meant nothing at all to Gherring. He didn't even understand what she was talking about. He was really just keeping her warm. That physical contact hadn't affected him at all. He had no idea something that simple was distressing her, and now she had as much as told him he made her hot and bothered. She couldn't even bring herself to look at him.

Gherring offered to buy dinner for the whole group, so the young people jumped on the idea. He took off his hat and glasses and immediately procured a table for six in a restaurant with a two-hour wait. He had easily spent eight hundred dollars for the meal with appetizers, wine and desserts. Everyone was laughing and joking, and Anne pretended to enjoy herself, while avoiding eye contact with Gherring.

After the limousine dropped the boys off, they returned to the apartment. The girls were exhausted but excited from their eventful day in New York.

"Hey Mr. Gherring," said Charlie. "I hate to ask and you can say 'no' if you want to. But can Mom take a picture of us with you?"

Gherring grinned. "Okay, but only if you send me a copy."

Anne looked through the camera viewer at her two beaming girls standing next to Steven Gherring with his arms around them. She felt a lump in her throat, and she wasn't sure of the cause. She snapped the picture and handed it back to Charlie. Even on the elevator, Anne kept her girls between her and Gherring. On the tenth floor the doors opened, and they started to depart.

"Can I talk to you alone for a second?" asked Gherring.

"Sure," said Anne, but her heart started pounding in her ears. When Emily and Charlie had gone, Gherring gestured toward a pair of chairs in the elevator foyer. Anne sat down with her back stiff, studying the pattern on the rug.

"Ms. Best, I'm sorry I was so forward with you tonight." He leaned toward her, but she refused to look at him. "You're quite different from any other woman I've known, and I'm not really sure how to act around you."

"It's okay—"

"No wait, I want to finish. I want to correct a couple of things you seem to believe about me."

"I'm sorry I said that stuff. I was just rambling—"

"The first thing is I haven't dated thousands of women." He held a finger to her lips when she started to protest.

"The second is I do remember the women I've dated, and that's because of the third thing. I'm a very careful man. Everything I do... Remember this... Everything I do *means* something to me."

He stood and took a few steps toward the elevator, before turning back. "Oh, and that last thing I said on the boat—I'd never let you freeze to death, no matter how stubborn you were."

With those words, Gherring got on the elevator and closed the doors, leaving Anne very much alone with her worries.

Chapter Ten - Sightseeing

ANNE AND THE GIRLS SLEPT LATE on Sunday morning. "Let's go to Central Park today," said Anne. "We can walk from here and, we'll make a picnic lunch. After that we'll go to Grand Central Station and the Empire State Building."

"Okay," said Charlie. "Today is picture day. We've got to get lots of them, because I haven't posted many. And this may be our last chance to see New York. Who knows how long Mom's going to keep her job?"

At Anne's distraught look, Emily gave her mom a hug. "Mom, she was just teasing. Mr. Gherring seems to like you a lot. You're not going to lose your job."

"I'm not so sure. I just can't seem to think straight around him. I'm always putting my foot in my mouth and making things awkward."

"Mom, I've just got to ask you... Do you like Mr. Gherring?" asked Emily.

"Of course I like him. Don't you?"

"You know that's not what I mean."

"Yeah Mom," said Charlie. "I think maybe you like him a little more than that. I couldn't blame you if you did."

"No, of course I don't *like* him. Not *that* way. I'm not falling for him or anything like that."

The girls exchanged looks and crossed their arms simultaneously, and she squirmed beneath their inspection.

"I mean, I do appreciate all the things he does for me, I mean all the things he did for *us* this weekend. That was really all for y'all. He's just a great person. Anyone can see that. That doesn't mean I have feelings for him."

"'The lady doth protest too much, methinks,'" Emily quoted.

186

"What about Henri? Do you still like him? Are you still going to visit him in Paris?" asked Charlie.

Anne felt her stomach churning. "Yes. I'm going to Paris."

"Well don't be so excited about it. It's not supposed to be an execution. You don't have to go to Paris, Mom. If you don't want to go anymore, just tell him."

"You don't know Henri very well. He's a hard man to say 'no' to. And anyway, Henri likes me. And I like him, too."

"You do? Or do you like Mr. Gherring?"

"I like Henri. And it doesn't matter what I think about Mr. Gherring, because he doesn't like me."

"Why do you think he doesn't like you? He bought us play tickets. He went climbing with us. He drove us around in his limo. He went on a tour with us. He paid for dinner." Emily ticked off these points on her fingers.

"He did all that for you girls."

"But he didn't even know us. He did that because we're *your* daughters," argued Emily.

"He never had any children. I think he does stuff like that because he doesn't have children of his own."

"Okay. What about on the boat last night? Y'all looked pretty cozy over there. I don't think he did that for us." Charlie arched her eyebrows.

"I was just cold. He would never let a woman freeze to death. And besides, y'all were cozying up with Spencer and Mark."

"That's because Emily likes Spencer," said Charlie.

"I don't either!"

"Well he sure as heck likes you."

"I can't believe I was so off on that one. I just knew Spencer would hit it off with you," Anne told Charlie. "He's such an outdoorsy adventurous guy."

Charlie laughed. "So if they get married, you won't get credit for their match, Right?"

"Hey," Emily protested. "We're not getting married."

"It looked like you and Mark were getting along pretty well."

"Yeah," said Emily. "Mark likes you, too."

"Maybe, but Mark didn't get my cell number and email address. Has Spencer texted you this morning?"

"I don't know." Emily's cheeks reddened.

"Ohmygosh! He's already texted you. He's really fallen for you."

"He just wants to add me to his groupies. Mom said girls hang all over him all the time. Besides, he lives in New York City. And I'm way too practical to get involved in a long distance relationship. Look at the mess Mom's in."

"Hey," Anne protested. "Are you calling me a mess?"

"If the shoe fits..."

The sun was out. With no wind blowing, the rays felt warm despite the nippy air. "This is beautiful. I can't believe how big this park is. It just goes on and on. It's hard to believe we're in the middle of Manhattan." Emily leaned her head back, basking in the sun.

Anne looked up from her book in time to see Charlie make an amazing catch for her pick-up team of Ultimate. "She'll need a shower before we go anywhere else."

"No problem, she only takes ten minutes to shower and dress. An extra five to dry her hair. It really is kind of like you gave me a little brother."

"It's a good thing, since *you* used to spend hours in the bathroom, mostly just twirling around in front of the mirror."

"You should've put a big mirror in my room. Then I wouldn't have monopolized the bathroom."

"So... about Spencer..."

"Don't want to talk about it."

"Okay." Anne and Emily turned back to their books.

"So... about Steven Gherring..."

"Don't want to talk about it."

Emily grinned. "Let's talk about Charlie instead."

"Great idea!"

Charlie took her good camera to Grand Central Station and the Empire State Building. She made some artistic shots in Grand Central Station, but they got a stranger to take some photos of the threesome.

"This one's really good," said Charlie. "You can see the clock and the glasswork."

"Not that one," said Emily. "My eyes are half closed. I look like I'm nauseated."

"Sorry sister. I look best in this photo. It'll be my new profile picture."

"No way—I'm deleting it when you aren't looking."

"Why didn't I have boys?" complained Anne.

"Mom, don't say that. You know you wouldn't have as much fun with sons," said Emily.

"Yeah Mom. And think how silly you'd look wearing our clothes if we'd been boys."

"And if we were boys, then when we got married, we'd always go spend holidays with our wives' families."

"And we wouldn't read all the good books with you and discuss them afterward."

"And we wouldn't be able to give you fashion advice."

"And—"

"Stop, stop," laughed Anne. "You win. I'm glad you're girls. At least most of the time."

At the top of the Empire State Building, Charlie got serious with her photography.

"Charlie, you've taken enough pictures. Surely you've used up all your memory by now," said Emily.

"No, I've got room for five hundred more pictures."

"You're so busy taking pictures you're missing the experience," said Emily. "It's romantic, like *Sleepless in Seattle*."

"Oh really? Maybe I should call Spencer and ask him to join us," Charlie teased. "He'd probably be willing to take the stairs up here if he got to see you again."

"He doesn't like me. He's just flirting."

"Ohmygosh, Em! The boy asked questions about your boring accounting job for an hour. No guy would suffer like that on purpose unless he'd seriously flipped for a girl."

"He's hasn't flipped for me. We live fourteen hundred miles apart. It's not like he's planning to come visit."

"He didn't mention seeing you the next time you visit Mom?"

"Yes, but Mom's only here on a trial basis."

"Hey, that's not nice," said Anne.

"Sorry, Mom. I just wanted to shift her attention off me."

"She's right, Mom. You're the one with some crazy-hot French guy with dreamy green eyes, who's willing to fly you to Paris just so he can see you. One would almost think he's expecting more than a kiss this time."

"Tell me again," said Anne. "Why am I glad I had girls?"

Gram sent a limousine to pick up Anne and the girls at the apartment at five thirty. Anne's heart fell when she realized Steven Gherring was not going with them. He'd never said he'd be there, but she must have secretly hoped. Then she scolded herself. Why did it matter whether Steven Gherring was with them on Sunday at Gram's dinner? She would see him Monday at work. That was better. It would remind her Gherring was her boss and nothing more. Plus, with Gherring absent from the dinner, it would be easier to conspire with Gram about their matchmaking efforts. She needed Gherring to find a wife—the sooner, the better.

The ride to the Gherring Estate was thirty minutes along the Hudson River to Yonkers. As they drove up to the two-story mansion at the top of the hill, they could see the lights twinkling a warm welcome in the courtyard. Anne counted four chimneys on the rooftop.

Charlie exclaimed, "This place is ginormous!"

"Mom, did you know she lived in a place like this?" asked Emily.

"I had no idea, but I suppose I should have guessed."

Gram met them at the entry that opened into a huge main hall with an enormous grand staircase off to the left. Their footsteps echoed in the hall as they followed Gram across the marble floor.

"Come this way. We'll sit in the library and chat until dinner is ready."

The expansive library was lit with two large chandeliers that hung from an elaborately coved and painted ceiling. The twelve-foot walls were covered on each side from floor to ceiling with bookcases filled to capacity. The bookshelves even extended over the doorway. A seating area beckoned in front of a roaring fire in an ornate stone fireplace.

"Emily, Charlotte, this is Mrs. Gherring. And this is Emily, the oldest, and Charlotte."

"I'm Gram! I've told your mother already that Mrs. Gherring is the name of my grandson's wife." The girls exchanged confused looks, and Gram chuckled. "I always say that. Love to see people's reactions. You know, they think I might be senile and maybe I don't know my grandson is still single."

"We're working together, Gram and I, to find a 'Mrs. Gherring' for Mr. Gherring."

"Ah ha!" said Charlie.

"Emily?" Gram asked, shifting her attention to the other Best daughter who'd turned her head to study the walls of books. She quickly forced her eyes back to the short woman with the commanding voice.

"Yes ma'am?"

"I can see you're dying to peruse the book collection. Go ahead. I'll just grill your sister for a while."

"Yes ma'am." Emily flashed a smirk at her sister and hurried to survey the books.

"So your name is Charlotte?"

"Actually, I go by Charlie."

"Charlie? Isn't that a boy's name?"

"I think Charlotte sounds kind of weak, and I'm not a weak person."

"And I'm betting you like to compete with boys a lot."

"I don't compete with 'em... I beat 'em."

"Ha! That's my girl. I would've been just like you in my day, if I'd had the opportunity."

Anne pictured Gram as a modern day twenty-one year old, and laughed. She knew Gram's small size would never have prevented her from being a daunting adversary.

"Thanks, Gram. I hope I turn out just like you when I'm a grandmother."

"What do you do, Charlie?"

"I teach ski lessons in the winter and lead rafting and climbing trips in the summer."

"That sounds like fun. Plenty of time to settle down. Not like me. My Samuel swept me off my feet when I was sixteen."

"Wow, you got married at sixteen?"

"Yes, and I had my son, Steven's father, when I was nineteen."

"Our family's small." Emily rejoined the group. "Mom and Dad were 'only children' and we've lost all our grandparents except for Mom's father. I think maybe that's why we're so close. We're all we've got."

"And the Best name is dying out now, since we had two girls," Anne added.

"I don't know. I might just keep my maiden name. I can't imagine a guy that I'd be willing to give up my name for," said Charlie.

"Any guy that manages to catch you, with the fight you'll put up, deserves to have you take his name." Emily chuckled at her sister's feigned indignation.

"Ha-ha, sister. The poor guys can't even get you to pay attention to them. At least I look at them, over my shoulder, as I leave 'em in the dust."

"It looks like you've got plenty of work to do after we get Steven married," said Gram.

This broke everyone up, and they were still laughing when a butler came to announce dinner.

The dining room was so expansive it held three long rectangular tables. Their dinner was set up on one of the tables. As they took their places at the table, Anne noticed a fifth place setting.

"Dinner is served," said a familiar voice.

Steven Gherring appeared, wearing an apron and carrying a soup tureen.

"You cooked dinner?" Her heart gave a leap of joy at his presence, despite all her self-warnings.

Gram answered. "Steven is a fantastic chef. And we don't keep a cook on staff since I'm seldom here anymore."

"What's for dinner?" asked Charlie.

Gherring smiled. "The first course is lobster bisque." He set the soup down and headed back to the kitchen.

"You're not eating with us?" asked Anne. She kicked herself for sounding so eager.

"I'll be back in second. I just need to turn the burner down to simmer."

When the kitchen door closed behind him, Anne turned to Gram. "When are we going to work on our plan? I didn't know Mr. Gherring would be here."

"Steven made me promise not to attempt to set him up with a woman, so I'll keep my promise. However, I didn't promise not to help *you*, so I'll be your secret consultant—" Gram's voice dropped abruptly.

"How's the soup?" Steven strode back into the dining room.

"I love lobster bisque—it's my all-time favorite soup. And this is the best ever. What's the secret?" asked Emily.

"A little dry sherry," he replied. "It's also got Worcestershire and Tabasco. I can give you the recipe."

"Emily loves to cook," said Anne.

"Tell me about yourself, Emily. What do you do?" Gram asked.

"Well I have a Masters degree in Accounting and I've already passed my CPA exam. I just need to work another four months and I'll be certified."

Charlie said, "Yep, the family genius."

"Maybe I was just the one who actually put forth a little effort in school. Don't let Charlie fool you, Gram. She's just as smart as I am. But she never saw the value in studying."

"New subject... How did you learn to cook?" Charlie asked.

"It was that or starve to death," he laughed. "I guess I could eat out or order in every night. But cooking is a lot more challenging and a lot more satisfying. Although it's not a lot of fun to cook for one person."

Gram cleared her throat. "Yes, it would certainly be nice if you had someone to cook for."

Gherring glared. "Gram, we've talked about this."

"I meant, of course, you could stay out here with me."

"Sure Gram, except you're usually four hours away from here."

"You could cook for Anne."

Anne felt the heat radiating from her skin. Perhaps she could melt under the table, and no one would notice. The room was deathly silent.

Gram continued, "You do live downstairs from Steven, don't you Anne?"

"Yes, but Mr. Gherring has to deal with me all day, Gram. In the evening I'm sure he needs a break." She turned a hard stare at Gram. "Besides, if he was with me all the time, when would he have time to *date*?"

"You're quite right, dear. That would be bad. He does need time to date. However will he ever find a wife if he doesn't date anyone?"

"Gram! That's quite enough of talking about me as if I'm not sitting here at the table. We've already had this discussion, and you promised—"

"I did promise not attempt to set you up. But I didn't promise not to nag you about it. There's only one way to get me to stop nagging you. Get married." She paused to pat her lips with her napkin. "Or I guess you can keep waiting for me to die..."

"Yes I know, Gram. You're not going to die before I get married. Can we change the subject?" He looked at Charlie and Emily. "You see what I have to put up with?"

Charlie laughed, but Emily said, "I'd say you're pretty lucky to have someone who loves you that much."

"How can you take her side after that great dinner I bought you last night?" Gherring pretended outrage.

"I'd be more worried about the dinner tonight, Emily. He could spit in your food," said Charlie.

Giggles broke out all around and the mood was lifted again.

Gherring served a main course of almond crusted salmon with garlic-mashed potatoes and steamed asparagus. Dessert was chocolate mousse.

"I've died and gone to heaven! This meal was even better than last night's," said Charlie.

Gherring beamed at the praise. But Anne had been quiet throughout dinner, trying to settle her thoughts.

"Did you like the meal?" he asked her.

"It was amazing." Her answer was sincere, but she couldn't make eye contact.

"I have a little surprise for Charlie." Gherring stood, walking toward the door.

"What? Is it a present? What is it?" Charlie leaped to follow him.

"No, it's not a present. It's an experience. Come see."

Gherring led the group outside to the garage and opened the door. Inside was a white Maserati MC12. Charlie squealed at the sight.

"I thought you might want to go for a ride."

"Okay, she can go first, but I want a ride too," said Emily.

Anne watched as Charlie climbed into the passenger's seat.

"Now you won't go over the speed limit, will you?" Anne asked in her best worried-mom voice.

"Of course not. Although I'm fairly certain Maserati's have a different speed limit than the rest of the cars out there." He chuckled as he started the engine and spun the tires in the driveway before racing to the road.

"I can't believe he's got a Maserati," said Emily. "This is the best weekend ever. None of our friends will believe it. We've got to get pictures. I wish we didn't have to go home tomorrow."

"I'm going to miss you so much." Anne gave Emily a hug.

"Why don't you girls come back here for Thanksgiving? I'd love to have you."

"We've got to take care of Grandpa at Thanksgiving, because Mom's going to be in Paris."

"Paris! Why are you going to Paris?"

"She's going to Paris with this French guy named Henri who's really crazy about her."

"Henri? Henri DuBois?"

"You know him?" asked Anne.

"I know him. And he's not good enough for you."

"Gram," said Anne, "he's not as bad as you think."

Gram's expression was disapproving, and Anne's heart fell.

"Please don't be mad at me, Gram. He's been really sweet to me and to the girls."

"I know what he was like before. I can't believe he's changed that much."

"Even Steven found out some of the stuff he thought about Henri wasn't true at all."

"Humph! Well I don't like him."

"It's not like I'm planning to marry him, Gram. I'm just going to visit him."

"Humph!" They stood in uncomfortable silence until Gherring returned to trade passengers. Charlie climbed out of the driver's seat.

"He let you drive it?" asked Emily.

"I made the mistake of saying I would let her drive it if she knew how to drive a manual," Gherring chuckled. "Who knew she'd actually know how?"

"And I was pretty good, wasn't I?"

"I have to admit, you surprised the h—, the heck out of me." Gherring looked to see if Gram had noticed his near slip.

Instead of fussing about his language, she said, "I can't believe you let Anne associate with the likes of Henri DuBois."

Gherring started laughing. "Now you see what it's like to be on the receiving end of Gram's disapproval. Perhaps you'll be more sympathetic in the future."

"I suppose you drive a manual as well?" he asked Emily.

"Of course I do, but I'd rather just enjoy the ride."

"I think every girl should know how to drive a stick shift. All three of us drive a manual car at home," said Anne.

Gherring shook his head. "You never cease to surprise me."

When the Maserati disappeared again, Anne turned to Gram.

"Please Gram, don't tell Mr. Gherring about Paris. He doesn't know."

"If you think Henri is so great, why don't you want Steven to know about Paris?"

"Because he doesn't like Henri either, and it just upsets him. But Gram, Henri was a perfect gentleman. He acted like he had a huge crush on me and said a lot of things that made me feel... I don't know... attractive again. He made me feel special and beautiful. And when he calls me, I feel like I'm really important to him. I've just missed that, I guess. And he opened up to me and told me some things about how he's been hurt—"

"That's the real thing, Gram," Charlie butted in. "Mom can't stand to see anyone hurting. She just melts."

She gave her mom a hug. "But I love you for it."

"Humph! All right, I won't tell him. But I think you can do better than Henri DuBois."

"He's pretty handsome though—you have to admit that much."

"Handsome is as handsome does," said Gram.

"Anyway, I'm not looking for a new husband. I'm happy like I am. I've had one great love in my life, just like you. Right, Gram?"

This time Gram didn't respond.

When Emily and Gherring came back, Charlie pulled out her phone and took pictures of them with and in the Maserati. He asked Anne, "Did you want a ride as well?"

"No, that's okay—"

"Come on, Mom. It's amazing," said Charlie.

Emily said, "Mom, if you don't try it, you'll never know what it feels like. You'll probably kick yourself for wasting the chance."

He was already climbing in the driver's seat.

"I guess I'm going."

Charlie leaned in the car and took a picture of Anne and Gherring inside together.

"Ready?" asked Gherring. Before Anne could answer, he stepped on the gas and sped out of the driveway. Anne couldn't help a little squeak that came out of her mouth as she felt her back pressed into the seat. Gherring drove a short distance to a turn off on a deserted road that wound around through the hills. As he steered the car skillfully through the twists and turns, Anne found herself with a broad smile plastered on her face. And she couldn't stop smiling. Watching him control the powerful car, she thought of how strong he was. He handled driving as he did everything else in his life—with expert efficiency and absolute control. It made his masculine appeal even stronger.

Just for a moment she allowed herself to imagine what it would feel like to kiss Steven Gherring. Would he be soft and gentle, sweet and romantic? Or would he be strong and powerful, taking what belonged to him? Or maybe he would be subtle and teasing, drawing out her fervor until she surrendered her lips to be plundered?

"You look like you're really enjoying this," Gherring commented. Anne felt the blood rising in her cheeks and thanked God the light was dim. He'd caught her enjoying a bit more than a ride in a fast, powerful sports car.

"It's... It's indescribable."

"Did you want to drive?"

"No, I like watching you. I mean, I like watching you drive. I don't need to drive." She blushed even deeper. Thank goodness he couldn't tell. "So does this thing really 'do one-eighty-five', like the song says?"

He smiled. "I've had her up to one-eighty, and I think she'd do two hundred on a straight course."

"She?" Anne asked. "What's her name?"

"Gayle."

"Really? Why Gayle?"

"That was the name of my first true love—in fourth grade." He laughed. "Even now, in my memories, she's beautiful beyond imagination."

Anne grew quiet again. "I can't thank you enough. You've been amazingly generous this weekend."

"You're welcome. It was my pleasure." His eyes cut her direction. "I wanted this to be a special time for all three of you."

"It was, thanks mostly to you. You didn't go out and buy a Maserati just so Charlie could ride in one, did you?"

He laughed. "No that one was a lucky coincidence."

"Still, it was very nice, and the girls really like you."

"And do they, like their mother, freely bestow love and affection on everyone they meet?"

"What? I don't—"

"Really? You're going to deny this?"

"Well, I don't bestow on *everyone*—just *most* everyone."

"Name one person you've met in New York you haven't loved."

Anne thought for a moment. "Jeff Murphy!" She lifted her chin high.

Gherring chuckled. "Okay, but you were even nice to him at first. The original question was about your girls, though."

"Okay, the girls... Charlie bestows love pretty freely. But if you make her mad—watch out—she'll never forget. Emily is very careful and not very trusting."

Gherring nodded as if he was not surprised. "Well, they're lovely girls. I'd be very proud if they were my daughters."

He drove the sports car back into the garage. Gram and the girls had returned into the house, out of the chill air.

"This was really nice," he said. His voice was husky as he leaned toward her. "I really enjoy making you smile." His blue eyes were hooded as he reached his left hand out to brush against her cheek. Anne closed her eyes and held her breath while her insides quaked. Then his fingers slid gently down her neck, leaving a sizzling trail in their wake. He moved has hand slowly along her sweater-clad arm. Then she heard a click as he released her seat belt.

"Sometimes that latch can be stubborn."

She opened her eyes to see him smiling, dimples dancing as he watched her recover from his touch. He knew! He knew what he did to her. He was playing with her emotions. He'd enjoyed watching her squirm in her seat, wishing for something more—something that would never be. Overwhelming embarrassment soon gave way to anger.

"Thank you again, *sir*, for the ride. You have a beautiful vehicle."

She slipped from the car and escaped from the garage.

*****

"I can't believe it's over already," complained Charlie.

"Back to the grind tomorrow," said Emily.

"Yeah, ski season starts this week. Back to the grind." She giggled, while her sister glared at her. "You could always quit your job and move to Colorado with me."

"I don't need two kids with no health insurance," said Anne.

"Mom, you worry too much. I have insurance through the resort, so I'll be fine."

"Yes, but only during the actual ski season," Anne said. Charlie rolled her eyes, having had this discussion numerous times.

"Mom, it's almost seven fifteen," said Emily.

"Oh, right. Okay, y'all lock up when you leave and have a safe trip back. I'm going to miss y'all so much at Thanksgiving. I kind of wish I wasn't going."

"Right," said Emily sarcastically. "I'll bet you're going to miss us while you are having fun in Paris."

"Besides, Mom. You'll finally get to use your passport."

"Now, we may have to have 'The Talk' before you go and spend four days with Henri. Between those eyes and that accent, he's going to be hard to resist."

"Oh yes, I think I should definitely help give you 'The Talk.' This could be really fun," Charlie quipped.

"Once again—why am I glad I have daughters?"

"Because you love us so much," said Charlie.

"And because your life would be boring without us. Hmmm. Well, maybe not anymore."

"So speaking of your life not being boring... Are you going to talk to us about what happened on that car ride with Mr. Gherring last night? Did you wreck the car or something? The tension was pretty thick when y'all came back."

"Nothing happened. I was just tired, that's all."

"Come on, Mom. Something must have happened. You'll feel better if you talk about it," said Emily

Anne thought for a moment. Perhaps it would be best to get the whole thing off her chest. To get her feelings out in the open. Maybe it would sound better if she told the story to someone else. Maybe she wouldn't feel so foolish.

No, this was a problem she needed to handle by herself. After all, she was the mother, and they were the children. She couldn't be asking them for advice about how to control your emotions.

She turned to the girls and forced a smile. "Don't worry. It really was nothing. Now, come give me hugs. I've gotta go."

Upon arrival at her desk, Anne found a sticky note from Gherring requesting she come to his office. With tension permeating her body, Anne knocked on the door.

"Open," ordered his deep voice. She found him in conference with Jared about the Switzerland presentation.

"Ms. Best, we need to work together today on Jared's part of the presentation. I understand he's given you the bulk of his material for the PowerPoint. If we could get a copy of what you have so far, I was hoping you would finish his portion and then see how much of Jeff's part you can prepare on your own."

Gherring spoke as if nothing at all had happened between them. He didn't act awkward in any way. Of course it had all seemed like a big joke to him, so why wouldn't he be fine? Well, two could play at that game. She could be a cool cat if that's how he was going to be.

"Yes, sir. I'll get that for you right away. Are y'all working in here or in the conference room?"

"I think we'll work in my office and leave the conference room for you since Jeff's materials are all organized in there. Are you okay working on your own?"

"Absolutely, sir. I prefer it that way." She noted with some satisfaction the slight wince on Gherring's face.

She sent a copy of Jared's PowerPoint to Gherring's computer and perused the additional material he'd given her. She estimated she could finish his portion easily in an hour, and then she would tackle Jeff's part. She'd show Gherring she wasn't some secretary to

200

be trifled with. She might not have had any business classes, but she was smart and she learned fast. She'd figure out what everything meant without even asking for Gherring's help. She was smart enough to use her resources. Tanner and Sam could clarify the difficult concepts for her.

Since Jeff's proposal involved a choice between acquisition and contractual cooperation, she'd have to understand the material to show which option would be optimal. Because of tax consequences, the most favorable option for Gherring Inc. would be a contractual cooperation with a company formed by the merger of two existing Swiss companies. Anne's data needed to prove this would also be the most favorable option for the two companies. Otherwise, Gherring Inc. would simply buy out the two companies and merge the acquisitions. It was very complex, but she would study until she understood it, backwards and forwards. Taking a deep breath, she started working with relish.

"Here's your lunch," said Sam. "I can't believe you're doing this all on your own. Why isn't Mr. Gherring helping you?"

"I really appreciate your help. Mr. Gherring didn't say he wouldn't help me. I just wanted to prove I could figure it out myself. Besides, he's really busy working with Jared today. This will be Jared's first big presentation, and I'm sure he's nervous. I would be—I hate public speaking."

"Well, you seem to grasp the basic concepts pretty well. It's all very complex. I'm sure even Jeff didn't understand all the international laws that are involved. Mr. Gherring is the only one who really does. I've already taught you everything I know. But I'll pass on your questions to Randy. His specialty is mergers and acquisitions."

"Hey thanks. Maybe after I talk to Henri, I'll run up there and pick his brain. Would you ask him for me?"

"Sure thing. So things are still going strong with Henri? I still can't believe you snagged him. Women around here have been falling all over him for years. You show up, and he's following you around like a puppy dog. Do you have some secret aphrodisiac?"

"She certainly seems to," Steven Gherring's deep voice carried from the doorway of the conference room.

"Oh… Hi, Mr. Gherring. I was just leaving." Sam made a small gesture to Anne indicating she would call her later.

"Are you making progress?" he asked.

"Yes, it's coming along."

"Unfortunately I have to go to a meeting with some investors this afternoon. You know I don't expect you to do this on your own. I'll tackle it tomorrow and try to get it into a form you can put in the PowerPoint. Sound okay?"

"I'll just keep plugging along. And Katie is handling all the day-to-day stuff."

"Great." His jaw flexed, causing his dimples to appear despite the distinct lack of a smile. "Do we… I think we need to talk… about last night."

"Mr. Gherring, the last thing I want to do is talk about last night. I'd like to forget about it, and I'd appreciate it if you'd help me do just that. So let's make an agreement *not* to talk about anything."

"We can't not talk about *anything*."

"Of course I don't mean that. I'm your secretary. So, we can talk about work-related subjects."

"You're my executive assistant," Gherring huffed as his hands balled into tight fists. "And I'm *not* agreeing to *not* talk. I won't press the matter right now, because I've got to get to this meeting. But I'll promise you this much—you *will* talk with me. Or if you prefer you can sit quietly and pretend to listen. It's your choice. Just not today."

He left the conference room, shutting the door just a little harder than usual.

Anne realized her hands were shaking with adrenaline. At least she'd managed to put off the discussion until tomorrow. She felt so humiliated. What she needed was a pep talk, and she knew just where to get it—Henri.

His face appeared on the screen, still sporting his scruffy look. "I am so happy to see you. You look amazing. Those deep brown eyes, they are fathomless."

"Thanks, Henri. I needed an ego boost. And how do you know a word like 'fathomless'?"

"I have been reading English poetry. And why do you need an ego boost? Someone as beautiful as you should not need boosting."

Anne didn't want to share the real reason for her distress. "Surely even someone as handsome as you has doubts every once in a while."

Henri appeared to think hard. "No... no I've always known I was perfect." He laughed. "Sure I do, and you are very good for my ego." Then his face fell. "I hate to bring you down, when you need a boost, but..."

"What's wrong, Henri?"

"It's my niece, Anna-Laure. She said that her leg was hurting, and we thought it was from riding the pony. But now the doctors are afraid it may be something worse. It might even be cancer."

"Oh no! Are they doing tests? When will you know?"

"She's already had some blood tests today, and she is scheduled for some scans later in the week." Henri looked absolutely destitute. "I don't know what I'll do if she has cancer. I can't lose her. And her mom and her brother will be devastated."

"Don't jump the gun, Henri. It might not be serious. I'll pray for her—I promise."

"I wish you were here, just to hold my hand and tell me that everything will be all right. At times like this, I feel so alone. You understand now, don't you? You see why I feel strongly for you? I knew from the beginning you were different from the other women. There are many women who want me, who offer themselves to me. But they are selfish, as I am selfish. But you are not selfish, and you make me want to be like you."

"I'm not perfect either, Henri. You just don't know me well enough. If you put me on a pedestal, you'll be very disappointed when you see the real me."

"I am not so young that I am naïve, *mon ange*. I know you are human, not a real angel. You will see when you come to Paris."

"I wish I could come tonight, Henri. I'd hold your hand and cry with you. But I hope by the time I come, you'll have good news."

"If you would come tonight, I would buy your ticket. But you will not come, will you?"

"I... my job..."

"Your job." Henri's expression was sour. "Gherring does not appreciate you. You are more than a secretary. You have a degree in

Chemistry, so you must be very intelligent. Anyone else would know you could be so much more than a secretary."

Anne took a deep breath and let it out slowly. "Henri, I agree with you. I could be more than a secretary. But a Chemistry degree and no job experience except being a part-time travel agent and a mother doesn't qualify you for many positions. I'm lucky to have this job."

"Still, Gherring does not know how valuable you are. He uses people. He plays with their lives. That is how he makes his living."

"Henri, I don't think he's as bad as you think he is."

"Of course, my angel, you will defend him. He does not deserve your loyalty. Let me ask you a question... Has he never done anything to keep you in his control? Has he never made you feel foolish? Has he never made you think he was your friend, and then done something to hurt you?"

She didn't answer, struggling with her emotions as she considered Henri's questions. He continued, "But a better question is this... Have I ever done any of those things to you? I pray the answer is no. If I have, I fall on my face and beg you to forgive me."

"No Henri, you haven't ever done any of those things."

"But? There is something you are not saying."

"But... But you push me, Henri. I don't like pressure. It makes me nervous."

"I am sorry."

"You don't look like you're really sorry."

Henri laughed. "Life is short, and I have wasted much of it. I do not want to waste another day. So I may try to hurry you along."

Anne tried to keep a stern countenance, but failed. "Okay, Henri. You're forgiven."

His smile was unrepentant.

Sam set up Anne's meeting with Randy. With his help, she gained a greater understanding of the proposal. He gave her his cell number, so she could call him with questions as she worked. Having acquired some basic knowledge, she attacked the project with a vengeance. She had slides to show the actual profits from the five prior years. Then she organized the PowerPoint with comparison tables to show

204

the projected profit with the merger and cooperative contract. She had organizational charts and slides with tax consequences.

Occasionally some of Jeff's notes would look like a foreign language to her, but so far Randy had been able to clarify the issues. Anne was tired but extremely pleased with her progress. She started reading a particularly tedious stack of notes. The information was random. Some pertaining to the physical plant while others referred to economic trends. She read until her eyes were blurry.

"Oh my God! What are you still doing here?" Gherring's voice startled her from her trance.

"I was… I was just working. What time is it?"

"It's nine thirty! There's no one here but the night guards. How were you planning to get home?"

"I don't know. The subway, I guess. I didn't know it was so late. What are you doing here?"

"I tried to call you, and you didn't answer your cell. You weren't at the apartment and Rayna hadn't seen you come in. Gram didn't know where you were. I even called Emily, and she hadn't heard from you. Everyone was worried."

"You had Emily's cell number?"

"Yes, I… That's not the point. No one knew where you were. You can't stay here this late by yourself."

"Okay, I'm sorry. But look what I got done. I've almost finished Jeff's whole PowerPoint."

"I don't care about the PowerPoint. I care about—"

"You darn well better care about this PowerPoint! I've sweated blood over this thing, and you're going to look at it whether you want to or not!" She glared at him with her arms crossed, until he finally gave in.

"Fine. Let me see what you've got." He leaned over the computer. "You do remember I said I would do this tomorrow?"

"Yes, but that doesn't give you time to practice the presentation." Anne brought up the PowerPoint, flashing quickly through the slides and summarizing the information. "Okay, that's not quite all of it, but most of it. What do you think?" She held her breath.

He was staring at the computer screen, scrolling though the PowerPoint. "How did you do this? How did you put this together using those crappy notes Jeff left? How did you know how to organize this or what this stuff even meant?"

"I just did a little research, and then I got Randy, from the international accounting department, to explain the concepts and the laws and such. I mean, some of it still seems like Greek to me, but I've got the gist of it." She paused for a breath. "Is it good?"

His eyebrows arched high, and he smiled, his dimples announcing his pleasure. "It's actually great. I can't believe it—just when I think I'm finally getting to know you, you surprise me again. I mean, every day it's something new." He shook his head, and then he forced his face into a stern expression. "But that doesn't mean you're out of trouble for scaring me to death. Oh, and you'd better call Emily. I'll call Gram."

Anne rode home with Gherring in the limousine. She was so tired she didn't argue with him about her mode of transportation. Relaxing in the back with the vibration of the car, she felt herself nodding off, even though the ride only lasted fifteen minutes. She woke with a jolt when the car stopped and found herself leaning against his shoulder.

"I just moved over so you could lean on me. Your head was tilting at an awful angle."

"Thank you." She felt awkward and shy at his sweet and gentle manner.

"It's the least I could do. After all, I'm the reason you're so worn out. Let's get you upstairs."

Gherring supported her elbow as they walked in. Anne felt warm even from that small contact on her arm. When they walked into the lobby together, Rayna spotted them immediately.

"Anne! Oh, thank goodness you found her. Is she okay?"

"Yes, I'm fine."

But Gherring had stopped cold.

"Steven," said a soft female voice.

Anne turned to see the owner. She was blond and beautiful. Anne knew immediately she was wealthy. By now, Anne knew the look—soft, self-assured, impeccably dressed, sophisticated demeanor, a subtly powerful presence.

"I've been waiting for you. I hope you don't mind." She walked confidently to Steven and kissed his cheek, before her glance slid

206

questioningly to where Gherring's hand still supported Anne's elbow. "Have you rescued some fair maiden?"

Gherring broke from his reverie. "Michelle, this is Anne, my uhmm—"

"His secretary. I'm his secretary." Anne spoke in a flat, emotionless tone. She removed her elbow from his hand. "I think I can make it upstairs alone. Thank you, sir... for the ride home."

Anne started for the elevator. She heard Michelle talking in a low voice to Gherring. "Can we go up? It would be nice to have some privacy."

"Do you have a hotel room?" His voice sounded gruff and a bit impatient.

"No, I was hoping..." Her voice trailed off and a sob escaped.

Escaping into the elevator, Anne turned around to face the lobby and let her eyes fall on Gherring. He was standing frozen in place, but Michelle had thrown her arms around him, crying inconsolably. For just a moment, his eyes locked with Anne's. The doors closed, shutting off her view and vaulting her back to reality.

*****

Anne arrived at the office on Tuesday, feeling fatigued. She'd been unable to fall asleep, finally drifting off at two o'clock. Then her eyes snapped open at five o'clock, and she knew the fight was over. She went up to the gym and ran for thirty minutes, then showered and headed for the office. Anne immediately headed into the conference room, with the intent of finishing the Switzerland project. She'd been working undisturbed for almost an hour, when Gherring came to the door.

"Good morning, Anne," he said hesitantly.

She nodded, but didn't return the greeting.

He sighed. "I hate to do this to you, but Michelle would like to talk to you."

This got her attention, and she turned stunned eyes to Gherring. "Why does she want to talk to me? I'm nobody."

Gherring frowned. "Don't say that—"

Michelle pushed her way into the room. "I'm sorry! I'm just asking if you'd be willing to talk to me."

Anne scrutinized Michelle, her quivering lips, her reddened nose, and her still-swollen eyes. Perhaps her night had been as bad as Anne's. Her heart softened.

"Of course you can talk to me. I just don't know why you'd want to."

Michelle nodded at Gherring, and he closed the door, leaving the two women alone. "Can I sit down?"

"Sure. What do you want to talk to me about?"

"I... I want to... I need to ask you about Henri."

"Henri? Why do you—" Anne's mouth fell open. "Oh—you're *that* Michelle!" Now Anne remembered Katie's story about the broken engagement between Michelle and Gherring.

"So, I understand... Steven told me... you're dating Henri."

"Well, I don't know if you can call it dating. I went out with him a few times while he was here, and I've talked to him on Skype. But I'm here, and he's in Paris. And you've probably noticed, I have a job. So I can't just drop everything and move to Paris."

"But Henri likes you, doesn't he? It's not like him to pursue someone. I know him. He doesn't just pursue anyone who comes along. He must really like you."

"Look, I don't know the whole story about y'all. But I understand you used to date Henri, and you also dated Steven. Word has it you turned both of them down. Is that about right?"

"Yes. But I've come to realize I still have feelings for Henri."

"It's not really any of my business. I try not to be a judging person, so you don't need to explain your reasons to me of all people. And if you and Steven have decided to marry after all, I think that's good. He needs someone. I hate he's alone. And it's really not my business, because I'm just his secretary."

"But that's not it at all! Just let me explain." She looked behind her as if to be sure no one else was in the room. "I met Henri, and we were crazy about each other. But I knew he was a real player, so I didn't really trust him. I broke it off."

She stood up and began to pace. "And I ran to Steven's arms, sort of. We'd grown up together like a big brother and little sister—he's ten years older. Neither of us had anyone else to marry, so we thought the perfect solution was to marry each other. Our families were thrilled, and we almost went through with it."

She seemed to grow more upset as she shared her story, swiping at the tears rolling down her face. "But then I realized I still loved Henri. So we made up this story about me wanting children and Steven refusing, just to keep my parents and Gram from hounding us. And we called off the marriage."

Anne nodded. "I can see you'd have to take desperate measures with Gram. She can be pretty tenacious."

She stopped to search through her purse for a tissue to wipe her face, collapsing into a chair next to Anne. "Six months later, I decided to go to Paris and give it a try. For a couple of weeks it was perfect. Henri was perfect. And he was rich enough I knew he didn't love me for my money. I know that sounds snobby or stupid, but that kind of thing happens all the time. I've been burned so many times."

She looked so miserable Anne put her hand on her arm to comfort her. "I'm sure it's hard. That sounds terrible."

She blinked away a few tears and continued. "One day I noticed Henri was always gone for an hour at the same time every afternoon. So, I know this sounds awful, but I followed him. And I saw him with two kids, a boy and a girl, and the boy looked just like him. I knew they were his kids, and I was just furious he hadn't told me. We fought, and I wouldn't let him explain. So I left. The press assumed I'd caught him in an affair, and so did the rest of the world, including Steven."

Michelle took a deep quivery breath. "But the thing is, I found out later those weren't Henri's kids. Do you know about them?"

"Yes, he told me about his sister's kids. They live in his house now, all three of them. And I think Henri is wonderful for loving those kids and his sister like that."

Michelle's expression was wretched, tears spilling from her eyes. "I know... You're right. I was so blind and I wouldn't even let him explain. And then, when I found out the truth, I was too proud to admit I was wrong. And I know I really hurt him."

"Henri said you'd found someone else. He thought you'd found someone who'd make you happy. What happened?"

"He was a jerk. Just like always, he loved my money more than me. And I wish I could go back in time and do that all over again. You know... swallow my pride and let him explain. I was such an idiot."

"What do you want from me?"

"I don't know... I guess... Did you say he mentioned me?"

"Yes, I think you're the reason he was so wild before he met me. I think you really hurt him. He likes me because I could see what a great guy he was, behind all that playboy façade."

"I think he's the only man I ever *really* loved."

Anne was thinking this woman didn't even begin to understand the meaning of the word.

"I'm going to see him next week, during the Thanksgiving holidays. Mr. Gherring doesn't know. I haven't told him because he doesn't like Henri, as you well know."

"That's mostly my fault. It really hurt Steven when I went back to Henri after we broke off the marriage, even though it was a mutual agreement. It hurt Steven's pride for me to be with Henri. And I probably hurt him again last night by telling him about my feelings for Henri. Steven is so good to me. He only wants what's best for me. I really wish I could love him the way I do Henri. I think I've waited too late now, anyway."

Her heart hurt, not for Michelle, but for Mr. Gherring. He must still have feelings for her, and it must have killed him for her to profess love for Henri. As much as she hated the idea, if he loved Michelle, she would help them get back together.

"Maybe you should forget about Henri and try again with Mr. Gherring. It's obvious that he still cares for you."

"Actually, if you and Henri aren't dating seriously, I was hoping you might put in a good word for me with him."

"I can't make any promises, Michelle. He's going though a lot right now, and he really needs someone supportive. I don't think he could handle it if you broke his heart again."

"But I wouldn't... Not this time!"

Anne grimaced. "Okay. I'll try to put in a good word for you if we get a chance to talk."

Anne worked alone in the conference room until lunchtime. She was about to order take-out from Papa's when the door opened abruptly.

"Come dear. It's time for lunch," Gram demanded.

Anne thought about arguing, but she knew it would be fruitless. "I'm coming, Gram. But I need to get back quickly. I have a lot of work to do."

"I've already spoken to Steven and informed him he's been giving you too much work. The very idea of you working here alone until nine thirty last night. You can take all the time you need for lunch, and Steven can and will take some of this workload."

"It's not his fault." Anne grabbed her purse. "In fact, it's kind of my fault."

"What do you mean?"

"He had to fire this guy who was being fresh with me, and it left us with a crisis right before the big Switzerland presentation. And they're leaving tomorrow evening."

"Humph! I don't believe it was your fault Steven fired someone. He's not a rash man. He's infuriatingly deliberate about his decisions... Well, usually."

"I know you didn't invite me to lunch to talk about work. Have you made some progress on our project?" Anne spoke cryptically since there were other passengers on the elevator.

"I've made some progress, but there've been some setbacks." She gestured with her eyes to the others in the elevator. "We'll talk during lunch."

May chatted happily with Gram, leading them to the private room in the back. They ordered quickly, with Anne trying the new special—crab-stuffed whitefish.

"So what's up?" asked Anne.

"I had a long talk with my grandson Sunday night, and I believe some of my advice is finally sinking in. He admits, at least, he doesn't want to be alone for the rest of his life. But he says he'll find the right person his own way in his own time." Gram screwed up her face. "If I let him do it in his own time, I'll be long gone before he finds someone."

"Well, at least it sounds like he's open to the possibility. What about Michelle?"

Gram looked surprised. "Michelle? What about her?"

"Well, she's in town. She was with Steven last night, and she was here this morning."

"That's great information. I'll give her a call. She owes me a visit anyway."

"And after Mr. Gherring comes back from Switzerland, I'm going to introduce him to my friend, Ellen. I think she'd make a good match."

"I'd still like to know why you're doing all that work by yourself in the conference room. Why isn't Steven helping you?"

"Well, partly because he's just swamped. But I also think it's partly because he doesn't want to work with me. We had a... misunderstanding. I guess I have a bit of a temper, and I'm sure he's uncomfortable."

"Sunday night?"

"Yes."

"What happened?"

"Let's just say I don't appreciate being the butt of a joke. I know I'm probably too sensitive, but I can't help it. Especially with Mr. Gherring."

"Well, that answer is hogwash. Steven wouldn't explain it to me either."

"It doesn't matter. I can be professional, and I've proven I can get the work done."

"It *does* matter. We need to clear this up, or my plan is never going to work."

"But I'm still on board with the plan. I'll still help you find him a wife, I promise. After all, I have to protect my reputation as the world's best matchmaker. This one will be my crowning achievement."

Gram's chin jutted out. "I'm afraid you'll never win that title away from me, dear."

Katie came in the conference room that afternoon carrying coffee from the downstairs shop.

"Coffee! Is that a latté? I love you, Katie!"

"I haven't seen you for days. Aren't you going stir-crazy in here? Is there something I can help you with?"

Anne stretched her arms, arching her back. "Ugh! I *am* getting a little stiff. But I think I'm almost finished."

"Well, the president of the company from Bern just called. Gherring's on the line with him now. There's some kind of scheduling problem, and they may cancel the whole thing."

"Ohmygosh! After all this work?"

"I'm sure they'd reschedule on a later date. But Mr. Gherring wanted to get this thing done before the end of the year. Postponing would get us into Thanksgiving, and December is really tough, with all the end-of-year business to wrap up. We'll see soon enough. Here he comes."

His hair was mussed as if his hand had been pushing it in all directions.

"I don't know what we're going to do. One of the companies involved has a conflict on Friday. We can't move it up to Thursday because we aren't even finished with the presentation."

Anne said, "I'll stay tonight and work late. We can finish everything. I'm almost done with Jeff's part, even the last stuff you interpreted for me. By the way, thanks for clarifying that mumbo-jumbo."

Gherring shook his head. "I've done this a lot. I'd rather postpone the presentation than show up for a meeting with jetlag."

"I'll call the pilots, and maybe you can fly out tonight. Just check with Jared and see if he can leave a day early," said Katie.

"And you can give me the additions you and Jeff have. I'll keep working tonight and email the PowerPoint," said Anne.

"Absolutely not. I want that PowerPoint on a flash drive, and I prefer to have it on my computer already. I've had that backfire on me before," Gherring frowned. "I think I'll reschedule. It may have to be January."

He strode to the door, but froze in his tracks. "Or... you could just go with us."

"Me?" Anne's heart turned over in her chest.

"That'd work," said Katie. "I'd volunteer to go in a heartbeat, but I have a meeting with the caterer on Thursday and a shower on Friday."

"And you already have a passport, right? I heard you tell Johanna you have one," said Gherring.

"You were listening?"

"I just happened to overhear. So you do have one, right?"

Anne nodded, numbly. "I guess I'd better get to work, then."

"No," said Gherring. "Ms. Carson, you call and set everything up with the jet, the pilots and the hotel. I'll talk to Jared and call the company in Bern. Ms. Best, you need to gather everything here in some organized fashion and be sure we have everything else we need for the presentation. Then we'll get home and pack. We'll leave as soon as possible."

Anne felt dizzy. Things were happening too fast.

"Are you okay with this Ms. Best? Is there some problem I don't know about?" Gherring studied her with concern lining his forehead.

"No."

"We'll finish the presentation tomorrow at the hotel in Switzerland. I'll have a suite, and we'll have plenty of room to spread out and work. Okay?"

"I'm going to Switzerland?" she asked in a squeaky voice. "Tonight?"

Gherring's face broke out in a broad grin, flashing his dimples. "Yes, you're going to Switzerland. Tonight."

He stepped out of the conference room door, closing it behind him. But he stuck his head back inside and added, "With me."

"I can't believe it, Mom! You're going to Switzerland? You're so lucky! Switzerland this week, Paris next week. What's next? Venice?" Charlie was so excited Anne saw her dancing around on the computer screen.

"Yes, and I don't have any time. I tried to get Emily, and she didn't answer. Will you tell her for me?"

"Oh, don't worry your little head about that. I'll be glad to call Em and tell her all about your fabulous surprise trip to Bern, Switzerland. On a private jet. With Steven Gherring."

"It's for a presentation, and it will be me and *Jared* and Mr. Gherring. You make it sound like a tryst."

"If I'm telling the story, I'm telling it *my* way. Besides, it sounds so much better like that. So, have you told Henri yet?"

"Ohmygosh! No, I forgot. I've got to hang up with you so I can call him."

"Bye, Mom. Skype me from Switzerland, okay?"

"Absolutely. Love you."

Anne contacted Henri on Skype. She felt guilty when she spied the dark circles under his eyes. "You are calling really late tonight. But I am glad because I missed your call earlier. I was at the doctor's office, with my sister and my niece."

"What did they say? Do they have test results yet?"

"The numbers do not look good, but we do not know for certain. They are doing the scans tomorrow and Thursday. We will know something on Friday."

"Henri, I'm so sorry. I'll keep contacting you every day, but it may be at a different time. I'm going to be in Switzerland tomorrow through the weekend."

"And why will you be in Switzerland?"

"It's for work. We're doing a big presentation in Bern."

"Yes, I know. You have told me about your work, but you were not going before. Or you did not tell me."

"It's an emergency. It's a long story that starts with Jeff Murphy..."

"That man is scum. What does he have to do with this?"

"I didn't even realize you knew him. But Gherring fired him. He was... he was making suggestions to me about... you know..."

Henri's brows furrowed. "Gherring should have never hired that man. I am glad he is gone."

"But Jeff was doing part of the presentation, and the date got moved up, and I have to go so I can help them finish tomorrow because the presentation's on Thursday. Please don't be upset, Henri."

"You are going with Steven Gherring?"

"Yes, with him and Jared. It's not like we'll ever be alone. It's my job, Henri, and it's important to me."

Henri's face relaxed. "I am sorry, angel. I do not want to cause you stress. I will not say any more about it. But if he does anything to hurt you, he will answer to me."

"Thanks, Henri. Maybe I'll get to practice my French in Bern. I'll be ready for Paris."

Henri waggled his eyebrows. "I am hoping you will practice your French with me, *mon ange*."

"If Anna-Laure is really sick, will you still want me to come next week?"

His smile fell away. "If she is sick, I will *need* you to come. Even more."

"I'm praying for her, Henri."

"*Merci!* Please be safe. I don't want to lose you. I think I could not handle any more pain."

"Okay, Henri. I'll talk to you soon." Anne hung up, with more than a little concern. Henri seemed to be more and more dependent on her. She needed to be there for Henri because he didn't seem to have anyone else.

Anne finished packing her bag and checked for the fourth time to be sure she had her passport. Then she picked up a pillow and held it to her face. She screamed into the pillow at the top of her lungs, "*I'm flying to Switzerland tonight! Ohmygosh! Ohmygosh! Ahhhhhhh!*"

She threw the pillow back onto her bed with a grin. "There—now I'm ready to go."

Chapter Eleven - High Flying

ANNE WAS TOO EXCITED TO SLEEP. Her first time to fly in a private jet. Her first time to go to another country. Her first time to get to use her passport. Her first time to visit Switzerland. Her first time to be a part of a huge business presentation involving millions of dollars' worth of assets. As if that wasn't enough, she was travelling with Steven Gherring, whose soft cashmere sweater only enhanced the appearance of his broad shoulders and hard muscles. She was grateful Jared Hanson was on the trip with her. He was almost as excited as she was, tempered only by having to leave his wife and new baby daughter behind. Despite the fact this was his first big presentation, he seemed more eager than nervous.

"This is great, isn't it?" Jared explored the spacious main cabin. "These chairs are so comfortable. And they recline. And look, this part pulls out and it will lie flat, like a bed."

"You should sleep now," said Gherring.

"But it's only eight o'clock," said Anne. "I thought we'd work for a while."

"We'll sleep on the plane, and work when we get there tomorrow. We've got an eight-hour flight and we're losing six hours. So it'll be ten o'clock when we get to Bern. Sleeping now will cut down on jet-lag."

"There's no way I can go to sleep now. I'm way too excited." Indeed Anne felt adrenaline pumping through her veins. She needed to go for a run to expel some excess energy.

"Not me," said Jared. "I'm perpetually tired. I love Emery, but she still doesn't sleep at night. I can fall asleep any time I want, and sometimes when I don't want to." He stretched his seat into a bed, grabbed a blanket, lay down, and promptly began to snore.

Meanwhile, Anne started reclining her chair, but Gherring stopped her. "Let me give you a sleeping pill. You really need to sleep, because I need you sharp tomorrow."

"I don't know. I'm kind of sensitive to drugs. I might over-react."

"Oh yeah, I remember the Benadryl incident. How about half a pill? That should just make you relax."

"Okay, I'll try it. But don't leave me behind on the plane if you can't wake me in the morning."

"I promise. But I'm taking a whole one. I need it."

"What if we oversleep?" She swallowed the proffered half-pill with a swig from a bottled water.

Gherring laughed. "The pilots would wake us up, but I've already set my watch alarm to go off forty-five minutes before we get there. Come with me, and I'll give you a quick tour first."

Anne followed him from the main cabin through a small area with a compact kitchen on one side and a table and seating area on the other.

"There's a bathroom here. Even has a small shower in the back. And the master bedroom is back here."

"Wow—this is amazing. I can't believe there's room for this on the plane. And you have a flat screen TV in here. Why am I not surprised?"

"We've got a great selection of movies and shows to watch. Not very good television reception on overseas flights."

"And do you have black lights in here and mood music? The world's richest playboy's private love plane?"

"The music starts automatically when I say the words, 'You're the most beautiful woman I've ever seen.'" He reached his hand over and felt for a button on the wall. The room was immediately filled with the sound of bagpipes. Anne giggled hysterically.

"Oops, I must have said the wrong words." He fumbled with the buttons while he spoke. "I think the correct phrase is, 'Oh baby, you're the best.'"

The music changed to soft jazz.

"Much better," she said. "You'd better remember what to say. What if someone said, 'Stop it! Stop it!'?"

He flipped the channel back to the bagpipe music.

She started giggling again. "Oh baby, you're the best."

She was rewarded with the soft jazz again, and she lay back on the bed. "What? No mirror on the ceiling? What's a love nest with no mirror on the ceiling?"

He lay down next to her and locked his fingers behind his neck. "The mirror is actually hidden under that padded panel." He pointed at the ceiling. "I've forgotten the magic words, though."

"Hmmm, let's see... *Gosh, you're really kind of fat.*"

He grinned. "Nope, that's not it. *Oh, you don't believe in shaving?*"

She chortled noisily. "*Ooo! Have you seen a doctor for that?*"

He laughed and quickly countered. "*So you actually paid good money for those?*"

This time she laughed so hard she snorted, and he cheered, "I scored—I made you snort."

They both laughed until there were tears in their eyes.

"Oh," said Anne as the music changed. "That's Norah Jones. I love her voice. So smooth. I used to listen to her all the time. Who's your favorite singer?" She relaxed, absorbing the music, letting her tension melt.

"I like listening to the Beatles, James Taylor, and old classics like Frank Sinatra. Really, I like jazz and rock and classical too. Just depends on the mood."

They studied the ceiling in silence. "You know, I hope everything comes out good with this meeting. I'm so afraid they'll hate it, and it'll be all my fault for not making a good PowerPoint."

"I'm not worried at all. If they don't go for it, I'll just buy them out and do what I want anyway. It's simply more profitable for me this way. Anyway, your presentations are great. And I'm really impressed with your grasp of the concepts. I think you've been hiding something from me. Maybe you secretly have an MBA you didn't mention. I bet you're some kind of corporate spy."

"That's it. You found me out—I'm a pie. I mean I'm a spy." She giggled. "And you, too—you're Double-O Steven!"

"Have you been drinking?"

"Hmmm? What'd you say?"

"Are you drunk?"

"No, I'm not..." She turned on her side. "It's kind of cold..."

Anne felt someone shaking her arm. "Anne... Anne you need to wake up now."

She stretched and pried her eyes open. She felt warm and cozy under her blanket. "Mmmm, I think I'll just sleep here tonight. It's a really big bed." She chuckled, reluctant to move in her relaxed state.

"Anne, you *did* sleep here. You've been asleep here for seven hours."

"What!" She jerked up, frantically looking around. She'd slept in a bed with Steven Gherring. And he didn't have a shirt on. What else had she done? She tried desperately to remember.

"I thought you might want to go pretend to be asleep out there before I wake Jared up. Not that it matters to me—being the world's richest playboy and all—but I know you worry about these things."

"Ohmygosh! Did we...?"

"Of course we didn't. You're still dressed aren't you? So am I." Her eyes fell on his bare chest. "Okay, I'm mostly dressed. I still have my pants on."

"Why didn't you make me move?"

"Really? Are you kidding? When you go to sleep, nothing will move you." He shook his head. "At least when you take a sleeping pill of any sort. Even half a pill. Anyway, do you want to go protect your reputation?"

"Yes, I do." She hurried toward the main cabin where Jared was still snoring softly in the same position. Anne lay down on her reclined chair.

He walked up behind her with a pillow and blanket and whispered, "You've got about ten minutes, if you want to snooze a little more."

"I don't think I can sleep now. My heart's beating kind of fast."

"Mine, too." His breath on her ear sent a chill down her spine.

Anne unpacked in her room at the Bellevue Palace, pausing long enough to admire the accommodations. She hadn't done a lot of traveling, but this was by far the nicest hotel she'd ever seen. Her room was small, but nicely decorated and furnished with pieces that looked custom rather than mass-produced. A relaxing blue color coated the walls, and the queen bed was covered with a lovely duvet. There was marble in the bathroom, and a guest bathrobe hung in the closet. Anne thought she'd be quite comfortable here, noting her view was similar to that of her New York apartment. She quickly freshened up and changed clothes, preparing for a long day working with Jared and Gherring in his suite on the top floor.

When Anne knocked on Gherring's door, Jared opened it with a broad smile.

"Wait 'til you see this room—it's awesome. It's even got bullet-proof glass. There're two bathrooms. And there's a view of the Bernese Alps over the Aare River. Come see."

Anne followed Jared through the suite, allowing him to give her the grand tour. His enthusiasm was contagious and Anne had the same sensation she'd gotten when visiting Gram at her estate. It was rather dream-like and surreal. She observed Gherring's amused expression as Jared exclaimed about all the great features of the Presidential Suite.

"The view is gorgeous," she agreed. "But I really love the chandelier and all the furniture. Are you sure it's okay to sit on this stuff?"

Gherring gave her a bemused smile. "We could order up a metal folding chair for you if you'd be more comfortable."

Anne had already stretched out on the couch with her laptop in her lap. "Nope, I'm fine right here." Then a terrible thought occurred. "Oh no—did Katie change the reservation for the meeting room to tomorrow?"

"Ms. Carson has taken care of all those changes with the hotels and the companies. You need to concentrate on the presentation. We can't go to sleep tonight until we're done."

"So I guess we're working though lunch and dinner?" Jared asked.

"No worries. The room service here is amazing. We'll have to hold back so we don't eat ourselves into a stupor."

The three started working in earnest, stopping for a quick lunch around two thirty. Anne had finished Jeff's PowerPoint and was entering the last of Jared and Gherring's information on slides. They were planning the logistics of the actual presentation at the meeting.

"So I guess I'm free to wander the city tomorrow." Anne was excited about the chance to explore Bern, even by herself.

"Well, actually I think I want you to be in the meeting tomorrow," Gherring said. "I've found through experience a team presentation is more easily accepted. Somehow, if it seems the ideas are just coming from me, people feel defensive. So it's very important you don't come across as a secretary. Or even as an executive assistant. You're a team member in the Contract, Merger, and Acquisition department, just like Jared."

"But you and Jared will do all the talking, right?" Anne felt a little light-headed.

"I think you should have at least a small part," Gherring said. "Nothing to be nervous about. You can just give the introductory information, and then I'll take over before we get to the parts where there can be questions."

"I don't think that's a good idea. I have this fear of public speaking. I could blow this whole thing for you."

"There are several female executives who'll be present tomorrow. They won't like it if you don't say anything at all. They'll see me as being anti-feminist and repressive. I would've brought Shanna Matheson if she weren't out on maternity leave. So this could actually be a lucky thing for us." His blue eyes bored into hers. "Of course, I won't force you to speak if you don't want to."

"I'm not refusing. I want to help, but—"

"Great—then it's settled," said Gherring with a satisfied smile. Anne felt her heart beating franticly, but made no further protest.

Jared, who'd been silently observing the exchange, winked at Anne. "Thanks for the lesson in negotiation, Mr. Gherring."

When Gherring turned his back, Anne stuck out her tongue at Jared, who laughed and reciprocated in the same fashion.

By five o'clock the group, feeling stiff from inactivity, decided by consensus to take a short break. Anne slipped her coat on and walked onto the balcony to call Henri.

"I'm standing on a balcony, overlooking the river and the Alps."

"I wish I could be there," he said. "It kills me to know you are so close. Are you at the Bellevue Palace? That's where he usually stays in Bern."

"Yes—it's amazing. We're in the Presidential Suite."

"We? You are staying with Gherring in his room?"

"No, don't be silly. Jared and I are working in the suite with Mr. Gherring. I have my own room."

"I still don't like it."

"Come on, Henri. Jealousy doesn't become you. There's nothing to be jealous of, anyway. Unless you think I'm the kind of girl who'd be in a threesome."

"Hmmm," Henri pretended to think. "No. The girls I've had threesome's with were nothing like you."

"Henri! You've actually—"

"I am teasing you. You are so easy to tease. I cannot resist. You believe anything."

Anne chuckled for a moment before sobering at the thought of Henri's niece. "Do you know any more about Anna-Laure?" Did she have more tests done?"

"She had a bone scan today. And now they've scheduled an MRI tomorrow."

"So when will you know something?"

"Probably not until Friday."

"Well, we'll be here until Saturday, I think." She realized she hadn't asked Gherring if they would return earlier since the presentation was a day early. Gherring might have scheduled a Friday return. Certainly Jared would be anxious to get home to his wife and baby Emery. "Anyway, you can call me as soon as you know something."

Back inside, Anne discovered Jared hadn't yet returned, so she got on Skype and managed to connect with Charlie.

"Just look at this room." She circled the room while aiming the camera outward. "Isn't it amazing? And that's the Alps over there. You can see them past the river."

"Wow, Mom. It's beautiful. Have you gotten to tour or shop or see anything?"

"No, but hopefully I'll get to see something on Friday before we leave. We have the big meeting tomorrow, so I'm guessing that's an all-day thing."

Gherring walked up behind her. "We don't need to leave early. I love Switzerland, even in November. We can wait until Saturday to leave."

"Awesome," said Anne. "I guess I'll see Bern on Friday."

"Did you finally get a stamp in your passport?" asked Charlie.

"I did, but we had to ask them to do it. I didn't know they don't automatically stamp your passport when you fly on a private plane."

"So, now that's off your bucket list. What's next?"

"I don't know. I also got to fly on a private jet, and that wasn't even on the list. Hmmm, maybe seeing my girls married and having grandkids."

"Oh no—you don't get to put us on your bucket list. That's strictly for things *you* can do."

"I guess that means you don't want to go hang gliding with me, then."

"Heck, yeah. I'm going with you."

"Well, either you're in the bucket with me or you're not."

"Fine, I'll promise to get married and have kids one day in the far, far future, if you'll take me with you when you go hang gliding."

"Deal."

Gherring spoke from across the room. "Emily doesn't want in on this?"

"Not hang gliding. Not Em," said Charlie.

Anne said, "Unless maybe I bribed her with a first edition of *Little Women* or *Pride and Prejudice*."

"I used to be able to talk her into anything, but she's gotten really stubborn lately," complained Charlie.

Gherring said, "I think she gets that from her mother."

"Absolutely," Charlie agreed.

"Hey, wait a minute. No ganging up. Him, I can't control." Anne nodded toward Gherring. "But you're still partially on the payroll."

"Just kidding, Mom. No need to play the money card. But even Grandpa says you've always been stubborn. He says you got it from Grandma."

"Luckily for you, Jared is back. So I'm going back to work. Otherwise we'd be having a little talk."

"Oh great. I'd love to give you 'The Talk.' Do you really think you're ready for 'The Talk'?"

Anne blushed crimson, and mumbled in a low voice, "Charlie, stop it. They might hear you." She picked up the laptop and started for the second bedroom.

"Too late! We already heard!" Jared was chuckling along with Gherring. "So this is what happens when your sweet baby girl grows up... She turns on you."

Two hours later, Anne was making a few final changes on the slides. Gherring had Jared practice his presentation, which took about an hour without questions or discussion. The bulk of the PowerPoint slides were devoted to the portion that had been Jeff's responsibility. Gherring said, "Jared's part is first, of course. Then we'll have a short break. Anne, you'll start at the beginning of part two with the introduction and just keep going for a while. Probably to about slide fifteen. When they ask a question you can't answer, I'll step in as if we planned to switch at that point."

"What about introductions and opening the meeting?" asked Jared.

"I'll do all the prep work and introduce the two of you. Jared, you've met about a third of these people, but Anne won't know anyone. I'll know all but a few."

"And they're all going to speak English?" asked Anne.

"Yes," said Gherring. "French will be their primary language, but all of them will understand English. Most will be pretty fluent, and I'm pretty fluent in French as well. Most of these people speak at least three languages."

"I didn't know you could speak French," Anne said.

"Oh yeah, he speaks French, German, and Spanish, too." He looked at Gherring. "You speak anything else?"

"I'm passable in Italian and Portuguese. I know some Mandarin Chinese, but I'd never try to conduct business in it."

Anne wondered what else she didn't know about Steven Gherring.

"I guess I should try to practice." Her hands were already shaking. Having always had an irrational fear of public speaking, she'd managed to avoid taking speech class in high school and college as well.

She started the presentation, reading from her slide notes in a tentative voice.

"Look up," said Jared. "You wrote that stuff. I know you mostly know it."

Anne tried to look up, but Gherring's stare made her incredibly nervous. Her mouth was dry, and she couldn't process her thoughts properly.

Gherring said, "I don't think that's right. Are you sure your notes are correct? Maybe you were a little careless copying from Jeff's notes. We may have to start over and double-check everything."

Her temper flared. "No, my figures are correct. Look here on the next slide, you can see how the numbers changed from year to year. That's exactly what I said. And on slide five, you can see the totals averaged over five years. I didn't make any mistakes." She fumed with indignation. She'd poured her heart and soul into that presentation, and she knew there weren't any errors.

"We're going to need to make her a little angry. She's quite fearless when she's ticked off…" Gherring grinned at Jared.

Jared's eyes were wide. "Yeah, I noticed."

Anne began to chuckle and felt the tension leave her body. "Okay, I can do this. You don't have to provoke me on purpose." After that, she kept going through the first hour of the presentation.

Gherring held up his hand. "Okay, that's enough for tonight. I'll probably take over long before we get to that point. There'll be a lot of questions on this part." He stretched. "Eight o'clock—not bad. I say we go out to eat instead of ordering in. We'll go someplace casual. Let me call the concierge, and we can meet downstairs in, say, fifteen minutes?"

Less than a ten minute drive brought them to Restaurant Meridiano. Anne was happy to let Gherring order for her, as long as it was "something good I can't get in the United States." She had a four-course meal with a matching wine for each course. She started with Vietnamese spring rolls, followed by redfish and then Simmentaler veal with a basil mash. Dessert was a chocolate bombe filled with ice cream, Grand Marnier, crunchy crisps and cream. She was absolutely stuffed, but refused to leave a morsel of the delicious dessert on her plate, no matter how miserable she felt. Both men ordered a tasting menu with twelve different entrees, and appeared equally sated and wretched.

On the way back, Jared asked, "Did you ever see that really old Alka-Seltzer commercial? I can't believe I ate the whole thing."

"I'm just glad I didn't try to actually finish all that wine. Y'all would be carrying me to my room," said Anne.

"I always eat too much at that restaurant. Every time I tell myself next time, I'll be more judicious. But it's too good to resist," said Gherring.

"Well there won't ever be a next time for me. I've got to eat everything I can on this trip," Anne said.

"You don't know you won't ever be back. You didn't even know you were coming here until two days ago," said Gherring.

Anne smiled. "You have a point. My life has changed so much in the past six weeks, I guess I really can't predict my future."

"I hear you might be living in Paris someday," teased Jared.

"Where did you hear that? That's not true," said Anne, grateful for the darkness to hide her crimson face.

"It's all the talk in the break room. All those women have evidently been after Henri DuBois for a long time. They'd only heard rumors until someone saw you talking to him the other day when they were getting coffee. It's true isn't it?"

"We've become friends, that's all." Anne glanced at Gherring as he scowled out the window. She could see him flexing his jaw muscles.

"Whatever you say…" Jared smirked. "That's not what I heard. I heard—"

"Could we change the subject, please?" Gherring interrupted. "We need to plan tomorrow morning. We'll meet in the suite at eight o'clock. I'll have a light continental breakfast there. The meeting starts at nine." He spoke with an edge of sarcasm to Anne. "Do you think you'll have trouble waking up?"

"No *sir*. I'll be fine. No need to worry."

Oblivious to the tension between the other two, Jared said, "I'm gonna sleep like a baby. No, not like a baby, because they wake up all night. I'm gonna sleep like the parent of a baby."

He chuckled to himself, while Gherring and Anne stared silently ahead, refusing to make eye contact.

"But don't worry, Mr. Gherring," Jared said. "I'll set my alarm and wake up in plenty of time."

Anne was terrified as she sat in the meeting room, waiting for the group to arrive. She'd been unable to eat any breakfast, instead pushing a crescent roll around on her plate, tearing it into pieces. Jared seemed unaware of her anxious demeanor. He chatted happily and showed her a picture of his baby his wife had emailed the night before. She tried to act interested in the photo, but her heart was pounding so hard she thought she might have a stroke. She kept her hands clenched in her lap to hide their shaking, but Gherring was not fooled. She knew he was counting on her, and she couldn't let him down. Unfortunately, this thought made her even more nervous. Why hadn't she simply refused when he told her she needed to speak? She was going to make a fool of herself and Gherring as well.

When the group arrived, trickling in, she fought the urge to run to the bathroom and throw up. She'd decided that was exactly what was going to happen, when Gherring pulled her aside and spoke in an urgent tone. "I'm worried about Jared."

"Why? What happened?"

"It's just that once before, during a previous meeting, he said something inappropriate. You know how he is. He speaks without thinking. And then he panicked and blanked out. He couldn't even finish."

"Oh no! Why did you even bring him? You should have left both of us at home."

"I just had to give him another chance. You know, with a new baby and everything."

"What do you want me to do?"

"Just stick with him while we're mingling and make sure he doesn't stick his foot in his mouth. Then be prepared to bail him out if he blanks during his presentation."

Anne nodded and hurried to guard Jared, who appeared totally at ease. Perhaps he was too much at ease. She listened carefully as he talked. Whenever he seemed to be getting a little too casual in his conversation or seemed to be ready to tell a story, Anne jumped in and asked questions, steering the talk back toward business. Several of the female board members came to join the group, asking Anne about herself. She bypassed the questions about her work experience, but talked readily about her children. The other women were older and had grown children as well, and soon they were sharing pictures of children and in some cases grandchildren. She tried to listen in on Jared's conversation as well, but so far he seemed to be pretty tame. She wondered just what Gherring meant by *inappropriate*. She breathed a sigh of relief when the time came for the presentation to start.

Gherring stood up and addressed the group in fluent French. Anne caught a few words, but mostly just laughed when everyone else laughed, as did Jared. She'd never seen Steven Gherring speak to a group before. Even though she couldn't understand what he was saying, she was drawn to him. She couldn't take her eyes off of him. His blue eyes were so clear. It was like looking at the sky. His voice was powerful, his presence magnetic. Everyone in the room was hanging on his words. It was an amazing thing to experience and observe. Finally, Gherring began introducing Jared and Anne. He switched to English for their benefit.

"So you will hear first from Mr. Jared Hanson, and later from Ms. Anne Best. As I said, this is informal. Please feel free to ask questions at any time. If your particular question will be answered further along in the presentation, we can let you know. But otherwise, we want to answer your questions as they occur." He turned the podium over to Jared.

Jared began his presentation. Although he was only thirty years old, he was smart, confident, and well spoken. Was he overconfident? Perhaps that's what got him into trouble. Anne listened carefully, ready to jump in at the first sign of trouble. She was so concerned with Jared she forgot about her own upcoming presentation. She'd worry about that later. There were a number of questions Jared fielded easily. He hadn't shown any sign of going blank up to this point. Then someone asked a question Anne knew was answered on an upcoming slide.

"I believe that's on slide forty or forty-one. Am I right Jared?"

Jared looked ahead on the presentation. "Yes, you're right as usual, Anne. That answer is coming up three slides from now." He sent her a grateful smile, but he didn't look particularly stressed. She wondered what it took to make him forget everything. Or perhaps he'd already figured out how to prevent that from happening again. She had to make sure he did well. He needed this job to support his family, especially since his wife had chosen to stay home with baby Emery.

Finally, Jared got to the end of his section and answered all the questions, with Gherring fielding a few and putting off some questions until after the next presentation. Gherring declared a fifteen-minute break and refreshments were served in the back of the room. Since Anne no longer felt the need to worry about Jared, she began to get nervous about her presentation again. She felt the blood drain from her face and her tongue felt as if it were sticking to the roof of her mouth. Gherring approached her with glass of water. She took it with trembling hands, and he watched her take a sip.

"Thanks for helping. He did quite well this time. Much better than before."

Anne nodded her head, but her mind was racing along with her heart. She was starting to feel a bit faint again, when Gherring suddenly grabbed her hand. Startled, she turned to look at him and noticed his face looked pained.

"What's wrong?"

"I don't know." He let out a slow breath. "I have a pain in my abdomen. But don't let anyone know."

"What if it's appendicitis?"

He gave her a strained smile. "It's going to have to wait. I'm going to sit down right over there next to you." He took another deep breath and grimaced. "Walk with me, okay?"

She followed and watched him sit down gingerly. "How are you going to be able to finish the presentation? You're in pain. This is ridiculous. We should cancel—"

"No, this is important to me. Please... I'll be fine. Just go as long as you can with the presentation. Maybe if I rest a bit, the pain will ease up." He bit his lip and breathed slowly. "It's time. You've got to do this... for me."

"Let me tell Jared to call a doctor..."

"No," he hissed. "Don't say anything." He frowned at her, but she returned the glare.

"Okay, but I'm watching you. I'll put a stop to this whole thing if I think I need to."

"It's easing up a bit. It may just be that twelve-course meal from last night."

She could see the pain etched on his face, even though he said it was getting better. He was probably lying to keep her from calling off the meeting. She needed to hurry this thing along and get him some medical treatment.

"Excuse me. *Excusez-moi*! If we can gather again, please. Feel free to bring your refreshments with you."

The board members obediently returned to the table. Anne glanced at Gherring, who was studying his handout. At least he wasn't clutching his abdomen. She forced herself to focus on the presentation. Gone were the nerves that had plagued her earlier. She pulled up the first slide and started speaking, while keeping Gherring in her side vision. Anne proceeded through ten slides before the first question came up. She glanced at Gherring, but he averted his eyes downward. He must be feeling worse. She fielded the question and continued on.

She was so preoccupied with concern for Gherring she went through the presentation on auto drive. She'd spent so many hours on the preparation and study to understand the concepts she didn't really need to think about what she was saying. She noticed Gherring moved slightly and sat back in his chair. From the corner of her eye he almost appeared to be relaxed and smiling. But when she glanced his direction the smile dissolved into a grimace and his right hand was pressed to his side. Anne tried to recall which side the appendix was on. Wasn't it the right side?

Someone directed a question at Gherring, but Anne rushed to protect him. "I believe the answer to that question is coming up here on the next slide."

She proceeded far past the point she'd originally aimed for. When the door opened, she noticed with relief it was one o'clock. Time for lunch. She could check on Steven and get him to a hospital if need be.

To Anne's surprise, when Gherring stood, he appeared to be pain-free.

"Ladies and gentlemen, it seems lunch is served next door. We'll take up where we left off after we eat. This door will be locked so you can leave your things at the conference table."

As all the board members filed out the door, Anne grabbed his arm and forced him into his chair.

"You shouldn't be standing. Should I call the doctor now?"

"Oh, no. I feel quite fine now." He grinned.

"I don't believe you could suddenly feel fine. You were in pain the entire time. You can't risk your health for a meeting, no matter how important you think it is."

He gave a hearty laugh. "I assure you, I have no pain whatsoever. It must have been indigestion."

But Anne was trembling now. "I know you're covering something up. No one recovers like that. You were holding your side five minutes ago—your right side. Isn't that where your appendix is?"

Gherring stood up and grabbed her shaking shoulders and forced her into the chair. "I'm sorry. I lied to you—"

"I knew it—" Anne tried to jump up, but he kept pressure on her shaking shoulders to keep her seated.

"No, I lied to you when I told you I was hurting."

"What? What do you mean?"

"Well... You were just so nervous. I had to appeal to that selfless nature of yours and get you worried about someone else. I knew you'd be great if you weren't thinking about it."

"But... But I saw you... I watched you the whole time."

Gherring immediately demonstrated a pained look and pressed his hand to his side. Then he changed back again to his smiling, smug demeanor.

"I can't believe you! I can't believe you'd let me worry about you for two hours!" Now Anne was trembling from anger rather than fear. "You let me go twice as far as I was supposed to go—I was worried *sick* about you!"

"But can't you see I did it for your own good? Look what a great job you did. You weren't nervous at all, right?"

"You manipulated me!"

"What's up guys?" Jared approached the pair.

"Mr. Gherring lied to me to distract me. He made me think he was having an appendicitis attack."

"Really? Awesome job, Mr. Gherring. You must be a great actor. I'm learning a lot from you."

"It's not funny at all! He probably said something to you as well. I noticed you didn't have any trouble suddenly going blank this time."

Jared seemed confused. "Well I don't ever really get nervous, but this is the first time I've done one of these. Still, I never expected to forget my presentation—Ow!" He looked at Gherring. "Why'd you kick me?"

"But Mr. Gherring told me that last time you..." Her voice faded and she skewered Gherring with her eyes.

"Now Anne, can't you see it was for the best?" he pleaded.

She whipped around and stomped out the door, slamming it behind her.

Anne was furious, but she was also hungry. She hadn't been able to eat breakfast. Darned if she was going to miss lunch because of Gherring. She clomped into the adjacent room, searching for a table with one empty chair. She certainly wasn't going to let Gherring sit by her.

This is just what Henri warned her about. He'd told her Gherring used people. What was it Henri had asked? "Has he ever done something to keep you in his control? Has he made you feel foolish?" Yes, he certainly had. And this was not the first time, either.

Anne's furrowed eyes brightened when she heard someone call her name. Henri was standing in the doorway.

"Anne, there you are." He reached her in three steps, picked her up in a bear hug and swirled her around, to the delight and entertainment of the company board members.

"Ohmygosh! What are you doing here?"

"It is only three hours on the train. I could not have you this close and not come to see you. Good surprise? I was afraid you would tell me not to come."

Anne hugged him again, all the stress of the morning causing tears to form in her eyes. "Oh Henri, it's the best surprise. Can we go somewhere for lunch? I'll have to come back, but I really need to get out of here."

Henri looked at her puddled eyes. "What is wrong? No do not tell me now. Wait until we are alone. Come. I know the best place just down the block."

He took her hand, leading her out the door toward the lobby exit.

"Where are you going?" Gherring's strained voice called out before they could reach the revolving door. Anne halted in her tracks, cringing at the irritation in his tone.

She remained motionless, but Henri turned around to face Gherring. His voice cut the air like a knife. "I am taking her to lunch. I will bring her back when she is ready. No sooner." He put his arm around Anne's trembling shoulders and ushered her out the door.

"What happened? What did he do?" Henri asked when he got her outside.

"I didn't say it was him…"

"You did not have to say. I could see it. I could see how you reacted to his voice. Did he make a pass at you? I will kill him for hurting you."

"No, it's nothing like that. He didn't even touch me." Anne searched for the right words. "It's… It's like you warned me. He manipulated me. He lied to me. It wasn't a big thing, and I suppose it turned out okay. But he made me feel like a fool. After I worried about him for two hours."

"Why would *you* be worried about Gherring?"

"He pretended to be in pain. He was holding his side and making a terrible face. I thought he had appendicitis."

"But why would he do that?"

"He did it so I would be thinking about him instead of thinking about how nervous I was. You know… when I was giving the presentation."

"Gherring let you give the presentation? Why did he do that?"

"Something about needing to win over the female board members. It was all just like you said. He used me to get what he wanted."

"And how was your presentation?"

"I think it was okay. It was all just a blur to me."

"I am so proud of you. Did I not say you were worth so much more than just a secretary? Did I not say? So Gherring has finally seen that you are valuable. And now he will try to take you from me."

"Oh he's not trying to take me. Believe you me. I'm just a big joke to him. You should have seen him afterwards, laughing because I believed his act." Anne couldn't decide if she was more embarrassed she'd fallen for his ploy, or she'd been so ridiculously nervous in the first place.

He stopped walking and drew her into his arms. He held her there while pedestrians passed around them, hurrying to their destinations. "You are not a joke to *me,* my angel."

Anne felt the tension drain from her body, and she relaxed in his arms. "Thank you, Henri. Today, you're *my* angel." She smiled at him. Then she took his hand and pulled him along the sidewalk. "Now come and feed me. I'm starving."

But he stopped her again. "I know he hurt your feelings. But I was so afraid he had... I thought he had hurt you in a different way. I was afraid you were starting to fall in love with him."

"I'm not in love with Steven Gherring. Henri, I've only said 'I love you' to one man in my life. You've got to understand, love is more than a word or a feeling to me. It's a commitment. I don't expect to say those words again unless I'm positive I'm willing to commit to a life-long relationship." Anne held up her chin and spoke with passion. "I hope that scares you just a little."

"I should probably be afraid, but somehow I'm not." He held her face in his hands. "But I have not said the words to you yet, and I will take your pledge to heart. If you hear the words from me, they will have the same meaning." His gaze was so intense she had to look away.

When the food came, Anne attacked her plate. "I can't believe how hungry I am."

"It is from the adrenaline rush. You will get used to it. You learn to let the nervous energy help you to be sharp. You channel the nerves to help you think."

"Well I don't plan to ever do that again. It's way too stressful."

"So you say now. But you will see. It is addicting. When you go back and Gherring closes the deal and you know that you had a part in that—you will want to do it again." He leaned in close. "I am willing to make a wager..."

She was immediately suspicious. "I don't think I'm very good at bets. I probably shouldn't."

"I know some of those people. We have met before. One of the women... Gherring is right... Some of the women demand to have another woman playing a role when they work together."

"They don't know I'm his executive assistant. They think I'm part of the CMA group."

Henri raised his eyebrows. "Is that so? I think I can use that information to my advantage... Oh don't look distressed. I will not spoil Gherring's deal. But I think I can bargain for something good."

"Don't make him mad at me. I still have to work for him."

Henri looked at her with a devious twinkle in his eyes. "Trust me, *mon ange*."

Anne and Henri walked in the conference room door just as Gherring was about to begin the afternoon session. The smile Gherring gave to Henri didn't reach his eyes. Henri, however, grinned and shook Gherring's hand, pulling him to the side to speak to him. Gherring's eyes narrowed, his lips pressing together in a hard straight line, but he nodded assent. Anne had taken her place at the head of the table next to Gherring. Henri strolled around the table chatting to his friends and acquaintances before making an obvious point of placing a chair for himself next to Anne's. Her face hot and her pulse throbbing in her temples, Anne pretended to study her handout.

"Let's begin now," said Gherring, commanding the attention of everyone in the room. "We're delighted to have Henri DuBois visiting with us. I know many of you already know him. If this is your first time to meet Henri, let me just say 'I'm sorry' in advance." Gherring laughed and the group joined in... even Henri, who seemed to relish the introduction.

Gherring continued, "As you may know, Monsieur DuBois' company, La Porte, has had a cooperative agreement with Gherring Inc. for a number of years. This association has been fruitful and profitable for both companies, as I'm sure Henri can attest. He will be an excellent resource should you have any questions about that option."

After this introduction, Gherring plunged forward in the presentation. Anne found herself mesmerized by him, even though she'd prepared the PowerPoint herself. The time passed quickly. Questions were answered. The companies deliberated privately and questioned Henri about his association with Gherring Inc. And Gherring closed the deal by seven o'clock, without ever threatening to actually buy out the other two companies, although perhaps they knew he was considering the possibility.

"You were right," Anne told Henri. "It was exciting. It was fun to be a part of it all. At least it was fun after my part was over."

One of the female board members approached Anne and Henri. "Henri, someone is finally going to tame you?"

"Only because I asked you so many times, and you turned me down. How is Charles? You are ready to leave him for me?"

"One day, Henri, I might say 'yes'. Then what will you do?" She laughed, and turned to Anne. "Ms. Best, it was so nice to meet you. Watch out for Henri! I am looking forward to working with you in the future. Do you have a card?"

"No, I don't have a card with me, but if you need me, you can reach me on the main line."

"Excellent. And here is my card."

Anne took the card, the first of many. Soon Gherring joined their group along with Jared, exchanging greetings and promises of future communication. Gherring kept a close eye on Henri and Anne, until the last person left the room.

Henri clapped his hands with glee. "Well done, Gherring. That should bring a few billion more into your coffers. Where are you taking us to celebrate?"

"Us?" asked Anne.

"Yes," Gherring spoke with obvious irritation. "Henri *suggested* he should be allowed to participate in the second half of the meeting and the celebration after, in exchange for keeping his mouth shut about my *secretary*."

"Yes, and I believe I did my part to help close the deal. It was Sir Walter Scott who said, 'O what a tangled web we weave, when we practice to deceive.' He was correct—*N'est-ce pas*, Gherring?"

Gherring narrowed his eyes, and Henri said, "And the other part of the deal?"

"I have *already* apologized to Ms. Best, but I will say it again." He turned to Anne and caught her chin with his hand, turning her to face him. "Ms. Best, as I have told you before, everything I do *means* something to me. I wasn't making light of you. I simply wanted to make you feel better. I never meant to cause you more emotional stress."

Their eyes locked together, and for a moment Anne was lost in a blue ocean. She floated into their depths and forgot anyone else was in the room. She regretted her harsh judgment of his actions. It was Henri's turn to look annoyed.

"Ah-hem!" said Jared. "Aren't you going to apologize to *me* for making up that story about how I blanked out on a presentation? Only don't grab my neck—I'm afraid you'll choke me."

Gherring dropped his hand from her face.

"I'm *so* hurt!" Jared used an effeminate voice and started chuckling.

The tension broke as the others joined in.

Anne giggled. "Really, Jared. My feelings weren't hurt. I was just indignant for *you*. And the appendicitis thing was exciting. After all, I've never actually gotten to see one burst open before. I could've marked that off my bucket list. Could've been even better than getting my passport stamped."

Jared said, "Now about that celebration..."

A dinner that could have been awkward, with a glaring contest between Gherring and Henri, was instead incredibly jovial. No one was able to maintain a glum attitude for more than a few seconds with Jared constantly entertaining them. One could almost imagine Gherring and Henri were friends. Almost.

"... And we looked everywhere for that pacifier. Finally, at midnight, I was going out to the car to buy a new one from the store. But when I sat down in the car, I felt this hard lump in the back of my underwear..."

Anne had tears pouring out of her eyes, her mascara long gone after a night of sidesplitting stories about Jared wrestling with newfound fatherhood.

"Stop, Jared! I need to catch my breath!" She giggled and wiped her face with her napkin. Anne waited until Jared was telling a new story to Gherring. Then she leaned over and whispered to Henri, "When do you have to go back? Tonight or tomorrow?"

"I have to go back tonight. We meet with the doctors tomorrow. They will tell us the results."

238

Anne reached out to take his hand. "I don't know if you'll feel like talking, but call me if you do. I'm praying. I want to know."

"I will call you. I'm so afraid. They haven't said the word cancer, yet. But…" Henri choked a little. "She doesn't deserve this. I wish it was me."

Anne squeezed his hand, but Henri excused himself from the table and went to compose himself. Gherring and Jared turned questioning eyes to Anne.

"I don't know if he'd want me to tell you…" Anne started.

"Well I overheard the word *cancer*," said Jared.

"Please don't say anything, Jared. It's not him—it's a family member. And they don't know for sure yet. Just act like everything's normal."

"The bill's paid already. We'll leave when he returns. We won't ask any questions," Anne was relieved to see sympathy in Gherring's eyes.

"I'd never say anything. I'm not *that* insensitive. I'm thinking what if it was Emery."

When Henri returned, the foursome went to the car. The mood had turned somber, and no one seemed inclined to talk. Henri asked, "Can you take me to the train station on the way back?"

"Henri, if you want to stay the night, Gherring Inc. will pay for a room. You really did help close the deal today. I never actually thanked you."

"No, I need to be back before the morning. But thank you for the offer."

At the station, Anne walked in with Henri while the others waited in the car. Out of Gherring's sight, she hugged him hard, and they shed a few more tears together.

"I'm praying, Henri. I wish I could do more. You rescued me today, and I won't forget it. I owe you, now."

"You are still coming next week, right?"

Anne smiled. "I've got the ticket taped to my bathroom mirror! I look at it every day. But Henri, you don't have to entertain me when I come. If you need to be at home or at the hospital, I'll be there with you."

"Of course you would say that, *mon ange*. I will have time to show Paris to you, no matter what happens."

Anne stood on her toes and kissed him on the cheek.

"I cannot believe that I, the great Henri DuBois, am reduced to a kiss on the cheek. Next week, I hope to kiss these again." He touched her lips gently with his finger before he turned and departed.

When Anne returned to the car, Jared and Gherring were discussing the schedule for the next day. "I'd love to see Switzerland, don't get me wrong," said Jared. "But I miss my wife and my baby girl. So I was thinking about getting a commercial flight home. You said I was getting a bonus if we closed the deal. You could just take the extra cost out of my bonus."

Anne said, "You don't have to do that—I feel bad. Mr. Gherring, it's okay if we go back tomorrow. I still got a stamp on my passport, even if I didn't do any sightseeing."

Gherring silenced them without raising his voice. "Jared, you can go back any time you please, and Gherring Inc. will pay for the ticket. This will be a lucrative deal at some point in the future. I am certain of it. However, Anne, as I was telling Jared, I have plans to go to Jungfrau tomorrow. You can come along," he offered, his blue eyes twinkling with mischief, "or go back early with Jared if you prefer."

"Well, I don't know what Jungfrau is, but I'm going!" She grinned so hard it hurt.

Anne was so excited about the trip she arrived twenty minutes early to Gherring's suite for breakfast. She knocked gingerly on the door, and listened for sounds of stirring inside. Then the elevator door opened and the breakfast cart emerged, heading for the Presidential Suite. This time she rapped loudly on the door, and Gherring opened the door clad only in a towel, his hair still dripping. The butler was unfazed by his state of undress, pushing the cart into the room and setting up the grand breakfast on the table.

She lagged behind, expecting Gherring would hurry to his room to change. Instead, he lounged casually and chatted in French with the butler before giving him a tip. She tried to act nonchalant. After all, she'd seen his chest and his legs before, in the gym. Why was her heart racing this time? It was nothing new. Just a chest. Well, not just a chest. A very nice, well-muscled chest with a firm stomach underneath. He certainly didn't have the stomach of a fifty year old. There didn't seem to be any flab there at all. Didn't all fifty-year-old men have at least a little paunch? He looked very fit, but it was nothing she hadn't seen before. Maybe it was the fact he had on a towel. There was that vague idea it was *only* a towel, and it might somehow fall off. Not that she hoped it would. It was just that it might—you never knew. But it looked like it was tucked in pretty well. It probably wouldn't fall off. Not that she wanted it to.

"… Hello… Anne… Are you in there?" He was talking to her. Ohmygosh, he was talking to her! The butler was gone already. When did he leave? How long had she been standing there staring at his towel?

"Oh! I'm sorry. I was thinking about being hungry—I mean—thinking about breakfast." Anne could hear her own heartbeat in her ears.

Gherring, however, acted totally oblivious. "You're hungry? Let's see what they've brought us." He walked between her and the table and bent over to examine the contents under the silver domes. This afforded her a fantastic view of his backside. Under that towel. And when he bent over… Did the towel shift a little? Was it lower than before? Ohmygosh, what was she doing?

Anne promptly turned her back to Gherring. "I think you should go and get dressed. I shouldn't have come so early."

Gherring made a sound behind her. Was he laughing? She whipped around, but Gherring's face was unreadable. "I'm sorry if I made you uncomfortable. You've seen me shirtless before."

"Yes but… it's different… you're in a towel."

"Well, you can't see through it, can you?"

"No, it's just… Please go get dressed."

Gherring smiled enigmatically. "As you wish."

And he disappeared into the bedroom.

With Gherring properly attired, Anne was once again able to focus on what she really loved—food. They had eggs benedict—her favorite. And it was the best eggs benedict she had ever tasted.

"Wow." Gherring's dimples peeked out as he watched her eating. "I'm not sure I've ever made a woman look that happy before. All that effort and all it took was eggs benedict."

"This is not just eggs benedict. It's the best ever. I don't know what they did to it, but… Wow!"

"I guess seeing the glacier at Jungfraubroch will be a letdown after the eggs benedict."

"Oh, what time are we leaving? I need to brush my teeth."

"The train leaves at eight a.m., and we'll be gone all day. Dress warmly. Bring gloves and a hat."

Anne rushed downstairs to pack her day bag.

"This is amazing! It's so beautiful!" Anne felt like a broken record. She couldn't help herself. She kept exclaiming about the scenery from the window of the train as it sped along the railway. "What's the name of this lake?"

"That's Lake Brienz. Our first stop is Interlaken, which is on the lake. But we won't tour there until we're on the way home. I want to get you up to the top of Jungfrau before the afternoon clouds roll in. Hopefully, we'll have an incredible view."

Anne smiled so much her cheeks hurt, still mesmerized by the scenery. The grass was still green, and the Alps had a sprinkling of snow on top. Gherring said, "You should come back in the winter. It looks like a picture postcard, especially up in the mountains."

Gherring shifted a bit to point out the window, and she suddenly became aware of his leg pressing against hers.

"What did you say? I... I missed it." She tried to concentrate on his words, but she could only hear a distant sound in her head. Why did he still affect her this way? She'd tried to make herself see Gherring objectively. It worked for her brain, but her body just wouldn't listen. She could still picture him wearing nothing but a towel. What was he saying?

Anne nodded her head and fabricated an all-encompassing answer. "I see." She hoped that comment would make sense with what he had told her. It was probably some factoid about the geography or the history of Switzerland. He seemed to be a walking encyclopedia.

"You see?" Gherring looked at her quizzically. "I asked if you'd like to take a hike along the lake this afternoon. What did you think I said?"

Anne's cheeks filled with color. "Oh, I'm sorry. I must still be groggy from that Benadryl I took last night."

"Really? I thought you said you were never taking a sleeping pill again."

"I did say that didn't I?" Why did she ever try to lie? It always backfired.

"Yes, you did. And having observed you after taking sleep aids, I think you should avoid them at all costs." Gherring actually looked concerned, and Anne felt guilty for lying to him.

"Sure, okay. You're right. I won't do it again."

"But why were you having trouble sleeping? Are you worried about Henri's family member?"

"No, I wasn't... I mean, yes I was worried, but that didn't keep me from sleeping. I slept fine, really. I just... Ohmygosh! I'm such a terrible liar. I'm surprised I made it through my childhood. Although, I guess I really didn't lie as a child either. I've just never been good at it, you know..."

Gherring was baffled. "You lied about being worried? Just because I asked about Henri? I'm not such a terrible person I'd be upset when you're worried about something like this. Even if it is Henri! I don't wish bad things on him or his family. Why would you lie about it?"

"No, I didn't lie about being worried. I lied about the sleeping pill. Okay? I didn't take a Benadryl, and I don't even remember why I lied about it anymore." Just one more little lie. Please let it work this time. "Now *please*, can we just change the subject?"

Gherring studied her with narrowed eyes. "Sure. What would you like to talk about?"

Anne racked her brain. She needed to think objectively about Gherring. "Let's talk about you. When was the last time you went on a serious date?"

"I don't think I care for this topic."

"How about something more general. What characteristics do you think make the ideal woman?"

"A woman who minds her own business."

"No seriously, this could be fun."

"Okay, then you go first. How would you describe your ideal man?"

"Hmmm." Anne twisted a strand of hair around her finger. "You know, I've never given it much thought. I've always been good at picking out people who go together. But I picked out a man so long ago…" She gave Gherring a challenging look. "You have to list as many characteristics as I do. Deal?"

"Deal."

Anne contemplated her list. Obviously handsome and a great body would go on her list, but she wasn't going to mention that first. "Hmmm… well-educated, great conversationalist—"

Gherring grinned. "Ditto."

"No way—you have to think of your own. You go next, that way you can't cheat."

"Beautiful, with a great body. What else matters?" He laughed.

"Ditto," Anne chuckled.

"Now who's cheating?"

"Okay, how about this one? Someone who'll put me first and someone I would be willing to put first in my own life."

"No, that's too hard to measure. How about hair color, eye color?"

"Blond and brown," she replied quickly. She certainly wasn't going to say dark hair and blue eyes.

"Oh." Gherring's dimples appeared suddenly. "Too bad for Henri. Shall I be the one to break the news?"

She chuckled. "Stop it! Now don't you want a woman who isn't interested in your money?"

"Why would I want that? I'm an old fart now. Women aren't really interested in me for myself anymore. Money's my only real asset."

"That's not true at all. There's a lot more to you than your money."

Gherring looked away, dejected. "If I wasn't rich, no woman would look twice at me."

"You can't really believe that. You're smart and handsome and you…" Anne stopped talking when she noticed Gherring's shoulders shaking with laughter. "And you did it to me *again*!"

"Don't stop now. I'm really enjoying your evaluation." He chuckled, but grabbed her hand and squeezed it. "No, please, don't be mad. I'll cooperate this time."

He heaved a great sigh.

"I want someone I won't be bored with after six months. I'd like someone who'd be fun to grow old with. I want someone who helps me to be the best man I can be. I want someone who needs me as much as I need her."

"Wow... That's really good." Anne was acutely aware of his hand holding hers, yet she maintained her composure. "But talk about hard to measure. How would you ever know?"

"Well, in the past, I would've said you couldn't really know. You'd have to be willing to take a chance."

"But now?" Anne attempted to slide her hand away casually, but Gherring maintained his firm, yet gentle, hold.

"But now I'd say I'd never met the right woman."

This time Anne succeeded in slipping her hand away to gesture with it. "You see—that's exactly what Gram and I said. We just need to find you the right woman." She smiled with satisfaction.

"And what about you?"

Anne felt herself blushing, and leaned down to re-tie her boots and hide her face. "What about me?"

"I gave you four more qualities. Now you owe me four more. And they have to be really good ones." When she met his gaze, the intensity made her breath catch in her throat.

"I'd want someone... someone I could trust. They'd have to love my girls, too. Someone with integrity. And someone who'd hold me when I cry and not be awkward about it, because sometimes I just need to cry."

Gherring left her alone with her melancholy reflections for several minutes before speaking. "Would you like to change the subject again?"

She released a big breath. "Absolutely! I'll do better this time. I've got a great question. Where are we going for lunch?"

The scenery was increasingly beautiful as the journey progressed. Anne exclaimed at the quaint towns, waterfalls, and lakes peppered among the mountain slopes and valleys. At Lauterbrunnen, they boarded a cog train that took them to Kleine Scheidegg. From there, another cog train traversed up a steep incline for the last leg of their journey. Eighty percent of the fifty-minute ride was inside a tunnel carved deep in the solid mountain rock. The train arrived at the Jungfraujoch, the highest train station in Europe.

"This is great," he declared as they exited the train. "I don't see any clouds. Let's go to the observation terrace first."

Even with her hat and gloves and heavy coat, the wind whipped through to her skin. But the views from the terrace made her forget the ice and cold.

"We're at eleven thousand three hundred and sixty-eight feet here. There's no view like this anywhere else in the world."

But she needed no convincing. Despite the cold, she stayed on the terrace for almost thirty minutes, until he urged her to follow him inside.

"I'm starving," she said.

"I don't know how you stay so thin with that appetite of yours."

"I'd rather run a few miles so I can eat more. Wouldn't you?"

"You've got a point."

The food was warm and filling, if not spectacular cuisine.

"I think I feel better now. I was a little light-headed."

"Could be the altitude. Drink the rest of your water."

"I don't really like drinking much. It's always been a problem."

"So prove to me you aren't stubborn, and drink the rest of that water."

"What about you?" She pouted, pointing at his water bottle. He immediately upended it and drank the entire content. His brows arched as he looked at her still-full bottle of water.

"Fine," she said. "I'll drink... as much as I can, anyway."

It took five minutes for her to drink half of her water. He checked the time. "Oh, the ice palace is closing soon."

"Ice palace? Let's go now. I don't want to miss the ice palace. What *is* the ice palace?"

"We'll go as soon as you finish your water. Maybe it'll still be open."

She rolled her eyes and chugged down the rest of her water. "Let's go, and don't look so smug."

Entering the ice palace, she noted the hours, commenting they'd been in no danger of missing it.

"Hmmm... What do you know? I must have been mistaken about the hours."

246

They walked through a long tunnel carved in the glacier to reach a large hall with several chambers and small connecting passages. Everything was made of ice—the floor, ceiling, walls, and arches. Everywhere were magnificent ice figurines of birds and animals, so intricately carved they were almost life-like. The lights cascaded through the ice and reflected from the shiny surfaces. Some sculptures were enhanced with colored lights, as well.

Anne studied every carving, while Gherring studied Anne.

"Why aren't you looking at the ice sculptures?" she asked. "Are you bored?"

"No. But it's more fun to watch you. You're like a little kid. You get so excited about everything. I've seen it all before, but now I can see it through your eyes." He paused. "You know, Anne—"

"Look—a bear! Will you take my picture with it to send to the girls?"

He sighed, reaching for her phone. "Sure."

"Too bad it's November," Gherring said as they changed trains at Lauterbrunnen. "We could stop here and go see Trammel Falls, but they close at the end of October. In the summer, we could hike through Lauterbrunnen Valley. It's about a three-hour hike and there're seventy-two waterfalls. And if it was January, we could go stay in Wengen and go skiing—it's such a beautiful place to ski. There's this great little bakery you can stop at on your way back from a day of skiing." He heaved a big breath. "I've got to bring you back."

"Since everyone here thinks I'm in the CMA department, I guess I'd have an excuse. That is, if you ever had to come over here for business again."

He frowned. "I could bring you here—"

Her phone trilled, interrupting his thoughts. "Oh no, it's Henri." She took the call with trembling fingers, while Gherring moved to allow her some privacy. "Henri? Hi, did you hear something?"

Anne could hear him trying to catch his breath. "They have to do a biopsy to confirm, but they say it is most likely cancer." Henri was choking back tears.

"Oh no, Henri. I'm so sorry. She's so young." Her own tears were falling freely. "What... What does this mean? What will they do for her?"

"I do not know yet. They said… They said possible amputation." Henri's voice cracked. "And we would be upset about that, but they talked about better survival rates… And we can't lose her! I can't lose her!" He sobbed now, and Anne cried with him. "I… You will still pray?"

"Yes, of course I'll pray for her."

"The biopsy is tomorrow. They could schedule surgery before you come, or while you are here. I… My sister is calling me. I have to go. Please pray."

Anne disconnected and sat staring at her phone with tears streaming down her face.

"Anne?" His voice was tender as he sat beside her. He opened his arms, and she fell against him, crying as he held her, gently rubbing her arm. He didn't complain when his shirt was wet with her tears, but pulled her closer and tucked her head against his chest.

He didn't ask her any questions, but when her tears began to diminish, the story of the little girl she'd never met spilled out from her broken heart. The sweet Anna-Laure who'd just gotten a pony for her seventh birthday. The uncle who loved her like a father. The terror of the word—*cancer*.

And still he held her. Silent. Listening. His presence somehow soothing her aching soul. She began to cry again, because it felt so good to be held. But she knew it was an empty promise. He held her because that was the kind of man he was. He would do the same for any woman in distress. It didn't mean anything. For a moment, she imagined how it would be if he loved her. And then she cried for herself, for the woman who'd stood alone for fifteen years with no one to hold her.

Anne was still feeling glum when they departed the train at Interlaken, but she didn't want to ruin the trip for Mr. Gherring. He seemed content to stroll the streets and go into the shops. Her mood began to brighten as she shopped for presents. She found an entire store devoted to music boxes, and chose two small ones for Emily and Charlotte. The decorative boxes fascinated her with exposed mechanisms that played intricate tunes and harmonies.

One store displayed alphorns, and the merchant let her blow on one. She was thrilled when she *finally* produced a semblance of a horn sound. Gherring snapped a picture of her face as she strained to play the cumbersome instrument. She found a shop devoted to Swiss Army knives, and purchased a small one for her father.

When the stores closed, Gherring took her to Restaurant Benacus, where he ordered a seven course tasting meal for each of them. Despite her protests to the contrary, she managed to eat a significant portion of each sampling. She declared this to be the 'best food so far!'

Back on the train, she struggled to stay awake for the hour-long trip back to Bern. But she finally succumbed to exhaustion, physical and emotional, and fell asleep leaning against the window. When she awoke, she was somehow oriented the other direction, with her head against Steven's side. She sat up abruptly, apologizing under her breath.

"Thank goodness you're awake," he whispered. "You know you're really heavy, and you snore profusely."

"I do? That's awful. I didn't know. How embarrassing—"

"Anne, I'm teasing you. You're not heavy, and you don't snore."

"Stop doing that—I can't tell when you're being serious and when you're teasing."

"It's just so easy. You'll believe anything. But you know, you do drool a bit."

"I do?" This time she looked at him, and huge tears formed in her eyes and rolled down her cheeks.

"Wait, don't cry. I was just teasing, again. I'm sorry. I didn't—"

Anne began to laugh. "Gotcha! And it serves you right."

"Now that was pretty low. Those were real tears."

"Just another of my many hidden talents."

"Why are we leaving so early?" Anne grumbled as they boarded the jet at five a.m.

"You'll be glad tomorrow. The jet lag is much worse going back because we lose six hours. This'll help you go to sleep at a normal time tonight."

"No it won't, because I'm going right back to sleep."

"No, you're not, because I'm not going to let you."

"Ha! You can try." She pulled the lever to lean her seat back.

"We have things to discuss—like how we're going to handle your transition."

"What transition?"

"Your transition to CMA. The problem is I still need an executive assistant."

"You're moving me? To Contract, Merger and Acquisition? I thought that was just a ploy."

"Well, you've already proven yourself. And we'll need you to work with these companies in the months ahead, now you've established a working relationship."

"But I don't have any business education. No one in that department would have any respect for me."

"Yes. I've been thinking, you might want to take some night courses. Gherring Inc. would pay for them."

"Wait! Just stop for a second and let me think. This is a bit too much all at one time." She put her head in her hands, rubbing her forehead.

"And I'll have to get another executive assistant. We can probably still get the candidate I planned to hire before you arrived and shook things up. I think her name was Lana Stewart. Don't you want this? You'll get a raise, of course."

"I... I just need to think..."

"Well, you've got six hours to think. Are you awake now?"

"Oh, yeah. I'm awake for sure."

Anne's heart was contracting in her chest. Was this a promotion? She guessed so, but maybe it was simply his way of getting rid of her. In the CMA department, she'd hardly ever see him. She couldn't turn this down—it was the opportunity of a lifetime. He'd even offered to pay for further education. She could eventually get her MBA. Her dad had always been a little disappointed she didn't use her degree. He'd told her, "You were made for great things!" But she'd felt fulfilled just raising her children. And now her children didn't need her anymore...

Wasn't this what she really wanted? A chance to be challenged? A chance to be more than just a secretary? Why wasn't she thrilled? She knew the answer. She'd looked forward to seeing Steven Gherring each day, even when they didn't interact a lot. Now, after spending so much time with him, she realized how much she was going to miss him. She felt desolate already.

The plane's engines droned, and her head hurt. Maybe it was from lack of sleep, or maybe it was from worrying about his plans to move her to a new job in a new department. But whatever the reason, it hurt so much she couldn't think anymore.

She glanced at Gherring, who was reading a newspaper. "Do you have anything for a headache? Ibuprofen? Aspirin?"

Gherring's eyebrows knit together. "Sure. Is it a migraine?" He didn't wait for an answer, but started for the back of the plane and returned quickly with two ibuprofens and a bottle of water.

"So, how bad is it?"

"It's not a migraine. I think it's just a tension headache."

He sat down next to her. "Okay, call me crazy, but you don't seem too happy about this promotion. What's going on?"

What could she say to him? *I just want to be your secretary so I can stay close to you?* Ha! That would go over like a lead balloon. She could never let him know. He would send her farther away than the CMA department. She already knew the best thing she could do was to find a wife for him. Maybe it would be easier to let him go if she didn't see him every day. She needed to work fast while she was still with him. Being in the other department, she wouldn't have many opportunities to set him up with the ideal woman, whoever that was. Since he'd shared his thoughts on the subject, she felt she needed to search harder and be more scrutinizing.

But why had he decided he didn't want to be around her anymore? Maybe it was because she'd become so involved with Henri. But Henri really cared about her, and he really needed her. She wouldn't desert Henri just so that she could pine for Gherring every day.

"Anne? What's wrong?"

"How soon would we make the switch?"

"Well, it depends on how soon I can find a replacement for you. And how soon you can get him or her trained."

He covered her hand with his, and her skin sizzled. She remained still with great effort. "You know, you're really gifted. They loved you. You can't believe how many people told me they want to work with you in the future. You should be really proud. So why aren't you happy? Are you nervous? Because I know you'll do a great job. I'm never wrong about these things."

What could she say? How could she explain to him why she wasn't thrilled? She couldn't even explain it to herself. She thought of a practical question. "Who'd be training me?"

"I thought maybe Shanna Matheson might take you under her wing. She'll be back from maternity leave in December. Jared's a little green or I'd pair you with him. Would you rather have someone else?"

"You do realize I don't know anything except the stuff I learned in one day? Just the stuff I needed to understand how to prepare Jeff's presentation? I don't really understand all the different concepts."

"What impressed me was not your understanding of the concepts, but how easily and quickly you managed to grasp those ideas. Some people study for years to learn what you picked up in a few hours."

"Oh... Okay."

He frowned. "Usually people respond more positively to my praise." He bent his head toward her. "What gives?"

"I... I don't know. I'm really honored and flattered... I mean... Thanks, I'll do my best. I'll try to get my replacement trained quickly." She bit her lip.

"Are you afraid? Is it too much responsibility?"

"No... Maybe... Yes, I guess that's it." She peered into his eyes. "What if I can't do it? And then..." She looked back down. "And then you'll already have a new executive assistant..."

One side of his mouth quirked upward. "I guess we could wait to get your replacement."

"Really?"

"You don't have to take the promotion at all if you really don't want it."

"You mean you'd let me stay if I wanted to?"

He looked up at the ceiling and blinked his eyes. "I really don't understand you at all." Then his eyes locked with hers. "Is that what you want?"

She couldn't look away. "No, I think I want the job. I... I just... It seemed like you might want..." She finally blinked and averted her eyes, "You seem to want a different executive assistant..."

"So you *do* want the job? But you *don't* want me to get a new executive assistant? I'm so confused—"

"Ha! You think *you're* confused!" She wanted the new job, but she didn't want to quit her old one. And she wanted him to offer her the promotion, but she wanted him to be at least a little sad about it. He just seemed too happy about replacing her—like he wouldn't miss her at all. But of course he wouldn't miss her, not like she would miss him.

"Ms. Best?" his deep intense voice compelled her attention.

"Yes, Mr. Gherring?"

"What would make you happy? What job would you really like at Gherring Inc.?"

"Honestly? Mr. Gherring—*you* are Gherring Inc. Right now I help you with everything you do. Aren't I more valuable as your assistant than I would be in CMA?"

"Well, I don't know. You've done quite a bit more than an executive assistant usually does. You've learned technical specifics about an area of the company and accomplished work I would've had to do myself. That's way more than being a personal executive assistant."

"Oh, wow! That's a great idea!"

"What idea?"

"That I'll be your expanded-duty executive assistant. I can learn about everything you do and take some of your workload—that sounds awesome!"

"Is that what I said?"

"That's what I heard. Isn't that what you said?" Then she sat up and grabbed his arm. "Oh, just one thing—do I still get a raise?"

He closed his eyes for a long moment and then started chuckling. "I really have lost control, haven't I?" After he caught his breath, he turned back to her. "So, Ms. Best?"

"Yes, Mr. Gherring?"

"Are *we* going to need a secretary?"

Chapter Twelve - What's Important

GHERRING DIDN'T TALK ANYMORE ABOUT expanding Anne's job description and keeping her as his assistant, but Anne began to worry. For the rest of the flight, there was no discussion of work, but she wondered what he was thinking. Since she'd spilled the whole story of Henri's niece, he'd be more suspicious than ever. She had to make sure he didn't hear about the Thanksgiving trip to Paris. Even though he obviously felt sorry for Henri and his niece, he'd still be upset she was going to see him. Perhaps she could help mend the relationship between Gherring and Henri. That would certainly take some strain away.

But how on earth was she going to keep a handle on her feelings for Gherring. She'd be spending more time with him than ever before. She tried to think of him objectively. But she couldn't deny her body's response when something happened to remind her he was a man, and not just her boss. She definitely needed him to keep a lot of clothes on, although his broad shoulders and muscled chest were hardly disguised, even in dress clothes. But it was absolute disaster to see him in workout clothes. And thank goodness she'd probably never see him in a towel again—that'd been the worst. And she needed to make sure they never came into actual physical contact.

The best thing she could do would be to find a wife for him. If he were attached, she'd be able to put all those thoughts out of her mind. It was like a switch in her head would be turned off. She'd never be attracted to a married man. She was almost certain if Gherring were married, she'd lose all that physical attraction she felt for him right now. Then maybe she could let herself be attracted to someone else. She didn't believe she'd ever find someone like Tom, someone she could really love and trust, someone she would be willing to marry. But maybe she could find a man she could be a really close friend with. Maybe even Henri. But first she had to eliminate Gherring from her system. He really messed with her perception.

It was seven thirty p.m. in New York by the time they arrived back at the apartment. Gherring still hadn't mentioned anything more about the job. Anne debated whether to ask about it as she dragged her weary body into the lobby.

But Gherring broached the subject as they entered the elevator. "So, I guess we should get together and talk about your new job description before Monday."

Anne panicked. She'd already decided she shouldn't spend anymore time with Gherring outside of work, but she could hardly refuse. "Should someone else be at the meeting with us, like maybe Katie?"

His brows pinched together. "I don't think Ms. Carson needs to be involved. After all, she's leaving in mid-December. Why don't you just come up for dinner tomorrow night? We can iron out the details."

"Okay."

He slanted a suspicious look toward her. "Unless you have other plans? Maybe you're planning to talk with Henri at that time?"

"No, I don't have other plans—"

"Six o'clock? Seven?"

"Seven is okay." She heard the words come out of her mouth.

"Or, I guess if you'd rather, you could come up earlier and run while I work out."

Anne felt all the blood drain from her face. "No, I don't think that's a good idea. I mean, that won't work for me. I'll see you at seven for dinner."

"See you tomorrow night, then," he said as she exited the elevator. She didn't respond but she noted his self-satisfied expression before the doors closed. What on earth had she gotten herself into?

Henri had left her a message on her phone to call him in the morning. He sounded weary. And Anne discovered her most recent email from Johanna.

Dear Anne,

I must hear what happened on your trip to Switzerland! How did Mr. Gherring behave toward you? Do you think I am right he is interested in you as more than a secretary? And what about Henri? Was he jealous you went to Switzerland with Mr. Gherring? What did Mr. Gherring say about your plans to go to Paris next week to stay with Henri? Are you still going?

My life here is boring, so write back soon! I am trying to talk Alexander into visiting New York in December. We must get together!

Yours truly,

Johanna

Anne quickly jotted a note back.

Dear Johanna,

Switzerland was beautiful! I have a stamped passport now! Mr. Gherring was extremely considerate. And no, I am certain he is not interested in me as more than a secretary. In fact he tried to move me to a job that would have meant we seldom even worked together. I negotiated for something a little different. I am getting a kind of promotion, with expanded duties, as a reward for long hours of work on the presentation. I am a little nervous about living up to his expectations. Henri surprised me with a visit in Bern. Mr. Gherring and Henri got along fine, considering the circumstances. I still plan to leave for Paris on Tuesday night. I would love to see you in December. You could perhaps help me clear some confusion from my head with your sage advice.

Thinking of you,

Anne

Anne was exhausted from the travel, but she knew she needed some exercise if she wanted to sleep well. So she changed quickly and made her way to the gym. It was mostly deserted on a Saturday night. Only one other soul, and he was busy with the free weights. She knew most people in the building had something to do and someone to be with on Saturday nights. But she was glad to have a chance to clear her mind. She set the treadmill for forty minutes and started her run. Soon she was in her zone, concentrating on the smooth repetitive motion propelling her feet forward on the belt, consciously minimizing extra movement, relaxing her shoulders. She felt the initial burn in her leg muscles and pushed through it until she no longer felt any discomfort, just warmth. Her mind relaxed along with her body, and she let her thoughts wander.

She was certainly overthinking the problem with Steven Gherring. She was not some young hormonal girl who couldn't control herself. She was a strong, determined woman. She'd already proven herself in her education, her marriage, her motherhood, and now in this new job adventure. She was smart enough to handle any challenge put before her, and she wouldn't let something like a little physical or emotional attraction to Steven Gherring cause her to make a misstep. She'd raised two children by herself for fifteen years. During that entire time she hadn't let herself even look at another man. She was disciplined *before*, and she could be disciplined *now*.

Anne finished her forty-minute run and cool down. Feeling much more positive and relaxed, she picked up her bag and stopped by the water cooler for a drink. She realized she even enjoyed the feeling of being drenched in sweat with her hair plastered to her head. It was a feeling of accomplishment. She opened the door and slammed her sweaty body into someone entering the gym.

Steven Gherring had arrived at the gym with his shirt off, and now she'd smeared his chest and abdomen with sweat.

"Ohmygosh! I'm so sorry," said Anne.

"That's okay. I'm gonna be sweaty in a minute anyway. You're leaving already?"

"Yeah... but what are you doing here?" She tried to keep her eyes on his, but her gaze kept drifting downward.

"I live here. I own the building. I can use the gym, can't I?"

"But you have equipment upstairs in your apartment. Why are you using this gym?" she asked, as once again she felt her eyes fall toward his bare chest.

"Maybe I just wanted a change of scenery or a little company."

Anne glanced back into the gym. "It's dark outside, and there's no one else in here." She couldn't stop herself from gazing at his muscled abdomen. She felt her heart racing. "And why don't you *ever* wear a shirt?" Without waiting for an answer, she turned and stomped down the hall.

"Hey Mom, I missed you." Anne could see Emily's pouting face on the computer screen. "I can't believe you went to Switzerland and you're leaving for Paris in a few days. I wish you could take me with you."

"That wouldn't be too adventurous for you?"

"Mom, you know I love to travel. I just don't like doing things that involve bodily injury or death."

"I know, just kidding. You would've loved it. I'm determined to save up money and go back with both of you. Or else you can marry a rich doctor, and he can take all of us."

"Well, don't hold your breath. I haven't even dated in a year."

"And whose fault is that? I'm willing to bet you've been asked out more than once."

"But those guys all have something wrong with them. What is it about me that attracts creepy guys?"

"Surely they weren't *all* creepy, were they?"

"Trust me on this. If they were cute, then they were either stupid or arrogant or players. And I tried to make myself like this one guy who had a great personality, but there just wasn't a spark. It would've been like dating my brother."

"But you don't have a brother. How would you know?"

"Mom!"

"Just kidding. But seriously... What about Spencer? Have you heard from him? I just wondered."

"He's texted me a few times. But he lives in New York. And he's probably got something wrong with him—I just don't know what it is yet. And speaking of long-distance relationships how is Henri? Did he have a fit when he found out you were going to Switzerland with Mr. Gherring?"

"Actually, he took the train to Geneva and surprised me."

"What? Are you kidding? That's so romantic. *And* he's rich *and* he's hot. *And* he must be crazy about you."

258

"Yes, but things are really rough for him right now. He just found out his niece, who might as well be his daughter, has cancer. And she's only just turned seven."

"Oh, that's awful. Will he still want you to come if he's dealing with that?"

"I think he really needs me, and I want to be there for him. It's gonna break my heart, though."

"No kidding. You'd have to be pretty hard-hearted to prevent that." Emily made a sad face. "Tell me something happy."

"Okay... I'm kind of getting a promotion."

"What do you mean?"

"Well, it's a long story, but Mr. Gherring thought I did a good job on the presentation, and he offered me a position in the Contract, Merger, and Acquisition department. Then we came up with an alternative where I still work with Mr. Gherring, but I'm more of an assistant than a secretary."

"What's with that? You turned down an offer for a real job and decided to stay an assistant?"

"It's not like that. I'll be doing important stuff. Mr. Gherring's work is the most important part of the company."

"But you'll still just be an assistant. I would think you'd be excited about working independently. It sounds like an amazing opportunity." Emily paused for a moment. "Unless... Unless you didn't want to leave Mr. Gherring. Is that it? Are you starting to fall for him?"

"No, that's not it."

"Really? And what would you say if I decided to be an assistant to the president of our company instead of being an accountant?"

"That's not the same at all. You've got a degree in Accounting. My degree is in Chemistry."

"All the more reason you should have jumped at the chance. But you didn't." Emily frowned at her mom. "Okay, Mom. You denied liking him when we came to visit you in New York. You're a terrible liar, so tell me the truth. Or are you lying to yourself?"

Anne felt slightly nauseous. This was exactly the kind of thought pattern she'd been avoiding. "Okay, okay. The truth is... The truth is I *am* physically attracted to him, but so are about a million other women. I'm not kidding myself. I know there's no future for me with him. That's why I'm sticking to my plan. Gram and I are going to find a wife for him. After that, I'll be fine transferring to another department."

"Are you sure you're not in love with him?"

"No. I'm not in love with him. I don't just fall in love. I've never loved any man except your father. And I probably never will."

"Oh Mom, don't say that. I know you loved Dad a lot. But I hope someday you'll love again."

"Don't feel sorry for me. I'm happy—I have my girls. Maybe after you two are married, I'll fall in love again. But I just don't need that in my life right now."

Emily shook her head. "Well, congratulations on your promotion of sorts, I guess."

She recognized the need for company. Like her younger daughter, Anne seldom spent more than a few hours alone. Instead, she thrived on constant companionship and activity. Luckily, Ellen answered her phone and jumped on the idea of lunch at Papa's.

"Catch me up," demanded Ellen after May seated them, promising to return after the rush.

"Well, there's not much to tell. After the girls went home, I worked like crazy, ended up going to Switzerland, rode on Mr. Gherring's private jet, toured around Switzerland on trains, rode back in the private jet, and got a promotion—kind of."

"Are you kidding me? That makes my life sound downright dull, and I was feeling pretty good about it." Ellen leaned in close. "Details, I want details. What was it like to ride on Steven Gherring's private jet?"

"Ohmygosh, it was amazing. But you know, if you were to meet Mr. Gherring and y'all hit it off, you could find out for yourself."

Ellen rolled her eyes. "Are you still on that kick? And tell me again why *you* don't want to date him? What's the secret? What's wrong with Steven Gherring? Does he have some hidden deformity? Does he swing both ways? There must be something wrong with him, or you'd be going after him yourself."

"There's nothing wrong with him, I promise."

"Then why has he never gotten married before? Or maybe he *has* been married before?"

"No, he's never been married. He was engaged before, but they broke it off."

"But in the magazines and newspapers, he's always got some girl hanging on him. Every time, it's a different girl."

"That's just it. He doesn't really date. It's like he thinks every girl out there is only after his money, so he doesn't give them a chance."

Ellen laughed. "Only half of them are after his money—the other half are after his body. Have you ever seen pictures of him without a shirt?"

Anne felt her face heating up. "Yes, I've seen him."

"Ah, ha! You're red. You've seen him up close and personal without a shirt. When was this? On the private jet? Just how *private* was this jet?"

Anne scrambled to cover her blunder. "No. When we went climbing, remember? Didn't I tell you Mr. Gherring went climbing with me and the girls the morning before we came to meet you at the bookstore?"

"Maybe... I don't remember that. But anyway, what's wrong with him? Why don't you want to date him?"

Anne sighed. "I just know I'm not his type. For one thing, I'm older than the other women he dates. The oldest one I know of is Michelle, and she's still five years younger than me. It's not like I wouldn't date him if he asked me. But he's known me for two months, and he hasn't asked me out. So I don't think that would ever happen."

"Why do you care whether he has someone to date or not?"

"I just care about him. I want him to be happy, and I know finding the love of your life can do that for you. It worked for me. And if I'm right and y'all hit it off, then you'll find the love of your life as well. And just as a bonus, he can provide financial support for your plays."

"Anne, I'm perfectly willing to meet him, and we can just see what happens. You said Gherring Inc. supports the arts? Have they underwritten plays before?"

"I'm almost positive they have. I can certainly find out. But even if he hasn't done it before, he might do it for you."

"There is one other little complication."

"What's that?"

"I kind of have a crush on my leading man."

"You do?"

"Yes, but he's not interested in me. So I guess it doesn't matter."

"Well if things don't work out with Mr. Gherring, I'll figure out a way to make this guy notice you."

Ellen laughed. "You know, I think you'd really do that. It's a deal. When do I meet Mr. Gherring?"

"How about next Monday, after the Thanksgiving holidays? Lunch at Papa's? I'll do my best to get him there, but no guarantees."

"What should I wear?"

"Wear a dress and show off those dancer legs."

"You've got it. And if it flops, you have to help me catch Ben's attention."

"Deal."

By the time the lunch rush was over and May came to join them, Ellen had to leave.

"Do you need to go too, Anne? I'm sorry I was tied up so long," May said.

"No, I'd love to stay and chat," said Anne.

"Tell me all about your trip."

"Do you mean Switzerland? Did you know about that?"

"Yes. Although I think I found out through the grapevine. I'm pretty sure Spencer told me about it."

"Spencer knew?"

"Sure. He found out from talking to Emily."

"He was talking to Emily? She just told me they texted. She didn't say anything about talking to him."

"Oh, he's been talking to her alright. He's talked to her every day since she left. He's saving up his money to fly to Texas."

"Does she know that?"

"Well I don't know. I only hear about it from Spencer. But he's crazy about her, I think. I've never seen him act like this before."

Anne stared at May. "I've got to talk to her and see what's going on. Either she's hiding something from me or she's leading him on. I don't want Spencer to be hurt."

"Or it could just be Spencer's moving a little faster than she is. When he makes a decision, that's it. He jumps in with both feet."

262

"Oh… Not Emily… She thinks about everything and then thinks some more and then maybe she'll try it. Just test the water with her toes."

"I don't know, they don't sound too compatible, do they?"

"I disagree—I think they could be really good for each other. Strike a great balance. Hmmm…" Anne drummed her fingers on the table. "I need to find a way to get her back out here."

"If this works out, we'd be aunt and mom-in-laws together."

"I'd love to be related to you and George. Woo hoo—this is fun!"

Anne made sure she was five minutes late to dinner with Mr. Gherring. She didn't need to catch him in any state of undress. She wanted to compose herself and reestablish their professional relationship. As soon as the door opened, her senses were assaulted with the aroma of food cooking. He let her inside and hurried back to the kitchen.

"Make yourself comfortable. Dinner's almost ready."

She followed him into the kitchen, noting he was fully dressed in khaki pants and a dark blue sweater. Still, she remembered exactly what his chest looked like under that sweater. She could see his muscles flexing through the fabric, even when he was just cooking dinner. She was hopeless.

"That's smells wonderful. What is it?"

"It's a stir fry with shrimp, steak, chicken, and veggies. Hope you like it."

Her stomach rumbled noisily. "If it tastes as good as it smells, I'll love it."

"Could you set the table? You'll have to look around for placemats and such. I don't ordinarily use the dining table."

She went into the dining area and searched through the buffet and found two linen placemats, napkins and silverware. There was a china cabinet with glassware and plates. Gherring had already set out a bottle of wine and two wine glasses. He came in with the steaming food just as she finished.

"Wow, I haven't seen this china in a long time."

"Is it okay? I found it in the bottom of your china cabinet. You have another set, but I really liked this one." The plates were a simple design, white in the center with cream-colored rims and gold encrusted edges.

"These belonged to my parents. It's a Minton pattern. I think it's called Buckingham. And it's great to use them tonight. I dislike owning things I don't use."

"My folks were too practical to own china. And I don't even remember my mom. She died when I was three." She took a bite. "Oh, wow—this is so good. I'd be fat if I could cook like this. I'd just eat all the time."

He chuckled. "I doubt that seriously. You and your girls look like you've got metabolisms that works overtime. You're fortunate."

"Oh that's true. I'm so lucky, because I really eat like a horse." Anne covered her mouth. "Oh that sounded kind of crude. Sorry."

"No problem. I've already told you I prefer horse-like eaters to bird-like eaters." He grinned. "As long as you don't actually look like a horse."

"So… about the job. I've been thinking. Are you having regrets about this? I mean, we're talking about creating a whole different position that doesn't fit into your current framework. I can be a bit impulsive at times. I want you to be honest with me."

His dimples flashed. "Why don't you hold that thought until after dinner? I think I know you pretty well. If you start thinking too much, you won't be able to eat."

Her mouth hung open. He was right—her stomach often refused food when she was upset about something. "Okay. We'll wait. So what shall we talk about? Should we go with… qualities you would like in a wife?"

He laughed. "Not again—that one upsets *my* stomach."

"Tell me about growing up with Gram."

His expression grew contemplative. "That's a good one. Good memories. Gram took me out of boarding school when my parents died. I grew up in Gram's house—the one where you had dinner."

"And Michelle?"

He frowned. "What about Michelle?"

"She told me you were family friends."

"That's true. I used to change her diapers. She was born when I was ten years old."

"I see—so you've *always* liked younger women."

His mouth twitched up on one corner. "We didn't date until long after we were grown."

"Mmmm. Okay, where did you go to college?"

"Columbia and Harvard Law."

"Really? I didn't know you went to law school."

"That was my rebellious stage."

"You rebelled by going to law school?"

"I thought about going into politics instead of running the family business that had been waiting for me. It felt like I didn't have a choice. But in the end, it was in my blood. I had a knack for it, even more than my father."

"And then, you absorbed yourself in your business and forgot to get married and have a life."

"That's what Gram would say. But the magazines reported my life was too wild, and that's why I never got married. It just depends on who you believe."

"And are you happy?"

"I've spent my life building an empire. Our charitable foundations have done a lot of good things. And you're the only person I know who looks at me with pity, even though I'm a billionaire."

"Let me ask you this. If you had to choose between being rich and having Gram in your life, which would you pick?"

He answered with a shake of his head.

"You see—you don't even have to answer. I know you know what's most important in life. I'm glad you have Gram. I'm just sad you never got married. But I'm just as sad for people who've only had bad marriages. There's nothing like finding the love of your life, who loves you back the same way." She sighed. "Even if you lose them after ten years."

"I don't disagree with you. You and Gram, both—you act like I've never tried to find a wife. I've looked, but—" He stopped abruptly. "Why am I discussing this with you? This topic is officially off limits. And I'd better not catch you trying to set me up with a potential wife."

Anne's mouth went dry. This hadn't gone well at all. She'd have to proceed very carefully and be extremely subtle. Subtle—fat chance. She would just be sneaky instead. The wheels began to turn...

After dinner, Steven settled Anne in front of the fireplace with a cup of cocoa. "Dinner was incredible, and now, hot cocoa and a fire. I'm in paradise."

A pleased expression on his face, Steven lounged next to Anne on the buttery-soft leather couch. "I'm glad you enjoyed it. I like to be appreciated, and it's fun to make you smile."

"So, about the job. I feel like I may have forced you into this."

"Ms. Best, I've never been forced into a business decision by anyone in my entire life. Rest assured your influence, while formidable, does not equal compulsion."

Anne's spine stiffened. "Mr. Gherring, I certainly feel chastised for my presumptive assertion. Please accept my sincerest apologies. I was not suggesting your manhood had been detached. I was merely offering you an opportunity to withdraw the proposed job alteration with aplomb and promising not to take unwarranted offense."

Gherring held up his hands. "I surrender! I bet you always win when you play Scrabble, don't you?"

"As you said, I'm formidable."

"So, about the job. If you went to CMA, you'd start at eighty thousand, since you don't have a degree or job experience. I'm willing to give the assistant position a try for three months. It's an intriguing idea. If it works, you'll get at least a ten thousand dollar raise, plus bonuses. If it works really well, you could make as much as you would in CMA."

"What if it doesn't work?" Anne asked in a small voice.

"Then you'd be terminated."

Anne felt a rock in her stomach. "I'm a pretty confident person, but I'm not *that* confident. I don't think I want to take the risk—"

"Anne, really? You think I would fire you? If it doesn't work, we'll renegotiate." He chuckled at the relief on her face. "How did you ever live this long when you're this gullible?"

"I'm not really sure."

"But there is one caveat." His expression grew serious. "This deal we've made with Bern... You and Jared will need to work with those two companies, just as if you're in the CMA department with him. I have yet to think what title to give you, but we'll come up with something."

"I feel better. And the secretary work?"

"I'm afraid you'll have to cover that as well until we get some help."

"Katie's gonna flip out. She's already been through heck trying to get you to agree on a secretary—I mean, personal executive assistant."

'I'll just let you and Ms. Carson pick someone for me, and I'll give the final approval." He caught her hand and narrowed his eyes. "And you'd better find me a secretary and not a potential wife."

She blushed furiously. Especially since her thoughts had indeed been heading in that direction. He released her hand and leaned back on the couch, stretching out his arms along the back. She was acutely aware of the lightest contact of his arm against her shoulder. That familiar tingle began where she felt his touch and spread downward causing her heart to flutter. Her breathing became shallow with anticipation. What was wrong with her? What was she anticipating? Nothing was going to happen.

Gherring leaned across her to set his wine glass down on the end table, sending thousands of alarms throughout her body.

"Anne." His voice seemed deeper, slightly raspy. Or maybe it was her imagination. "Anne, you know, we've spent—"

A loud rapping sound on the door interrupted his speech. He looked puzzled. "Excuse me. Let me see who's at the door." Anne watched from the sofa, but couldn't see the person.

"Steven!" said a soft feminine voice. "I hope I didn't come at a bad time. I really needed to see you. We really need to talk. You see, I've been thinking a lot about my feelings. You've always been the one that understood me, the only one. And I know I can talk to you about anything. And your idea, the one about trying again, giving it another shot. I think I'm ready. I just need to be more selfless and understanding—"

"Wait, Michelle. Actually, this is kind of—"

"I was just leaving," said Anne, slipping through the doorway. "Thank you, Mr. Gherring. I'll see you at the office. Michelle—it was good to see you again."

Monday morning, Anne left early for the office. She wanted to get a head start on the administrative work so she'd have time to begin training for her new workload, whatever that might be.

Meanwhile, she wrestled with her feelings about Michelle's appearance at Gherring's apartment the previous night. On one hand, this could be an answer to her problems. Her arrival had certainly put a damper on Gherring's escalating lure. But she worried Michelle was too fickle for him. Hadn't she been crying about Henri just the week before? In Anne's experience, you couldn't love one person one week and another the next. She didn't want Gherring to be caught in a bad marriage. Especially one based on Michelle's chameleon emotions.

Steven Gherring didn't arrive until almost ten o'clock. And when he came, he came with a vengeance.

"Ms. Best," he said as he breezed by her desk. "In my office please."

She meekly followed him inside and he shut the door. "I've gotten caught up a little. I've already returned the phone calls from last week. We've had a few schedule changes, but nothing major—"

"Ms. Best, what are your plans for the Thanksgiving holidays?"

Anne swallowed hard. He wanted her to work during the holidays. And she was going to be in Paris. She'd simply have to lie and tell him she'd be in Texas.

"Well, I'm flying out tomorrow night, but I could be available to work by phone and Internet if you need me."

"You're going to see your family for Thanksgiving?"

"Well, the girls and I always get together with my dad for Thanksgiving." So far, so good. She hadn't actually lied yet.

His eyes narrowed. "So you're flying to Fort Worth tomorrow night?"

"My plane leaves at six thirty. I was planning to leave work a little early. I hope that's okay?"

This time his voice was strained. "Ms. Best. Are you flying to Texas tomorrow night, or are you flying to Paris?"

Her throat constricted. "Who… Who told you?"

"Michelle told me, but that's quite beside the point. The point is, why didn't *you* tell me?"

Anne's temper rose. "Because I didn't think it was any of your business where I went for Thanksgiving."

"So on one hand you want to know everything I do in this company and work with me on every business transaction and investment. But on the other hand, you don't think it's my business if you have an affair with the head of another company?"

"First, it's not an affair. And second, I thought you had a cooperative agreement with La Porte. Doesn't that make him sort of a part of your company?"

"Exactly! I think I need to know what's going on between my employees."

Anne's wrath came bubbling to the surface. "Well, in that case... Mr. Gherring, sir. Please let me inform you I'm flying to Paris tomorrow to spend four days with Henri. And I plan to tour Paris and visit a very sick little girl in the hospital. And I'll be sleeping in my *own* room at Henri DuBois' house."

Now passionate tears began to spill onto her cheeks. "And I'll probably hug him frequently, and I might let him kiss me. And maybe you'd also like to know I haven't let anyone else kiss me for the past fifteen years. So maybe I'm a weak person to let him kiss me, but it feels nice. And maybe it's just something I need right now."

He'd taken a few steps back as her frantic tirade began. Now he came toward her and held out his hands in supplication. "I'm sorry. I didn't mean—"

"Will there be anything else, sir?" She backed away from him and looked away, swiping at her tears.

"Anne... I didn't want—"

"I'm afraid I need to visit the ladies room. I'll be at my desk if you need me for anything else of vital importance." She walked out the door without closing it behind her.

Gherring didn't bring up Henri or Paris again, but their conversations were tense and stilted. Both made an effort to talk only about business. He acted as though their exchange had never occurred, discussing her new job responsibilities and how to inform the other employees.

"I've decided to name your position as a new department in the company. I'll call it Coordination, and you'll start out as the only team member. Then if we don't think it's successful, we'll just dissolve the department. At that point, would you be willing to move to CMA?"

"Sir, I'm willing to move to CMA at any time. It's entirely up to you," she replied without emotion.

He sighed. "Ms. Best, if we're going to work closely together, you'll find I have more than a few imperfections. I get stressed and irritable. I may sometimes get a little testy. I might say things that offend you."

He caught her eyes. "I need to know you'll be able to overlook an occasional lapse in my demeanor and comportment."

Anne's eyes softened. "I'm sorry. I know I have a temper. I'm usually able to control it, but with you... I don't know. You just seem to push my buttons sometimes, just like my kids. But I can forgive your slip-ups, if you can forgive mine."

"It's a deal." His eyes crinkled in the corners.

"Oh... and one more thing."

"Yes, Ms. Best?"

"I'd appreciate it, if you'd forget most of what I said earlier today."

He chuckled. "I'll try. But you do make an impressive speech when you're angry."

As predicted, Katie was not pleased at the prospect of searching for another secretary for Gherring.

"I can't believe I have to find you a *new* executive assistant. Do you know how long it took me, how much work I had to do to get you to hire Ms. Best?" She was on a rampage.

Gherring said, "Ms. Carson, you seem to be a bit more outspoken than you used to be—"

"I just want you to know if this is a trick to make me stay here after I'm married, it's not going to work."

He commented to Anne. "I think perhaps you're rubbing off on Ms. Carson. I'd better keep you far away from my next secretary." Anne started to protest, but he let out a chuckle.

"Katie, please. I promise to make it easy this time. I've finally accepted you're leaving me. You and Ms. Best can choose someone for me from the candidates we've already interviewed. Just set up one quick interview appointment with me. It will be on a three-month trial period."

Anne said, "You mentioned that one girl, Lana something..."

"Yes, do you remember, Ms. Carson? Lana Stewart?"

"Her name was Lana Seward. She was extremely qualified and experienced, attractive, well-spoken."

"How old is she?" Anne asked.

"I think she was about thirty-five," Katie replied.

"She sounds perfect," said Anne, already contemplating the possibilities.

"And I do believe she's married," he said with a sideways smile at Anne.

"Oh," Anne replied. She turned her head and stuck out her tongue at him.

He chuckled and said, "Score one for Gherring."

"What?" asked Katie.

"Nothing," said Gherring and Anne in unison.

"Will you mind if I read all your business email?" Anne asked Gherring. "I know it won't make any sense at first, but eventually it'll all fall into place."

"Yes, and just sit in on my meetings. But that'll need to come later. First I need you to meet with Jared and get an understanding of your responsibilities with the Swiss companies. These first few weeks are really critical. They could still back out of the deal. I've already sent out an office-wide memo and spoken to HR about the new department. And I've set up for you to meet with Jared this afternoon."

"What did Jared say about my new job?"

"Why would he say anything about it?"

"I just thought it might bother people for me to get some sort of promotion when I don't have education and experience."

His face darkened. "No one here would dare to question my decisions."

"No, of course not." But Anne had her doubts. "Okay, I'll go meet with Jared."

Working with Jared was even more entertaining than she'd expected. His constant jovial attitude, funny stories, and clever quips made the time pass quickly. But Anne was surprised both at the amount of work they accomplished and the knowledge she gained in a single afternoon.

"Let me ask you something, Jared. Will you be honest with me?"

"Sure thing. What's up?"

"I just want to know if you think I can do this job. Almost everyone here has an MBA and, I don't know…"

He smiled. "You can do anything. I've never seen any other employee with the b—, I mean gumption to chew out Mr. Gherring." He laughed. "And then you end up with a promotion."

"Yes, I'm trying to learn to control my temper," she said, averting her eyes from his curious inspection.

"But seriously, you catch on to everything really quickly. I didn't even understand some of the stuff you talked about on Jeff's part of the presentation."

She smiled gratefully. "Thanks, Jared. You've got a really encouraging personality. Do you have a younger, single brother I could fix my daughter up with?"

"Ha! Nope, I've got five, count 'em, five older sisters. That's why I laugh about everything. In my house you had to learn to laugh to survive."

Gram called just as Anne was about to leave for the day. "I'm picking you up for dinner. We need to talk."

When she climbed into the back seat with Gram, she noticed Gram appeared to be upset.

"It's about Michelle," said Gram. "She's back in town again… And I think she's set her sights on Steven again."

Anne swallowed. "Well, I guess that's good, isn't it? Didn't you want them to get married?"

Gram frowned. "I'm not sure I trust her anymore. Last week she was going on about Henri DuBois." She spat out his name like it tasted bad. "And I know you like Henri and you think I'm misjudging him, but there's no comparison between him and my Steven."

Gram was obviously waiting for her to agree, so she nodded her head in response.

"She's a manipulator, that one. Oh, I've loved her since she was a baby, but I've always known her parents spoiled her rotten. She's always had her daddy wrapped around her finger so tight he's still bent when she lets him go. And she always gets her way."

"So you don't want Steven to marry her?"

272

Gram squinted. "I think he can do better, don't you?"

She had to agree. She felt like Michelle was using Steven to fill a void left by Henri. "I guess I concur."

"So what do you think we should do?" Gram asked.

"Well, I'm leaving for Paris tomorrow…"

"Steven's a grown man who hasn't had much female company in the last few years. I'm afraid if she offers herself, he won't be able to resist. She's beautiful, you know."

She knew just how beautiful Michelle had looked when she visited Gherring last night. And she sounded so needy. Gherring was a sucker for a woman in need. And she was unscrupulous. She'd told Steven about Anne's trip to Paris after promising she wouldn't. Maybe she'd already offered herself to Gherring. Maybe she'd spent the night with him last night.

Her head swam at the thought, but she replied, "There's certainly nothing I can do if he can't control himself. I'm planning to introduce him to my friend, Ellen next Monday. But I don't have any other ideas."

"Humph!" said Gram. "I was thinking you might flirt with him a bit before you left. You know, you could just keep him distracted so Michelle can't get her hooks into him again."

She felt the blood rush to her face. "Gram, I just can't do that. Please don't ask me to."

Gram stared at her for a long time. "No, I guess that wouldn't be much like you to do something like that. Well, it was worth a try." She huffed a bit. "Don't be too distressed, I'll just keep him distracted while you're gone. Maybe I'll fake a heart attack or come down with some other life-threatening disease."

The astonishment must have shown on Anne's face, because Gram patted her arm and said, "My dear, desperate times call for desperate measures."

Anne packed her bags for Paris that night. She tried to call Emily to wheedle some more information about her relationship with Spencer, but she didn't get an answer. She'd just have to wait until she got to Paris. She knew Charlie was flying into the Dallas/Fort Worth airport on Tuesday afternoon to spend the holidays with Emily and Grandpa. Anne planned to Skype with all three of them together on Wednesday and on Thanksgiving Day. Perhaps she could pin her daughter down and pry the truth out of her. Both her daughters seemed to have an innate ability to tell untruths without being detected, a skill that had obviously not come from their mother.

Tuesday morning dawned, and Anne was filled with excitement. Paris! Another stamp in her passport. She wished the circumstances were not so dire for Henri and his family. But Anne felt drawn to bring all the comfort she could to Henri.

Gherring suggested she work in his office that morning so he could begin to teach her about the investment side of Gherring Inc. She listened with rapt attention to everything he said, but she quickly decided she needed a crash course in basic economics. Surely she could buy a book, or maybe Spencer could lend her a book. She texted him and he promised to bring one to Papa's at lunchtime.

Anne fielded her first phone call from one of the companies in the Bern transaction. Fortunately, the question had to do with specific information she had covered in her presentation. She breathed a sigh of relief. But secretly, she felt like a poser in a cardboard house that would soon fall over in the wind.

She planned to leave work at two o'clock, so she worked through lunch. She called Sam and asked her to pick up the Economics book at Papa's Place. After lunch, Sam dropped the book by her old desk, where Anne was working for the short afternoon.

"Anne? I need to ask you something?" Sam's eyes were scrutinizing. "Are you sleeping with Mr. Gherring? I won't tell anyone, but—"

"No! Ohmygosh. Why would you ask me that?"

Sam shrugged. "It's not a big deal... Well, it could be a big deal, I guess... People have just been saying you and Mr. Gherring spend a lot of time together, and you were in Bern together, and now you're getting promoted. You know, it just sounds like maybe—"

"Well it isn't. How could you think that about me?"

"Anne, don't be such a prude. I'm not thinking anything *bad* about you. If you got the chance to sleep with him, you'd be crazy not to. Any girl I know would jump at the chance... I mean, any single girl. Not me, I like Tanner." She smiled benignly.

Anne couldn't breathe. She felt the room closing in on her.

"Hey, Anne? What's wrong? You look terrible. Are you sick? Let me get you a wet towel for your face."

Sam ran to the bathroom to retrieve a wet paper towel. Gherring wandered out of his office with a scowl affixed to his face.

"Ms. Best," he said without looking at her, "I hope you aren't planning to leave for Paris before you—" He spied her slumping at her desk. "Anne! What's wrong?"

Sam came running over with a paper towel. "I can't believe it— she actually passed out."

"What happened?" he asked.

Sam cringed at his intimidating expression. "Mr. Gherring, sir, I think I should let her tell you about it, if she wants to. It's like a girl thing."

He cringed, asking no more questions as Anne was coming to. Sam came around in front of Anne and lifted her head gently. "Anne, are you okay?"

"Yes, I don't feel very good. What happened—Wait—I remember... Please, Sam. You *have* to tell everyone I didn't sleep with Mr. Gherring. He's never been anything but a *perfect gentleman*."

Sam paled a bit at his foreboding face, poised just over Anne's shoulder. "Okay, I promise." She hurried to make her escape. "I'll see you next week. Happy Thanksgiving."

Anne held the towel against her forehead and tried to breath slowly. She startled at Gherring's voice behind her. "I'm sorry that happened—I should've known. They don't mean anything by it, they just don't know you."

"But aren't you angry? They were accusing you as well as me."

He grimaced and turned away. "Anne, I'm not as innocent as you. It's not like I've never slept with a woman before. Or a secretary for that matter." Then he turned back with a fierce expression. "But Henri's no better than me, and I've changed a lot in recent years."

She breathed in and out slowly, contemplating his words. "I guess this is what it feels like to lose your naïvety. It had to happen sooner or later, but I don't like it."

He struggled for words. "Anne... I..."

"I'm leaving work at two o'clock this afternoon," she said. "That's thirty minutes from now. Did you have something for me to do before I leave?"

"So, you haven't changed your mind?" he asked with a hint of sarcasm.

She looked up, her eyes swimming with unshed tears. "I really want to make everyone happy, but I can't do that. So instead, I'm going to keep my promises as much as possible. That'll have to do."

Gherring nodded and returned to his office. When the door shut behind him with a quiet click, it resounded in her head like the closing of a tomb.

Anne made it home safely with plenty of time to spare. She planned to take a taxi to the airport, leaving at three thirty to allow plenty of time to get to the airport and check in before her international flight. She'd packed efficiently with one checked bag and one carry-on. She double-checked her packing list and added some snacks for the trip. Then she heard a sharp knock at her apartment door.

She thought it must be Rayna, letting her know her cab was here. Her cell phone must be turned off. "Coming!" she exclaimed, as she hurried to open the door.

Steven Gherring was standing outside the door. His clear blue eyes burned into her and held her motionless. "What... what're you doing here?" she asked.

"Anne..." he said, his voice breaking. "Don't go to Paris."

She stared at him, speechless for a moment. Then she turned around and walked back in the apartment and picked up her suitcases, one in each hand. She faced him again. "We've been through this, Mr. Gherring. I have to go. I promised Henri, and he needs me right now."

"Has Henri been a perfect gentleman?"

"What?"

"You said I'd been a perfect gentleman. Has Henri been a perfect gentleman?"

"I don't know... I guess so. Maybe not. It doesn't matter—I still have to go to Paris, even if he hasn't been a perfect gentleman." She still stood unmoving, suitcases in hand.

He crossed the floor in four steps to stand in front of her. "Don't go. Please. I don't want you to go."

She stood straining her neck to look up at him. He was so close to her she could feel the heat radiating from his body. She opened her mouth to reply, but her mind was foggy. She couldn't form a coherent thought.

Suddenly, he grabbed both of her arms with his hands. His voice was gravely and deep. "Anne—"

He pressed his lips to hers, claiming her mouth with his. This was no gentle supplication, but a heavy, needy demand. She froze, shocked by his incursion. And then the heat began to spread through her body, warming her deep inside. Her bags fell from her fingers, and her hands rose of their own accord to press against his firm chest. She felt his heart pounding under her touch. Her own heart was answering, fluttering like a captured bird. Her lips softened, and she heard a small whimper. Was that her? He groaned in response and deepened his kiss. His tongue was probing her soft lips until they parted and allowed him entrance. His breathing was quick and heavy. He moved his hands to embrace her and crushed her body against him. She clung to him, feeling his hard body pressing intimately against hers as his mouth continued to assault her senses, his tongue swirling and stroking. A deep ache arose in her core as she caressed his tongue with her own.

Abruptly, a strident song rang out from Anne's cell phone, and they sprung apart, breathing heavily. "I… I should get that. It's Charlie." He nodded, clamping his eyes shut and rubbing frustrated fingers through his hair.

She rummaged through her purse to find her phone. "Hello? Charlie?"

"Mom! Mom! Grandpa… He was in a car wreck! I don't know how bad, but they called me from the hospital! He was coming to pick me up and…" Charlie sobbed. "Mom, I don't know! I don't know! They're in surgery! Emily's going! I'm getting a taxi! But we don't know—I think it's bad!" She sobbed again. "Mom—"

"I'm coming! I'm coming as soon as I can get a flight! I'm coming, baby! Let me hang up and call the airline. I love you, baby."

She hung up the phone and fell sobbing into Steven's arms. Her mind was flooded with memories of the Thanksgiving fifteen years before, when a similar phone call had ended her fairy tale life. She was consumed with terror and began to shake even as he held her.

"Did you hear?" she choked.

"I heard, I heard. I'm sorry." He held her close and caressed her head with his hand. He held her until her weeping lessened slightly. Then he urged her toward the couch to sit.

"I'll make the calls," he said. "I'll get your flight changed."

"I… I should…"

"You sit. Give me your ticket. I'll take care of you."

Chapter Thirteen - Phone Issues

"ANNE, ARE YOU OKAY? Have you had anything to eat?" Steven asked as he strapped her into the seat on his private plane. Anne stared at him, unhearing, and nodded her head. "I'm sorry I can't come with you. But Gram called last night and told me she's been having chest pains. So I just can't leave her here alone right now." He watched her closely, noting her lack of reaction. "You haven't heard anything I've said, have you?"

He held her face between his hands and bent over to speak closely. "Anne, I need to know you're hearing me, okay?"

This time she made eye contact with him. "Okay," she said, as a single tear rolled down her cheek. He rubbed it off with his thumb.

"Okay, I need for you to repeat this. It's very important for you to remember. So repeat this back to me. *When the plane lands I will turn my cell phone back on and check my messages*. Can you say that?"

"When the plane lands, I will..."

"*Turn my phone on.*"

"Turn my phone on."

"*And check messages.*"

"And check messages."

"Okay, now listen. I gave the pilot the name and address of the hospital. He'll get a taxi for you and make sure you get there. Unless one of the girls comes to get you. Emily's going to call your phone and leave a message as soon as she knows something."

"Okay. Thanks. Thanks for—"

"No need for thanks. I want to help." He straightened up. "Anne, there's one more thing. Will you let me call Henri and tell him what happened? It'll be awfully late in Paris by the time you get to Fort Worth."

"Okay. Thanks."

"And will you call me when you get to the hospital?"

Tears began to tumble down her cheeks again. He walked to the back of the plane to find a box of tissues. He pulled one out and dried her face, handing her the rest of the box. His own shirt had a salty tearstain on the chest.

"Are you going to be okay?"

"Sure," she said. But she'd never been more unsure in her life.

He spoke again to the pilot and left her alone on the plane. She couldn't think clearly. So much had happened. Her mind was so clogged with terrifying images of her father in a mangled car, she couldn't process her earlier scene with Steven Gherring. He had kissed her? Had that really happened? What did that mean? She decided she wouldn't think about that. She wouldn't think about anything else, until she knew about her father. Right now, that was all that mattered. Later, she could deal with other things—things like Steven Gherring.

When the plane finally landed and Anne checked her messages, she heard Emily's quavery voice. "Mom, come as soon as you can. Charlie's here. Grandpa's alive. He's in critical condition."

The taxi ride seemed interminable. But she dared not ask the driver to hurry. Every time he changed lanes or used the brake she caught her breath, especially since the roads were wet. She called Emily from the car and both girls were waiting in the lobby for her when she arrived.

"You're here," cried Charlie, muffled from their group hug. "Everything's gonna be okay, now."

"That's how I feel, too," said Emily. "Everybody was talking to me like I was a grown-up, and I just wanted to cry like a little girl. I'm so glad you're home."

Anne wept and hugged her girls and peppered them with kisses. "Take me up there."

She was shocked to see her dad, bandaged and bruised, with tubes coming out of him and surrounded by flashing electrical gadgets. When Tom and his parents were killed in the car accident fifteen years previously, they'd been pronounced dead at the scene. She hadn't experienced seeing her loved ones, unrecognizable, in the alien-like hospital environment.

She bent over to place a tender kiss on his head in an unbandaged spot. Arriving to check his vital signs, the nurse informed Anne of his condition.

"We're keeping him unconscious right now. He came through the surgery pretty well for a sixty-eight year old. It's fortunate he was so healthy—his heart is strong. He has a broken arm, compound fracture. We've already set it. He also has some broken ribs and a punctured lung. We have some low-pressure oxygen to help keep the lung inflated while it heals. His spleen was ruptured, but the doctors only had to remove part of it. He lost a lot of blood, and he's not out of the woods yet. But he has a good chance of surviving."

She patted Anne on the arm. "You look terrible, dear. It could have been much worse. A number of people died in that accident."

"There were other people? Do you know what happened?"

"As I understand it, there were at least ten cars involved. It had just started to rain and the bridge immediately iced-up. Those cars were going seventy miles an hour when they hit the ice. They never had a chance. Most of the ambulances came here, but I understand some went to other hospitals. So I don't know exactly how many people were injured."

"I was so worried about Dad I didn't even think about other cars being involved."

"Understandable. But I think you can relax a little. He's a fighter, and it takes a real fighter to battle back from something like this. It's already past visiting hours, so I'm afraid you'll need to come back tomorrow. We have your contact information, right? We'll take good care of him and call you if there're any changes. Tomorrow or the next day, he may get to move to a room. Then you can stay with him as long as you like." She smiled as she ushered them out.

Anne breathed a sigh of relief as they walked toward the elevator. But she saw Emily and Charlie exchange a worried look. "What is it? What aren't you telling me?"

"Mom," said Charlie, with huge tears falling from her golden eyes. "Gandalf was in the car."

Emily was driving to the veterinary office while Anne, in the passenger's seat, was jumping at every move the car made. It was like reliving a nightmare. She'd refused to drive for a month after the accident that killed Tom.

"Mom, you've got to relax a little," Emily complained. "You're making me nervous, and I need to concentrate."

"Sorry, sorry… I'm trying."

Do you know where this animal hospital is?" asked Charlie.

"I've got the address in my GPS. I've never been there before. Some Good Samaritan drove Gandalf over there. I got a call on my cell because my number was associated with his ID chip."

"And what did the message say?" asked Anne.

"The message said to call because they had Gandalf. But I called them, and the nurse said they were going to do surgery. He'd lost a lot of blood from internal bleeding, but they couldn't do surgery until they'd gotten my permission." Her lip quivered. "He may have died because it took so long for me to call them back."

"Oh honey, no! It was an accident, and you were busy keeping Grandpa alive. It's not your fault."

Charlie was crying. "Y'all stop talking about him like he's already dead. We don't know for sure."

"But he's so old. He wouldn't be strong enough to recover," said Emily.

Anne struggled to find a dry spot on her last remaining tissue. "It had to happen sometime. We've had him for nine and a half years—that's pretty good. Most Irish Wolfhounds only live five to ten years."

On their arrival, the clinic appeared deserted. But there was a single light burning inside. "They said there might be someone here until ten o'clock, and it's almost ten now. If not, we'll have to come back tomorrow," said Emily.

They rang the night bell and waited for several minutes before they heard the sound of movement inside. A light flipped on and the door opened. A small bespectacled man who looked to be at least seventy years old stood in the doorway. "Can I help you?"

"We're here about Gandalf? The Irish Wolfhound?"

"Oh, yes. The Wolfhound. The car accident. I'm so sorry. Come in."

He walked ahead of them down a long dim hallway.

"Are you the doctor?" asked Anne.

"Oh, yes, I'm Dr. Williams. This used to be my practice, but I sold it to a great young doctor named Christine Stephenson. I'm just here to check on the surgery patients one last time before bed."

"And what about Gandalf?" Anne asked, dreading the answer.

He opened a door. "He's still in here. I thought you'd want to see him."

Anne's heart fell as she passed through the doorway with her girls. Gandalf's limp body lay sprawled across an operating table. Blood was smeared on his fur, although it was obvious someone had tried to clean him up. The IV tube had been disconnected and was hanging loose. Anne looked at his still body and tried to connect this image with the joyfully rambunctious dog Gandalf had been.

Though she meant to be strong for her daughters, a sob escaped. She leaned over his head and kissed him, her tears wetting his fur. Emily was weeping audibly. Charlie threw her arms around him, crying out, "Gandalf!"

Emily rubbed his head and kissed his nose. "He's still warm. He must've just died!"

Anne heard Dr. Williams behind her. "Oh, he's not dead—I thought you knew. He's just so big I can't move him by myself. I was trying to figure out what to do when you rang the bell."

"What? He's alive?" asked Anne.

The girls began sobbing anew and kissing Gandalf all over.

Anne grabbed Dr. Williams and squeezed him in a bear hug. "Thank you, thank you!"

He blustered a bit and patted her back. "It wasn't really me. It was Dr. Stephenson that did the surgery. Of course, I taught her everything I know."

Anne's phone rang, and she answered quickly, thinking it might be the hospital.

"Hello?"

"Anne?" Steven Gherring's voice sounded anxious. "You didn't call. I—I was worried."

She froze. With the news of the accident, Anne had blocked out all other thoughts. But now, hearing his voice, a flood of memories and images and emotions invaded her head. She remembered. Everything. He hadn't been shocked when he heard the rumor they were sleeping together. He'd told her he'd slept with his secretary before. He'd come to her apartment. He'd kissed her. And she'd kissed him back. And she'd pressed herself against him and her kiss had become manic. What must he think now? He must think she'd be willing to sleep with him. Is that what would've happened if the phone hadn't interrupted them? She remembered the deep ache that had threatened to overwhelm her senses. Somehow she couldn't control herself around Steven Gherring. How far would she have gone if Charlie hadn't called? What would she have done if her father hadn't been in a near-fatal car accident?

"Anne? Are you there?" Steven's voice was insistent, even frightened.

"I—I—" Suddenly Anne burst into sobbing tears. She ran from the room, handing the phone to Emily, who had been watching her mom with mounting fear.

"Hello?" Emily asked in a tentative voice.

"This is Steven Gherring calling. Who are you? Is this Emily?"

"Yes, this is Emily. What did you say to Mom?"

"I'm pretty sure I just said *hello*. What happened? Is he… Is he dead?"

"No, he's alive!" shouted Emily, and her words followed in a torrent. "We thought he was dead at first because the doctor thought we knew and he didn't tell us. And he was just lying there on the table, all covered with blood and so still. And then I kissed his nose and it was still warm. And I said, 'his nose is warm', and the doctor said, 'Oh, he's still alive'. But he was too big to move, so they left him on the table. We thought he wouldn't make it because he's so old. But he's alive!"

"How old *is* your grandfather?"

"Not Grandpa. Gandalf! Gandalf's alive! But Grandpa's alive too!"

"Gandalf… You mean your dog?"

"Yes, Gandalf was in the car, too. They're both alive, but it was a bad accident. At least ten cars. We were lucky. Grandpa's still in CCU, but they think he's gonna be okay."

"What about your mom? What's wrong with her? Why was she crying so hard?"

"I don't know. But we all thought Gandalf was dead just a few minutes before you called. So I guess she's been worried for so long she just fell apart when she heard your voice."

"Okay... Well, could you have her call me when she gets herself together?"

"Tonight? Or tomorrow?"

"Tomorrow, I guess. It's after midnight here. But if she wants to talk tonight, she can call and wake me up. I don't mind."

"Okay. Thanks, Mr. Gherring. And thanks for flying her here. We really needed our mom. I don't like facing things without her."

"I understand how you feel," said Steven. "Be sure she calls me."

"Mr. Gherring really wants to talk to you." Emily unfolded her couch into a bed for her mom.

"I know. Thanks for letting us stay here, since it's closer to the hospital."

"You're welcome. And you're also evading the topic. Why did you freak out when Mr. Gherring called you?"

"I don't know. Why did you neglect to tell me you'd been talking to Spencer on the phone?"

"You've been talking to Spencer?" cried Charlie. "Sister! You're keeping secrets from me."

"Nice try, Mom, but I asked you first," said Emily.

"Oh, we kind of had a scene before Charlie called, because he didn't want me to go to Paris to see Henri."

"What kind of scene? Like a yelling scene? Somehow I don't see Mr. Gherring as the type of guy who'd yell at a girl," said Charlie.

"No, he didn't yell, he just asked me not to go. And I insisted I was going, because I'd promised Henri. Besides Henri really needed me. I feel terrible he's going to be alone, when he thought I was coming. He's so upset about Anna-Laure."

Emily crooked her head at her mom. "You know, somehow I don't think you've ever been entirely honest about Mr. Gherring. Even from the beginning, your interview story was kind of fishy..."

"No, we really did have a scene. And then Charlie called, and I came here instead of going to Paris. And Mr. Gherring flew me here. It's all kind of awkward. I don't know what he wants."

"Maybe he just wants to talk to you, like he said. Did he hurt your feelings or something? He really sounded kind of pitiful to me." Emily tossed her a pillow.

"You kind of owe him, Mom. You probably wouldn't have been able to get a regular flight at the last minute. You might not even be here yet, if it weren't for Mr. Gherring," Charlie reasoned.

"I know I owe him. But I don't owe him *that* much."

"What do you mean?" Charlie asked. "Did he ask you to pay him?"

"No, of course not. I'm just talking about... I don't know. I don't want to feel obligated to him."

"But he seems so generous," Emily argued. "I don't think he expects anything in return. You worry too much, Mom."

"Okay, I'll call him tomorrow. Now about those phone calls with Spencer..."

"I'll tell you all about it tomorrow. Right after you call Mr. Gherring."

Anne's phone rang as they were driving to the hospital in the morning. She held her breath until she checked the caller ID.

"Hi, Gram."

"Anne, dear. How is your father? Steven says he's in CCU."

"Well, he's got a broken arm and broken ribs, a punctured lung and he lost part of his spleen. But we feel pretty lucky he's alive. Hopefully today we'll get to talk to him. He was unconscious yesterday. We're on our way to the hospital now."

"I'm so glad, dear. I know you must've been pretty frightened."

"Yes, I barely remember most of what happened yesterday." As soon as the words were out of her mouth, she recalled her encounter with Steven in the apartment. She labored to breathe.

"I thought I'd give you a report on our little project," said Gram. "My little ploy worked like a charm. Thanks to my 'chest pains', Steven's been very distracted. And Michelle is supposed to fly out tonight. So I think we're safe for now."

"That's great, Gram." She still wondered if it might be better if Steven reunited with Michelle. Then he wouldn't approach Anne again when she returned. What would she do if he tried to kiss her again? She'd barely kept her wits about her the last time. Too late now, since Michelle was leaving New York.

"So what do you think our next step should be?" asked Gram. "I was still thinking you could be a bit of a distraction yourself. You

286

wouldn't have to actually flirt with him, but perhaps if you spent some time with him outside the office—"

"No, I think that's a terrible idea."

"Why is that?"

"Because he knows about me and Henri. And he might decide to go back with Michelle. Yeah, that's it. Seeing me outside work would remind him of Henri, which would remind him of Michelle. And there you go—Steven's marrying Michelle."

"I'm not sure I agree with you. Steven doesn't ever make rash decisions."

"Yes he does. Maybe he used to never make rash decisions, but I *saw* him make a rash decision recently." Anne swallowed hard. "We can't be too careful."

"Do you have a better idea?"

"You should keep him distracted until Monday. I mean, *really* distracted. You probably shouldn't even give him enough time to call me. You know, so I won't remind him of Henri and he won't call Michelle and beg her to come back."

"Or, you could break up with Henri, and then you wouldn't remind Steven of Henri all the time," suggested Gram.

"I can't break up with Henri—we're not even really together. It's not like he's professed love to me or anything. We're only friends."

"Humph! What happens on Monday?"

"That's when I'm gonna introduce Steven to my friend, Ellen, the actress. Remember?"

"Humph! I don't know this girl. I may not like her."

"We'll have to cross that bridge when we get to it. I'll call you on Monday, okay?"

"Okay. Hope your father recovers quickly."

"Thanks, Gram. Bye now."

Anne hung up the phone with a sigh of relief. Charlie was staring with her mouth wide open. Emily was frowning as she drove.

Charlie started in. "What the heck was that, Mom? You want Gram to keep Mr. Gherring from calling you?"

Emily added, "And you suddenly think if Steven Gherring talks to you, he's going to marry this Michelle girl? That's a bunch of cr—"

"Emily!" Anne scolded, eliciting a chuckled from the back seat.

"Out with it," said Emily.

Her phone began to ring again. Spying Steven's name on the caller ID, she rejected the call.

"Why didn't you take the call, Mom?" questioned Charlie.

"It was no one important. I'll call them back later. We're almost to the hospital."

"Mom, we're on your side, you know. If you can't talk to us, who can you talk to?" Charlie leaned forward, her face earnest.

"Yeah, Mom. I'll start, okay? I've talked to Spencer on the phone a couple of times and on Skype a couple of times."

Charlie started to squeal, but Emily silenced her with a look.

"The jury is still out. I don't know if I like him or if I even trust him. But I'll tell y'all as soon as I decide. Okay?" She glanced at her mother. "Now it's your turn. Why don't you want to talk to Mr. Gherring?"

Anne contemplated. Charlie was right—if she couldn't talk to her girls, who could she talk to? No one. She couldn't tell her girls what had happened. She didn't even know herself what had happened or what it meant. And she had no one she could talk to.

"Can we just say I'm afraid to talk to him right now and leave it at that?"

"Hmmm," said Charlie. "I don't know. Sister, what do you think? Could we leave it at that?"

"No. Probably not. That doesn't really sound like us."

"If you're afraid to talk to him now, and you don't talk to him during the Thanksgiving holidays, what's gonna happen when you go back to work on Monday?"

"I'll act like nothing ever happened and go to work."

"Which means, of course, something *did* happen," smirked Emily. "And what would that something be?"

Her phone rang again. Her heart hammered until she realized Henri was calling. Grateful for the reprieve, she answered quickly.

"Henri… I'm so sorry I couldn't come. How's Anna-Laure?"

"She is okay. But I am calling for you. What happened? Gherring told me that there was a car accident. Your father? What happened?"

"He's alive, but in intensive care. And I'm so sorry. The timing was awful, and you wasted all that money on a plane ticket for me."

"The money is nothing. I am so glad your father is okay. And you? Are you okay? You must have been very afraid. If I were there I would give you a hug. Like you gave me a hug. You give very good hugs." She could almost picture his smile over the phone.

"Yes, I was terrified, but I'm okay now. We're on the way to the hospital, me and the girls. But tell me about Anna-Laure. Has she started chemotherapy?"

"She had a treatment today. She was *très courageux*. Brave, she was brave. And it did not make her sick. Tomorrow may be worse."

"I'm praying for her every day."

"Me, too," said Charlie.

"And me," said Emily.

Anne smiled. "Charlie and Emily want you to know they're praying, too."

"We need all those prayers—every one. When will you go back to New York?"

"I hadn't really thought about it. But if Dad is doing well, I guess I'll go back on Sunday night. I really have a lot of work to do, especially with my new job and still having to do the other stuff. And I've got to work out the final details for the company Christmas party."

"I think I will still come to New York. I have a ticket already for that weekend. If I think that Anna-Laure will be okay without me, then I will come. I would like to come. I would like to see you."

"That'd be great Henri. I'd love to see you, but I'll understand if you can't come because of Anna-Laure."

"I hope I can come. I hope I can see you. I need you, *mon bel ange*."

"My gosh, Mom," said Charlie as they walked into the hospital. "Henri's voice is so sexy, with that French accent. I don't know how you can resist him."

"A problem made easier by the fact there's an ocean between us. But you may be right. Who knows what would've happened if I were in Paris right now?"

"You see, I told you we needed to have 'The Talk.'" Emily waggled her eyebrows.

"Really though Mom, you're so strong. You've never even dated anyone since Dad died. You must be amazing at resisting temptation."

"Or maybe she's terrible at it, and that's why she never dated." Both girls chuckled at Emily's comment. But Anne cringed at how close to the truth Emily had come.

"I've never really been tempted, but I'm sure I could resist." She rushed to change the subject, hoping to cover up her lie. "I'm so worried about Grandpa—I'll feel so much better when he's awake and we can talk to him."

"He's awake, and he doesn't like the tube in his nose. I hope you can help him calm down a bit." The attending nurse frowned in obvious disapproval of his antics.

"Daddy?"

"Annie, baby," he croaked. "I'm sorry baby. I didn't make it to the airport to get Charlie."

"I'm here, Grandpa." Charlie arrived on the other side of the bed.

"And me," said Emily.

"Do you know what happened, Dad?"

"I remember the car sliding sideways, but nothing after that. What about Gandalf?"

"He's at the animal hospital. He had surgery, too," said Charlie.

"Dr. Stephenson said it's a miracle a Wolfhound his age survived the trauma. We're gonna visit him later today," said Emily.

"I think I really messed up Thanksgiving for everyone. I don't suppose my car survived?"

"I don't know, Dad, but it was probably totaled. That was a huge accident. It started to rain, and the bridge iced over. Ten cars or maybe even more were involved. You're lucky to be alive."

"Does it hurt much?" asked Emily.

"I feel kind of like I got tossed into a dryer with some rocks and knives." He chuckled. "Ow! It even hurts to laugh."

"You had surgery. I bet your stomach is going to hurt for a while," said Anne.

"Yep. Nurse Brume Hilda over there told me all about what they did to me."

"Dad, be nice. She's just trying to do her job and keep you alive. I heard you were fussing about that tube."

"Oh, and she's a tattle-tale, too."

Charlie giggled. "Grandpa's grouchy—he's back to normal."

The girls sat in the room with Grandpa and chatted until the nurse came in again. "He needs to rest now. You can come back this afternoon."

"I don't feel like resting," he gruffed.

"You're not going to give me any more trouble for a while." She smiled as she injected into his IV tube. Before he could even protest, the medicine began to take effect.

"That does feel better." He winked at the nurse before he fell asleep.

Anne asked, "Do we know when he'll get to move to a room? Are we going to talk to a doctor?"

"The surgeon was in earlier to check his stats. He's in surgery now, but he'll be back to talk to the family this afternoon. I'm guessing your dad will be out of CCU by Thursday."

On the way to see Gandalf, Anne noticed Steven had called twice while she was in the hospital. She listened to her messages.

"Anne, I hope you'll call soon. I'm worried about you. I hope your dad is okay and... and I hope you'll call me."

Then the second message. "Anne, I guess you can't talk because you're in the hospital. Please call me as soon as you can."

Just as Anne was tucking her phone away, he called again. Her heart started pounding, she turned the ringer off and stashed her phone in her purse.

Charlie raised her eyebrows. "Who was that?"

"I don't know. Probably a wrong number."

Emily's phone began to ring, and she handed it to Charlie. "Will you get that, Sis?"

"Hello?" said Charlie.

"Hi, this is Steven Gherring," said a relieved voice. "Is this Emily?"

Charlie smiled. "No, it's Charlie. Emily's driving."

Anne was waving at Charlie, mouthing *I'm not here!*

"I've been trying to reach your mom."

"Oh, you're in luck. She's sitting right here."

Charlie grinned as she handed her mom the phone. Anne gave Charlie the dirtiest look she could muster, while Emily giggled in the driver's seat. Anne stared at the phone she held in trembling hands. She took a deep quaky breath and held it to her ear.

"Hello?"

"Hi Anne. How're you doing? I've really been worried. You were so shaken up when I put you on the plane. I really wanted to go with you, except for Gram. I told you, but you probably don't remember. She's been having chest pains. She wants me to stay in the house with her. She doesn't want to go to the doctor, but she doesn't want me to leave her for a moment. And she seems really worried about you. She keeps telling me to call you. I don't know why she doesn't just call you herself." He paused for a breath. "Are you there?"

"Yes, I'm... I'm here." She took deep breaths, trying to slow her heart rate. She could do this. Steven wouldn't bring up *the incident* over the phone.

"How's your dad?"

"He's okay. He was awake today." She tried to keep her voice light and even. The girls were listening closely. She didn't want them to hear her nervousness.

"And Gandalf?"

"Alive, as far as we know. We're going to see him now."

"And you? How are you?"

"I'm fine." She thought her voice sounded odd and squeaky.

His pitch dropped. "I mean, how are you, really? I know you're probably feeling awkward after what happened. But Anne, I don't—"

"Oh, we're here. I've gotta go—I'll talk to you later. Thanks, Mr. Gherring."

She handed Emily's cell phone back without looking up.

"Well that was certainly interesting," said Emily. "Wasn't it, Sis?"

"It certainly was... Very interesting."

"No time to talk." Anne hopped out of the car, thanking God for the reprieve while hurrying inside to check on Gandalf.

The girls were cheered to find him awake, and even happier when he wagged his tail in greeting, albeit a weak wag. Dr. Stephenson's report was good, and they made plans to visit the following day.

"Where to now?" asked Emily, as they left the animal clinic.

"Lunch first. Then back to the hospital, I guess," said Anne.

"Although, I don't think you should be allowed to eat until you explain that little conversation with Mr. Gherring," said Charlie.

"I said 'later', and this is not 'later' enough. And if I'm not allowed to eat, I don't think I'll be paying, either."

"Fine, you can eat. But my curiosity is killing me," Charlie complained.

"We don't really need Mom. I could hear everything Mr. Gherring said. What would you like to know?"

"Emily!" Anne's voice sounded a warning.

"I couldn't hear what he said after Mom said she was fine," said Charlie.

"Charlie, that's enough—" said Anne.

"He asked her how she was *really* doing. And then he said, 'You must feel awkward'. And then Mom cut him off in mid-sentence," said Emily.

She squeezed her eyes shut. How was she going to cover her awkward conversation with Steven?

Emily began, "Mom, you can tell us the truth. Are you—"

"No, I'm not sleeping with Mr. Gherring! Why does everyone think that? I wouldn't do that."

"What are you talking about? I was going to ask if you were in *love* with him, not if you were *sleeping* with him. Who thinks you've been sleeping with Mr. Gherring? Is that what this is about?"

Tears welled up in her eyes. How could she possibly have any tears left?

"Mom, please don't cry," said Charlie.

"Yes, you know we'll both cry too," said Emily. "And I'm driving."

She studied her hands for a moment and then snuffled. "People at the office were saying I slept with him. Sam told me Tuesday. It's silly I care so much, but I can't help it. They think that's why I got the promotion." She swiped angrily at a tear on her cheek.

"How could they think that? That's awful." Charlie sniffed a few times. "Does Mr. Gherring know?"

"Yes, and he said he was sorry. But he wasn't surprised. I, on the other hand, was totally shocked. How can I be forty-five and still be this naïve? Of course that's what people would think. I just hope…"

"What, Mom?" urged Emily.

"I'm just afraid he… That he gave me the promotion because he *wants* to sleep with me." Saying the words out loud was even more devastating than simply thinking about the possibility. "Really… I mean, why else would he promote me? I'm just a mother from Weatherford, Texas. I don't know anything about business or investments or mergers or acquisitions. It's really the only reason that makes sense. Now do you see why I don't want to talk to him?"

"Mom, I really think you're selling yourself short here," said Charlie.

"Yeah, Mom," said Emily. "And Mr. Gherring, too. He just doesn't seem like that type to me. I know what the magazines say about him. But after spending time with him, I don't believe it."

"And let's face it. If Steven Gherring wanted sex, he'd never have to go to this much trouble to get it."

"I don't know." Of course, her girls weren't aware of that kiss in the apartment. The one that made her doubt her own self-control. "But for now, can we *please* change the subject?"

Anne felt guilty about returning to New York on Sunday, leaving Emily with so much responsibility.

"Okay, so Ms. Minnie and Mr. Greenly are going to keep Gandalf until Grandpa is better," Anne told Emily. "Are you sure you're going to be able to handle having Grandpa here at the apartment for a week or two?"

"We'll be fine. He's just planning to park on the couch so he can watch TV. The hardest thing is going to be keeping him from moving around too much. Especially while I'm at work and I can't keep an eye on him."

"Yeah, the doctor said he needs to be pretty still for at least another week and a half while his lung is healing," Anne agreed. "The real problem may start when he goes back to the house by himself. He's not supposed to do anything strenuous for six weeks."

"Right—good luck with that," said Charlie.

"He can be almost as stubborn as Mom."

"Yes, Mom. Explain to me how you managed to avoid talking to Mr. Gherring again during the entire holiday?" asked Charlie.

"I talked to him."

"You texted him. That's not the same," said Emily.

294

"We were usually at the hospital, and I didn't want to be on the phone. I haven't talked to Henri since Wednesday either."

"Mom, I have to tell you something," said Emily. "Don't be mad, okay? Mr. Gherring called me again just to check on you. So I covered for you this time. I told him you'd stayed up late and you were sleeping. But... I think he's really worried you aren't talking to him. Are you planning to resign or something? You can't let silly rumors about you and Mr. Gherring ruin your life."

"No... No I'm not going to resign. Although I have to admit, when I came back here and I was with Dad and both of you, I was tempted to stay. I've missed y'all so much, and it would be so easy just to go back to my old life. But I don't want to be a coward and run away."

"That's more like it. I've always thought my mom was exceptionally brave," Charlie said. "And besides, don't you want to check on Gram? Didn't Mr. Gherring say she's been having heart problems?"

"Oh no, that was just Gram trying to keep Mr. Gherring distracted so he wouldn't end up with Michelle."

"Are you kidding me?" asked Charlie. "Gram's just pretending to have chest pains?"

"It wasn't my idea. That was *all* Gram's doing. She's a little frightening sometimes. But she really loves Steven, and she wants him to have a good wife. There's nothing wrong with that."

"Well no danger you're gonna end up like Gram someday," Emily said. "Because you can't lie worth a flip."

"Yes, that's been a bit of a problem for me. I could learn a lot from my eldest daughter, it seems."

"Emily's not that great at lying either. I can always tell when she's fibbing... Well, almost always. I didn't know about the Spencer thing."

"There's nothing to know about Spencer. But you're the one who's really talented at telling white lies."

"Yeah, I'm so good you don't even know I've ever done it."

Anne lifted one eyebrow. "I'll be on alert from now on."

"Are you ready to go to the airport? We need to leave now so we can drop Charlie off, too."

Anne looked grim. "As ready as I'll ever be, I guess."

Chapter Fourteen – Back in New York

ANNE FELT EXTREMELY GUILTY at being the sole occupant of the luxurious jet. She wished vainly Steven had managed to put her on a commercial flight.

She was so tired she could barely keep her eyes open, but she refused to go back and lay down in the master bedroom. She was determined to avoid the thoughts that would surely invade her mind if she were to lie down in Steven's bed. She planned to grab a taxi and go straight home to sleep. She was too fatigued to even eat dinner. Maybe she'd take just one Benadryl to make sure she could sleep tonight. If she didn't get some rest, she'd never make it through the hectic week ahead. The plane landed smoothly, and she waited for it to taxi to a stop. She already had her suitcases in hand when the pilot came back to open the door. He exited down the ladder in front of her carrying her large bag and she followed behind. When she reached the ground, someone took her carry-on from her hand.

"I've got the car warmed up, waiting for us," said Steven.

Anne felt a rock lodged somewhere in her chest. She'd hoped to avoid being alone with Steven Gherring before going to work on Monday morning. Now she had no choice but to follow him to the waiting limousine. Still, she was grateful for the expedited trip back to the apartment. Perhaps she could keep the topic of conversation on safe ground. Work... she had to talk about work.

She crawled into the car and sat down in the middle of the shorter side seat. He took a seat on the opposite side, per her plan. She decided to be proactive in guiding the dialogue.

"I'll bet we've had some calls from Bern during the Thanksgiving holidays. I plan to start on that first thing in the morning. I'll be at work early."

"That sounds like a good plan, if you feel up to it. You're probably exhausted. Are you sure you're ready to go back to work tomorrow?"

"Oh, I'm fine. I'm not tired at all." She stifled a yawn. "That was just the power of suggestion. We've got the Christmas party this Saturday night. Oh? I forgot to ask if I'm supposed to contact the publicist about an escort for that party."

"No, I usually don't take a date to the company Christmas party... unless I'm actually dating someone. Are you planning to take someone to the party?"

"Maybe. But I'm not sure. Henri may be coming to New York next weekend."

His brows creased. "Henri? I thought he... Did he tell you he was coming next weekend?"

"He said he wanted to come when I talked to him on Wednesday. But with Anna-Laure's chemo, who knows."

"Wednesday? Have you talked to him since then?"

"No, but I'll talk to him tomorrow. Why are you asking?"

"I need to talk to him about a business matter, and I wondered if he was back at work. It's nothing. I'll email him tomorrow."

She struggled to get her heavy coat off. "It's warm in here. Ow— my hair's caught on something."

He sprang across the car to help her. "Wait, it's caught on this button. There I've got it."

He pulled the coat from her shoulders and, to Anne's alarm, remained sitting next to her. She wracked her brain, trying to think of a safe topic.

"Oh! How's Gram?"

"She's absolutely fine. I finally insisted she see a doctor and get checked out. They didn't find anything wrong with her. And by Thursday, she said she was 'hunky-dory.'"

"That's great."

"Anne, I think we should talk about last Tuesday."

"Oh, you mean the office rumor about us sleeping together? I've come to terms with that. I mean I can certainly see why everyone would think that."

"No, I meant... Wait—what do you mean, you see why they would think that?"

"Well, you're you, and I'm me. I got a promotion. Why else would you promote me, right? Only you and I know that would *never* happen."

"Because you wouldn't sleep with a man unless you were married, right?"

Anne was relieved. Maybe he actually got it now. "Right. So if you decide you don't want to promote me after all, I'll understand."

"What do you mean? Why would I decide—" The muscles in Steven's jaw began to flex and she could see him breathing hard. When he finally spoke again, his voice was full of hurt. "Are you implying I actually promoted you so you would sleep with me? Is that what you think of me? After all this time together, you actually think that little of me?"

"Well… no, but—"

"I can't believe it, Anne. Why would you think that?"

"I'm sorry. I didn't know what else to think. After you… you know… And I was embarrassed because I was so… you know…"

"So you put two and two together and came up with thirteen?"

"Well—"

"There are other logical conclusions you could have made."

"Logic has never been my strong point."

"No kidding! And I sent you on my jet to Fort Worth because?"

"I don't know. I feel really bad about that. I wish you'd gotten me a regular ticket. I'll find some way to pay you back."

"I don't *want* you to pay me back."

Her throat tightened. "But I owe you so much. I'm a proud person—I don't like to feel indebted. You just don't know how that feels."

"Did it ever occur to you I *like* doing things for you?"

"I know. You really are a good person—a generous person. You really are *sweet*."

"You've got to be the most infuriating woman on the planet!" He ran his fingers through his hair until it he appeared to have been in a hurricane. Then he looked at her, piercing her with his cold steel blue eyes. She was caught like a deer in headlights—she couldn't look away. He reached out slowly with one hand and brushed away a tear from her cheek. Then his hand dropped down, slowly trailing along her chin, falling down to her neck. She held her breath, afraid to move. Her skin was scalded where his fingers brushed her skin. He moved his hand slowly, gently around the side of her neck until his fingers splayed on the back of her head.

His face was close. She could feel him breathing. She had to stop him now. Just a word and she knew he would retreat. His eyes searched hers. Searched for a sign. Then she felt his fingers twist in her hair, and he pulled her face toward his until their foreheads pressed together, their lips almost touching. Her breath was coming faster, almost panting. She trembled from head to toe. Still he waited, holding back, teasing.

She lifted her hand and tentatively touched his neck. What was she doing? This was a bad idea. He was her boss. If she couldn't stop him from kissing her, how would she stop him when he wanted more? Yet she moved her mouth toward him, like parched lips seeking water. Her lips parted as she touched them to his—shy, timid, seeking.

He spoke to her in a stilted groan, breathing the words into her mouth. "I... am... not... sweet!" His hand tightened behind her neck and he pressed his lips firmly into hers. His tongue invaded her mouth. He kissed her hard. He kissed her thoroughly. Then he released her, pulled away with an expletive, and sat back against the seat, his chest rising and falling with heavy rapid breaths. She felt bereft—empty—with the departure of his lips. A pain as if a bandage had been torn away from a wound.

He turned to capture her gaze again. "And this time, *you* kissed *me*."

They didn't speak the rest of the way home. He seemed as lost in his own thoughts as she was in hers. Her emotions were in turmoil. What did this mean? He'd as much as told her he wasn't trying to sleep with her. Yet, his kiss said something entirely different. And the way her body reacted to him, she knew she was standing on a slippery slope. Hadn't she warned her own girls not to put themselves in a position where they had to make important decisions in the heat of passion? No one was that strong. And she certainly wasn't that strong after denying herself for fifteen years.

Only one thing was certain, Steven Gherring wasn't interested in a long-term relationship with her. If he were, he would have told her. He'd had plenty of opportunities, but he'd never said anything. Even now, in the car, he sat in brooding silence next to her. He seemed to be physically attracted to her. He couldn't fake his reaction any more than she could. But that's where it ended. He cared for her, and he was concerned for her, but no more. And more than anything else, she still wanted him to find happiness and love.

She needed security. She needed someone she could trust. Her encounters with Steven had left her floundering in confusion. She wished he would say what he was thinking. Did he kiss her simply to toy with her emotions? To show her she wasn't in control of her own body? To prevent her from falling in love with Henri?

Regrettably, she realized all these things had been accomplished, even if they weren't his ultimate goals. But even if Steven was just teasing her with these physical episodes, she still wanted him to be happy. She still wanted to find a match for him. She wanted him to find true love, even if she could never find the same for herself.

The car stopped in front of the apartment, and she climbed out. He followed her, carrying both bags. On the elevator, they stared silently at the numbers above the door until they arrived at the tenth floor. She started to take her bags, but he deftly scooped them up and led the way toward her apartment. She had no choice but to follow him and unlock her door. She turned to take her luggage from him, but he pushed his way through the door and deposited her bags on the living room floor. Then he walked back to where she stood just inside the door, watching him with wary eyes.

"I see from your expression you still don't trust me. What did you think? That I would come in here and kiss you again?" He leaned in close and his voice became coarse. "And then did you think I would wait until you were limp with desire and take you to your bed?"

Shocked by his words, she couldn't respond. She couldn't even think.

"Maybe you're right not to trust me. Because believe me, I thought about it." His breathing became shallow, his voice strained. "It would be so easy, so good... I would kiss your lips." His hand caressed her face and his thumb slid lightly back and forth, tracing her lips. "And then I would kiss your neck right here under your jaw." His fingers trailed down, following the path of his words. "And then I would shower kisses here on your shoulder." Now his hand seared a path down her neck and edged under her collar to explore the hidden hollow on her shoulder.

She was breathing rapidly through her mouth, her eyes closed. She should stop him now, but instead she stood frozen in place—waiting, anticipating. Abruptly, he withdrew his hand. A small cry escaped her lips, and her eyes flew open. His face was inches from hers.

"And afterward, you would look at me with regret and disappointment. I'd become the man you accused me of being earlier tonight. So—" He pressed his lips in a gentle caress to her forehead. "I'll earn your trust, instead." He slipped to the door and waited to catch her eyes. "I'll see you in the morning."

Anne dreamed about Steven Gherring. She was *incensed*. He wasn't satisfied with ramping up her desires and dousing them with cold water, or speaking in cryptic words that left her head spinning. Now the man was invading her sleep. She couldn't remember exactly what she'd dreamed, but she knew he was there, and she knew she was exhausted.

For the first time in weeks, Anne tripped when exiting the elevator at Gherring Inc., almost spilling the contents of her arms. She caught her balance and laughed it off to the spectators. But she was secretly frustrated she appeared to have lost the poise she'd worked so hard to attain since she'd arrived in New York. Perhaps it was due to her acute awareness of the curiosity of several of the elevator occupants. Were all of them wondering if she'd slept with Steven Gherring? It would almost be more bearable if the rumor were true, since everyone appeared to believe it anyway. Then at least she'd have some satisfaction to go with her embarrassment. Instead she had only humiliation, confusion, and a healthy dose of frustration.

Although she arrived at seven fifteen, Steven still managed to beat her to the office. She texted Ellen to confirm their lunch plans. Perhaps she'd get really lucky and he would hit it off with Ellen. Then he'd stop making advances in her direction. Anne was thoroughly convinced she possessed the willpower of a cornflake in the presence of Steven Gherring.

She worked with him all morning. He appeared to be totally unaffected by their physical encounters, addressing her as *Ms. Best* and keeping a healthy distance throughout the entire morning. As lunchtime approached, she casually asked him if he'd like to join her for lunch at Papa's Place. His entire face brightened. His eyes sparkled and his dimples danced as he accepted her offer.

"I'd love to eat lunch with you, Anne."

"I need to go down a few minutes early and talk to May about something. Would you mind meeting me down there? May will give us a table in the private room."

"Sure. What time?"

"Oh, if you came down about twelve fifteen, that'd be perfect." She flashed him a nervous smile.

Hurrying down to meet Ellen, she spotted her long straight glossy locks as soon as she started down the sidewalk toward Papa's. She'd evidently also caught the eyes of several young men, judging by the way they peered over their shoulders for a second look when they passed by.

"Oh great, you're on time. Steven is coming, but he doesn't know you're going to be here."

"Terrific." Ellen's voice was dripping with sarcasm. "I'll be his unpleasant surprise. That's a great way to start."

"It's the only way. Trust me."

Inside Papa's, May spotted her and hurried over. "Anne, you're back. You must tell me all about Paris."

"Oh. I didn't get to go, May. It's a long story, but my dad was in a car accident and he almost died."

May and Ellen gasped simultaneously. May asked, "Is he okay?"

"Yes, but several people were killed in the accident. A highway bridge iced over when it started raining. It took out at least ten cars."

"Anne, I didn't know. I'm so sorry. And you didn't get to go to Paris either? That's a pretty awful Thanksgiving." A frown formed a wrinkle between Ellen's eyes.

"Well, my dad is still alive, and I got to see both of my girls. So I'm just counting my blessings."

"You need to come and catch us up on everything that's happened. George is pouting because he didn't get to talk to you the last few times you dropped by," said May.

"I promise to come soon. We also need to chat about Spencer. But today, I have a favor to ask. Can we sit in the back room? Mr. Gherring is coming."

"No problem."

"One more thing. Mr. Gherring doesn't know Ellen is with me. I'd appreciate it if you wouldn't mention that fact to him."

May lifted her eyebrows high and gave Ellen the once over. "So I'm guessing you're trying to make a match with Mr. Gherring and your friend, here?"

Ellen's cheeks reddened. "It's not my idea—I think she's crazy."

"I tend to agree with you," chuckled May. She turned back to Anne. "Honey, I won't breathe a word."

Anne's palms were sweating as they waited for Steven to arrive. Perhaps if she were casual enough, he might think it was an accidental meeting rather than a planned setup. After all, this was the first time she'd actually tried to introduce him to someone. He might not be suspicious.

May led him into the back promptly at twelve fifteen. His pleased expression fell when he noticed Anne had company at the table.

"Hi, Mr. Gherring. I hope you don't mind, but I ran into a friend of mine outside."

"Hi. Steven Gherring. Nice to meet you." He held out his hand and presented a forced smile.

Ellen shook it firmly. "Sorry for imposing, Mr. Gherring. My name is Ellen Dean."

"Ellen's an actress."

"How is it you have so many friends? You've only been in New York for a few weeks." His voice betrayed his irritation.

"Ellen was the only person on the subway who would talk to me."

He glanced at his watch. "You know, I have a pretty busy afternoon. Why don't you just bring something up to me, and let me leave you both to a peaceful lunch?"

He started to turn, but Anne put out her hand. "Oh you should stay. Ellen is very interesting. Like I said, she's an actress. She's got the leading role in a play that starts next week."

His brows flew for a moment, and then understanding dawned on his face. His expression turned fierce and dark. Anne felt her fingers trembling. Perhaps this hadn't been such a great idea.

"May I speak to you privately for a moment, Ms. Best?"

She followed him to the door, scrambling for a cover story. "I'm sorry Mr. Gherring, I didn't think you'd mind—"

"I know exactly what you're doing. This is just part of your little plan with Gram, right?" His voice was quiet, but left no doubt of his anger.

Anne's face was burning. "No, I—"

"Give it up. We both know you can't tell a lie."

"But you can't leave now. It would be rude."

"I can't believe you still want me to... After all that's happened..." His eyes hardened into cold blue slits. "Fine! I'll meet your friend, if that's what you *really* want."

Striding back to the table, he slid into a chair next to Ellen. "It turns out one of my appointments has cancelled this afternoon. I have plenty of time for lunch, after all. Tell me about yourself, Ellen. You're in a play?"

"Yes, it's my first role. I'm trying to break into the business. I have the lead, but we're a really small production."

"What's it called?"

"*Rainbow Junction*. Have you heard of it?"

"No, I'm afraid not. But that's no matter." He flashed his deep dimples at her. "What's that fragrance you're wearing? It's intoxicating."

"Oh. It's called 'Rain'. Do you like it?"

He picked up her hand and lifted her wrist to his nose. "That's really nice. It's light and sweet. It suits you." He held her hand a moment longer before he released it.

Anne kept a smile plastered on her face as she observed their interaction.

"Thank you, Mr. Gherring." Ellen's blushed, a pretty rose color rising to her cheeks.

"Please. Call me Steven." His smile was devastating. "You know Ms. Dean, I just might be interested in supporting this play of yours financially. We should get together and talk more about it."

"Oh, thanks Mr. Gher—I mean, Steven. We could really use some financial support. It's a great play, but it's so far off Broadway no one knows about it."

"Ellen, I have a terrific idea. I have a benefit dinner tomorrow night. Why don't you accompany me? We could talk more about your play."

Anne jumped into the conversation. "Wait. You have a dinner tomorrow night? I didn't know about that—"

He pinned her with cold, angry eyes. "No, you didn't. That was not an accident. I purposely left it off your calendar."

He turned back to Ellen. "Can you believe that Ms. Best has been plotting with my dear grandmother to set me up with a potential wife? Yes, it seems she's even resorted to meddling with my dinner escorts. Unbelievable, right?"

"That's pretty crazy, I guess."

"Yes, indeed. It seems she's working overtime to get me hitched. To someone. To anyone who'll have me I suppose. Despite the fact I specifically forbade her from interfering. So are we on for tomorrow night?"

"Sure." She glanced nervously at Anne.

"Great." He smiled, his sky blue eyes studying Ellen. "Your hair is really striking. Do you do something to straighten it?"

"No, I'm one quarter Asian. It's naturally straight."

He reached out and lifted a lock of her long hair in his hands, gazing as the silky strand slipped through his fingers. "I hope you'll wear it down tomorrow night. I really like it."

"Sure... okay..."

"Ms. Best," he said without taking his eyes off of Ellen. "I'll need Ellen's contact information."

The waitress arrived with their orders, but Steven stood. "I'm sorry for the inconvenience ma'am, but I'll need mine boxed to go."

He turned to Ellen, and lifted the back of her hand to press it against his lips. His clear eyes caught hers in their trance. His voice was low and resonant. "Mademoiselle... Until tomorrow night, *ma jolie fille*."

Anne barely touched her lunch. She supposed her stomach was upset because she knew Steven was angry with her. Still the meeting seemed to have gone extraordinarily well. Ellen was excited the show might be getting some much needed funding and chatted with great animation throughout the rest of the meal. But instead of the elation she ought to be experiencing, Anne felt a gnawing pain in the pit of her stomach. Why wasn't she thrilled? Steven appeared to be enthralled with Ellen? If his date went well on Tuesday night, Steven might never try to kiss her again. Wasn't that what she wanted? More importantly, she wouldn't have to worry about what that kiss might lead to. She pushed her food around on her plate until she finally gave up and asked for a doggy bag.

Steven's office door was closed, so Anne decided to Skype with Henri.

"Hello Anne." Henri's smiling face appeared on the screen. Still sporting the scruffy look, he smiled with tired eyes.

"Hey Henri. I missed hearing your voice. How is Anna-Laure doing?"

"She has had a rough time today, but hopefully the worst is over. But she loves the book you sent her. Where did you find it?"

"I ordered it online. A seven-year-old with cancer wrote it, and it's been translated into three languages. I wanted to do something. And since I couldn't come to Paris, I had it sent straight to you. So she really likes it?"

"I think so. She has read it four times already."

"So will you be able to come this weekend?"

Henri hesitated. "Yes... I am planning to go to Chicago for business on Wednesday. I will be in New York for the weekend."

"So if you're here on Saturday, would you like to go to the company Christmas party with me? I'm kind of expected to go, since I planned most of it."

"Well... maybe... But I am not feeling much like a party."

"It's okay if you don't want to go. We can just wait and see how you feel."

"Okay, that's a good idea."

"So, when will I see you? That is, assuming Anna-Laure is fine and you get to come over here."

"I am not sure. Probably, we will get together on Friday night. That is when I first come into the city."

"That sounds great. I'm excited to finally see you again. I'd better get back to work before I get caught. Bye for now."

"Goodbye, *jolie fille*."

Back at her desk, Steven addressed work issues, not mentioning the lunch incident except for retrieving Ellen's contact information. Still, Anne couldn't relax in his presence. He chose the afternoon for a lesson using his email correspondence. He was constantly brushing his arm against her while leaning over to identify specific terms on her computer screen. At one point he stood behind her and leaned across her shoulder, his face almost touching hers. For his part, he seemed totally unaware of the casual contact, but Anne felt a growing discomfort. He'd ruined her. Now his close proximity stirred memories of just how good his kiss had felt. She tried to concentrate on work, but was frustrated at her lack of progress and grateful when it was time to leave.

Arriving at the apartment building after her long subway commute, Rayna hurried out to stop her before she got on the elevator. "Hey, Anne. What are your plans tonight?"

"Well, not much. I'm planning to change clothes and go for a run on the treadmill right now. But I'm free later if you want to get together and talk. Is something up?"

"No, I just feel like we've lost touch. I like to know what you're up to."

"Should I call you later?"

"Sure. That'd be great."

Anne changed quickly and headed for the gym. She needed a good run to release some tension and get all thoughts of Steven out of her head. She chose a treadmill and started her run. She planned a forty minute run, but she might go forty-five or fifty if she was feeling strong. She'd been running for about five minutes when Steven Gherring walked in front of her treadmill, blocking her view out the window. He was shirtless, *of course*. He leaned his elbow on the front of her treadmill, his biceps flexing.

"Hey, Anne. Just thought I'd say hello before I start my ride."

Anne made a vain attempt to keep her eyes locked on Steven's face. "Hello."

"I'm planning to ride for an hour. I've gotten behind on my training." He stretched his arms above his head, flexing every sinewy muscle in his chest and arms. Anne watched him, mesmerized, and stumbled a bit on her track.

"Is there something wrong with the fancy exercise bike in your apartment?"

"Yes, it's broken."

"Should I call someone for you to have it fixed?"

"No, that's okay. I don't mind coming down here." He stretched again. "Well I'd better get started on that long training ride. You could come and talk to me when you're finished if you'd like." He bent over to touch his toes and did a lunge stretch on each leg. Every individual strand of his clearly defined leg muscles seemed to dance and flex. Then he sauntered over to mount an exercise bike.

Anne felt faint. It was probably a lack of food. Surely it had nothing to do with Steven's effortless but effective assault on her senses. He did have an amazing body. And she'd seen him in nothing but a towel. Unbidden, an image invaded her mind. Steven was bending over the breakfast table, his body still damp from his shower, muscles flexing, straining the limits of the towel tucked low around his hips. She missed another step on the treadmill and barely caught herself before falling. She'd better cut her run short before she broke something.

She turned off her unit and dashed out of the gym quickly, avoiding eye contact with Steven. It wasn't until she reached her apartment she realized she'd left her cell phone and keys upstairs in the gym. She returned to retrieve them, hoping to slip in quietly and escape another encounter with him. But when she arrived, his bike was empty, and he was nowhere to be seen.

She had to escape… to get away from everything that reminded her of Steven. It was dark outside, but still early. There were plenty of people on the streets. Surely it would be safe to go visit Mr. Hamilton. She hadn't even run on the treadmill long enough to break a sweat, so she changed quickly and hurried out the front door, waving at Rayna who was busy talking to another resident. Antonio stopped her at the door.

"Hi Beautiful! Where're you off to? Should I get you a taxi?"

"No thanks, Antonio. I'm just going a few blocks. And I'll be back in an hour."

"Are you sure? It's already dark."

"I'll be fine. Tell Rayna I'll call her later."

She walked rapidly, but she didn't feel any danger on the busy New York City street. Mr. Hamilton's light was on, but the door was locked. So she rang the door and waited. Soon she heard footsteps and he appeared at the door.

"Come in, come in!" His eyes crinkled in a huge smile. "I'm so glad you came by. I was just making dinner. Would you like to join me?"

"Oh, I don't want to impose," she said, but her stomach gurgled at the scent of food drifting down the stairs.

He laughed out loud. "Your stomach says 'yes', so come on up."

She followed him to his friendly kitchen and flopped into a chair at the table. He dished up two plates of spaghetti with meatballs and put a large bowl of tossed green salad on the table. Then he opened the oven and removed a pan of broiled garlic and cheese bread.

"If you don't like Italian food, you're out of luck."

A loud growl answered him before Anne could speak. She giggled. "My stomach and I both love Italian. Thanks!"

She felt the tension melting from her shoulders as she chatted with Mr. Hamilton over dinner. She told him all about the stress of learning about the accident, and not knowing the outcome until arriving in Fort Worth. They discussed her new job and her misgivings about her abilities. But she purposefully avoided the subject of Steven Gherring, the source of a great deal of her anxiety at the moment.

After dinner, they went downstairs and he pulled out a vinyl record of The Lawrence Marable Quartet, entitled *Tenorman*. The sweet sounds of jazz filled the shop. He carved while Anne browsed through the shop. Once again, she was thoroughly fascinated, examining the precise fit where each of the puzzle-like carved figures intertwined. She went back to her favorite carving, Inseparable Love, marveling once again at the intricate pieces carved from a single piece of wood. A new sign, *Not For Sale*, had replaced the seventy-five hundred dollar price tag.

"How come you took the price tag off this one?"

He smiled. "A man actually tried to buy it from me last week. I had to make up a story about saving it for someone else. So, I decided to play it safe, since I don't really want to sell it anyway."

"Just out of curiosity, how much would it take for you to sell it? A million? Not that I'm planning to buy it or anything," she chuckled.

"I don't think I could ever sell it. I might give it to my granddaughter someday."

"Wow—lucky girl." Her cell phone started ringing, and she ran to dig it out of her purse.

"Hey Rayna. What's up?"

"Oh great, you answered your phone. I called thirty minutes ago, and you didn't answer. I thought something might have happened. Are you okay?"

"I'm fine—I must've left my purse downstairs during dinner. I just had Italian food with Mr. Hamilton. He's the one I told you about. You know, he lives above his woodcarving shop. You should come and see it sometime."

"Okay sure. But are you coming home soon?"

"Yes, I didn't realize I'd been here for two hours already. I'm leaving right now."

Anne heard muffled voices in the background and Rayna came back on the phone. "You really should take a taxi. It's dark outside."

"Maybe. But I'll probably just walk. I need the exercise. I didn't manage to finish my run tonight. Anyway, it's a beautiful clear night, and I have a warm coat and hat and gloves. I'll see you in a few minutes."

Rayna started to protest again, but Anne disconnected the call. She turned to Mr. Hamilton. "I guess I need to go. My friend Rayna has suddenly gotten very motherly." She bundled up and gave Mr. Hamilton a big hug before dashing out the door.

Making her way down the deserted street, she had some misgivings about her decision. She would have hailed a cab, but there were no cars to be seen. She began to get a little nervous when a man across the street seemed to slow down as she came his direction. He was probably just looking at the street sign, but it appeared he was studying her, instead. She scolded herself for being paranoid and picked up her pace a bit, slipping her hand into her purse to find the comfort of a can of mace she'd had for ten years. Who knew if it even worked after this much time? The streetlights made shadows under the awnings, and she began to imagine someone hiding in every darkened doorway. Perhaps it would have been wise to get a taxi after all.

She saw a figure coming toward her on the same side of the street. He was making rapid time, although he didn't appear to have on running attire. She stepped into a sheltered doorway to remain undetected as he passed by. But when he got closer, she recognized his face.

310

"Mr. Gherring?"

"Anne!" He almost fell down as he skidded to a stop. He darted to her hiding place and pulled her into his arms. She sank into their safety and comfort, holding on as if she were drowning.

"You can't be this stupid. You're a grown woman—a mother! What would you tell your daughters about being alone on a deserted street in New York at night?"

"H-how did you know?"

"Because Rayna... She happened to be talking to you when I was walking out the lobby door."

"Well, you didn't have to come," she said stubbornly. "I only had another block or so. I would've been fine."

"Really? And that's why you were hiding in that doorway when I came by?"

"I have my mace." She pulled the can out of her purse.

"You should keep that, but you should never put yourself in a place where you need to use it." He kept his arm around her and started guiding her back toward the apartment building.

She began to shiver.

"Are you cold?" He pulled her closer.

"No," she confessed. "I think it's that adrenaline thing, like what happened after Jeff made that pass at me. I suppose it's *possible* I might have gotten a little afraid when this huge thug came running toward me at a marathon pace."

He chuckled. "I'm a huge thug now?"

"When you're alone on a deserted street at night, everyone is a huge thug." She sighed. "You're *right*. I should've taken a taxi."

"You could've called me. I would've gone with you."

"I didn't want to... to inconvenience anyone."

"How do you know Mr. Hamilton, anyway? Wait, Gram introduced you. Of course."

"I love his shop. His carvings are amazing."

"I should visit the old guy. I haven't seen him in a long time."

They arrived at the apartment building. "Thanks for walking me safely home. You really are *sweet*, just like I said. I'll see you later. Where was it you were going?"

"Oh—you mean where was I going before?"

"Yes, when you were going through the lobby?"

"I was headed to the drug store down the block to... to get some... aspirin. That's right, I needed aspirin. But come to think of it, I have some in the apartment." He walked into the lobby with her.

Rayna grabbed her arms and squeezed, scolding, "Anne, you mustn't go anywhere again without talking to me first."

She stared at Rayna as if she had two heads. "What on earth has gotten into you, Rayna? You never used to worry so much."

"I don't know. Aren't we friends?" Her voice was distressed as she cut her eyes toward Steven.

"Oh sure we are. I didn't mean anything by it. Thanks for caring."

But secretly, Anne was baffled by her friend's sudden excessive controlling behavior.

Chapter Fifteen - Tuesday

GRAM CALLED TO TAKE ANNE to lunch on Tuesday. "Time for another emergency meeting."

"Everything's an emergency for you, Gram."

"That's because I don't know how much longer I'm going to be alive. I've got to get things done as quickly as possible."

She laughed. "Okay, what's the emergency this time?"

"This time the emergency is you."

"Me?"

"Yes, I've decided it's time you married again."

"But Gram, I'm fine alone. I've already had the love of my life—ten wonderful years. And I've been fine for fifteen years without anyone. You should understand. You're just like me. You're single and happy and independent."

"Well, I have Steven to take care of me. And who knows, I may not stay single for the rest of my life."

"What?" Was Gram contemplating marriage at the age of ninety-five?

"But we're here to talk about you. You're always taking care of other people. You're taking care of your dad and your girls. You have to take care of my Steven at work. And now, you're taking care of Henri even though he's in France."

Anne looked startled at her last statement. "Gram, what—"

"Steven told me about Henri's niece. What is her name? The poor dear..."

"Her name is Anna-Laure. But why would Steven tell you—"

"Last night on the phone, I was discussing you with Steven, and complaining about Henri."

Anne felt her cheeks redden. "Gram! Why would you discuss me with Steven? I really don't want y'all to discuss me."

"Steven seemed to find it amusing we were discussing you, instead of you and I discussing him."

"I'll bet he did," she retorted with dripping sarcasm.

"Anyway, my point is you take care of everyone else, and there's no one to take care of you."

"I have my family—"

"Pish-posh. Your family doesn't live here. And your girls are grown. They have their own lives. They'll probably be married soon."

"Well my dad is kind of a wanderer. He never lives in the same place very long. But he always comes when I need him."

"But you need someone to take care of you every day. You need a husband. And I intend to find one for you." Gram crossed her arms, and Anne knew she had a battle on her hands.

"Gram, I have plenty of people here who care about me. There's George and May, Rayna and Antonio, Katie, Ellen, Sam, and you. And Mr. Hamilton has been very sweet to me as well."

"And Steven?"

Her face and neck grew hot. "Yes, of course Mr. Gherring has been very helpful and encouraging."

"You don't need encouragement—you need a husband."

"Gram, I don't think you—"

"Don't worry, dear. I'll be very discreet."

Anne sighed in defeat. "Fine Gram. How about I just keep you informed if anything happens on that front."

"That'll be your part, and I'll do mine."

"And what was that you said about you not staying single? Are you planning to get married again?"

"It's always a possibility," she said evasively. "Or… maybe we'll just live together in sin."

"Ms. Best," said Steven, sticking his head out of his office door. "Would you double-check my tux is being delivered to the apartment tonight?"

"It's *that* kind of benefit? Mr. Gherring, I'm not sure Ellen owns an appropriate dress for a formal event."

"She does now. I bought her one."

"Oh, I see." Her stomach churned a bit. "And what time do you need the tux?"

314

"The dinner's at seven, so five o'clock is fine. Thanks. Oh, and Ms. Best?"

"Yes sir, Mr. Gherring?"

"I want to apologize for getting so angry about lunch yesterday. I'm really glad you introduced me to Ellen."

"You're welcome, Mr. Gherring. I'm really happy for you." Her words should have been true. Perhaps if she said it enough, she'd believe it.

The rest of the afternoon, Anne worked alone at her desk. Every time she thought about Steven and Ellen together she had a queasy feeling in her stomach. Why wasn't she happier they seemed to be hitting it off? Maybe she was second-guessing their compatibility. Ellen hadn't done much traveling, and she didn't know anything about business. What would they find to talk about? Somehow that thought made her feel better.

By the end of the day, her body felt drained. Standing to stretch her tired muscles, she heard her cell phone ring.

"Hi, Johanna. What are you doing calling me? Especially at this time? Isn't it pretty late at night in Germany? Is something wrong?"

Johanna laughed. "If you slow down for a moment, I will actually answer you. Surprise! We are here in New York. We just got in town. I talked Alexander into bringing me to see the Christmas tree at the Rockefeller Center. Would you like to come with us? They are lighting it tonight."

Her fatigue vanished. "Oh, I'd love to go—I'm so excited. And I can't wait to see you and talk to you. To tell you the truth, I was feeling a little glum before you called. And I've never even seen the Rockefeller Christmas Tree."

"I am so pleased. You can come and eat with us, as well. Do not dress up. Just dress warmly." She hesitated and then added, "Feel free to invite someone along. Mr. Gherring, perhaps?"

"He's busy tonight. He's going to a benefit dinner. It'll probably just be me. Is that okay?"

"Absolutely, dear. It is you I wanted to see. Alexander can talk business another day."

Anne was practically floating as she walked toward the elevator. There were several other employees leaving at the same time, and all of them greeted her cordially. No one was acting awkward, so she felt relieved. Perhaps everyone had forgotten the rumor about her and Steven. Just as the door was about to close, Steven came running to the elevator and slipped inside. At his appearance, the elevator became stiflingly quiet.

He turned to Anne. "What are your plans for the evening, Ms. Best?"

"I'm going to see the Christmas tree lighting ceremony at the Rockefeller Center." She couldn't hide her growing excitement. "I've never been before. I mean, I've never even seen the Rockefeller Christmas tree."

"You're going by yourself?"

"No sir. I'm going with Johanna and Alexander. They just flew in from Germany."

He seemed annoyed. "Well that's good. Sounds like you'll have a good time. I'm glad you won't be sitting at home alone." His voice sounded as though that's exactly what he wished would happen. Was he jealous of Johanna and Alexander?

"I think they would have invited you as well, sir. Except you have that important benefit dinner tonight." She added, "With Ellen."

"Right. We'll have a fabulous time, I'm sure. Please give my regards to the Kleins."

"I will, I promise." At his glum expression she added, "Johanna mentioned something about Alexander wanting to talk business. You should call him tomorrow."

"Thank you, Ms. Best." Everyone else in the elevator remained quiet. They all seemed to be listening to their exchange.

In the lobby, Steven exited first, and the quiet tension relaxed as the riders dispersed. One of the women Anne knew from the Personnel Department stopped her before she could leave the lobby.

"Anne. What's with you and Mr. Gherring? Did you have some kind of fight?"

"No, not at all. What do you mean?"

"Well, aren't you dating?"

Her face was burning. "No, Lisa, we aren't dating. We never have. That was just a rumor."

"Aren't we just talking semantics here? And there's no company rule against dating the boss, you know. It won't get you in trouble with the Personnel Department. I hate to be nosy, but I've given up and accepted it as part of my personality. So, you and Mr. Gherring don't have romantic feelings for each other?"

Anne chose her words carefully. "I think I'd know if we had that kind of relationship. He thinks of me only as a secretary, an employee. In fact, I'm the one who ordered his tuxedo for his date tonight with a friend of mine."

"Okay, I guess we had it wrong after all."

She was relieved. Perhaps she'd finally put those rumors to rest.

Anne was waiting in the lobby for Johanna, when Steven came downstairs in his tux. Her heart leaped in her chest. He was achingly handsome in a tuxedo. For a moment she tried to decide whether he was more handsome in a tuxedo or in a towel. But the pounding of her heart reminded her this was a dangerous thought pattern.

"You look very sharp, Mr. Gherring," she said sincerely. "I hope you have a good time tonight. You know, I'm really glad you're keeping an open mind about this. Ellen could be *the one*." She wondered at the way her heart clenched when she said those words.

"And that would make you happy? You'd be happy if I was with Ellen?"

"Well yes, I... I really, truly just want you to be happy. Whatever it takes. That'll make me happy. So yes, I'd be happy if you and Ellen were together, if she's the one who can do that for you."

"And it wouldn't bother you?"

"Of course not. I mean, I'm the one who wanted the two of you to date, right?"

"That's right. You're the one who wanted it." He tightened his lips, closing his eyes for a moment. "Have fun at the Christmas tree lighting."

"Oh, I will—I can't wait. Just imagine, a bazillion lights coming on all at once. I've seen it on TV, but never in person. I'm going to take a video on my phone and send it to Charlie and Emily. They'll be so jealous. And the weather is perfect. It's going to be so beautiful."

Steven smiled a bit dejectedly. "I wish I could be there to see it."

"Oh, I'm sure you've seen it plenty of times. It wouldn't be exciting for you."

"No," he said. "I wish I could be there to see *you* see it for the first time."

"Oh!" Anne cried with thousands of others as the huge Christmas tree sprung to life with over thirty thousand lights. She joined in the cheers and clapping, forgetting she was taking a phone video as she jumped up and down with glee. Johanna and Alexander seemed to enjoy watching Anne as much as the tree. They stayed for thirty minutes until the show was over and the crowds began to disperse.

"Will you take my picture with the tree in the background? I want to prove I was actually here."

Alexander snapped several pictures of Anne and Johanna together with the glowing tree in the background. Then they walked a block away to their dinner reservation. Anne was engrossed in the stories of Johanna's grandchildren, a set of twin boys, aged three, and a one-year-old girl. She totally forgot about Steven and Ellen on their inaugural date. Two glasses of wine also contributed to her relaxation. But over dessert, Johanna asked a few probing questions about her *love life*.

"How is Henri? Are you two still an item? And most importantly, are there sparks?"

Anne hesitated. "Well. I know I emailed you about my dad's accident and me not getting to go to Paris."

"Yes, and you told me your father is expected to make a full recovery. I am so glad." She reached out to touch Anne's hand. "Did things not go well with your father?"

"No, it's not that. It's just that... well, I didn't go to Paris. And somehow I feel like something is different between Henri and me. He's coming here this weekend. I guess I don't feel those sparks with him. But then I think maybe I would if we spent time together. He's incredibly good-looking." She looked up at Alexander. "I'm sorry to put you through this. Your wife is a good counselor."

He laughed. "Oh no. I am used to this. Back home, Johanna is *die Liebe Arzt*—the 'Love Doctor.'"

"But what were you going to say?" urged Johanna.

"I just feel like Henri and I will never be anything but friends. But I don't want to tell him that right now, not when he's dealing with his niece who has cancer."

"Oh, I don't think you mentioned that. How terrible... His niece?"

"Yes. Well his sister and her two kids live with him, so he's practically her father instead of her niece. And she's only seven."

"And they just found out? About the cancer?"

"Yes. So you see why he needs me right now?"

"He is coming this weekend, and you will see him in person? Right? If the sparks are not there, you must tell him the truth. He needs the sparks as much as you."

"You're probably right," she agreed, but she felt like a heel. She couldn't break his heart at a time like this.

"But you have not told me about Steven Gherring."

"What about Mr. Gherring?" Blood rushed to her face, and she concentrated on her plate.

"The last time I was here, I told you I thought he might be attracted to you. It was the way he looked at you when you were dancing together. Was I right?"

Anne could feel her pulse in her temples. "No... I mean... It depends on what you mean by attracted. He's... I don't know."

"Yes, I see."

"You see what?"

"With Steven Gherring, there are sparks," she said with a smug smile.

"Oh no. There are no sparks. Well not the kind of sparks that mean anything. He may have kissed me, but he's the world's richest playboy. He's kissed plenty of women."

"I see."

"And tonight, for instance, I set him up on a date with one of my friends. And he really likes her. Would I do that if I was in love with Steven Gherring?"

"Interesting leap you made. I asked if there were sparks. I did not ask if you were in love with Steven Gherring." She chuckled at Anne's gasp. "But I do not know why you would set him up with your friend. Why did you do that?"

"Because he needs someone who'll love him and take care of him. He's already grown tired of dating women who only value him for what he can give them. He deserves the kind of love I had with Tom. I want that for him."

"I see." Johanna smiled.

"You see *what*?" Anne demanded.

"I just see. That is enough." She patted Anne's hand. "Do not worry—we will talk again. Alexander and I will be here several days."

"Hi, Anne." Rayna greeted her when she came in. "Where've you been?"

"I went to see the Christmas tree lighting ceremony at Rockefeller. It was amazing."

"Were you on a date?"

"Hardly," laughed Anne. "I was just the third wheel—I went with a couple that are visiting from Germany."

"Oh, sounds fun."

Anne asked casually, "Did you see Mr. Gherring? I mean, has he come back from his benefit dinner?"

"Sure. He's been back for an hour."

"Did he look like he was happy? Like he had a good time? Or was he in a bad mood?"

"I don't know. He's so serious all the time. I think he's always in a bad mood."

"Oh, he's not like that, really. He's really fun and witty, if you get to know him."

"Okay honey, no offense. He's kind of my boss, since Gherring Inc. owns this building. So I'm a little afraid of him."

"Well, I'm beat. I'm headed up to bed. Goodnight, Rayna."

Anne had just opened her apartment door when her cell phone rang. It was Steven, and he never called late at night.

"Hello? Mr. Gherring?"

"Anne, I'm sorry to impose. Are you already asleep?"

"No, I just walked in the door. What did you need?"

"I really need to check something at the office, and I can't get my laptop to turn on. Would you mind bringing yours upstairs for just a minute?"

"Sure, I'll be right there."

Anne threw her coat and gloves off and grabbed her laptop, heading for the penthouse apartment. She knocked on the door and Steven opened it immediately, blocking the doorway. He was still in his tuxedo pants, but his tie was off and his shirt was unbuttoned, hanging open. His chest was almost more appealing when only partially exposed, like a teasing entreaty. She had an insane urge to put out her hand and feel those firm muscles. She felt that familiar tingle as his fingertips brushed against hers when he took the laptop from her hands. He opened it and made the connection to the office computer, pulling up his daily schedule.

He muttered something about checking his schedule for the next day. "Oh good, I don't have anything scheduled during lunch."

"Oh, I could have just told you that. I almost never schedule anything during your lunch. I think it's too important for you to eat well."

Steven turned around and took a few steps inside. "Good news, Ellen. I'm open for lunch tomorrow."

Anne's eyes followed Steven's. They stopped when they fell on Ellen, sitting on Steven's soft leather sofa with a glass of red wine in her hand. Her expression, as she returned Anne's gaze, was incredibly awkward.

Anne's eyes took in the atmosphere. Ellen's bare feet, her sexy dress, the wine, Steven's open shirt, and soft music on the stereo. She turned around slowly and walked away. She heard Steven's voice behind her, but she ignored it. Instead she kept walking past the elevator to the stairway, and started down the stairs.

She needed to get control of her emotions. She should have been ready for this, but she wasn't. Was she crying? She breathed slowly, concentrating on stopping the tears. This was what she wanted. It was for the best. Ellen was a good match for him. She'd done her job well. Anyway, it was just one date. Who knew if this would really lead to anything? But didn't she want it to lead to something? Didn't she want Steven and Ellen to be together? What did she want? She wanted him to kiss her again. At least, that's what her body wanted. But her mind knew she wouldn't be able to stop with a kiss. It was better this way. It was better for him to be with Ellen.

She walked all the way down the stairs to the lobby. In a daze, she moved through the lobby and outside the door. Her tears dried on her face in the chilly wind. She was standing outside in the cold, when Antonio came out to talk to her.

"Hey, Anne. Are you expecting someone? Why don't you wait inside? You're going to freeze out here without a coat."

Anne turned glazed eyes to Antonio, trying to comprehend what he was saying.

"Aren't you cold?" She looked down at her hands and noticed she was shivering. "Do you want to wait inside?"

"Okay," she agreed, but her body didn't respond to her brain.

He took her elbow and led her inside the door. "Why don't you come and sit over here, out of the wind for a second? Who are you waiting for?"

"Waiting for? No one. I wasn't waiting for anyone. I was just... I was just hot, I guess."

"Are you okay? Rayna's gone upstairs, but I could get her for you."

"No, I don't need anyone. I'll go home." Anne rose and headed for the elevator. After a few steps she stopped and turned back to Antonio. "Do you love Rayna?"

He blushed. "Yes. I'm going to buy her a ring soon. But don't tell her—it's a secret."

She smiled. "I'm so glad. It really does make me happy when two people find each other. It really *does*."

"Okay." Antonio's expression was full of confusion. Then he shook his head and added in a low voice, "Wow, I really don't understand women."

Chapter Sixteen – Wednesday, Thursday, Friday

ANNE SLEPT FITFULLY. When she woke up at five a.m., she knew sleep was a lost cause. She thought about working out, but she really didn't feel well. Her body felt tired and achy, almost feverish. She made a cup of hot tea, poured it into an insulated mug, and headed to work without attempting to put food into her churning stomach.

Arriving at the office, she was so early the night guard had to let her inside. She sat down and started into her backlog of work, gaining some level of satisfaction from her productive activity. She dreaded having to face Steven, and had practiced looking nonchalant and happy about his successful date with Ellen. She tried hard not to imagine what must have happened after she left them alone in his apartment—that really wasn't her business. Like she'd told herself before. Steven was a man. He had needs she couldn't meet. No, that wasn't right. She could meet those needs, but she wouldn't. It was her choice, and now she had to live with the consequences of that choice.

Katie was still coming in to work part time, and she arrived before Steven. Anne pulled up a chair for her and started asking her every question she could conjure. Her ploy worked, for when Steven arrived, she was still deep in conversation with Katie. He stopped at her desk, as if waiting for an opening to speak.

"Yes sir? Did you need something?" she asked without quite making eye contact.

"I… I wanted to give you your computer back. Thanks for your help."

"Sure, I was happy to help you." Anne hoped she succeeded in sounding upbeat.

Steven remained standing at her desk, until Katie finally looked at him and rolled her eyes.

"Mr. Gherring, did you want to talk to Ms. Best alone?"

Anne attempted to skewer Katie with her eyes, but she smiled back.

"Yes, thank you, Ms. Carson. And tell Gary I said hello."

Anne found herself alone with Steven. She was grateful they were at least in the common area and not in his office. He leaned over to get her attention, but she kept at her task, never raising her eyes.

"Yes, Mr. Gherring? What did you need? I'm really busy today. I have so much to do."

"I... I wanted to be sure you're okay. You left in a hurry last night. I thought—"

"Yes I'm okay. Is there anything else?"

"I was thinking maybe we should talk."

"Aren't we talking now, Mr. Gherring?"

"I think you know what I mean."

She was still trying to form an answer in her head when the elevator doors opened, and Michelle stepped out.

"Steven," she cried, crossing quickly to him and throwing her arms around his neck. "It's awful!" She began to sob. "Oh, Steven! You have to help me. It didn't work. He's—" She took his hand. "Please, I can't talk about it out here." She cast red-rimmed eyes in Anne's direction.

Steven couldn't hide his frustration as he followed Michelle into his office. He paused and turned back to Anne. "This conversation isn't over."

That was all the warning Anne needed. She had to find a place to hide for the rest of the day.

She called Jared and arranged to spend the entire morning training with him in the CMA department. Sending him off to lunch at twelve, she remained working at Shanna Matheson's desk. She was glad Shanna hadn't yet returned to work after her maternity leave. Her goal was to avoid talking to Steven alone if possible. Also, she didn't want to see him immediately before or after his lunch with Ellen. She just wasn't sure she could control her emotions. She certainly wasn't going to eat next door at Papa's Place. Steven and Ellen could be going there for lunch.

Anyway, she wasn't the least bit hungry. She felt much the same as she did after learning of Tom's death, a little in shock. She reasoned her emotions just needed time to adjust to this new reality. It's not like those few kisses she'd experienced had been satisfying in any way. On the contrary, she felt a longing and a distinct dissatisfaction. Pursuing more physical contact with Steven Gherring would bring nothing but disappointment. The only logical conclusion to a physical relationship with Steven was to either stand by her convictions and experience frustration, or give in to temptation and experience temporary physical pleasure, followed by guilt and self-condemnation. She'd made her decision. Now she just had to learn to live with it.

Johanna called, but Anne let the call go to her voicemail and turned her cell phone off. Johanna was too astute. She'd sense immediately something was wrong. She needed to gain her composure before talking to Johanna.

When Jared returned from lunch, he brought something for her to eat. She thanked him profusely for the thoughtful gesture, and pretended to eat something. But the thought of actually swallowing food made her gag. As had happened in the past when she was upset emotionally, Anne became almost robotic in her work. She functioned quickly and methodically, churning out data reports and comparative charts.

When she asked Jared to check her work, he whistled.

"Wow, Anne. You did all that today? If you keep this up, they'll fire me and Shanna, both."

"But it looks correct? I just want to make sure I'm doing it right."

"It looks perfect. Why don't you take a break? You look a little tired."

"No, I want to tackle the yearly estimates, taking the tax changes into account."

"Well, okay. But we usually let the Accounting department do that one."

"I'm not sure. But I think my new department is supposed to cover that as well. Anyway, I'm going to try—"

"No, you're not," Steven's voice rang out behind her. "You're not expected to do that report. And it's time you took a break to eat something."

"You were right, Boss—she didn't touch the lunch I brought her."

Anne glared at Jared, but he grinned, shrugging. "Sorry, Anne. Us guys have to stick together. Beside's he pays me."

"Did you even have breakfast?" Steven demanded.

"It's none of your business what I do or don't eat," she pouted. "What do you care anyway, as long as I get the work done?"

Steven's face grew red and the veins stood out on his neck until it looked as if he might explode.

"Oh, that's my cue. I'm outta here." Jared melted out the door.

"I think I've shown I care what happens to you," Steven said evenly. "Now I'm going to pretend you didn't say that, and I'm going to ask my question again. Did you eat breakfast today?"

"You don't understand. I can't eat. My stomach is upset."

"And did you drink anything today?"

"Yes, I made a cup of tea this morning," she said defiantly.

"And you drank it?"

"Of course."

Steven pulled a familiar insulated mug from behind his back and shook it. "It seems full to me."

"Oh…" Anne was confused. "Maybe I forgot…"

He pinched her arm.

"Ow—that hurt!"

"You're dehydrated. Look at your skin—it doesn't spring back." He heaved out a huge breath. "Wait here."

He disappeared through the door and came back moments later with two bottles of water.

"Ughh—please don't make me drink that. You know I don't like to drink water. I don't feel well right now. It'll make me throw up."

"You can drink this water or I'll drive you to the hospital and hook you up to an IV. Your choice."

Anne opened her mouth to protest, but she quailed at his fierce expression. She obediently reached out to take the water bottle.

"And your hand is shaking. You can't do this, Anne. You have to take care of yourself."

"It's not like I was going to die," she retorted, forcing down a small amount of water. "I've been taking care of myself for a long time, without any help from you or anyone else."

"And evidently doing a poor job of it." He started pacing, stopping every so often to glare at her until she obediently swallowed some water. "I meet you after forty-five years, and it turns out you're only alive by lucky happenstance."

She started to protest again. But he shot her another look, and she took another sip of water instead.

"We still need to talk, but I can see this is not the time for it. And I suppose you turned off your cell phone. Alexander and Johanna came by. They wanted to take you and I to lunch, so we went without you."

"But I thought you were going to lunch with Ellen?"

"No, she had to work through lunch."

She could tell he was watching for a reaction. Her heart gave a little leap of joy, but she tamped it down with her brain. Steven was hitting it off with Ellen, and hadn't that been her plan all along?

"I'm sorry that didn't work out."

"You are? I thought maybe... Oh never mind, drink some more. You've barely touched that water." He paused to watch her sip some more. "Johanna wants you to call her."

"Okay," Anne reached for her cell phone, but Steven grabbed her hand. An electric jolt shot up her arm, and she jerked her hand away.

"After you drink your water."

"This is silly. I know you have more important things to do than to babysit me while I drink water. You go, and I promise to drink it."

He sat down next to her and pulled her computer toward him. "You're right. I do have work to do. I just don't have anything more *important* to do. So I'll work right here until you finish drinking." He began sorting his email.

She sighed and forced another gulp into her protesting stomach. Staring glumly at the daunting bottle and a half of water in front of her, and knew she could never down that much water. At least she wouldn't be able to keep it down. She picked up the water bottles and said, "I think I'll just take these to the lounge area. Maybe if I had some crackers, I could drink more."

Without taking his eyes off the computer, Steven reached into his pocket and pulled out a package of her favorite cheese crackers from the vending machine. He waved them in the air, until she snatched them from his hand with considerable irritation.

She snacked on the crackers and drank her water until all of one bottle and most of the other was gone. But he continued working on her computer, ignoring her completely. She turned on her cell phone and found two missed calls from Johanna, two from Steven, and one from Sam. She decided to return Johanna's call first.

"Hi, Johanna." At Steven's glare, she grabbed the water and took a swallow.

"Hello Anne. We are so sorry we missed you at lunch. But we have tickets to go to a jazz club show tonight. Do you like jazz?"

"I love it—that'd be fun." She really needed the distraction. Anything to stop thinking about Steven.

"Dress warmly. To get good seats, you have to arrive early and be in the front of the line."

"Okay, what time?"

She heard Johanna confer with her husband. "We will pick you up at six thirty. Okay?"

"That sounds great."

Next, she called Sam, swallowing more water to pacify Steven as she waited for her to answer.

"Hey Anne. I wanted to apologize I didn't believe you the other day when you said you weren't with Mr. Gherring."

"That's okay, Sam. I know you didn't mean anything by it. But I'm glad you believe me now."

"Well, after I saw Mr. Gherring's picture in the social column this morning, I knew you were telling the truth."

Her mouth went dry. "What picture?" She peeked at Steven to ensure he wasn't listening in.

"You should see it. He's with this beautiful girl with amazing long, straight hair. She looks kind of exotic. He has his arm around her and he's actually smiling. You know, he looks like he's posing for the cameras. Usually, he looks really grumpy in the pictures or else they get a candid shot when no one is looking. And here, I'll read you the caption. *Steven Gherring is always shopping for new talent. This one is actress, Ellen Dean, from the new play, 'Rainbow Junction'. Don't they look cozy? Maybe New York's most eligible bachelor will be off the bachelor list soon.*" She prattled on, full of excitement "So, do you think he's really going to marry this girl? Everyone was kind of pulling for *you* before, but this girl's really beautiful. They'd have amazing-looking kids together."

"Oh... Yes, I hope that works out." Anne tried to keep her words neutral for Steven's benefit. "Well, I'd better get back to work."

Overwhelmed by a sudden intense nausea, she flung her phone down and dashed for the ladies room, barely making the toilet before her stomach emptied its contents. She was humiliated at the gagging sounds she made, since there appeared to be someone else in the bathroom. So she hid in the stall until she was certain no one would see her make an exit. At the sink she washed her mouth and face, startled by the stark appearance of her sunken eyes in the mirror. She tried to improve her looks, smoothing her hair around her face. Finally, she gave up and exited the restroom, only to find Steven pacing outside the door.

"Are you okay?" he said, grabbing her by her arms. "Do we need to go to the hospital? Someone said you were throwing up."

She was mortified he knew she vomited. Mortified other people knew. She was mortified about everything.

"Great... Now the whole office will think I'm pregnant and the baby is yours."

"It doesn't matter what anyone thinks. I... *Could* you be pregnant?"

"Well yes, if you believe in Immaculate Conception," she sniped.

"No—I mean—I thought you were too... Don't you eventually get to the point where you can't have children?"

Her cheeks flamed. "I haven't gone through menopause yet. That's usually around age fifty. And I can't *believe* I'm discussing this with you." She stomped back toward the CMA department.

Steven arrived a few minutes later with two more bottles of water. "Come on, I'm taking you home. I'm sorry, but you're going to have to start drinking again, now that you threw up that last water." He lifted her from the chair by her arm and urged her toward the door.

She'd finally had enough of his controlling attitude, and she'd had way too much water. "There's no possible way I can drink any m—"

"If we don't get some fluid into you and keep it down, we won't be able to go see the jazz show tonight."

"We? *You're* going?"

"Neither of us is going, if you aren't better. So start drinking."

Her knees felt weak. Was it dehydration? Or was it the news she'd be spending the evening with Steven.

"But last time we went somewhere with Johanna and Alexander, someone took our picture and put it in the social column. That could mess things up for you and Ellen."

"I don't care," Steven forced the words between his teeth. "Let them speculate. More gossip will be better publicity for Ellen, anyway." He stomped toward the exit.

"Oh. I hadn't thought of that." She was following him out the door, when she grabbed his arm, pleading. "Could I get something else to drink besides water? Please? Maybe some iced tea?"

His expression softened. "Sure, we'll get some tea to go from Papa's on the way out."

Anne worked hard to drink the enormous cup of Papa's iced tea. Papa's was the only place she'd found in New York City that offered sweet tea that tasted just like what she had back in Weatherford, Texas. By the time she walked into the lobby of the apartment with Steven, she felt a little less queasy. On the elevator, he pinned her with a look.

"Do you promise to finish that tea? Or do I need to come and sit with you until it's gone?"

"I promise," she said meekly. "I don't mind drinking sweet tea so much."

"You've got two hours before we're supposed to be downstairs. I'm coming to your apartment thirty minutes early to evaluate whether I'll let you go tonight."

Anne's hackles rose at the authority in his voice. "No thank you. I'll make that determination myself and call you."

"You'll pardon me if I have little faith in your judgment at the moment. You'll do as I say, or…" He stopped and let out a little frustrated grunt. Then he began again in a tired, pleading tone. "Ms. Best. I've been quite worried about you this afternoon, and it's taken an emotional toll. Frankly, I'm exhausted. If you could just roll with me on this one thing, I could relax and take a nap and look forward to our show tonight."

Immediately her demeanor was assuaged. "I'm sorry… I didn't mean to be selfish. You go take a nap, and I'll do whatever you tell me to do."

With relief evident on his face, she exited the elevator under his watchful gaze.

She finished the tea and set her alarm to take a quick nap. Her body was physically and emotionally spent. She fell asleep immediately and woke confused at the sound of her clock beeping. Moving to the bathroom, she regarded her drawn face with alarm. Perhaps a quick shower would help. She hopped in and washed her hair, quickly donning some clothes before Steven was scheduled to arrive. He knocked on her door precisely at the prescribed time. She dashed to answer it, flinging the door open.

"I'm sorry," she said, peeking through a mass of unruly wet waves. "I decided to take a nap and a shower, so I'm not ready yet."

He eyed her critically. "How do you feel?"

"I'm fine," she said, hurrying to the bathroom to continue her preparations. "Really, I feel a lot better. I'm not trying to hide anything. And I drank all of that ten gallon cup of tea you bought me."

He followed her and leaned against the bathroom doorway, watching the proceedings. "It wasn't quite ten gallons," he bantered. He observed her with interest as she applied mascara. "Why do you hold your mouth open wide when you put that on?"

"I don't know—it's just something you have to do somehow when you put mascara on. Everyone does it, I think."

"You don't really need make-up. You don't wear much anyway, do you? I mean, I guess you had on more that night you went to the gala. And you looked good. But I think you look beautiful without it."

Anne watched her face turn red in the mirror. She started coughing to distract attention from her flush. "Thanks. That's a sweet thing to say."

"Maybe, but I didn't say it because I'm *sweet*. I could prove that to you again if you'd like." His smile was wicked.

She'd thought she couldn't get any redder, but she was wrong. "Maybe you should wait in the other room while I finish getting ready."

"But this is so interesting," he protested with a grin.

"Yes. But you're distracting me and I won't be ready on time."

He reluctantly removed himself to the living area. When she emerged, he was standing by the bookshelves holding a photograph. "I guess this is Tom with you and the girls?"

"Yes, it's one of the last ones we took together as a family before... before we lost him."

"I can see him in the girls, especially Charlie. I thought they looked just like you, but now I can see where they get some of their features from him." He placed the photo back on the shelf. "You have a lot of family photos—I guess family means a lot to you. I just wondered... Why did you decide to apply for a job in New York and leave your family behind?"

"Wow, I don't know how to answer that. Let me think." She contemplated his question as they strolled to the elevator.

"I guess maybe boredom. Dissatisfaction. Feeling like I'd lost my purpose with the girls gone. Wondering if there wasn't something else out there... But to be honest, I never dreamed I'd actually get the job. It was just a lark. A chance to go to New York."

She challenged him, "So now, you tell me. Why did you hire me?"

"Same reasons. Boredom. Dissatisfaction." HIs dimples grew deep. "Let's just say I enjoy a challenge, and I hadn't had one in quite a while."

"Oh, so I was a challenge?"

"Yes. I had to treat you like a skittish wild animal, draw you in, earn your trust. And just when I think I've got you all figured out—tamed the wild animal—you do something I don't expect. You're hard to control, that's for sure."

"Maybe that's because I don't care to be controlled," she bristled.

"No doubt... Thus, the challenge." He waggled his eyebrows until he elicited a giggle.

"Stop that—don't make me laugh when I'm trying to be mad," she complained, suppressing a smile.

"Or instead, you could just stop trying to be mad. You never manage it for more than a few minutes anyway."

"I know. My kids figured that out early on. They knew I was too soft and took advantage of me. I wasn't good at discipline."

"I think your kids turned out great. Maybe it's a good thing to have an explosive temper that peters out immediately afterward."

She stiffened at the description. "Is that really what you think? That my temper is *explosive*? I don't think I'm any worse than *you* are."

"Really?" Steven raised his eyebrows and started laughing.

She started to retort, but then she deflated. "Oh. I see what you mean."

They traveled through the lobby and out to Steven's waiting car.

"I thought the Kleins were picking me up."

"I called them and told them we would me them there."

"Mr. Gherring? About tonight... Have you told Ellen? I mean I don't want her to think it means anything—us going to the jazz show with the Kleins. Because we know it doesn't mean anything, but she might not know. She doesn't know you know Alexander from business and all. And I just wouldn't want her to think I set you up with her and then I was trying to mess things up—"

"Ms. Best, I'll deal with Ellen Dean as I see fit. If she's the kind of woman who gets jealous over something like this, we won't last long."

"Okay... Sorry." They sat in uncomfortable silence for a while. She wished she hadn't brought up the subject of Ellen. Now images of Steven with his open shirt and Ellen with her sexy dress invaded her mind. What had happened in Steven Gherring's apartment? It was none of her business. They were two consenting adults. But she wondered, did Steven compare her to Ellen? Ellen wouldn't have been stiff and afraid when Steven kissed her. She would have responded with passion, like any other normal red-blooded woman. He wouldn't have to stop himself to protect her. And Ellen was young and beautiful, exotic even. She realized she was hyperventilating. She had to stop thinking about it.

"Perhaps," said Steven, "now would be a good time to discuss last n—"

"Nope! Nope! Not a good time," Anne said, keeping her voice light. She tried breathing slowly in and out through her nose. "Maybe tomorrow, maybe never..." she said, between breaths.

Steven watched her with wide eyes, but made no further comment before they arrived.

The show was great, and Anne was enchanted with every moment. They sat near the stage, so there was little conversation. But Anne was too enthralled watching the musicians to notice anything else. The saxophone player sauntered over to the table and played while looking directly at Anne during one of his sexy solos, much to her embarrassment. After the song, Anne clapped and cheered and let out one of her wolf whistles for his benefit. Steven ordered drinks and appetizers, with water for Anne. But she barely sipped on anything and the fried calamari looked too greasy to her tender stomach.

When the show was over, Johanna wanted to grab a late dinner so they could talk. Anne started to respond she was too tired and had to be at work early, but Steven usurped her authority.

"I think that's an excellent idea. But we need something very light. What sounds good to you Anne?"

"Nothing really. I'm not very hungry."

"Which is interesting since you haven't eaten all day. And this from the girl who won't let me skip lunch anymore."

She started to protest and mention she'd eaten cheese crackers, but she remembered they hadn't stayed down. She gave in without argument. "Anything would be fine."

Steven remembered a place that had great soups and breads. When their orders arrived and Anne swallowed a few bites of creamy potato soup, he gave her an approving nod.

"So Mr. Gherring," said Johanna. "Alexander says he has invited you to visit us in Germany. Do you think that might be in your plans soon? Perhaps after Christmas?"

"Perhaps we could come visit you when we come to Switzerland to ski in January."

"Yes, we have a wonderful guest cottage with a fireplace. Very cozy for two." Johanna smiled.

Anne's heart lurched as she thought of Steven and Ellen skiing together in Switzerland and staying in the Klein's cozy cottage. But Ellen's play might still be running in January. In fact, she hoped it would run for many months.

"But Mr. Gherring," Anne said. "Isn't Gherring Inc. underwriting *Rainbow Junction*, now? Hopefully, the play will run for a long time. And I know Ellen said one of the actresses has a sick child. They all really need the work. Ellen probably won't be able to get off for a trip in January."

"As always, Anne, you're on top of every detail, although sometimes you seem to miss the big picture." He chuckled with the Kleins, while Anne wondered what she'd missed. "Yes, if the play does well, Ellen certainly wouldn't be able to make a trip in January. I'll keep that in mind."

Johanna touched her hand. "Anne, you had not been working at Gherring Inc. for very long when I first met you. How do you like your job? Are you planning to stay? Or will you go back to Texas?" Her eyes twinkled with mischief as she queried her. Anne took it as an opportunity to give Steven a hard time.

"Most days I like my job just fine. But the boss can be a bit controlling at times. One time he even tried to tell me what I should eat and drink. Can you believe that?"

Steven replied, "Personally, I feel sorry for your boss, never being able to predict just what you might do next. He must have to work very hard to stay ahead of you."

"Oh, I don't mean to complain about him. He's very misunderstood. People think he's really scary, but he's actually very *sweet*."

Steven's dimples pulsed as his jaw muscles contracted. "I think he's scarier than you realize. I've seen him lose his temper when someone is too stubborn for their own good."

"If that were true, he'd be angry with himself. I've never seen anyone more stubborn in my life."

"Ah-hem!" Johanna cleared her throat loudly. "Anne, how do you like your soup?"

Thursday was uneventful at work. Anne finalized the plans for the Christmas party for Saturday night. Emily called to tell her

Grandpa was out of the hospital, at her apartment and doing well. Anne tried Charlie's cell phone several times, but she never got an answer.

Henri called when she was in Steven's office. Anne answered, but tried to keep her conversation generic. "Hi, how are you?"

"Hello, *ma jolie fille*. I will be in town tomorrow as I thought. We can have dinner together? Seven o'clock?"

"Seven. That sounds great."

"I will pick you up at your apartment lobby at seven. *Oui*? I think I have much to tell you. Anna-Laure is through her first chemotherapy session. She has two weeks off before she begins another session. You are still praying?"

"Yes. Every single day."

"I will see you tomorrow."

"Okay, bye."

Steven was observing her with interest. "Hot date tonight?"

"Yes. I plan to get very hot with my treadmill tonight. Or to be more precise, I'm getting hot with *your* treadmill."

A grin appeared on his face. "That conjures some very interesting images."

"Well, stop looking at them, please."

"I can't help it. When I close my eyes, the images are still there." He clenched his eyes shut to demonstrate. "Wait, I can see even better with my eyes closed. Wow! I didn't even know that was possible. You're more flexible than I realized." He flinched when Anne's ink pen flew across the desk and hit him in the head.

"You can't blame a guy for watching when he gets a chance like that," he chuckled.

"Stop it!" she ordered, but the corners of her mouth twitched as she suppressed a smile. "So... you've really hit it off with Ellen, huh?"

"Oh, yeah. She's a great girl. Very talented. Beautiful. Sophisticated. She's pretty perfect, I guess."

Her heart turned over at his words. But she was glad, wasn't she? Yes, of course. She was glad she'd brought them together. She'd done a great job of matchmaking.

"But... I might wish she was a bit older," he added.

"Older? Why would you want her to be older?"

336

"Well, you know, she hasn't had a lot of life experience. There's not as much to talk about with younger women. But then again, if they're beautiful, I guess you don't need to talk. Still, age has some advantages... But other than that, she's really perfect."

Anne worried a little. She'd thought Ellen was just the right age. Had she been off on her calculations? But he still seemed to like her.

"And it's too bad she hasn't had children."

"What? I thought you'd want someone who hasn't been married before."

"Oh, I guess that'd be nice—divorce can be so messy. But women who haven't had children usually want to start a family after they get married. I just don't know if I want to do that at my age. I could change my mind I guess, or maybe Ellen might change her mind. Maybe she'd be happy without children. But really, other than that, she's perfect."

Anne racked her brain. Had Ellen said whether she wanted children? Probably not right away, but surely she would want children someday. How old would Steven be by that time? Or would he insist she never have children?

"And I'm sure she won't mind giving up her career."

"What?"

"Well, you know, if we were to stay together, I'd want her to be available to travel with me. I travel all over the world. I wouldn't want a wife who has a job that ties her to the city. In fact, I might not want her to work at all. I mean, I've got plenty of money, so why would she want to work? But Ellen's pretty perfect. I really underestimated you. I'm sorry I gave you and Gram such a hard time."

"Sure. No problem..." Ohmygosh. Would Ellen want to give up acting? She'd barely even gotten started. If she agreed to give up her career now, would she resent Steven for it someday in the future? Maybe she should consult with Gram. Perhaps they needed to start over with this new information.

"... Anne. Did you hear me?"

"Huh? No, I'm sorry. What did you say?"

"I asked you where you're going with Henri on Friday."

"What? How did you—did I say I was going out with Henri on Friday?"

"You must've mentioned it. But you didn't say where you were going."

"I don't know. Just dinner, I guess."

"Dinner and then *coffee* upstairs?"

The blood rushed to her face. "Just dinner."

"No *coffee*?" he teased. She'd had quite enough of his mocking. "Well, as a matter of fact. I think we might have *coffee* after all. I've got some new flavors I'd like to try. Some of them sound sooooo delicious. You know, the kind that makes your mouth water just thinking about them. Mmmmm! I just love experimenting with something new. I'll bet Henri has a lot I've never sampled before. I'm glad you suggested it. I'm sure Henri will be grateful as well."

Steven's smile was gone. "Stop. You win." His face was sullen. "I don't really want you to have *coffee* with Henri. Or dinner either for that matter. I was only trying to be a good sport about it." His brows crumpled together. "And it turns out I'm not a very good sport after all."

Rayna called her over when she came home from work. "Hey, Anne. How was work today?"

"Routine. How about you? You and Antonio seem to be doing well."

"I've always heard Italians were hot-tempered, but Antonio is hot-blooded instead." She giggled. "But he's also really romantic. He took me on a great picnic in Central Park. And he's nothing like Eddie."

"I've got the magic touch," Anne bragged. "I've got a great track record. Maybe I should start a match-making website."

"Maybe so. What are you up to tonight? Big plans?"

"I think I'm going for a run right now. I'm just planning to eat in the apartment. You could join me if you want."

"No thanks. I'm watching the lobby tonight. And Antonio's bringing me dinner."

"Then I won't interfere with your tryst." Anne winked at her.

Just as she entered her apartment, her cell rang. "Hey Gram. What's up?"

"You're having dinner out here tonight. Sorry for the late notice, dear. Emergency session, you see."

"But—"

"Dress nice for dinner, dear. The car's coming for you in forty-five minutes."

"But—"

"I'll see you soon, dear." And Gram was gone.

Anne was unsure what it meant to "dress nice" for dinner. She didn't have that many nice things to choose from, so she opted for a straight wool skirt with a soft cream-colored sweater, and boots. She hoped wearing a skirt instead of pants would suffice as "nice".

When Gram greeted her at the door of the mansion, she grabbed her hand and pulled her along. "Come, dear. Let's warm you up by the fire."

"I'm okay, Gram. I was only outside for a second. Is this outfit okay? I hope it's dressy enough." She took in Gram's silk dress, with a lovely contrasting scarf.

"You look wonderful, dear."

"So, what's the emergency?"

"Michelle is back. I thought she was gone for good. But she's back."

"Gram, I saw her at the office yesterday. She was crying over someone else, I think. So, surely she's not really after Steven."

Gram raised her eyebrows. "And how do you think Steven responds when there's a woman in distress?"

Anne considered her question. She knew exactly how he would respond—he'd do anything to help her. "But isn't she gone now?"

"No, she came here to see me last night. And she was all sweet and considerate, fawning all over me. I think she wanted me to invite her to stay here while she's in New York. She's not planning to leave until next week."

"Oh." She considered the problem. She'd once thought it might be all right for Steven to marry Michelle. But now she'd changed her opinion of the woman. She might be a problem. But he was dating Ellen now. Was he the kind of man who would be with more than one woman at a time?

"Gram, he started dating my friend, Ellen. Surely he wouldn't... I mean, he wouldn't *be* with Michelle, while he's dating Ellen. Would he?"

"He's dating Ellen? He didn't mention her when I was grilling him." She was quiet for a minute. "Humph. I don't think this Ellen girl is a good match."

"But Gram, you haven't even met her."

"Well… She might be okay as a distraction to keep Michelle out of the way. But then we'll need to get rid of her." She grabbed Anne's arm. "Come dear. I need your help before dinner."

Gram led Anne into the dining room. Anne surveyed the ornate place settings on the antique table. "Gram, there are three place settings. Who else is coming?"

Steven came through from the kitchen with a crystal salad bowl. Gram said, "My chef, of course."

Anne's eyes bored into Steven's. "You could have given me a little warning."

He laughed. "I only got the call at five o'clock myself. I'm merely the dutiful grandson slash chef." He returned to the kitchen.

Anne attempted to pin Gram with a stern look, but she urged her to the china cabinet. "Quick, quick. Help me put out another place setting before Steven comes back."

She rushed to assist. "Who else is coming, Gram? Michelle?"

The doorbell rang, and Gram disappeared toward the front door. Steven came in from the kitchen, still wearing his apron. "Who's that?"

They both trained their eyes on the dining room door until Gram reappeared, followed by a tall, handsome man with sandy blond hair, wearing an expensive-looking suit.

"Hello, *cousin*." The man stressed the word, smiling while his eyes twinkled with merriment. "Great to see you."

"Evan," said Steven, his voice conveying disdain.

"Play nice, boys. I won't have a fight at my table tonight." Gram led him toward Anne. "Anne, this is my grandson, Evan Sterling. Evan, this is Anne Best."

"Grandson? I guess I didn't think you had…"

"You didn't think she had any other grandchildren, did you?" asked Evan. "That's because Steven is the favorite grandchild. His father and my mother were siblings. And I have two sisters, as well."

"Enough," said Gram. "I practically raised Steven as a son. Your mother moved with her husband to the West Coast until you were in high school. And I'll not be criticized in my own home."

Evan grabbed her in a bear hug and swung her around in a circle. "I'm sorry Gram. You know I love you. It's not your fault—I know that. But I've always been a little jealous of Steven, growing up in this house with you. And I promise not to spoil your dinner for you."

"You've already spoiled mine," muttered Steven.

Gram said, "Anne, you're sitting there. And Evan, you're next to Anne. Steven, you'll sit on this side next to me."

Evan grinned. "There's an advantage to not being the favorite. I get to sit next to this beautiful woman. You were right, Gram. She's gorgeous."

Anne blushed furiously. "I... I'm not..."

Evan's eyebrows arched high. "And not conceited either. How incredibly rare." He took Anne's hand and led her to her place at the table. "Come. Tell me about yourself, Anne."

Steven's fury was palpable. Gram said, "Steven, dear. We're ready to eat now, if dinner is served."

"Cousin," said Evan with a sly smile, when he tasted his first bite of seared tuna. "You're an amazing cook. I can see why you never bothered to marry. So self-sufficient." He leaned his head toward Anne, speaking in low tones. "*Stevie* has always been the best at everything. If he couldn't be number one, he didn't bother to do it."

He flinched at the nickname. "I wasn't that great at everything, cousin, but you were always around to make me look good in comparison."

"Quite right. Stevie made it a personal goal to show everyone he was better than me." He made a martyred face. "I've learned to accept I'd always have to live in Stevie's shadow. Everyone loved Stevie best, you know. Even my own mother was disappointed I wasn't more like him. Whenever he bested me in school, she'd not speak to me for weeks at a time." His voice cracked. "I used to cry every night..."

Tears welled in Anne's eyes and she put her arm on Evan's. "That's terrible—children need their mother's approval. I'm so sorry..."

"He's lying, Anne," said Steven with irritation.

"I'm not lying," he declared, putting his hand on top of Anne's to hold it in place. At Steven's violent expression, he relented. "Okay... perhaps I'm exaggerating a bit. But it's the sort of thing I've always had to do to get attention when Stevie's around. I'm sorry. It does feel awfully nice to have your sympathy, even if I don't quite deserve it." His fingers caressed Anne's.

Steven sat in barely restrained rage, slicing Evan to pieces with his eyes.

"Steven, will you pass the rosemary potatoes, please?" asked Gram.

Anne slipped her hand away. She tried to ease the tense atmosphere. "So y'all were in school together?"

"Yes," said Evan. "We went all the way through high school together. I was captain of the lacrosse team. That was the only sport Stevie didn't play, so I had a fighting chance." He winked at Anne.

"What about you, Mr. Gherring?" Anne asked. "What did you do in high school?"

He glared at Evan, who was laughing uncontrollably. "What's so funny?" asked Anne.

Evan chuckled until he caught his breath. "I'm sorry. It's just the way Stevie flinched when you called him 'Mr. Gherring'. It was priceless!"

"Well, he's my *boss*. I call him that out of respect. I doubt you'll hear me call you *Mr. Sterling*."

"Oh! You cut me to the core. I'll only ever be 'Evan' to you. Still better than 'Stevie' I suppose." He continued to chortle.

"I can come up with a name more suitable for you, if you like. But I won't be able to say it in front of Gram!" declared Anne, sparks flying from her eyes like daggers.

Now Steven's dimples made an appearance, and Evan promptly stopped laughing to don his most contrite expression.

"Please, Anne. I'm sorry. I only tease Steven out of habit. I really do love him, and he knows that. Won't you forgive me? I promise to stop." His face was the picture of penitence.

"Well, if you stop teasing..." She gave Evan a taste of her mommy-disapproval glare. "But this dinner looks good, and I haven't been able to eat a bite so far. And I get *testy* when something comes between me and my food."

Evans eyebrows lifted in good humor. "I promise, I promise! Gram, you didn't warn me about this temper. Had I known, I'd have been on my best behavior."

"It doesn't get any better," Steven muttered.

Evan chatted through the rest of dinner, regaling Anne with stories of him and his sisters growing up. He pointedly avoided discussing Steven again, unwilling to risk Anne's wrath. After dinner, he offered to give her a ride home.

"That won't be necessary, *cousin*," said Steven. "We live togeth—we live in the same building. I'll make sure she gets home *safely*."

"In that case, I'll simply bid the lady *adieu*." He took her hands in his and made as if to give her a peck on the cheek. But at the last moment, he brought his head around and brushed his lips against hers. Then he grinned. "Until next time, my fair lady!" And he dashed out the door while Anne stood in shock.

Steven muttered something about hating all his relatives, and Gram smiled as if nothing untoward had happened.

Friday morning Steven was in a bad mood. Perhaps he hadn't recovered from spending the evening with his cousin. Whatever the reason, he snapped at Anne several times. She stood her ground and fussed back at him until he foolishly delved into the subject of Evan's unforeseen kiss.

"You certainly seemed to enjoy Evan's company last night—especially at the end. I guess you'll just let *anyone* kiss you."

Anger surged in Anne's head, but it was quickly replaced by uncertainty and mortification. Had she led Evan on? Did she flirt too much? Henri had kissed her. Jeff had made a pass at her. Steven had kissed her. Maybe it was her fault Evan felt free to take that liberty. As all these conflicting emotions passed across her face, Steven watched with growing alarm.

"I didn't mean—"

"Yes you did." She blinked at sudden tears.

"No, I was just—"

"It's okay, really. I need to be more careful." She turned her face away. "Excuse me. I'm sorry—" She took a deep breath. Why did this bother her so much? Was it because she was insecure about how she interacted with men? Or was it because she'd disappointed Steven Gherring? Or was it just hormones? She certainly seemed to cry at the drop of a hat recently. She'd never been this emotional before. That's it, it was *hormones*.

Feeling much better with that matter settled in her mind, Anne let her ire rise up again. How dare he complain Evan had kissed her! Hadn't she seen Steven in his apartment with his shirt undone on his very first date with Ellen? She could only imagine what had happened after she left. And he hadn't been embarrassed in the least.

"I think now might be a good time to talk about Tuesday night." She raised her voice over the sound of blood pounding in her ears.

Steven, who'd been observing the visible manifestations of this thought process on Anne's face, responded, "Nope! Not a good time! Maybe never..."

She arrived home from work with only an hour to spare before Henri was scheduled to pick her up. Rayna stopped her on the way to the elevator. "So, tonight's the big date with Henri, right?"

"Yes, it's tonight," she said flatly.

"You don't sound very excited. We *are* talking about that incredibly yummy guy with the French accent, right?"

"I think... I think I may need to break up with him. Which is silly to even say since we've never really even been together. Just a few dates and talking on the phone." She thought for a moment. "Well, he did take a train from Paris to Switzerland just to see me..."

Rayna stared at her. "That's so romantic. Why would you want to break up with a guy like him? Is he two-timing you?"

"No, he's actually been great. He was probably that kind of guy in the past, but not now. It's just that, I don't think it's *going anywhere*, and I really don't want to lead him on. But he's got a sick niece he's really upset about, and he doesn't deserve another emotional blow. So... I don't know how to tell him. I may just not tell him at all." Her stomach was heavy, like lead.

"Well why isn't it going anywhere? Are you interested in someone else?"

344

"No… There definitely isn't anyone else. Although Mr. Gherring's grandmother is trying to find a husband for me now. She introduced me to another of her grandson's last night. I have to admit, he's handsome and very entertaining. He had me in stitches last night."

"But?"

"But I don't know. Maybe he's too slick for me? To tell you the truth, I'm not sure I met the real Evan. He and Mr. Gherring don't like each other, so there was a lot of verbal sparring."

"I thought you maybe kind of liked Mr. Gherring a little." Rayna's question sounded casual enough, but Anne noticed she was watching her response with a keen eye. She bottled up her feelings and put the cork in tight.

"No. I mean, I like him as a boss and all that. But we could never be romantically involved. That's why I set him up with Ellen. She's more his type."

"I guess you think you've got this figured out because you're some kind of master matchmaker, but I think your calculations may be a bit off on this one."

"You'll see," she said, with a confidence she didn't quite feel.

Anne went downstairs ten minutes early. She didn't want Henri to wait. Especially because she didn't want him to accidentally run into Steven. Exiting the elevator, she spotted Ellen sitting on a couch in the lobby. Facing the inevitability of the awkward encounter, Anne moved to greet her.

"Hi Ellen? What are you doing here?"

"Hi Anne. To tell you the truth, I don't know why I'm here. Steven picked me up at six thirty for our date, and then he told me he'd forgotten something at the apartment. So, here I am, waiting." She rubbed her hands in worried circles. "Anne, about Tuesday night—"

"No Ellen, that's none of my business—you don't need to explain anything to me. I'm the one who set y'all up, remember? I'm just glad you're hitting it off." Anne managed to say the words in a way that sounded believable. At least she hoped so.

"But I don't want you to think—"

"Hello, Ms. Best," Steven approached from the elevator, scouring the lobby. "Where's Henri? He didn't come?"

"He's not due here for another five minutes, so it looks like you missed him. I'm sure you're terribly upset, since I know how much y'all like each other."

"I like Henri just fine, as long as he stays in France," he bantered.

"Well I like Henri more when he's here," she countered.

"*Absolument!*" cried Henri, sauntering from the lobby door. "I am so glad you like for me to be here." He eased beside Anne, placing a possessive arm around her back and nuzzling her neck. "You smell divine, *mon ange.*"

Steven laid his arm around Ellen's shoulder. "Ellen, darling… I should introduce you to Henri DuBois. Henri, this is Ellen Dean."

Henri smiled at Ellen, but made no move to take her hand. "Ellen, you must be an amazing woman to put up with a man such as this one. My heart goes out to you." He slid his hand up to Anne's shoulder and gave it a squeeze, bending his head to kiss her hair.

Steven's smooth expression almost cracked, but he regained control. "I don't think Ellen's complaining too much so far."

Ellen took this as her cue. "Oh no. Steven's been wonderful. Tonight he's taking me to the Essex House." Anne almost gasped, knowing this to be one of the most expensive restaurants in New York City.

"And where are the two of you going tonight?" Steven's hand was stroking up and down on Ellen's arm, and Anne couldn't pry her eyes away.

"I have reservations at Daniel tonight. But only because I flew in town too late to go to Masa."

Steven scowled at Henri's stated plans, so Anne assumed the restaurants he mentioned were also expensive. The competitive testosterone was clogging the air in the lobby.

Anne said, "You know Henri, I don't care where we go. As long as we're together."

Henri smiled and kissed her ear in response.

Steven said, "So, Henri—will you be going with Anne to the Gherring Inc. Christmas party tomorrow night?"

"I wouldn't miss it."

"Really?" Steven frowned. "But—"

"And you must be going with Gherring, right?" Henri asked Ellen.

"I don't know. Am I?" she asked Steven, with confusion in her eyes.

"Of course... I thought I mentioned it before." Steven cast Henri an irritated glance. "In fact, I think you deserve a new dress for the occasion."

"If you will pardon us, I have not seen *mon ange* for too long. I have not greeted her properly."

Henri pulled Anne against him and kissed her full on the mouth. His tongue made its way gently between her shocked lips as he painted shivers up and down her spine with the fingers of one hand. Her arms locked automatically around his neck. Releasing her, he guided her out the door and spoke over his shoulder. "*Au revoir!*"

Henri's limousine was waiting for them. Anne crawled in and he sat on the opposite side. He wore a sad smile. "It is over, is it not?"

"What? What do you mean?"

"I am a Frenchman. I know when there is no passion in a kiss."

"I... I was shocked. I'm not used to public affection."

"No, my angel. I felt you respond to me before. This time..."

Anne felt tears welling in her eyes. "I'm so sorry, Henri. I didn't want to hurt you."

He crossed the car to put his arm around her. "*Non! S'il vous plait!* Please don't cry. I am okay." He patted her shoulder and sighed. "There is this nurse. From the hospital. And maybe I like her. She is very good to Anna-Laure."

She looked up through wet lashes. "Really?"

"Maybe. We will see. But I suspected already this might happen. From Switzerland. From our phone calls."

"Then what was all that back there with Mr. Gherring?"

"The pig! He thinks he knows something. He tries to make me look like a fool. He has talked to Michelle."

"Michelle?"

"Yes, Michelle came to see me last week. She told me she still loved me. And I realized..." he spoke with wonder on his face. "I realized I felt *nothing* for her. I do not trust her anymore. But she thinks it must be someone else—maybe you or the nurse. She cannot believe I would not come back to her, unless there was someone else."

"Good riddance, Henri. I don't trust her either. You can do better."

"At least, you still believe in me."

She sighed. "What a mess, Henri. What about tonight, the expensive restaurant? And tomorrow's Christmas party?"

He gave her the old devilish grin she'd grown accustomed to. "I plan to take advantage of your guilt from the cost of the food. Perhaps you will let me kiss you one more time." With her face turning red, she started to protest. But he put a finger on her lips to silence her. "I am teasing you. Well, unless it works…"

Chapter Seventeen - Saturday

SATURDAY MORNING DAWNED. Anne saw it transpire from the rooftop patio where she'd been sitting for an hour before it happened. She'd awoken at three and lain in bed tossing and turning for several hours before surrendering to her sleepless state. Deciding she needed to get away from Steven's apartment building, she went for a walk to clear her mind. She'd lost several pounds this week due to stress. Even her fancy dinner with Henri hadn't tempted her to eat in her normal fashion. Her stomach was definitely tied to her emotions. So she skipped breakfast again and didn't even miss it. After two hours of listless meandering on the New York City streets, she headed back toward her apartment.

She knew she shouldn't be depressed. She should be ecstatic. She'd finally found someone for Steven, someone who'd make him happy. He'd never have to be alone again. And Ellen was devoted to him—you could see it in how she looked at him.

Ellen was a great match for him. She was sweet and selfless. And her association with Steven was already helping her career. It was ideal. Everything was perfect. And Anne was the one responsible for making it all happen. Another matchmaking success story.

So why did she feel so miserable?

She heard a voice call from behind her. "Hey Anne! Where are you going? Aren't you coming in for coffee?"

Mr. Hamilton was leaning out the door of his shop and motioning for her to come back. She hesitated a moment, not really feeling up to socializing, but couldn't bring herself to disappoint him.

"I can't stay long today, Mr. Hamilton."

"Oh?" he asked with a broad smile. "Do you have a hot date?"

To his complete horror, she suddenly burst into tears. He was astonished, but quickly responded by wrapping her in his arms.

"Anne, honey, what's wrong? What happened?"

He continued to hold her and pat her on the back. When the sobs subsided into gentle tears, he tenderly led her to the chairs behind the worktable. Seated in front of her, he handed her a tissue and waited patiently for her to look up from her hands as she wrung them together in her lap.

"I don't know what's wrong with me. I should be happy everything worked out so well. You know, I think maybe he's really in love." She paused to take a deep shuddering breath.

"He's been so miserable and alone, and no one understood him before. He hides himself in his business and never lets anyone get close. He thought he was so self-sufficient, but I knew he needed someone who could break through all those barriers. Someone who could really love him. Someone who could understand who he really was. Someone who would love him for himself and not for his money or his power."

She stopped to wipe her tear-streaked cheeks. "I'm so happy for him."

"Are we talking about Margaret's grandson, Steven?"

"Margaret?" Did his face turn red?

"Yes, well, I meant Mrs. Gherring. Are we discussing her grandson?"

Her mouth tugged up at the corners, even as the tears continued to fall. "Yes, I'm talking about *Margaret's* grandson, my boss."

"So, are you saying Steven Gherring is in love, now? And this is why you're crying... because you're so happy?"

"Yes, that's it. I'm j-j-just s-s-so happy." She sobbed anew, covering her face with her hands.

Mr. Hamilton shook his head in confusion. "And who's he in love with?"

"Ellen. And sh-sh-she's wonderful. What's wrong with me? I love Ellen, I really do. And I'm so happy for them."

She attempted to make a proud face. "And I did it!"

"You did what?" He peered at Anne as if she might confess to murder.

"I matched them. I brought them together. I did it. I'm responsible for their love. That's why I'm so happy." She reached for another tissue to wipe her face and blow her nose.

"Well sweetie, I know I haven't known you for a real long time. But is this what you usually do when you're extra happy?" He waited quietly while she sniffed a few more times and took another deep quaky breath.

"Not usually," she admitted in a small voice.

"So, that means... maybe you aren't so happy after all?"

She should be happy, but she felt awful. "No, I'm not happy. I'm not happy at all. What's wrong with me? I don't understand. I'm *miserable*. I feel like all the air has been sucked out of the world. Maybe I need to see a doctor. That's it—a psychiatrist. There *is* something wrong—I've never felt like this before."

"Okay, honey. I believe you, because I've never seen you like this before. Everything will be fine, I'm sure." He scratched his head. "I thought... Well, that is... Margaret mentioned she thought Steven was in love. She didn't ever actually mention this Ellen girl."

"Yes, well it all happened so fast. Monday, I was trying to introduce them, and he was really rude to Ellen. Then he sat down and had lunch with us and asked her all kinds of questions." She paused to recount the events in her mind.

"Then the next thing I knew, he was flirting with her. And he asked her out. And he was showing her off to the social reporters. And they were in his apartment together." She felt herself blushing at this last memory.

"And they're going to the Christmas party together. And he's bought her two new dresses."

She put her hand on his arm. "That *means* something, you know. He said he doesn't do anything that doesn't mean something." She saw him flinch and realized she was gripping his arm tightly. Removing her hand, she saw the imprints of her fingernails remained behind.

"I'm sorry, Mr. Hamilton. But he looked so comfortable with her last night. So content. I can tell he doesn't need me anymore. Wait... Maybe that's the problem." She blinked a few times, suddenly excited. "Maybe it's like when your child grows up and leaves home and you realize you aren't needed anymore."

She went on in an enthusiastic voice. "That's it—for weeks I've been obsessing about Steven Gherring and finding someone for him. I wanted so badly for him to be happy. I guess I'm miserable because I've lost my purpose."

Mr. Hamilton tilted his head as he tugged on one ear. "Well, I guess that could explain it. You'd certainly have a right to be miserable after losing your purpose."

She nodded vigorously and felt her spirits lift a little. "Yes I would, wouldn't I? I'd be depressed and gloomy." She allowed herself a small smile as she watched him for confirmation. "And confused and sad."

He bobbed his head in agreement. "And sobbing and pathetic."

She stared at him. "Pathetic?" Her lips began to quiver. "I'm pathetic? Ohmygosh, I'm *pathetic*!"

She began to sob anew. Mr. Hamilton gaped at her and fumbled for a tissue, finally handing her the entire box.

Rayna spotted her the moment she entered the lobby. "Anne! Where have you been? I didn't see you leave."

"I just went for an early morning walk. Why? Did you need me for something?"

"No. It's just... you know... I feel like someone should keep an eye on you."

"Okay, Rayna." Anne eyed her friend curiously. "So... I'm going upstairs and I'm going to take a shower. And I'll probably take a nap, because I didn't sleep well last night. Okay?"

Rayna returned a sheepish smile. "Don't tease me. I'm just doing my j—." She coughed. "I mean, *duty*. I'm doing my duty to society to watch out for you."

Gram called before she made it all the way inside her apartment.

"I'll get straight to the point, dear. Are you going to the Christmas party with Henri?"

"No, Gram. We broke up. I'm not going to the party at all."

"Good. You can go with me."

"Thanks Gram, but I don't really feel like a party."

"You'd make an old lady go by herself?"

"You could go with Steven," she suggested.

"He's going with that Ellen girl."

Arguing with Gram was futile—she might as well give in. "Okay Gram, I'll go with you. But I think I'll go home early. Okay?"

"That's fine. Now let's go shopping. I want a new dress."

"I was going to take a nap..."

"Plenty of time for that after you take me shopping for a new dress. I don't want to wear the same one I wore last year."

"Okay, Gram. What time?"

"I'm on my way now, dear."

Anne waved at Rayna on her way out. She didn't take time to stop and chat, because Gram was already waiting outside in the car. Gram took her to a small exclusive dress shop. It was nothing like the second hand store Johanna had shown her. Gram rifled through the dress rack in the petite section, piling dresses into her arms. Not one dress had a price tag under five thousand dollars. Most were between seven thousand and fifteen thousand. The owner of the store spotted Gram and came quickly to take the selected dresses and set Gram up in a dressing room.

She chose a red brocade dress with a fitted bodice and a pleated A-line ball skirt whose hem swept the floor. The dress had a matching long-sleeved bolero jacket.

"At ninety-five, I don't really like those sleeveless gowns that are so popular. And I think this bolero jacket makes me look taller. Don't you?"

Anne stared down at the tiny dynamo of a woman. "Gram, I don't think you need to look taller. You're intimidating enough already."

The saleslady offered to bring out shoes, but Gram turned up her nose. "Your shoes hurt my feet. I have to get my shoes special-ordered for them to be comfortable."

Anne moved to follow Gram to the check-out counter.

"Now find a dress for my friend here," said Gram. "What size are you, dear? Four?"

She whispered to Gram, "I usually get my stuff from the second-hand store. It's just as nice, and I don't mind that someone else has worn it before."

"Humph! Well today, you're getting a dress from this store. Unless there isn't anything here you like."

"Gram, I can't spend five thousand dollars on a dress."

"No problem, dear. This is my treat. The short ones cost less, anyway. I figured on putting you in a cocktail dress."

She started to object again, but Gram fixed her with her piercing blue eyes. "Don't pretend you don't know how much money I have. I want to buy you a dress. I can afford it, and it'll make me happy."

"Okay," she agreed meekly.

"Alphonzo!" she called. "I want something special!"

"Yes, Mrs. Gherring! I have just the right thing for your friend. Not many people that tall and thin to pull it off. She will look stupendous!"

She was soon encased in a black dress with a sheer sequin-embellished silk yolk and long sleeves. The sheer silk continued downward, supporting a bustier paneled bodice, so the sides and back of the dress were also sheer. The formfitting jacquard skirt fell to her knees.

"Stunning!" declared Alphonzo, as the salesladies exclaimed.

"I don't know. An awful lot of this material is kind of see-thru." Anne crossed her arms over her chest.

"There's nothing hanging out that shouldn't be," declared Gram.

"Only because I don't really have much to hang out."

"We'll take it," said Gram. "And she'll take a pair of your uncomfortable shoes."

Anne entered in the lobby and strode toward the elevator, wrestling with her new dress and shoes. Before the doors closed, Steven somehow materialized beside her.

"New dress? For tonight I assume?"

"Yes," Anne refused to meet his gaze.

"Did you have a good time with Henri last night?"

"Yes, I did. And did you have a good time with Ellen?"

"Yes."

They rode for a few moments in silence. Then he moved in front of her, forcing her to look at him. "I just want to know something… When Henri kissed you…" His sky-blue eyes penetrated her with an intensity that burned into her soul. "When he kissed you, did it affect you like this?"

He reached out to take her face between his hands, capturing her lips with his. Stunned, she was powerless to stop him, not that she wanted to. Her hands still gripped tightly on the dress hanger and shoe bag. His tongue slid stealthily between her lips, and she welcomed the invasion. He pressed himself against her, forcing her back against the elevator wall. She felt his heart pounding against her own. He moaned as her tongue answered his invitation.

The bell rang, and the elevator opened on the tenth floor. Steven threw himself away from her and fell back against the elevator wall. Anne moved off the elevator in a daze.

Before the doors closed, she heard him say, "I don't dislike Henri anymore—I hate him."

Sitting on her couch, lost in confusion, her phone interrupted her reverie.

"Hi, Johanna," she said without enthusiasm.

"What is wrong, dear? You don't sound like yourself?"

"Nothing really. I just... Nothing makes sense anymore."

"Does this have anything to do with Henri and the Christmas party tonight?"

"No. Well, maybe. We broke up last night. So I'm not going with him."

"You're going with Mr. Gherring, then?"

"Oh no! He's going with Ellen."

"With Ellen? But I thought... Wait, I think maybe Mr. Gherring is toying with you."

"Oh, he's definitely playing some kind of game I don't understand. He... He kissed me again. Today, on the elevator. He kissed me, even though he's dating Ellen—I feel like I cheated with him!"

"I see. So I think we must teach Mr. Gherring a lesson."

"Oh, I don't know. I'm not good at playing games. And I don't want to mess up his relationship with Ellen. I'm not that sort of person."

"I understand, dear, but he needs to learn he can't play with women's emotions. Ellen would want him to learn this lesson, right?"

"I guess so. But I'm not very good at this sort of thing."

"It will be easy. Do you have a sexy dress?"

Anne chuckled. "As a matter of fact, I do."

"Wonderful! Now you need to do as exactly as I tell you..."

Anne was concentrating on steeling her nerves. She barely heard Gram chatting on the way to the party. She'd managed to delay their departure so she could make a grand entrance. That's what Johanna had said—to make a grand entrance. But she wouldn't look very grand if she were shaking like a leaf.

She went over the plan in her head. She had to find someone to flirt with, since Henri wouldn't be there. Johanna said Steven wouldn't learn his lesson if she stood on the side, alone like a forlorn rejected potted plant. She wasn't sure how, but she definitely had to avoid looking like a potted plant.

Approaching the door, Gram said, "Let me go in first dear. I want to make a grand entrance."

Anne thought maybe she should watch to see how it was done. But then someone might see her. No, she'd just have to wing it. She waited for what seemed like an hour, but was actually only about two minutes.

Her spiked heels were four inches high. She hoped she'd acquired some grace during her time in New York City or this grand entrance might be a magnificent fall.

Okay, the next step made her feel like an idiot, but Johanna had insisted this part was essential. She set her mind to the mantra Johanna had given her, saying it over and over in her mind in rhythm. *I'm way too hot to handle!* She took a deep breath and sauntered slowly through the doorway like she'd practiced at the apartment.

She stood inside the doorway and surveyed the crowd, as Johanna had directed her. *Act like you are checking everyone else out, to see who is worthy of your attention. Find your mark! He needs to be a handsome man without an escort. It doesn't matter how old he is—any age will do.* She started to panic when she saw Steven staring at her. But this time luck was on her side.

"Wow, Anne! You look really hot!" Evan Sterling strolled to her side, offering his arm. "Can I get you a drink?"

"Evan!" Anne smiled, grasping onto his arm. "You don't know how glad I am to see you!" She tried to remember her mantra, but it kept slipping out of her head. "I could really use your arm to make sure I don't trip and fall on these heels."

Evan laughed. "Anne, you're like a breath of fresh air. I don't remember meeting another woman so unaffected."

356

"What are you doing here? Do you work for Gherring Inc.?"

"No, Gram invited me. Steven will probably shoot me when he finds out. But it's worth it, just to have you smile at me." His eyes widened as he peered over her shoulder. "Speak of the devil. Here he comes."

"Hello cousin. Great party you have here."

"What are you doing here, Evan?" said Steven, with unveiled anger.

Anne swirled around to face him, tucking her hand around Evan's elbow. "He's my date. I'm allowed to bring a date, right?"

His expression was stormy. "I thought you were coming with Henri."

"Change of plans. By the way, where's *your* date? You're still dating Ellen, aren't you? After our little 'talk' on the elevator, I wasn't sure."

But he wasn't listening. He was staring... at her dress. Or at the missing parts of it. "What... What did you say?" He tore his gaze away from the sheer silk beaded panels and locked eyes with her.

Evan laughed. "Yes, cousin. She does look extraordinary tonight, doesn't she? Seems it's my lucky day."

Steven scowled. "No one asked y—"

"Hi Anne," said Ellen, coming beside Steven to take his arm. "Wow! Fantastic dress!"

"Thanks Ellen. I like yours, too. That cobalt blue is one of my favorite colors." Poor Ellen. Anne had set her up with Steven, thinking he was a man of principle. She'd be heartbroken to know he'd kissed her in the elevator today.

"Shall we get that drink now?" Evan led Anne away, throwing a smile over his shoulder. "See you later, Stevie."

As she walked she could feel Steven's eyes throwing ice daggers at her back. "Thanks, Evan. I really needed to get away."

"Yes, I wanted to get away from Stevie as well. And we really can get a drink if you like."

"I'm not really thirsty, yet. But you can get something."

"Why don't we dance, instead?"

Anne remembered another of Johanna's instructions. *Dance as much as you can. But don't dance with Mr. Gherring.* "I'd love to dance."

The band was playing a slow song, and numerous couples were on the dance floor. Evan and Anne moved smoothly into the undulating group. From a distance she could see Steven in an intense conversation with Gram. He didn't look very happy, but Gram seemed unmoved.

"You really do look great, tonight. This dress is… quite enticing." Anne blushed as his gaze fell down to the sheer silk panels. "And not many women have the figure to wear this."

"What you're actually saying is 'If you were a little more well-endowed, this dress would be really, really interesting.'"

Evan chuckled. "I can't believe how funny you are. Stevie's an idiot to be with that other girl, when he could be with you."

"Mr. Gherring's my boss and that's all. I'm not his type."

"Is that so? Well I'm glad to hear it, because you're certainly my type." He pulled her a little closer to him, placing his hands on her lower back and playing with the beading on the sheer silk.

Anne felt a little nervous. "Actually, I'm probably not anyone's type. I… I don't sleep around."

"I hear you saying that, but this dress says something else." He slipped his hands to the side of her dress, his thumbs fingering the peek-a-boo material."

Anne's face went white, and she clamped her arms down on his hands. "Stop it!"

"Hey, you can't blame a guy for trying."

His hands slid back to their proper place on her back. Anne was uneasy in his arms, but he seemed to be acting the perfect gentlemen, as they continued to dance and chat. Then his eyes focused behind her. He made an annoyed moaning sound, grabbing her elbow and leading her off to the side.

"What a bother. Stevie's coming to the dance floor. Let's get that drink now. What would you like?"

"I don't know—I don't drink much. Just something where I can't taste the alcohol."

He returned with two drinks and handed her one.

"What is this?"

"It's a Lemon Drop Martini," he said. "I think you'll like it."

She took a sip. "Wow, this is good."

She spotted Steven on the dance floor with Ellen, but his gaze was focused in her direction. His eyes seemed to reach past her carefully constructed defenses. Could he read her mind? Did he realize how much he affected her? How much he'd confused her? She took another gulp of her drink. As her stomach growled, she realized she hadn't had anything to eat all day.

"I need some food—I just realized I'm starving."

"Right this way." Evan guided her to the buffet table.

"Where can I put this," she said, referring to her now empty glass.

"You've already finished it?" He chuckled, taking her empty glass and handing it to a passing waiter.

"It was light and tasty—good choice. I don't usually like alcohol," she said, piling some carrots, cherry tomatoes, and cheese cubes on her plate.

"The good stuff is over here," said Evan, indicating a table with various meats, including boiled shrimp and roast beef.

"Ughh! I don't think I can eat anything that heavy." She popped a piece of cheese into her mouth.

Evan ate a few boiled shrimp while Anne munched on her veggies. But her appetite was quickly assuaged, and she found a waiter to take the plate from her hands.

"I think my stomach's shrunken. I haven't eaten much this week. Oh... I can feel that drink already."

"We should dance again. Some exercise to clear your head. Besides, Stevie's in the buffet line now."

She was a little wobbly walking back to the dance floor. But he held her close as they danced, and she felt pretty stable. Feeling drowsy, she laid her head on Evan's shoulder and relaxed in his arms. She thought Johanna had mentioned something about *dance with your head on his shoulder*, but she couldn't remember for sure. His hands traveled slowly up and down her back, and they swayed gently to the music. When the music changed to an upbeat song, he simply ignored the new music and continued to rock in a slow circle, until she was in a tranquil trance-like state.

She could almost imagine she was in Steven's arms again. She remembered how it had felt to dance with him at the gala. But he'd held her lightly, not tight and close like this. She would've liked

Steven to hold her more closely. And his hands were not on her back like this. Wait! Evan's hands were not on her back—they were back under her arms, toying with the beading on the sheer side panels. His thumbs were... Anne pushed out of Evan's arms abruptly.

"Stop it!" she cried, looking at him with a horrified expression. The room began to spin and she stumbled a little. He reached out to steady her, but she stepped back, out of his reach.

"I think the lady doesn't want you to touch her again," said Steven, somehow materializing by her side, his expression dark and threatening.

Anne was grateful for the reprieve, but she was fairly certain this hadn't been in Johanna's instructions. She knew she wasn't supposed to dance with Steven, so she quickly moved away from the dance floor. She saw Katie and Gary and headed in their direction. She'd just reached them when Steven caught up with her.

"Anne, could you spare me a second? I'd like to discuss something concerning work."

She panicked—Johanna hadn't told her what to do if Steven asked to talk to her alone. "I don't know..."

"Please. Just for a moment. It's important." His expression was so fierce, she feared he would make a scene.

"Okay, sure. Just for a moment."

She followed him to a relatively empty area near the doorway. "Why are you here with Evan? Do you purposely date men I detest simply to irritate me?"

"Gram introduced me to Evan and... Wait, you said you wanted to talk about work."

"This is about work. It's... It's about... Okay, I lied. I wanted to straighten out some misunderstandings."

"Are you going to explain what happened on the elevator today?" She remembered what Johanna had said. *Make him explain why he kissed you when he's supposedly dating Ellen.*

"Yes. Yes, that's part of it. Anne, I—"

"Because I really want to know why you kissed *me* when you're dating Ellen."

"But Ellen doesn't mind. She's—"

360

"Give me a break! I'm not that naïve! Did you tell her? Does she know you kissed me?" She was starting to get really angry. Perhaps the alcohol had made her lose her inhibitions.

"No, but—"

"Well, obviously you kissed me because you thought I was still dating Henri. So... *News flash*! We've broken up, okay?"

"I'm glad, but Anne I need to—"

"But I can't handle it anymore. Maybe it's easy for you to just kiss me and stir me up like that. But it's not easy to be on the receiving end—I haven't slept in days!"

"I haven't slept—"

"I don't want to hear about who you're sleeping with because here's another news flash... *I'm sleeping alone*!" She felt her lower lip quivering.

"I am too. I'm sleeping alone." He grabbed her shoulders. "Look at me. I'm telling the truth."

She squeezed her eyes shut as tears began to fall down her cheeks. "I'm tired, Mr. Gherring. I'm going home. Please don't do this. Ellen deserves better."

"Just wait. Okay? Just wait for a minute. Right here. Don't move. Okay? I'm going to get Ellen." He left her standing by the door. Alone. Crying. This wasn't anywhere in the instructions Johanna had given. She walked out of the door, out of the party, out of the hotel. Out of Steven Gherring's life.

Chapter Eighteen - To the Airport

THE TAXI TOOK HER TO the apartment building. "Just wait for me, okay? I'll be back in five minutes. I need to go to the airport."

"Okay lady, but you'll have to pay while I wait."

"That's fine. Please, just wait…"

She hurried into the lobby in her bare feet, carrying her shoes. She couldn't run in her new four-inch heels. Rayna watched her bolt past the desk toward the elevator.

"Anne! What are you doing? Where are you going?"

"To the airport."

"Wait, Anne. What are you talking about?"

She ignored Rayna, and dashed into the elevator, pushing the button for the tenth floor repeatedly in an attempt to make it move faster. When she got to her apartment, she threw her toiletries into a carry-on bag with some underwear and a change of clothes. She didn't even bother to change out of her dress, but put on some comfortable boots and a warm coat. In less than five minutes, she was back in the lobby and headed for the door.

"Anne! Wait! Where are you going?" Rayna caught her before she could escape.

"To the airport. I'm going to the airport." Her tears were coming in torrents.

"But where are you going?"

"I'm sorry, Rayna. I need to go now," she sobbed, moving toward the door.

Rayna grabbed her arm. "But wait. Why do you have to leave so fast? Where are you going?"

"I'm going… I'm going to Texas, where I belong. I have to go now. My taxi's waiting outside." She swiped at her tears and peered out the glass door.

362

"But wait. You don't have to leave this instant. Why are you leaving so fast? What happened?"

"I have to go. The taxi's waiting—"

"What time is your flight?"

"I—I don't know. I haven't got one yet. I just have to get away from here."

"You're running away? Really? The Anne Best I know would never run away."

She sobbed again. "She's a fake! I'm a fake! I came out here and pretended to be someone I'm not. I thought I wanted an adventure. I thought I wanted excitement. A new start."

"What happened, honey?"

"I did something really stupid..." Her tears were tumbling off her face and puddling on her coat collar.

"What? What did you do? If you're in trouble, I'll help you. Antonio will help, too. We love you. You don't have to do this alone. Are you pregnant?"

"No. I'm not. I almost wish I could be, though."

"What is it?" Rayna's eyes were wide.

"I fell in love with Steven Gherring!"

"What?"

"It's true. Can you believe it? Countrified widow, mother of two, from Weatherford, Texas. And I fell in love with Steven Gherring." She laughed bitterly. "I know. I couldn't believe it either. I kept trying to convince myself it wasn't true."

"Well, Anne. Doesn't he kind of like you, too?"

"No. He's dating Ellen. I should know. I'm the one who matched them together. Just like you and Antonio. And he... he was... you know... *with* her. And what am I supposed to do now? Huh?" Her voice rose to a hysterical pitch.

"You should go upstairs and go to sleep and decide in the morning what to do. My mother always told me you shouldn't make an important decision in the heat of passion."

Anne's mouth dropped open. "I always said that to my girls, too."

"So you'll stay? At least until tomorrow?"

"Rayna, this is not the heat of passion for me. If I stay, then I'll be passionate. I might even betray my friendship with Ellen and do something with Steven Gherring I'd regret for the rest of my life. I don't want to go, but I have to."

She hugged Rayna, who was now crying with her. "Please don't go."

"I have to," Anne said, picking up the carry-on bag she'd dropped on the floor. "I don't belong here. I don't know where I belong..."

"You belong with me." Steven's voice was firm as he strode behind her.

Her heart began to thunder in her chest. "No, I—"

"I took the liberty of paying off your taxi. But my car is outside. I'll drive you to the airport." He picked up her bag and took her by the arm, leading her toward the waiting limo.

Over his shoulder he said, "Thank you, Rayna. I appreciate your help."

"Rayna!" Anne cried, gazing accusingly at her friend.

Rayna silently mouthed, "Sorry," but she had a traitorous grin on her face.

Inside the warm interior, Steven sat across from Anne. She was wrapped tightly in her coat, hugging herself for comfort. He smiled at her.

"It's a long ride. You should take off your coat and get comfortable."

She didn't respond, but sat staring at her feet. He followed her gaze.

"Nice boots. But I really like those sexy sandals you had on earlier."

She refused to answer. Even talking was dangerous with Steven Gherring.

"I must say, you're very difficult to converse with. Either you talk so fast you don't let me get a word in edgewise, or you refuse to talk at all."

"There's nothing to say."

"Well, why don't you ask your questions again, and actually listen to the answers this time?"

She closed her eyes. "I'm not asking any more questions, because I don't want to know the answers."

"Fine!" He let his irritation show for the first time. "I'll do both parts. First question. Where's Ellen? Answer. She's with Ben."

Anne opened her eyes, regarding him with suspicion. "Who's Ben?"

"Nicely done. See how much more fun it is when you participate? Ben is Ellen's—wait for it—boyfriend. In fact, she already told you about him. He's her leading man."

"But…"

"Ah-ha! Now you have so many questions to ask." He wore a smug grin.

"So you aren't really dating?"

"Nope."

"And Tuesday night?"

"Nothing happened."

Anne contemplated his words, and suddenly she was filled with rage. "You pig!" She flew across the car and began to pound on his arm with her fists. "You made me believe you slept with her! You called me up there! I can't believe you did that!"

He grabbed her arms to stop the beating. "Wait! I'm sorry. I admit it wasn't the wisest decision I made. But you drove me to it!" One of her hands escaped to strike him. "Ow!" He secured the offending hand again.

"You were the one who set me up with Ellen after I asked you not to. I only wanted to find out if you'd be happy if I accepted your offer."

Anne was still twisting her arms to get them free. "Why would Ellen do that to me? We were friends."

"You were the one who forced her to meet me. She said she tried to talk you out of it. We just made a bargain. I'd help the play monetarily and get her some publicity, and she'd help me make you jealous."

Anne stopped struggling. "So you wanted to make me jealous? And then you kissed me to teach me a lesson?"

He pulled her hands toward him and placed them on his chest. "Do you feel my heart beating?"

She nodded—his heart was pounding almost as fast as hers.

"I kissed you because I couldn't help myself. And soon… I'm going to do much more than kiss you."

He pulled the coat off her shoulders and threw it on the floor.

"Did I mention how much I like this new dress? These little parts on the side where I can see your skin through the fabric..." He ran his fingers lightly up and down her side, dangerously close to her breast.

Anne's heart threatened to leap from her chest. She moaned, and then grabbed his hand and pushed it away. Tears began to fall anew.

"I'm sorry. I'm sorry. I just can't do this. I really want to. But I can't."

He groaned. "I know, but I've suffered for longer than you can imagine. Do you know how long I've wanted you?"

She shook her head, crying miserably.

"I think I knew after that first day, when you had no idea who I was. I knew I'd found something that had been missing all my life."

Her eyes were closed, but she felt the gentle pressure of his fingers on her jaw. "Look at me, please."

She opened her eyes and watched his face dancing through a shimmer of tears. His voice was soft. "I thought... I thought you wanted me, too. Was I wrong?"

She shook her head. "No, I *did* want you."

"But you don't anymore? I'm too late? I waited too long?"

She couldn't bear the devastation in his eyes. "It's not that. I just can't do what you want me to do. I can't be what you want. What you need."

"And what is that? What do you think I want?"

"I think you want me to... to sleep with you." Anne blushed almost painfully at the words.

"Oh no! I want you very much awake. But I do want you in my bed." His dimples appeared. "I don't want a one night stand, I want—"

"I'm sorry, I just can't." She began to cry in earnest.

"But I'm telling you—"

"I've thought about it. Believe me, I've thought about it. But it's just part of who I am. It feels wrong to me. I can't go to bed with a man I'm not married to."

"Yes, I know. But I'm not—"

"Don't you see? I can't stay here and watch you be with another woman. It hurts too much!" She buried her face in her hands.

366

"Anne... You're doing it, again."

"What? What am I doing?"

"That thing where you don't let me finish a sentence. You don't fight fair. It's my turn to speak."

"Okay, but if you—"

He halted her words with a forceful kiss, holding both of her arms securely in his hands. He withdrew his lips, and she tried to remember what she was going to say.

"You can't—"

He kissed her again, swallowing her words. His hands moved behind her head, tangling in her hair. This time his kiss lingered. He pulled back gently, his lips lightly caressing her mouth.

"Ready to let me talk again?"

She nodded, licking her swollen lips.

"I do want you in my bed. But I want you there every night for the rest of my life."

Her heart doubled its pace. "Are you... Are you asking me to marry you?"

"Well, sort of. Part asking, part begging, part demanding. Whatever will get you to agree." His sparkling blue eyes were full of hope. "So will you?"

"No. Absolutely not." Anne felt her insides churning as her heart fought against what she knew was right. "I won't have you making some rash decision you'll regret for the rest of your life."

He pulled a ring case from his pocket. "I don't make rash decisions. I told you, I'm a very careful man."

"You'd ask me to marry you, just to sleep with me? That's ridiculous! You'd regret it afterward. Heck, I don't even remember what to do anymore."

He smiled lasciviously. "I'd be happy to jog your memory. But that's not why I'm asking you to marry me. Don't you remember our conversation about this... in Switzerland? I told you exactly what I wanted in a wife."

He moved his head lower to catch her downcast eyes. "I said I wanted someone I wouldn't be bored with after six months. And I wanted someone that would be fun to grow old with. Someone who'd help me to be the best man I can be. And someone who needed me as much as I need her."

He pressed his lips in a gentle caress on her cheek. "That's you. Don't you know that? Can't you see? There's no one else in the world who'd be more perfect for me."

"But—"

"Now, the only question is—am I the someone for you?" He bit his lips, waiting for an answer. But she closed her eyes and squeezed out another deluge of tears.

"Okay. That wasn't quite the reaction I was hoping for…"

Somehow all her emotions seemed to be flooding her mind at once. She couldn't stop her tears long enough to speak. So Steven scooped her up into his lap and held her tightly, as if she might decide to flee again.

Finally the tears slowed, and she attempted to speak. "I… I've worked so hard to convince myself th-that it could never ha-happen. It just doesn't s-seem real."

"Do you remember your list? The one from Switzerland?"

She shook her head.

"Well I remember—I memorized it. You wanted someone who'd love your girls, and I do—I already love them. And you wanted someone to hold you when you cry. And I've done that—I even like doing it. But you also wanted someone with integrity and someone you could trust. I know that's me. But the question is, do you?"

Could this be real? Maybe she was only hearing the things she wanted to hear.

"I think so. I want it to be true. I need to be sure, though… Are you saying you love me?"

"Love is such a small word for what I feel. For the first time in my life, I have a reason to breathe. I'm enchanted with every part of you I know, and I only know a small part so far. I plan to spend the rest of my life searching out every hidden enchantment in your body and soul. And I'm going to cherish and protect you with every fiber of my being. So, do I love you? No… I lovelovelove you."

Even as her heart continued to pound, warmth spread throughout her entire body. What was that feeling? She'd felt it before…. When she'd married Tom. When her girls were born… *Joy.*

He smiled, his dimples deep and his eyes bright with hope, reaching out to brush a tear off her cheek. "So now, will you marry me?"

368

She grinned. "Well… I don't know. Let me look at that ring first."

He laughed, holding the ring case above his head, just out of her reach. "Trade ya."

"For what?"

"I'll let you have the ring, if you agree to marry me next Saturday."

"There's no way. Why the rush?"

"Because," he said, stretching out on the limousine seat and pulling her on top of him. "I don't want to *wait*. I don't think I *can* wait any longer than that. One more week, *tops*. I think I've shown a great deal of self-restraint with you, but I have my limits."

She felt his hard body pressed against the length of her, and she felt a now-familiar tingle deep inside. His hands edged up the outside of her thighs, pushing her dress hem out of the way. But before his fingers reached her hips his hands flew to her waist. Now his hands caressed their way up her sides, his thumbs rubbing on the sheer silk panels. She gasped for air. Had she been holding her breath?

Now he shifted beneath her and his mouth nuzzled her neck, sending chills down her spine. He flexed his muscles and pressed against her, igniting a fire in her center.

"Yes!" she said, breathing rapidly. "A week sounds great. Plenty of time. Maybe we shouldn't wait so long."

She moved her lips to his and kissed him. This time she was not tentative and shy. Her mouth was hungry and her lips couldn't get enough of him. She stroked her tongue against his and groaned with pleasure. Her body ground against him as if she could somehow get closer. Suddenly, he pushed her off and sat up, depositing her beside him.

"Whoa! I don't think you've forgotten much, after all. But I'm never going to make it a week if we keep doing that."

They sat alongside each other, dazed and panting, waiting for their hearts to slow.

Finally Anne said, "But what will Gram say?"

He laughed. "Gram? I imagine Gram is busy patting herself on the back right now. She knew I'd hurry up when she threw Evan into the mix."

"Gram wanted you to marry me? I don't believe that. She would never try to trick me like that."

"Sweetheart, you're so gullible, that's not a very difficult proposition. And you haven't known Gram as long as I have."

"What about my dad and the girls? I can't throw this at them in a week's time."

"Yes, I know. That's why I talked to them on Monday. Emily took the computer to the hospital so I could Skype with your dad." He gave a lopsided grin. "I was so nervous. I'm glad he couldn't see me sweating."

She giggled at the thought. "And Dad said okay?"

"Actually he made me tell him all about myself for about ten minutes before he said yes," he said with an astonished laugh. "It turns out your dad has never heard of Gherring Inc. either."

He continued, tapping off points on his fingers. "So, Charlie's got a flight booked. Emily says the Fort Worth Arboretum would be a good place for the wedding—"

"Wait… Wait a minute. You planned the whole wedding on Monday? With my daughters? Before you even asked me? I was still dating Henri."

"I know. I appreciate you finally broke up. Saved me from having to kill the guy. Murder can be so messy."

He pantomimed wringing Henri's neck, and she began to chuckle, laughing until she had to suppress a snort.

"Where is this limo going?" she asked.

"Nowhere. I told him to drive in circles until we decided."

This time both of them started chuckling.

"But what about work? What will people say?" Anne imagined facing all her co-workers after denying their relationship with such vehemence.

"Soon *everyone* will know… You're sleeping with the boss."

Chapter Nineteen - Company Pool

"Mom," said Emily. "You can't wear gloves and a coat over your wedding dress."

"Why would you plan an outdoor wedding for me in December when you know how cold-natured I am?"

"Sorry, I didn't get to consult with you. But Steven gave us strict instructions not to say anything."

"Do you know how hard it was to keep it a secret? Well, it was hard for me. Maybe Miss Perfect didn't have any trouble," Charlie complained.

"What would you have done if I'd turned him down?"

"Mom, we knew you were in love with him." Emily exchanged a glance with her sister.

"Really, Mom," said Charlie. "It was so obvious. I think you were the only person who didn't know."

"That's not true."

"Well, what did the people at work say when you told them?" Emily asked.

"Yeah, Mom. Were they shocked?"

"I'm sure some of them were shocked..." She racked her brain. Surely she could think of someone who hadn't suspected.

"Sam!" she proclaimed. "Sam was surprised. She thought Steven was dating Ellen."

"What do you expect from a girl who uses a boy's name?" Emily teased.

"Hey!" Charlie aimed a shoe at her sister.

"Anyway," said Emily, "the point is we knew you'd say yes. But poor Steven... I think he was planning on asking you Monday night. And then at lunch you pulled that stunt with Ellen, and messed everything up. I think he cut it kind of close, waiting until last Saturday."

Charlie said, "Mom, I think maybe there's a lot of stuff you never told us. Care to fill us in on a few details? Like, hmmm, was last Saturday the first time he ever kissed you?"

"Oh… Look at the time," Anne said. "We'd better finish getting ready."

"Eventually, we'll find out what really happened." Charlie grinned.

There was a knock on the door, and they heard a man's muffled voice. "Time to go!"

"Coming, Dad," said Anne.

It all felt a bit surreal after they arrived at the Arboretum Japanese Garden. She could see people sitting in white chairs and hear the light melodies of classical music. When the cello started playing Bach's Prelude in C, her dad said, "That's our cue. Are you ready, Annie?"

Anne took her father's arm, the unbroken one, and they started down the hill toward the small gathering.

"You look very beautiful, you know," he said, his voice cracking a little.

"Thanks, Daddy. You look so handsome in your tuxedo." She grinned up at him. "You know, maybe we should find a wife for you, too. You've been alone an awfully long time."

He chuckled. "I'm an old dog—too old. No new tricks for me."

"We'll see."

"You're shaking. Are you cold or nervous?"

"Just cold."

Her words were a lie. She was scared out of her wits. What on earth was she doing? She couldn't get married at her age. How could she get used to living with someone when she'd been alone for so long? What would they do during holidays? What if he lost interest after a few months?

Then she saw him. Steven Gherring was standing at the front, waiting. He had eyes for no one but her. And she could see it in his expression—he treasured her. This was a man she could trust. He would take care of her. He would lay down his life for her. The closer she got, the safer she felt. And when her dad deposited her on Steven's arm, she knew. This was where she belonged.

"You look amazing," he whispered in her ear, brushing her cheek with his lips.

"It's not time for that yet." Charlie's words sent a ripple of laughter through the crowd.

The pastor spoke. It must have been eloquent and meaningful, but she'd have to watch the video to find out. Anne was only aware of Steven. His hand was caressing hers where it rested on his arm. The flex of his muscles against her. The adoration and promise in his eyes. Sometimes he would squeeze her hand or lean over to kiss her head. She couldn't get close enough to him. How had they managed to stay apart for so long?

He had to nudge her every time she needed to respond, and she hoped she answered correctly. He slipped a ring on her finger, and she placed one on his. They promised to love each other until death parted them. Her heart turned over in her chest at that thought. She prayed it would be a long time before that happened.

But then, her face was in his hands. And he kissed her. And she lost herself in his kiss. At first his lips caressed hers gently, and then he couldn't seem to stop. He kissed her harder, and his mouth was demanding. He staked his claim on her, and his intent made her insides quiver.

"Ah-hem!" Emily cleared her throat. "Could y'all wait an hour, please? You're still my mom."

The preacher announced them as Mr. and Mrs. Steven Gherring. When they turned to face the crowd, Steven smiled and waved at a group of people standing a distance away, behind the bridge.

"Who's that?" asked Anne.

"That's the reporters. Let's give 'em a good picture." She squealed as he scooped her up into his arms and kissed her full on the lips, to the delight and applause of the guests and other observers, alike. And then he carried her down the aisle.

*****

"Are you sure you didn't ask her to marry you after midnight?" Katie asked Steven. "I was so close to winning the pool!"

"What pool?" asked Anne.

"The company pool on when you guys would get engaged," answered Jared. "I started it and today was my day—I should win something for picking the wedding day."

"Well, you were no help to me at all," complained Sam to Anne. "I was trying to get some inside information so I'd have a better chance of winning. And all you did was pass out on me."

"That's right," Tanner agreed. "And I made the mistake of listening to Sam. My day is still another month off."

Sam said, "And then Mr. Gherring got his picture in the social column with that actress. That really threw me off."

But Anne's mouth was still hanging open in shock. "There was an office pool on our engagement?" She turned to Steven. "Did you tell everybody except me?"

Katie said, "Are you kidding? I knew way before he did. The man is clueless." She chuckled. "Well, not nearly as clueless as you."

"Even I knew," said Gary, squeezing Katie's hand. "That night you brought her to climb with Steven. He's never been so interested in belaying before. And I've never seen him show off quite as much, either. You know he doesn't usually climb without a shirt on."

Jared chimed in. "I suspected even before we went to Switzerland. Sorry boss, but it was obvious."

Steven laughed good-naturedly. "At least I wasn't the last to know. That would be Anne, for sure."

"Well it all seems pretty surreal to me," Anne exclaimed. "It's a miracle I ever got the job."

"You're right, Anne, I can't even believe he hired you. But I really thought it was funny when you didn't know who he was." Katie turned to Gary. "You should have seen his face."

"Yeah, that was the best part," Gary said to Steven. "The great Steven Gherring having to work to impress a girl."

"I was impressed. He didn't really have to work hard." Anne squeezed his hand.

"I just thank God you somehow ended up in that group of interviews," said Steven.

Katie raised her eyebrows. "Well, God might have had a little help. You should talk to Gram..."

374

Anne and Steven found Gram and Mr. Hamilton talking to Mr. Greenly and Minnie.

"Minnie," said Anne as she hugged her. "Thanks for coming. And I don't think I've even thanked you for taking care of Gandalf."

"Oh sweetie, you know how much I love that dog. And we wouldn't have missed your wedding for anything."

"So you've met Mrs. Gherring?" asked Anne.

"We met a long time ago," said Gram, with a chuckle.

"You know each other?"

Minnie smiled. "Of course. This is my Aunt Margaret. I think I've mentioned her to you before."

Anne's eyes grew large as she gawked at Gram. *"You're* Minnie's Aunt Margaret? Gram? That's incredible! I wish I'd known you were Minnie's aunt! She always talked about you. In fact, she used to tell me you wanted to fix me up with your..." the words died on her lips as she recognized the truth.

Gram's expression was quite smug. "You're absolutely right. That's why I got Minnie to ask for a copy of your resume."

"Yes," Minnie laughed. "I think I gave you some story about sending your resume to a friend in Fort Worth."

Gram continued, "And then I just had to convince Katie to give your resume to the recruiter and make arrangements for your interview."

"But..." Anne's brain couldn't form a complete sentence.

Steven asked, "What made you think she'd even agree to go to New York for the interview, Gram?"

"Minnie encouraged me to go," said Anne with an eyebrow raised at Minnie. "She said I should go for sure since Gherring Inc. was paying for the interview trip."

"Gherring Inc. doesn't pay for interview trips for executive assistants," said Steven. He turned narrowed eyes to Gram.

"I did what I had to do." Her smile was benign.

Anne began to fit the pieces of the puzzle together in her head. "You were behind it all? You knew who I was that first day? You lied to me the whole time?"

"I never lied to you, dear. You just assumed I had no idea who you were. I never said that."

"But you said we were plotting together to find a wife for Steven."

"And we did plot together."

"But Gram, weren't you trying to fix me up with Evan? You never suggested anything about Steven..."

"No, I never intended for you to end up with Evan, dear. It was always Steven. I tried subtle suggestions, but you were all fired up about finding a *different* wife for him. I had to be creative to pull it off."

"And when you bought me that dress and invited Evan to the Christmas party?"

"Humph! I just needed to light a fire under Steven to get him moving."

"Well your little fire almost got Evan killed," Steven said. "I can't believe you let Anne wear a dress like that around him."

"The dress was for *you*, Steven. And it worked quite well. You can't blame me for Evan's behavior. I didn't tell him what to do. He did that all on his own."

"And when you kept saying you didn't like Henri? Was that part of your plan?" asked Anne.

"No," chuckled Gram. "I really don't like him."

"At least we're in agreement on that, Gram," Steven grinned. "That's why I sent Michelle over there during the Thanksgiving holidays. I thought I'd kill two birds with one stone, if they got back together."

Anne looked at her husband in shock. "You never told me you sent Michelle to be with Henri."

"Sorry honey," he said, without a hint of sincerity. "But you forgive me, right?" He planted a firm kiss on her lips.

"I don't know. But I like the way you apologize."

She asked Mr. Hamilton. "And were you in on the plot, too?"

"Well, Margaret tried to explain it to me, but I don't quite understand how women think," he said with a perplexed smile. "You had me pretty confused when you dropped by the shop on Saturday morning."

"Not nearly as confused as *I* was."

Mr. Hamilton handed Anne a gift bag. "I know you don't usually open presents at the wedding reception, but I'd like to explain this one."

Anne was delighted. "It's heavy... Did you carve something for me?" She dug into the large bag and pulled out a beautiful pair of carved wood figures.

"Oh!" she exclaimed, as tears sprung to her eyes. "I can't accept this, Mr. Hamilton. This is 'Inseparable Love'. You said you were going to give it to your granddaughter."

"Well," he said with a sly wink, "soon, that'll be true." He put his arm around Gram and gave her a little squeeze.

"Ohmygosh! Y'all are getting married?" cried Anne, and she hugged first Gram and then Mr. Hamilton. Steven picked his Gram up by the waist and twirled her around.

"Put me down this instant," fussed Gram. But she was laughing in spite of herself.

"When?" asked Anne. "When are you getting married?"

"We've got to get married pretty quickly," said Gram with a straight face. "Before I start showing... People will talk."

At this, the entire group fell into hysteria.

The wedding couple found Ellen and Ben. Ellen gave Anne a sheepish grin.

"Have you forgiven me, yet?"

"I don't know..." Anne teased.

"I hated doing it. It was the hardest acting job I've ever had."

"Wow," Steven chuckled. "I didn't know I was that bad."

"You know what I mean," said Ellen. "She just looked so hurt. I felt awful. No offense, Anne, but you'd make a terrible actress. You couldn't hide your emotions at all."

"I don't know," said Steven. "She had me convinced she was done with me at the party."

"That's because I *was* done with you."

"And I still owe Ben for letting me borrow his girlfriend." Steven extended his hand. "Thank you."

"You're welcome. We're already sold out for two weeks, thanks to your support and the extra publicity."

"I'm glad. But I got the best end of the deal." Steven gave his wife a squeeze.

"I guess I don't get credit for your match with Ben, do I? You managed to get his attention without my help," Anne said to Ellen.

Ben said, "You mean *I* managed to get *her* attention. I kept asking her to do special rehearsals with me, just so I could spend time with her."

"I thought you were worried about the play, because I kept forgetting my lines every time you touched me," said Ellen.

Anne spotted Johanna and hurried toward her, with Steven trailing behind.

"Johanna! I'm so excited y'all came. All the way from Germany to Texas."

"I would not have missed it. I am surprised it took Steven so long to make it happen."

"You owe Johanna, too," Anne declared to Steven. "She was the one who came up with the plot for me to teach you a lesson at the Christmas party. Although... I did keep forgetting the plan."

"Johanna!" Steven complained. "You already knew the truth. Why were you plotting against me?"

"If I had not stirred up her anger a little, she would not have even gone to the party. Am I right, Anne?"

"Wait, Johanna," said Anne. "You knew? Why didn't you tell me before the party? Why did you make me memorize all that stuff and follow that silly plan? Why didn't anybody just tell me?"

"Anne, dear, you still had not admitted to yourself you were in love. I had to get you to that party and force Mr. Gherring's hand. I knew if he saw you with another man, he would quit his little charade with Ellen."

Steven said, "It almost backfired when Anne ran away. It's a good thing I'd already enlisted *Rayna* to keep an eye on her and report back to me."

He laughed as Rayna and Antonio came up behind Anne to give her a hug.

"Rayna—you traitor," Anne teased her friend. "Seriously, that night, I was really mad at you."

"I know. But it's not like Mr. Gherring told me he was in love with you. I'd never have been able to keep that a secret. He just told me he was worried about you getting in trouble since, you know, you're not really a New Yorker."

"And I was helping her," said Antonio, "because it turns out keeping track of you was a full time job."

George and May waved the newlywed couple over. "You look beautiful, Anne," said May.

"Yes, May cried through the whole wedding," said George. "My handkerchief is sopping wet."

"Now we've got you matched up, we need to get back to work on Spencer," said May.

"Has he said anything more about Emily?" Anne asked. "Because she's not telling me anything."

"I heard that." Emily sneaked behind her mom, wrapping her in a hug. "No meddling, Mom."

Charlie said, "Oh, I think Emily deserves a little meddling, Mom. Remember, she actually talked to you on the phone after she talked to Steven, and didn't breathe a word about his plans."

"You knew, and *you* didn't tell her either," Emily accused her sister. "You just didn't have my great acting skills, so you didn't answer her phone calls."

Anne turned aside to Steven and said quietly, "Hope you're prepared. This arguing goes on all the time."

Charlie said, "We're not arguing. It's just friendly banter."

"No, it's a quarrel, and I'm winning," declared Emily.

"No, it's a battle of wills, and I can last forever," Charlie countered.

"It's a mêlée and the reset of us are innocent bystanders. Have mercy!" Anne complained to Steven. "You see what I mean? They're constantly provoking each other."

"Like me and Evan?"

"No, that's more like mortal combat," Anne said. "Have you forgiven him yet?"

"For getting handsy with my wife? No!"

"Well, to be fair, I wasn't your wife, yet. I wasn't even your fiancée."

"*You* were the one who wasn't being fair. Teasing him with that dress."

"I didn't want to buy it—Gram picked it out."

"Well, from now on, you can only wear it in front of me. Although, I won't promise I'll let you keep it on for long."

*****

"Haven't we been here long enough?" Steven whispered in her ear as they sat at the table. "We've already had cake and toasts and thrown the bouquet. What are we waiting for?"

"Everyone's having a good time visiting."

He reached under the long tablecloth and fumbled with her skirt until his hand found the bare skin of her knee. Her eyes opened wide as he began to slowly edge his way up her thigh.

"I'm thinking they could have a good time without us," he breathed into her ear.

Her face heated, first from embarrassment, and then from the sparks that began firing in her nervous system.

"Steven!" she warned in a harsh whisper.

"What?" His voice was innocent, but his hand continued its slow progression. "We're married now, and no one can see what I'm doing under the table cloth. You only need to keep a straight face."

Her eyes closed and her breathing increased. She grabbed his hand.

"I can't control my expression when you touch me."

"I know."

"So you can't do that here!"

"I know. That's why we need to leave now." He kissed her ear and trailed his lips down onto her neck.

Anne attempted to push him away. "Steven, people can see you."

"Then take me some place where they can't see me," he urged while his hand attempted to move closer to his goal.

"Okay, okay!" she said, attempting to keep her expression neutral. "Just say something. Make some excuse."

He stopped the advance of his hand, and smiled victoriously. "It's a deal."

He stood and tapped on his wine glass to get everyone's attention, pulling her to her feet. She hastily adjusted the skirt of her dress.

"Ladies and gentlemen, friends and family. Thank you all for coming to share in this time of celebration. We hope you'll stay and talk and eat and dance for as long as you'd like. But I've waited fifty years to find this woman—my perfect match! And now... We're going to go make up for lost time!"

The crowd chuckled and applauded, while Anne's face flamed. But Steven swooped her up effortlessly once again into his arms and carried her away.

"I don't think you quite understood my intent when I asked you to make an excuse," she told him over the noisy approval of the guests.

"Well, let's make sure you understand *my* intent." He grinned at her as he walked. "I intend to take you to the hotel room. Shut the door and lock it. Then I intend to slowly strip off these clothes, starting with this dress. And I intend to kiss each parcel of skin I expose when I undo the buttons on the back."

"Steven, you can't talk about it."

"Of course I can. Then when the last button is undone, I intend to slip it off your shoulders and let it fall in a puddle on the ground. Then I'm going to feast my eyes on you, while you stand in whatever lacy little underthings you have on."

"What if I have on a girdle and granny panties?"

"Then I will rip them off with my teeth and burn them so you can never wear them again," he promised, waggling his eyebrows. "Should I stop and buy some matches?"

She giggled. "No, you were right. I've got lacy little things on under here."

"I *knew* it!" He groaned, stopping to place her on her feet and, drawing her into a kiss. He pulled her against him and pressed his hips so hard against her she gasped.

"We'd better hurry!" She took his hand and pulled him along behind her.

"Wait." He laughed. "I haven't finished telling you what I'm going to do. You know, after I take off those lacy underthings."

They made it to the limousine and crawled into the back. She sat down and patted the seat next to her, but Steven knelt on the floor in front of her. He lifted her foot and took off her slipper.

"What? No spike heels?"

"No, I decided against them. I'm somewhat better at walking in heels now, but you tend to keep me slightly off balance anyway."

"I thought I'd give you a little demonstration of that thing where I kiss your skin as I expose it," he said, lowering his mouth to her foot.

"Not my foot!" she exclaimed, trying to pull it away.

"Just trust me, I promise not to tickle."

He held her foot firmly, and pressed gentle kisses on top of her toes. Then he slid his lips on the top of her foot to her ankle. He softly touched his tongue on the inside of her ankle.

"I love the way your skin tastes," he declared. She watched his progress with hooded eyes.

He pushed the trailing dress upward as he slid his lips up the shin of her leg toward her knee. His hands caressed her calf softly, sending chills up her spine. Then he repeated the process on the other leg, until she was practically melting off of the seat.

"I don't want you to stop. You haven't even touched me above the knees, and I'm already going crazy."

"I know," he said, his breathing heavy. "Watching your face is making me crazy, too."

He dropped her foot and seated himself beside her, leaving her to mourn the loss of his touch.

"I'm not going to let our first time happen in the back seat of a car." Then he chuckled. "Maybe the fifth or sixth time, though... It's pretty fun."

"I'm kind of nervous," she admitted as he began unbuttoning her dress and applying the promised kisses.

"Why are you nervous?" he asked between kisses as he worked his way down.

"Well, because... look at you." He stopped his ministrations to stare at her.

"What about me?"

"You... your body... I mean no one really has a body like that. Your... your chest and your stomach—they're all muscles, and you

382

don't even have any fat anywhere. How can I compete with that? I'm afraid you'll be… you know, disappointed. You've been with younger women, and I'm afraid when you see me—"

He turned her and stopped her from speaking with a possessive kiss.

"Watch what you say. Don't start criticizing my wife." He kissed her again, and his mouth slid down her neck. She moaned and lifted her chin. His lips wandered down to her chest and his tongue explored the tender skin peeking out of the bodice of the dress.

"Now these breasts," he said as he ran his fingertips along the lacy plunge of the neckline. "I haven't actually seen them yet. But I have lain awake at night fantasizing about them and agonizing over not possessing them." He kept gliding his fingers gently back and forth, sliding them slightly under the edge of the lace, as her breath became shallow panting. Suddenly, he withdrew his hand, and she cried out in protest.

"Your body is mine now, and I love every bit of it. And now, I'm going to make love to every bit of it—every square inch of skin—until I've propelled every doubt from that worrying brain you have."

He kissed her again, plunging his tongue deep into her mouth and plundering her mind. Her legs started to give way beneath her, and he held her against him tightly. She was acutely aware of his hard body rubbing against her sensitized skin and pressing against her.

"And then when I've held out as long as I can…" He ground his hips against her and let out a little groan. "Actually, that may only be about a minute from now, the way things are progressing," he chuckled.

"But when I finally get to make love to you…" He held his face close to hers and gazed at her, his clear blue eyes, shining with affection. "You'll never doubt again you are perfect for me. That we fit perfectly together. That you were made for me."

He kissed her again. "And you'll have just a tiny glimpse of how much I love you."

*****

The sun was peeking through the curtains of the hotel room. Anne and Steven lay in a tangle of sheets, her eyes closed, her head resting on his arm, her body pressed against his. Drowsy, tired, content, blissfully happy. That's how she would describe herself. Was it really true? Was she really married to Steven Gherring? She looked at his sleeping form. Yes, it was true. And he loved her. He'd proven it to her. Over and over and over. And *over*. Perhaps she'd made him wait too long, after all. He seemed determined to *make up for lost time*.

Her mind drifted. She'd started out looking for a little adventure and ended up with a whole new life. Mrs. Steven Gherring. What could possibly be next? Travel. Meeting lots of new people all over the world. Helping Steven with his work. And he'd promised to make the girls a big part of their lives. He'd already offered Emily a job at Gherring Inc., although she was fussing about needing to prove herself.

But Anne still had work to do on the matchmaking front. Her girls needed husbands. And she hadn't found anyone for Spencer, or that sweet young man who played sad guitar music in the subway station. Who else? Hmmm...

"Michelle!" She sat up in bed, her mind alert with excitement.

"What?" Steven rubbed his sleep-heavy eyes. "What about Michelle? Is she here?"

"No, of course not. I just realized... Michelle would be perfect for your cousin, Evan."

He frowned until understanding dawned on his face. "I see I have work to do." He threw back the sheet and gazed at her with a wolfish grin. "I'm going to drive all thought of my cousin from your mind."

And he did.

Turn the page for the Bonus short story, *The Best Is Yet to Come* , the prequel to The Best Girls Series and an introduction to the high-powered world of Steven Gherring. Includes the interview with Anne Best from Stephen's point of view.

The characters and events portrayed in this book are fictitious. Any similarity to real persons, living or dead is coincidental and not intended by the author. To the extent any real names of individuals, locations, businesses or organizations are included in the book, they are used fictitiously and not intended to be taken otherwise.

The Best Is Yet to Come
by Tamie Dearen

Introduction

ONCE UPON A TIME IN NEW YORK CITY, there lived a rich and handsome prince. He worked hard every day, accumulating more and more gold for his kingdom. But when he stopped to survey his wealth and accomplishments, he always felt a sense of emptiness. His grandmother, the queen, knew the prince would never feel complete until he found his one-and-only, always-meant-to-be, lovely, delicate-but-strong-enough-to-stand-up-to-him princess. Although he had attended many balls, he had never discovered his Cinderella. By the time the prince had reached the ripe old-age of fifty, he had given up hope of locating her, and he had resolved to live alone forever with only his gold to keep him company. But the queen grandmother believed in fairy tales and happy endings and refused to accept her prince grandson would be forever cursed to live without knowing true love with his beautiful princess. And so, she meddled in his life...

Chapter One

STEVEN WAS IN THE ZONE, pushing his body to its limit. Sweat was glistening on his bare chest, dripping from his face. At the end of a two-hour ride on his training cycle, he reveled in forcing his body to submit, despite the pain and fatigue. As the tone sounded, indicating he'd met his goal, he exited the bike, toweling off while his heartbeat gradually slowed to normal.

He noted a number of surreptitious appreciative looks from various females working out near him, all of them at least fifteen years his junior. He knew he was in remarkable shape for a forty-nine-year-old. Like everything in his life, his approach to exercise was total discipline. He was careful with his diet, kept alcohol to a minimum and exercised five days per week. Six months of every year his training became more intense as he prepared for the Ironman competition. As a result, his six-foot-three frame sported broad shoulders with a tapered waist, every muscle sculpted from a variety of training, including running, swimming, cycling, and climbing.

In the elevator his cell phone vibrated, and he fumbled with his gear to answer it, knowing his friend would panic if he failed to answer. "Hey, Gary. I'm on my way up to the apartment to shower, and then I'll be ready to go."

"Great! Pick me up at nine? The grand opening is at twelve, but the ribbon-cutting is at ten. And thanks to you, there'll be plenty of press-coverage."

"Just doing my part, buddy."

"I'm still pretty nervous. I know it's not much to you, Gherring, but I've sunk everything I've got into this climbing gym."

"Come on, Gary. I've never made a bad investment. I wouldn't be putting my money into Climbing High if I weren't positive of the outcome. Quit worrying so much."

He laughed. "I'll be there in thirty minutes, and you can give me a pep-talk on the way. Oh, and *my fiancée* will be there, of course."

"You mean, *my personal executive assistant*, Ms. Carson."

"Not for long," Gary reminded him. "She says you still haven't hired a replacement, despite having two rounds of interviews."

"There weren't any good candidates." Irritation crept into his voice, despite his efforts to keep it hidden. "It'd be much easier if Ms. Carson kept working for me and we found a secretary for you at the gym."

"Steven... It's not happening. Katie's coming to work with me at the gym as soon as we get married, whether or not you find a new executive assistant."

"This is the thanks I get for introducing you to her?"

"I refuse to feel sorry for you. You own Gherring Inc. You're a billionaire. You can afford to hire any executive assistant you want."

"I don't want a new assistant."

"Okay, Gherring. That's the problem. You hate that for once in your life you're not getting exactly what you want."

Steven knew it was partially true. He liked controlling every detail of his life. He needed control. He seldom met a challenge he couldn't bend to his will. But the truth was he enjoyed the challenge. He liked the stimulation of conflict and competition. But he also liked winning.

"We'll see," he said, dismissing Gary's argument. "I need to take a shower now. We can talk about our options later."

"Gherring!" Gary's voice was annoyed. "This is not open for discussion."

"Sorry, gotta go," Steven said, disconnecting the call. He smiled to himself. Surely he could talk Katie into remaining at Gherring Inc. as his executive assistant. Maybe if he offered another raise. He had no intention of giving in on this one, even though Gary was his best friend. He planned to win, and he never failed.

As Gary predicted, a huge crowd had gathered in front of Climbing High, including a fair number of the press corps. Gherring was accustomed to media attention. It seemed the public was always enamored with news of the dashing billionaire's activities, no matter how mundane. But this event had attracted the mainstream media due to the presence of other important officials, including the mayor of New York City, and Alicia Esparza, a rising young prosecutor who was currently running for District Attorney.

Gherring felt a touch on his arm and turned to see Alicia sliding in beside him, her hand nestling in the crook of his elbow.

"Good morning, Steven." She flashed a smile toward the multitude of cameras.

"Morning." Gherring gazed out toward the crowd even as he spoke from the corner of his mouth to the woman at his side. She was tall, standing only a few inches shorter than him in her four-inch heels. Her glistening long, almost black hair framed huge exotic tawny eyes. Her sleek movements were almost feline in nature. She was also smart, driven, cold and calculating. With her fearless confidence, she would no doubt flourish in politics. At the age of thirty-two she was already a rising star in the New York City political machine.

"How are the polls?" he asked. "Have you taken the lead over Hastings yet?"

"Not yet." Her eyes never left the cameras. "But I have a plan."

Now she turned an adoring expression his way. "Are you going to the benefit for Mercy General Hospital tonight?"

"You know I am. It's my fundraiser. But I'm escorting someone else tonight. My publicist always arranges those things for me." He glanced at her and laughed. "Is that look for me or for the cameras? Are you trying to start a rumor we're having some sort of affair?"

"Maybe I'd like it to be more than a rumor." She put on a pretty pout. "And I talked to your publicist, but it seems you have some sort of silly rule against escorting the same woman to more than one event."

"Yes. I've found that works best. A second appearance with a single woman leads to speculation and false expectations."

"I totally understand, but I have a proposition for you." Her smile was dazzling.

"I don't think I'm interested." He kept his voice bland, refusing to rise to her bait.

"And I think you're lying. I think you're intrigued. You're at least interested in hearing what I have to say, even if you decide to turn me down."

He considered this idea for a moment. "Perhaps I'm curious enough to listen to what you have to say. But know this... I *will* turn you down." He pinned her with his most chilling stare, but she didn't flinch. Her inscrutable expression fascinated him.

"We are so much alike, you and I." She glanced at the cameras again and then turned her head to kiss him on the cheek. He barely managed not to draw back.

"I'll talk to you tonight." She chuckled as she slipped away to talk to the mayor.

Gherring hated these black-tie events, but at least tonight's fundraiser was for a cause he cherished—a new children's wing at the hospital. Although he detested the necessity for attending, he was completely in his element, making speeches, shaking hands, hobnobbing with the socially elite and powerful. Even as he mixed and mingled with the rich and influential, he knew he couldn't relate to anyone present. He was likely the wealthiest person at the event, yet he didn't really care about the power and prestige that came with that affluence. He never socialized with any of these people outside of public events. He had no interest in climbing social ladders or attaining political influence.

On the other hand, he did enjoy the luxuries his money afforded and the adrenaline rush associated with competition. But his business had grown to the point where he seldom had any true challenges at work. He found himself relishing the rare moments when he encountered someone who didn't bow easily to his intentions. He seldom met anyone who would stand up to him, thus he was curious to hear Alicia Esparza's proposition.

He glanced at the girl on his arm. She was tall and pencil-thin with straight blond hair. A model whose popularity was climbing, she wore her fashionable dress with confidence. She was incredibly attractive—stunning, in fact. Until she spoke.

"Ste—ven," she gushed. "This is sooooo nice. And it's sooooo nice that you're raising money for the children's home."

"You mean the children's wing."

"Oh yeah! The children's wing. What exactly is it for? I mean, like, are there going to be children living there?"

"It's a treatment center at Mercy General Hospital." He glanced at his watch... Fifteen minutes—the night had just begun, and he was already losing patience with his uninspiring escort. "Excuse me. I see someone I need to speak with."

He abandoned her with relief, crossing the room to join the small group surrounding Alicia, who was speaking with fervent animated gestures. On his approach, the circle opened, allowing him a respectful space.

Alicia lifted a brow in his direction as she finished her tirade and made an excuse to speak with Gherring. "Where's your date?" she asked, taking his arm and leading him away from the crowd. "What's her name again?"

"Darian," he said, looking over his shoulder. "She's over there, flirting with the paparazzi."

"What's her last name?"

"Darian." A wry smile slipped onto his face. "She told me her name was just Darian. She said she was like Madonna. She only has one name."

"I see," she said, noncommittally. "Sounds like a real winner. I can certainly see why you'd want to come with her rather than risk being seen with me again."

He rolled his eyes. "I'll admit this time my publicist's choice was less than optimal. She's... she's a bit..."

"Vapid?"

"Yes, that's the word. But still, my policy affords the protection I need, if not always the optimal companion for these tedious events."

She stopped walking as they reached a secluded alcove. "Ah, yes! Your policy... That's what I want to speak to you about. I want you to consider suspending your policy for a bit. I think it could be to our mutual advantage."

"I'm listening," he said, all of his defenses on high alert.

"My campaign manager informed me that settling down with someone respectable might be enough to swing the election for me." She paused for effect, "And I think you and I would make a great couple."

He laughed—he had to admire her audacity. "I'm not sure I qualify for respectable. And what exactly do you mean by 'settle down'?"

"Well, that's open for discussion. For starters, go with me to the Black and White Charity Ball next Saturday night. And before you tell me you've already got a date... Just call your publicist and have them cancel with whatever insipid girl he's arranged an escort."

"The next one might not be insipid. Didn't he make the arrangements for me to escort you to the American Cancer Society banquet?"

"So, he got lucky one time," she quipped. "Wouldn't you rather have a sure thing?"

"What's in it for me?"

She smiled, squeezing herself against his arm. "Surely, we could make our evening *mutually* beneficial," she said, deepening the innuendo with her suggestive tone.

"An interesting offer... And I hope you won't be offended when I turn you down. But I don't need to change my policy to find someone to warm my bed."

In truth, it had been some time since any woman had interested him enough to risk the repercussions, but that wasn't her business.

"Before you say no, consider all the possible benefits. Consider I'd be a good long-term partner." Her intense gaze burned into his eyes. "I'll be honest with you. The DA position is just a springboard for me. I have much higher aspirations. Together, we would be a daunting couple. Your money and influence, my talent and charisma! Plus..." When she continued her voice was husky, "I could keep you *very* satisfied in the bedroom, and our progeny would be both beautiful and intelligent."

Steven smiled in spite of himself. "And I thought no one was as impudent as I. That's quite a step from an evening at the ball."

"So, you'll consider my proposal?"

He hesitated. She was smart and attractive. He examined her attributes with undisguised appraisal, while she smiled without embarrassment. Yes, she was extremely attractive. Most men would jump at such an offer from a woman like her. But there was no spark, no thrill at the touch of her hand. Still... How much longer should he delay, waiting for some woman who was probably non-existent? For more years than he could remember, he'd dated one beautiful woman after another. But none had held his interest for more than a few weeks. Now, at almost fifty years of age, he found himself alone, with no prospects, still waiting for a relationship that would stimulate him as much as the challenge of turning Gherring Inc. into a multi-billion-dollar company.

"I'll go to the ball with you." He crossed his arms. "That's all I'm promising."

"Look, Steven. It's the end of September now, and the election is in November. What if we just went to all the obligatory functions together until after the election? I'll make it worth your while." She gazed up through her lashes, her lips half-parted, full and inviting.

"I'll go to the Black and White Ball with you next weekend. That's it. Take it or leave it."

"But you'll think about the rest?"

A sigh escaped. "I'll think about it."

Her smile was radiant. "Steven Gherring... We're going to make beautiful music together."

Chapter Two

"Happy Birthday!" said Gram, as she arrived at Steven's office door. "Where are you taking me to lunch?"

Steven shook his head ruefully at the diminutive gray-haired dynamo that was his ninety-five-year-old grandmother. "Gram, I have work to do. I can't just leave right now."

"Certainly you can. What will happen? Will your boss fire you?"

He chuckled. "I just might fire myself if I mess up this deal at a critical time."

"Your deal can wait," she said in a firm, no-nonsense tone. "I'm hungry now. And we have things to talk about."

Gherring was already rising from his desk to follow her, surrendering to her inescapable persistence.

"Anyway, it's your birthday. You knew I was coming," she complained, walking briskly out of his office. He followed her obediently onto the elevator, nodding to Katie as he passed her desk.

"But I thought you were coming for dinner. You surprised me, showing up early."

"Well, this is a very important birthday. Your fiftieth. Half a century. More than half of your life is over."

"Thanks Gram." He couldn't help the sarcasm that crept into his tone. "You sure know how to cheer a guy up."

"The critical point is you still don't have a wife."

"Gram. It's my birthday. Please don't start with that."

"I'm ninety-five years old. I don't have much time left in this world, and—"

"I know," he pre-empted her oft-repeated line. "You refuse to die before I get married. Gram, you may just have to live forever."

"No. I've decided you've had enough time to find a wife on your own. I'm going to find one for you."

"Gram!" he growled, towering over her five-foot frame. "You'd better not try to interfere."

Unimpressed, she glared up at him with her arms crossed. "You've left me no choice." The elevator opened and she marched toward the lobby doors, forcing him to trail behind her.

"You certainly have a choice." He struggled to keep up with her rapid strides toward the waiting limousine. "You can mind your own business."

Her serene expression belied her words. "That's exactly what I intend to do."

"What does that mean?" he asked, as warning bells chimed in his head.

"It means just what I said. I'm going to take care of my own business. And in this particular case, it means finding you a wife. In fact, I've already got the ball rolling."

"Well, you can just put the stops on that ball. I don't need your help. In fact, I may have a possible candidate."

"Who?" she asked, her brows knitted with suspicion.

"Just a woman I know. We've been out once. I'm just considering the possibility." He hoped his vague answer would satisfy his intimidating grandmother, halting her certain-to-be-disastrous plans.

"She's not the one," Gram declared.

"You don't even know her," he objected.

"I can tell by the way you're talking about her. She's not the one."

"Gram, first you want me to find a wife. Then you shoot down the one I'm considering before you know anything about her."

"I *wanted* you to find a wife. I've been telling you to find a wife for the last thirty years. You had your chance. Now it's my turn."

"Whom do you have in mind?"

"No need for you to worry about it. I'm handling all the details."

"Gram, need I remind you I'm a grown man who runs a multi-billion-dollar company? I won't tolerate your interference. And if you show up here with a woman who's been promised I'm going to marry her, she'll be in for a rude awakening. It's not happening. In fact, I'm telling you right now, I won't even go out on a date with her," he said, bombing her with a dark scowl.

The blithe smile on her face alarmed him despite the acquiescence in her words. "Yes dear."

"I mean it, Gram!"

"Yes, dear. Of course, dear. But, I have a present for you."

His eyebrows flew up. She usually didn't buy gifts since he invariably already owned everything he needed or wanted. "What is it?"

She handed him a small box, complete with gift-wrap and a bow. "Thanks, Gram," he said, planting a kiss on the top of her head. He quickly unwrapped the present, uncovering a small jewelry box. He lifted the lid to find a diamond ring with a large square center stone set within a ring of smaller diamonds.

"It was mine. Your grandfather gave it to me as an anniversary ring the year you were born. He died shortly after that." Her eyes misted. "I haven't worn it for a while, and I want you to have it."

She held up her hand as he started to object. "Even if you don't get married, I want you to have it. You can do what you like with it. Of course, I hope you'll use it as an engagement ring, or have it remade into one of your choosing. But if not... You can make it into a tie-tack or whatever you like."

Steven wrapped his arm around her small shoulders. "Thank you, Gram. This really means a lot to me."

"Good." She returned to her standard gruff tone. "You're a good boy, Steven."

"I'm not a boy, Gram," he said good-humoredly.

"You may be a man to all those people who work at Gherring Inc., but you'll always be my little Steven. And that's why I know it's not good for you to be alone."

He groaned, "Not again..."

*****

Gherring arrived at the Town Center Office Building at seven forty-five Friday morning. This was a game he played for his own amusement. Officially, the Gherring Inc. business day began at nine a.m. But Gherring enjoyed appearing a little early and lounging near the elevators to watch the employees arrive. As a result, the

398

employees began to come earlier, in an attempt to beat their boss to work. So, Steven began gradually pushing up his arrival time, and the employees correspondingly arrived earlier as well. Yet, he knew when he was out of town the entire company reverted to their normal start time.

It wasn't much, but it provided a bit of distraction in a life that had become increasingly dull. He wondered if Gram wasn't right, after all. He almost regretted he'd concentrated on business to the near-complete exclusion of his personal life. He couldn't help feeling something was missing. And now, Gary, his only true friend, was getting married. He knew he would feel even more isolated after the wedding, despite Gary's insistence nothing would change. And not only was Gary going to marry Katie Carson, but he was also planning to steal her away from Gherring Inc. Steven hoped he could influence her to stay.

"Good morning, Ms. Carson," he said.

"Morning, Mr. Gherring. I've confirmed your appointments for today."

"Thank you, Ms. Carson. You're efficient, as always. What do you and Gary have on the agenda for the weekend?"

Her face became animated. "We're working on addressing wedding invitations. At least I hope I can get Gary to help me. He's constantly down at Climbing High. I swear he might as well sleep down there."

"I'm glad to know he's putting in maximum effort to make our investment a success. But I never had any doubt."

"I'm looking forward to working there with him. Otherwise, I might never get to see him."

"So, about that... I've been thinking perhaps if I offered you a raise, you might be persuaded to stay here and find a new secretary for Gary. Obviously, you're much more valuable in your position here—"

"Mr. Gherring. I'm only staying here until after the wedding. We've been through this before."

"But, I'm prepared to offer a significant raise. How much would it take to convince you?"

"Mr. Gherring, I'm not changing my mind. I'm not irreplaceable. There are plenty of qualified candidates. We have another round of interviews on Monday. If you'll simply choose someone, I'll have plenty of time to train them before January."

"They're all simpering idiots." He'd already thought this through and made up his mind.

"They are not! I've even brought in people with business degrees who're willing to work as your executive assistant to gain experience."

"I don't want someone who simply wants to use this job as a stepping-stone."

"You're so difficult to please. Most of the candidates were experienced executive assistants, and every single one was smart, probably smarter than I am."

"Experience isn't everything. Personality is important. None of them were compatible with my personality."

"*No one* is compatible with your personality," she snapped. At his stormy expression, her face paled. "I'm sorry, Mr. Gherring. I didn't mean that." She rubbed her furrowed forehead. "If you'll simply have an open mind about Monday's group of interviewees, I'm certain you'll find your ideal secretary."

Gherring couldn't help but wonder about the truth of her statement. Perhaps there was no one with whom he'd ever be truly compatible. But in his mind, he was applying her words to his yearning for love. Maybe he could be satisfied with a more civilized union, instead of a passion-filled marriage. Perhaps a marriage to Alicia Esparza, more of a business agreement, would be good enough. In fact, it was probably the best he could hope for, though the thought didn't set well with him.

"Not a secretary—a *personal executive assistant*. And what if I don't like any of them?"

"You will—you have to." Her reply was firm and left no room for negotiation. "I have the resumes. Would you like to look over them today?"

"No," he said, with defiance still in his voice.

Katie moaned her frustration before changing the subject. "Oh, about tomorrow night. You have the Black and White Charity Ball, remember?"

"Yes, and you contacted Mr. Cooper about canceling the escort?"

"Yes, I did that on Monday, as soon as you told me." She hesitated. "So you're going on a second date with Ms. Esparza?" She couldn't hide the curiosity in her voice.

"Yes." He refused to elaborate to sate her inquisitiveness.

Katie remarked, "She's very beautiful, but..."

"But?"

"It's none of my business."

"You're right. It isn't." At the hurt in her eyes, he regretted his harsh reply, but he made no move to apologize as he turned to stalk into his office. Perhaps he should hire a male executive assistant. Women were entirely too difficult to control.

*****

Everyone who was anyone in New York City attended the Black and White Ball. The event raised money to help families of police officers and firemen who were injured or killed on the job. It was a perfect opportunity to see and be seen. Although no campaign speeches were given, every candidate in the local races was present, and all were taking advantage of the opportunity to work the crowd and gain free publicity from the plethora of reporters at the fundraiser.

Alicia Esparza was no exception. Gherring couldn't help but admire her ability to attract and hold the rapt attention of the small audience surrounding her. He recognized the skill since he possessed it himself. Her evening gown was carefully chosen to be attractive, yet not overtly racy. Her ample assets were highlighted, but not openly displayed. She artlessly flicked a lock of her dark hair over her shoulder to join the thick shining mass. She didn't cling to him, a trait he greatly appreciated. But when the dancing started, she arrived at his side.

"Dance with me?" She pressed a chaste kiss to his cheek.

"Certainly," he said, sweeping her into a waltz on the as yet uncrowded dance floor. They moved together smoothly and flawlessly.

"We fit together well," she remarked.

"You mean, on the dance floor?"

"I mean we fit together. *Everywhere.*" She emphasized her point by pressing her body closer to his.

He couldn't ignore the pleasant sensation of her uninvited advances. She was soft in all the right places, and her eyes spoke an open invitation.

"Have you been thinking about my idea?" she asked.

"Not really," he lied smoothly. He'd certainly been considering her proposal, but he had no intention of making a commitment. As an astute businessman, he knew not to tip his hand.

"Tell me what your objections are, and I'll change your mind," she said, with the assurance of one who was accustomed to winning arguments.

"First of all, there are too many possibilities in your offer. Which proposal are we discussing?"

"Let's start with the easy option. You've really got nothing to lose by agreeing to date me exclusively until after the election."

"But I do have something to lose. There's my reputation to consider. I don't do exclusive..."

"So you're worried you might lose your status as a player? Wouldn't that be an improvement to your reputation?" She laughed.

"Only if I cared about anyone's opinion where that's concerned. And I don't. My reputation as a player protects me from unwanted complications. I value my freedom."

"But dating exclusively also protects you from unwanted advances," she reasoned. "In fact, you'd be even safer."

"Perhaps... I would be safer from other women, but not from you."

"But you don't need protection from me."

"Au contraire. You've already expressed an interest in marriage."

"Only as one of many acceptable options. Yes, I will need to settle down and get married to advance my career. But, it doesn't have to happen with you." She chewed on her lower lip, "My initial need is simply five weeks. I only mentioned the long-term option in case it was more to your liking."

"So you aren't interested in marrying me?"

"I didn't say that." She stifled a laugh. "I'd be a fool not to be interested. I had to at least make the offer. But, my main concern is my career, and I think this is a trait we have in common. Through the election, a short-term relationship would serve just as well as long-term."

402

"I think I know the answer to this... But, why me?"

"Are you fishing for compliments?" she teased. "Seriously, though. It's probably not for the reason you think. There are other handsome single men with money and status, but all of them have either been embroiled in messy divorces or break-ups or caught in embarrassing situations with drugs, alcohol, or some other type of scandal. Your reputation is unblemished. The only thing you're guilty of is dating hundreds of different women, none of whom seem to be able to claim your behavior was unseemly."

"Interesting point," he admitted. "So my reputation as a hermit has earned me this unforeseen offer."

"I wouldn't call you a hermit," she soothed. "I would say you're... discriminating."

His hearty laugh drew a few curious stares. "So the question is, 'why would I want to change now?'"

The music changed, and Alicia used the opportunity to wriggle her body closer to his, moving her arms to link around his neck as they swayed in time to the music. Her perfume wafted upward, sweet and appealing. He could feel her heart pounding against him."

"Of course you told me you don't need what I have to offer," her breathy voice entreated. "But then again, you don't know what you're missing. Perhaps you might find I'm worth the small, temporary sacrifice of your freedom."

He was disappointed when he experienced only mild curiosity in response to her advances. He'd hoped he might find her irresistible and exciting. Perhaps it was because, like all the others, she was offering herself so freely. He longed for the thrill of the chase, the challenge of the fight, the exultation of winning.

"You also don't know what you'd be gaining. You might be disappointed."

She gazed at him with hooded eyes. "I highly doubt it. And I'm willing to risk it."

He heaved a heavy breath. "Listen, Alicia..."

"Wait. I know when I haven't made a good enough closing argument to win my case. Don't make a decision yet. Okay, Judge Gherring?" Her eyes twinkled. "You're being entirely too serious about this. Let's just agree to one more date. I have a fundraiser event next Friday night. Are you available?"

"I have to check my calendar. But, I don't know—"

"Steven, please! I'm not even upset you're rejecting my not-so-subtle offer, although I think we'd have had a really good time. I'm not some innocent, insecure girl. Just don't say no yet."

"I don't think it's a good idea for you to continue to pursue me if you need someone who'll commit to you through the election. I just can't guarantee that."

"What if I promise to look at other options? My campaign chairman believes this last week of speculating about our possible *affiliation* has helped me rise in the polls already. You could give me one more week. And who knows? You might even change your mind."

Steven didn't really think he would change his mind. But on the other hand, maybe he needed to be realistic about his options. As a potential wife, Alicia was ideal. Intelligent. Attractive. Poised. Charismatic. And she had a very practical approach to their relationship—mutual benefit. With Alicia Esparza, he wouldn't have to deal with a woman sobbing and crying about how he'd ruined her life and broken her heart. He chuckled to himself. In fact, if he ever actually fell for her, she would probably break *his* heart.

"Okay," he said. "I'll give you one more date, and I won't say no yet."

She squeezed her arms around his neck, nuzzling against his chest. "Judge Gherring, I think you've made a wise decision. Can we seal the agreement with a kiss?"

"For the benefit of the photographers?" he asked.

"Well, yes," she admitted. "But for my personal benefit as well. Just one kiss?" She lifted her lips toward him, and he obligingly lowered his mouth to capture hers. Her kiss was warm, passionate, and full of unspoken promises. His body responded to her, despite his efforts to remain aloof. He pulled away before their embrace became more ardent.

"That wasn't too awful, was it?" She maintained her composure, even as her breath came in little pants. "But, I suppose you like to always be in control, right?"

"Something tells me we have that in common."

"Yes, I suppose that's true. But I think it would be an interesting fight to determine the winner. Don't you?"

404

Steven didn't answer, instead regarding the cameras flashing in their direction. "I think you have your publicity in the bag. I hope you get the desired boost to your ranking. It might just backfire on you, you know."

She chuckled. "I don't think so. I know how to play the press. Now, if you dump me, I can always play the damsel in distress."

"But if they really knew you, they'd never fall for that."

She laughed, a melodic and happy tune. "Steven, I like you more and more. I sincerely hope our relationship extends beyond our next date."

Chapter Three

GHERRING IGNORED THE STACK OF RESUMES Katie placed on his desk when he arrived at the office Monday morning. He had bigger problems.

"What do you mean you don't have time to travel to Germany, Henri? What pressing engagement is preventing you from attending to business?" His voice was dripping with sarcasm.

The handsome Frenchman regarded him with open disdain before answering in heavily accented English, "I will not listen while you talk down to me. I have the matter under control. There is no need to travel to Germany to close the deal. I have already talked extensively with their CEO. She will not back out, I assure you."

The blood vessels were pulsing in Gherring's forehead. He rubbed it, wishing for some ibuprofen.

"Henri, sleeping with the CEO does not count as having the matter under control. She called me yesterday. Extremely upset! It seems she thought you were interested in a long-term relationship."

His face paled. "*Mais, non*! I never said such a thing."

"And yet she believed it to be true. So now, the question is, what are you going to do about it?"

"Perhaps it would be better if you were to go," Henri suggested. "I would not want to fuel such dreams."

"Oh, no. You started this, and you'll finish it. And you'd better not mess up this deal in the process. I think your father would agree with me on this."

Henri looked irritated. "You do not need to involve my father in this. I will take care of it." He started toward the door, but turned back to face Gherring. "Soon my father will pass the company to my control, and you will not be able to use him as a threat against me."

Gherring glared at him. "Your father is an astute businessman, and Gherring Inc. has enjoyed a profitable association with his company, La Porte. But you're forty-eight years old, and he hasn't turned over the reigns to you yet. I think he's still waiting for you to grow up, and I wonder if it will ever happen! Have you ever considered it might not be a good idea to sleep with every woman you meet?"

He had the audacity to laugh. "*Non*! No! I am only giving them what they ask for. It would be rude to say *no*. But you cannot criticize me for this. You are just like me."

"No Henri, I'm not like you." Steven sincerely hoped his words were true. But he knew he'd been less than discriminating in his younger days. Still, he reasoned, he'd never mixed sex with business. On the other hand, he knew he couldn't claim innocence in such matters. The realization made him even angrier.

"Ms. Carson!" he spoke into the intercom. "Monsieur DuBois will be making a detour on his way back to Paris. Please make a reservation for him on the next flight to Frankfurt."

"Yes, Mr. Gherring."

Shortly after Henri departed, Katie knocked tentatively on Gherring's door.

"Yes, Ms. Carson?" His head was pounding as he attempted to tamp down his still-revving temper.

"I'm sorry, Mr. Gherring. But Mr. Murphy is here about that matter we discussed earlier."

Steven felt his blood pressure rising as he massaged his temples. "Send him in."

Jeff Murphy entered the room, his expression arrogant and challenging. He strode casually to Gherring's desk and stood looking down at him from his six-foot height, his arms crossed casually across his chest. Why did every meeting today have to be a confrontation?

"Have a seat, Mr. Murphy."

"I prefer to stand."

Gherring rose to his full height of six-foot-three and leaned over his desk. "I asked you to sit, Mr. Murphy. It seems you're making a habit of flaunting my rules."

Cowed, Jeff sat down, although his entire demeanor remained in full scowl. "I've been falsely accused," he said. "I told Human Resources, already. I'm the victim here."

"Mr. Murphy," said Gherring, carefully controlling his voice. "Are you aware of the No-Tolerance Policy for sexual harassment at Gherring Inc.?"

"I'm telling you, I didn't do anything! That b—" He caught himself before the word left his lips. "That *woman* was lying."

As expected, the pig showed no sign of remorse for his actions. Growing up with Gram, Gherring had learned to have no respect for a man who took advantage of a woman sexually. Why hadn't he recognized these Neanderthal tendencies before he hired him?

"Mr. Murphy," Gherring repeated. "Are you aware of the No-Tolerance Policy for sexual harassment at Gherring Inc.?"

"Yes, but I didn't do anything! She's trying to ruin my reputation. She's just mad because we went out a few times, and now I've broken up with her."

"Her story is much different, Mr. Murphy."

"But there were no witnesses. It's her word against mine."

"That, Mr. Murphy, is the only reason you're still sitting in my office at Gherring Inc. rather than being escorted from the building. Consider yourself on probation. If you so much as blink in Ms. Latham's direction, you'll be terminated."

"But I'll see her every day in the break room." Gherring could see his anger in the flexing muscles of his jaw. He had no sympathy for the man after hearing Ms. Latham's testimony. Unfortunately, he didn't have enough evidence to fire him, but he would be watching him closely.

"Then you will need to take your break in your office. And further, you are not to be alone with any female employee at this office, at any time, for any reason."

"You can't control whom I see on my time off!" Gherring knew from his defiant attitude it would only be a matter of time before Jeff stepped across the line again.

"You're right, I can't control it. But if I find out you're alone with another female employee, even if you're sharing a cup of coffee, you'll be terminated."

"This isn't fair! I didn't do anything."

"What you didn't do is your job. You've made zero progress on the Bern merger, and I want that wrapped up before the holidays. Get your work done, Mr. Murphy."

"But I'm still saying you can't keep me from dating employees on my own time. There's no company policy for that."

"You're incorrect, Mr. Murphy. Our No-Tolerance Policy clearly states that in the case of any accusation, founded or unfounded, a no-dating policy will be enforced for the duration of employment."

Jeff sagged in his seat. "Fine. I'm not interested in anyone here anyway."

"Additionally, I want a report on my desk Friday morning concerning your progress on the Bern merger."

"Friday morning? I can't make any progress by then. Our business hours don't even coincide."

"I suppose that means you'll have some very early morning phone conferences. Perhaps you'll need to go to sleep early as well. The change of schedule could be good for you." He held his stare with the intensity born of a head-splitting migraine, until Jeff finally averted his eyes.

"Jared is supposed to be working on that deal, too," he contended.

"But Jared is new. You have the lead on the Bern merger, and you're responsible for the report. So don't try to push this off on him. This is your assignment." He turned his attention to his computer. "That will be all, Mr. Murphy," he said, without looking up.

Jeff made a comment under his breath, and left the room. A moment later, Katie entered with a glass of water and four ibuprofens.

He shook his head as he accepted her offering with gratitude. "Ms. Carson, how am I ever going to replace you? How did you know I had a headache?"

She chuckled. "Perhaps the fact you were holding your head with both hands when I glanced in the room a minute ago clued me in."

"Still... No one else would notice. And Gary doesn't need you like I need you." He tried to bat his eyes and look like a sad puppy.

Her eyes rolled around in her head. "Mr. Gherring, it won't work. I've enjoyed working for you... well, most of the time... but I'm leaving in January when Gary and I get married. But don't worry—I promise to train your new executive assistant to watch for signs of a headache."

When she left him alone, he laid his head on his arms and closed his eyes. He refused to think about losing her. He hated breaking in a new assistant. Why had he introduced her to Gary? He was losing his best buddy and his secretary at the same time.

Gherring heard Katie's voice on the intercom. "Mr. Gherring? Alexander Klein on line one."

"Thank you, Ms. Carson." He let out a sigh. Back to work. And he needed to be on his toes for this client. Klein was an important business prospect. Steven was extremely interested in forming a cooperative agreement with Klein's company in Germany. Although he could speak German, he knew Klein's English was flawless, so there was no need to speak Klein's language.

"Mr. Klein, it's good to hear from you."

"Please, call me Alexander."

"Great, and you can call me Steven, as well. So, you've read the material I sent you? Are you interested in further discussion about doing business together?"

"Yes. Actually, I was calling to tell you that we are planning to come to New York for your International Business Conference. My wife, Johanna, will be accompanying me."

"Yes, I remember Johanna. Your wife is a lovely woman. Please give her my regards. And you'll stay and attend the gala?"

"That is the current plan. So, we can find a time to talk privately during that week? I realize you will be very busy..."

"I will absolutely make time for a private conference. I'm looking forward to it. I'm going to connect you to Ms. Carson to schedule a time right away. My calendar is pretty crowded."

Satisfied prospects were good with Alexander, Gherring attacked his unanswered emails, determined to eliminate the task from his to-do list. He worked through lunch and was still engrossed when Katie came into the office with a determined expression.

"Mr. Gherring. It's almost time to begin the interviews. Have you looked at any of the resumes?"

"No," he replied, without glancing up from his computer. "I've been busy with more important things."

"Mr. Gherring." He glanced up to find Katie conjuring a stern expression. "There's nothing more important right now than these interviews."

He scowled back until she dropped her gaze. "Please, Mr. Gherring. Just give them a chance."

He pressed on his temples. Was his headache coming back? He gave in to the inevitable. "Bring the first one in."

Katie pushed open the heavy doors and called out a name. Gherring heard her heels tapping out a confident rhythm as the candidate approached the doorway, but he ignored her as he flipped through her resume and attached letters of recommendation. He didn't bother to look up, even after he'd finished perusing her papers. Instead, he went back to his emails, ignoring her presence altogether.

Katie said, "You can have a seat, Ms. Whitley. Would you like something to drink while you wait?"

This was a part of Gherring's routine. He liked to see how potential employees responded to uncomfortable situations, to test their poise and composure.

"No, thank you." Her voice was confident. Unruffled. Well, he'd see how long that lasted.

"Ms. Hartley, why do you want this job?" He deliberately called her by a different name to test her reaction. His eyes rose from his desk to fix her with a stare. She was a thin, beautiful blond, with flawlessly applied makeup. Her suit-dress was the perfect choice for an interview at a prestigious company. She looked... too perfect, he decided. This one was too perfect. She wasn't real. His gut told him if he hired her, she would surprise him with some nasty personality trait at a later time. He dismissed her without another thought, but he had to get through the interview.

She paused, flummoxed by his use of the wrong name. He saw her mind racing, trying to decide on the correct move. She decided to ignore the blunder, and answer his question.

"Mr. Gherring. I've studied Gherring Inc.'s prospectus thoroughly. I admire you and everything you've accomplished through this company. I would love to be a part of your work. I feel I'll be up to any challenge you present. Essentially, it would be a chance to study at the feet of greatness."

"I see."

He stared for a full thirty seconds of silence before turning back to his computer to answer a few more emails. After more uncomfortable silence, he looked up again, as if surprised to see her still sitting there.

"And why do you want to leave the job you have already. You're currently working for Barnes and Graves? Is there something wrong with your current job?"

"No sir, Mr. Gherring. I just feel this is an awesome opportunity. The kind of opportunity I can't afford to miss."

"And are you prepared to leave Barnes and Graves with a two week notice?"

"Yes sir. Absolutely sir."

"But what if they haven't found a replacement in two weeks? Will you leave them high and dry?"

"No sir. I mean, yes sir. I mean... I'm sure they can find someone to replace me."

"So you think you're easily replaced? Non-essential? Not very valuable?"

"No, I just think... I'm..."

"How much would you expect to be paid?"

"Well, the job description said the pay was commensurate with experience. And I've been an executive assistant for six years."

"So, what do you think you're worth, Ms. Hartley?"

"It's not..."

"Yes, Ms. Hartley?"

"I think I'm worth at least eighty thousand per year, but I would take the job for sixty."

"Very well." He spoke in a bored tone, carefully avoiding Katie's eyes. "That will be all. Ms. Carson. Will you see Ms. Hartley out?"

When Katie shut the door behind the interviewee, she marched to Gherring's desk with her hands on her hips.

"You'll never find someone if you keep this up. You didn't give her a chance. You were rude, and you called her by the wrong name, and you goaded her."

"Yes, I know. I'm not a very nice man, Ms. Carson. I need to know if my new personal executive assistant can cope with the fact." His smug response drew her ire.

"That's not what you're doing. You're just trying to sabotage these interviews. But, it's not going to work. At the end of this day, you need to choose someone. Either from this set of candidates or from the other two sets you've already interviewed." She fumed at him until he imagined steam pouring from her ears.

He regarded her with amusement. He seldom managed to ruffle her calm demeanor. He certainly would miss her if she left to work with Gary.

"Yes, Ms. Carson. Please don't yell at me." He winked and grinned.

The wind went out of her sails immediately. "You make me crazy! I can't wait to get out of here and work at Climbing High."

He pretended to be hurt. "But won't you miss me? Even a little?"

"Yes, Mr. Gherring," she answered, her cool control back in place. "But I'm going to leave you, anyway. No matter what. So you'd better take these interviews seriously."

"Of course, Ms. Carson. I always take my job seriously. You can send in the next candidate."

Katie called another interviewee into the room. Once again, Gherring refused to acknowledge the girl's presence until he had studied her cover letter, resume, and letters of recommendation. When he raised his eyes to the candidate, he found she was still standing before him, having refused to take the chair Katie indicated.

"Would you like to be seated?" he asked.

"Thank you, sir," she answered, her voice so soft he had to strain to hear her. Her eyes were wide and staring. She sat down slowly, feeling her way into the chair, never taking her eyes off him. What was that emotion he saw? Was it fear? Awe? He expected his employees to respect him, but he couldn't imagine having a personal assistant who became catatonic in his presence.

"Tell me about yourself, Ms. Everett." He opted to use her real name since she already appeared to be rattled.

"It's an honor to meet you, Mr. Gherring," she spoke, her voice almost a whisper.

"I'll need you to speak up just a bit, Ms. Everett. Can you tell me why you want to work at Gherring Inc.?"

"I just can't believe I'm really standing here," she said. "It's so surreal."

Steven decided he liked her better when he couldn't hear what she was saying. He returned his attention to his computer to answer another email. Then he turned back to the girl who still wore the same shocked expression.

"When would you be available to begin working if you were hired?"

"I could start right now!" She smiled with excitement. "Do I have the job?"

"No, Ms. Everett," he corrected, quickly. "I have to conduct the other interviews before I make a decision. Thank you, Ms. Everett." He nodded to Katie, who ushered the stiff gaited girl out the door.

"Okay," Katie said, ruefully. "I admit, that one was a dud. But the next one looks better."

He glanced at the top of his stack. "Enoch Grant? You really think I want to spend all day every day looking at a male secretary?"

"Don't try to pretend you're the kind of boss who choses a secretary for her looks. I know better."

"Perhaps not, but it does make my day more pleasant."

"I'm sorry Mr. Gherring, but I happen to know from my investigation you've had male executive assistants in the past."

He smiled. "Okay, I admit it's true. But I still maintain it's not my preference."

"Well you have two men to interview today. So, remember to keep an open mind."

Katie went to the door and called in the applicant. Once again, Gherring ignored him completely while he studied the components of the resume. This one had impressive credentials—too impressive. Even a Masters Degree in Economics. He wouldn't stay in the job for more than a year.

"Mr. Grant," he said, glancing up to find the man studying the diplomas on his office wall. "Are you quite through with your tour?"

"Excuse me, Mr. Gherring," he said, with a beaming smile. He moved to the desk with long, confident strides. "I couldn't help myself. I didn't know you had a degree from Columbia Law School. That's awesome." He held out his hand. "Enoch Grant. Nice to meet you. I know, Enoch is a strange name, but I'm kind of a strange guy so it fits. What would you like to know about me? I've got a Bachelor's degree in Business, and a Masters in Economics. I just got out of school, so I don't have much experience, but I can learn quickly. Oh, and I'm a whiz with computers. I really can do most anything you need around here. And I'm willing to work long hours, because I don't have a family or a girlfriend, even. Really, is there anything else you need to know?"

Gherring chuckled to himself and shook his head. "Mr. Grant, I'm going to refer you to personnel. If you just graduated, I think we have an internship available in our CMA department. If you succeed there, you'll have a chance at a long-term position."

"Are you kidding me? Just like that? Are you serious about this? Because I was willing to be a slave secretary for years just to get a foot in the door."

"Mr. Grant, you're overqualified for this position, and frankly it would be a waste of my time and resources to hire you as an executive assistant. But I've seen enough to predict you'll do well in CMA."

"Thank you, sir! Wow! This is the best day of my life!" He pumped Gherring's hand a few more times before allowing Katie to direct him to the personnel department.

The afternoon continued, until Gherring had dispensed with the last resume on his stack. He sat back in his chair and steepled his fingers on his chest.

"Ah, Ms. Carson. It seems we've come to the end of our possible candidates, and none of them are suitable for the position. Perhaps we should table our efforts until after the wedding. Although, I would say Ms. Jones could be a perfect fit for Climbing High."

"There's one more applicant." Katie handed him a single sheet of paper.

"I don't have time to interview another applicant." He refused to accept the paper from her hand. "We'll have to reschedule for another day. It's already five o'clock." He scowled and began to pack his briefcase.

"This one came from out of state. And she's been waiting for her turn since one-thirty. You'll simply have to stay and do the interview now."

"Fine!" he growled. "But I'm going to have a cup of coffee, first."

"But, she's been waiting all afternoon," Katie objected.

"Ms. Carson, a cup of coffee, if you please. With the mood I'm in right now, she won't want to meet me until I've had a cup of coffee." He glared at her until she placed the paper on his desk and moved to pour him a cup of coffee. He felt the blood throbbing in his head again. The ibuprofens had obviously worn off.

Unbidden, his eyes roved to the sheet of paper lying in front of him. Surely, this was a joke. The resume had more personal information than work experience. It was an older woman, according to the birthdate, forty-five years of age. Her education consisted of a Bachelor's degree in Chemistry. And she currently resided in Weatherford, Texas.

He smiled to himself. This would be fast and easy, and she'd be on her way back to Texas. And then he'd convince Katie to remain as his assistant. He had this under control.

Chapter Four

"OPEN THE DOOR, MS. CARSON. But, I'll call her in." Gherring decided he would make quick work of intimidating this woman, thus putting an end to this interview and this interminable day.

"Ms. Best!" he called out, in his most authoritative voice. Then he picked up a file and pretended to study it carefully, while ignoring her presence as he had all the others. There followed several minutes of tedious silence, during which time Katie refilled his coffee cup. The applicant was so quiet he wasn't certain she'd even entered the room. But he resisted the temptation to lift his eyes from the reading material on his desk.

He heard Katie say, "May I offer you some refreshments, Ms. Best? Coffee? Tea? Water?"

Oh, no. He didn't want the woman to be comfortable. He wanted this interview to end quickly. He frowned at Katie.

"That won't be necessary, Ms. Carson. Please, leave us alone."

"Yes, Mr. Gherring," Katie murmured, turning to leave the office. He knew she would leave the door open for propriety, but the woman would feel more unsettled if she was alone in his presence. He still refused to make eye contact with the applicant, but his side vision told him she remained standing.

"Wait," the woman spoke in a sharp tone. "Uhmm... Ms. Carson? Please wait. *Yes*, thank you. I would *love* some water."

His eyes flew up. The woman had countermanded his orders. Albeit, in a captivating Southern accent, she had nonetheless spurned his authority with her words. She stood with her back to him in defiance, waiting for Katie to respond. He took the opportunity to peruse her form. She was tall and slender, with thick brown hair. Her clothes weren't very impressive, but she had a nice pair of legs.

Runner's calves he surmised. To his surprise, he felt a bit of attraction. But he couldn't let that stop him from putting her in her place.

Katie was still standing by the door, frozen in place. She was probably waiting for him to erupt. But he held his temper back, as he spoke in a sarcastic tone.

"Well, Ms. Carson, what are you waiting for? Please retrieve some water at once for our honored patron, Ms. Pest."

The woman swirled around quickly and spoke with an acid tongue, while her body trembled with fury.

"My name is Anne *Best*. And I can see this interview is a waste of my time and a waste of your resources. Sorry to have inconvenienced you."

But when she locked eyes with him, his heart lurched in his chest. The woman was glorious in her anger. Her large, chocolate-brown eyes flashing passionately, while a few unruly brown locks escaped from their confining barrette to frame her face. She had a small, pert nose with high cheekbones. Her beauty was natural. He could detect little in the way of makeup, as opposed to the perfectly powdered, flawless faces of the previous applicants. He found himself studying her lips, and wondering if they were as soft and pliant as they appeared. He also wondered if she would kiss as passionately as she'd defended her name.

Suddenly, her entire demeanor changed. She began to blink at tears, mumbling, "Sorry. It was a mistake to come." Before he realized what was happening, she was trying to push past Katie. She was leaving. Before he'd even had a chance to talk to her.

"Wait!" he called out. Still she continued her retreat. He was moving toward her now. He had to stop her. He summoned all of his authority and placed it in his voice, "I said, *wait!*" This time she hesitated, and he reached her just as she looked over her shoulder.

"Please." Now he softened his tone. "I meant to say, *please wait*." He touched her elbow to guide her back into the room. His hand felt sparks where their skin met. He resisted the urge to pull her into his arms and hold her against him. He felt the need to comfort her, repenting of his efforts to cow her into submission.

"Please, Ms. Best, would you come back and sit down? I've obviously started off on the wrong foot with you. I've given you a bad impression."

He led her to sit down in front of the desk and motioned for Katie to bring water. Feeling satisfied he was back in control of the situation, he said, "And you've given me an *interesting* impression as well."

She flashed a grateful smile at Katie as she took the proffered water in trembling hands. He found himself jealous the smile wasn't directed at him. He tried to analyze her behavior. There was only one explanation. She didn't recognize him. She didn't realize she was interviewing with Steven Gherring. He hid his delight at the thought. It would be fun to watch her face when she realized who he was.

"Shall we begin again?" he said. "Do you know who I am, Ms. Best? Let me introduce myself. I'm Steven Gherring. I'll be interviewing you today for the position of my personal executive assistant."

He waited for the information to sink in. But instead of the surprise and embarrassment he expected to see on her face, her expression was blank. She gave him a fake smile and stuck out her hand.

"Pleased to meet you Mr. Gherring. My name is Anne Best."

He was confounded by her response. "Perhaps you've heard my name before," he suggested. But she denied his claim with a shake of her head. "Well, I'm sure you know of my company, Gherring Inc.?"

"Do y'all make car parts?"

"No. I'm afraid not. We're an international trade company with holdings..." His voice trailed off as realization flooded his consciousness. "You mean you really have no idea who I am? No idea at all?" He noticed Katie standing near the coffee pot, struggling to control her mirth.

"Well, no. I'm sorry. The recruiter just said y'all were in the Town Center Economic Tower, on the top floor."

"Yes," said Gherring with exasperation. "That's because we, or I, *own* the tower. I'm the chairman of Gherring Inc."

It was preposterous. Amazing, but preposterous. This woman who'd somehow captivated his interest in a matter of minutes had no earthly idea who he was. The one time when he would have been glad to use his fame to secure her attention, his notoriety had no effect whatsoever. He'd never felt so powerless.

"Nice to meet you, again, Mr. Gherring." She smiled sardonically. "You've probably heard of me as well. Anne Best? Sole owner of a twenty five hundred square foot home in Weatherford, Texas?"

He closed his slack jaw with effort. For the first time in his life, he had no idea how to proceed. "You're not what I expected, Ms. Best."

"Neither are you, Mr. Gherring." She clapped her hand over her mouth. He watched as a myriad of emotions flashed across her face. When two bright red spots appeared on her cheeks, she grabbed her glass and gulped the water so rapidly she began to choke.

"Are you alright, Ms. Best?" He thought to pound her on the back, but decided she might run away again if he attempted to touch her.

She nodded furiously, while obviously trying to regain her composure.

Gherring picked up the paper Katie had presented him before the interview. "Let's talk about your qualifications for this job. You have a B.A. in Chemistry, and you worked part time as a travel agent. Hmmm...."

He stared at her resume. Then he flipped the single page over to see the blank backside.

"You don't seem to have any actual experience as a personal executive assistant. Am I missing something, Ms. Best?"

Her eyes flashed with anger again and she propped her hands on her hips. He'd seen that look on Gram's face before, but no one else had dared to look at him like that.

"Well, if a personal executive assistant is someone who organizes someone's life and work, acquires all the needed tools and supplies, keeps the person's schedule, finds calm in the midst of chaos, and works countless hours in a thankless job... What you really need is a mother, and I have twenty-three years of experience!"

A painful silence fell on the room. He contemplated the woman, Anne Best, who sat a few feet away from him. He was at a loss. What was he supposed to do about her? She really had no qualifications for the job. But if he didn't hire her, she would walk out of the office, fly back to Texas, and he would never see her again. Something told him he would regret it for the rest of his life if he let her go.

420

Finally, he broke the silence. "Well, Ms. Best..." He spoke in a deliberate voice, but he couldn't quite hide the hint of a smile. "You make an interesting argument. Perhaps you're just what I need. It might be an absolute disaster. But somehow, I think I'd always wonder what would've happened if I didn't give you a try."

He warmed at the thought of having her near him every day. She would be tempting and trying, complicated and obstinate, sweet and gentle, alluring and aloof. Anne Best would be many things, but she would not be boring.

"You'll begin in two weeks on Monday at eight a.m. sharp. There will be a three-month trial period. Please talk to Ms. Carson about the details. Thank you."

He immediately turned his attention to his laptop, pretending to read and answer emails. He maintained a calm, unperturbed appearance, even as he felt his heart racing. He felt... What was it? He felt challenged. He felt anticipation. He felt *alive*.

From the corner of his eye he saw her stand up. She remained standing in front of the desk, as if she were waiting for him to change his mind. After several moments, he looked up, his eyes locked with hers in a powerful, magnetic gaze. He stood up unhurriedly, moving carefully so as not to frighten her. He leaned across the desk and reached out to touch her hand. He felt the sizzle of her touch deep inside.

"Did you want to say something else, Ms. Best?" He bit his lip to stop himself from laughing at her startled expression.

She jerked her hand away as if it'd been burned. "No... Just... thank you. You won't regret it!" She backed away awkwardly before bolting from the room.

"I hope you're right," he murmured, watching her fleeing form.

Katie stared at him, her mouth agape.

"What? I hired someone. Are you happy?"

"Yes, Mr. Gherring. Astonished, but happy," she said, as a huge smile slid onto her face. "Now, if you'll excuse me, I need to speak to your new personal executive assistant before the clock strikes twelve and her carriage turns into a pumpkin."

Chapter Five

"I'VE RESERVED THE BALLROOM for the International Gala," said Katie as they reviewed their progress on Tuesday morning. "And I reserved a bank of rooms at the Hyatt."

"And the conference rooms?" asked Gherring.

"We have conference rooms for large presentations on Thursday and Friday. But I'm assuming you'll have your meetings here earlier in the week. That's what you've always done before."

"We did?" He was so distracted. His concentration had been shot ever since the interview with Anne Best. He kept replaying the episode over in his mind. Remembering the thrill of the confrontation. Reliving the spark of her touch.

"Yes, we did. I can't believe you don't remember."

"Okay. But we might want to reserve one larger conference room for Tuesday and Wednesday, depending on what our attendance is. How's it looking?"

"Early reservations are up twenty percent from last year, so..."

"Right. Better to have the space reserved. We can always cancel if we need to. Now about flight reservations..."

"You know, Ms. Best will be taking over some of these responsibilities. She'll be here a week before the International Business Conference. And I'm going to be out several days the week of the conference."

He swallowed hard. He'd second-guessed himself multiple times about hiring Anne Best as his executive assistant. It was such an irrational choice. He'd never done anything so spontaneous where business was concerned. He always planned and calculated, carefully considering all of his options. Yet, he'd made this hiring decision based on his feelings rather than his intellect. And later, he realized he didn't even know if she was single. Her resume indicated she had two grown daughters, but it didn't mention a husband. He assumed she was divorced, but he didn't know for sure.

"Where did you make arrangements for Ms. Best to live?" he asked, attempting to keep a casual tone in his voice.

"I assumed you'd provide the apartment as part of the package like you normally do for new employees who move from out of town. Was that correct?"

"Yes, of course. Especially since we have her on a trial basis."

Katie narrowed her eyes. "Wait a minute... You're not planning to let her go after three months and try to get me back again, are you? Because I won't do it."

"No, no," he said impatiently. "I just wondered about her apartment."

"There's a studio apartment available in my building. I assumed you'd want her there, since it's close to work."

"But, will a studio be big enough? I mean, will she have any family living with her?"

"No, her children are grown," Katie said. "That was on her resume."

"Yes, but if she had a spouse, they would probably need a one bedroom instead of a studio," he reasoned.

Katie gave him a half-smile. "She doesn't have a spouse. She's a widow."

"Good," said Gherring. Then he realized what he'd said. "I mean... good that a studio will be big enough for her, not good that her husband is dead." Katie cocked an eyebrow, but said nothing. He blundered on. "When did he die? Do we know?"

"No." Katie grinned. "We don't know when her husband died. Do you want me to call and ask her?"

"No," he spat. "Of course not. I just wondered if... if she might need counseling or something, you know, if it hasn't been long. We have insurance that covers that sort of thing, don't we?"

"I really don't know," said Katie, shaking her head, her expression baffled.

He waved his hand, with irritation. "Anyway, I've been wanting to remodel that studio. It really needs updating. I think I'll put her at the West Fifty-Seventh location for now."

"You want her in *your* apartment building? But, it's a lot farther away from Gherring Inc."

"Just until we get the other studio remodeled. Bring in the architect we used on the East End project and have him put together a proposal."

"Okay," she said her voice full of confusion. "Do you want him to do the guest apartments as well?"

"Yes, sure." His mind was already spinning. He hadn't really intended to remodel the studio, although it was probably a good idea. But he felt Anne needed someone to watch over her when she moved to New York City. She was obviously innocent and unsophisticated. New York could be a dangerous place to live. No, she wouldn't be safe living all alone in the other building. At the West Fifty-Seventh location, he could keep an eye on her and make sure she didn't get into trouble. And she'd be none the wiser. It really had nothing to do with wanting to be close to her. After all, he barely knew her. And she really wasn't his type.

Another thought occurred to him. "Do you think Ms. Best can handle this job?"

Katie laughed. "It's kind of late to ask me that question. But, yes. I think she can handle it. It's not brain surgery. The most important thing is to be able to put up with your moods."

"I don't have moods, Ms. Carson." He realized Katie was getting more and more outspoken as the time came for her to leave her position at Gherring Inc. She sounded almost as feisty as Anne Best. He liked feisty, but he'd need to be careful to nip that attitude in the bud. He couldn't have his personal executive assistant being too rebellious.

"Sorry," she said with a sweet voice. "Wrong word choice. You don't have moods. You have varying amounts of tolerance for whatever doesn't go exactly as you planned."

He grunted in response. It was obviously too late to fix Katie, but he'd do better with Ms. Best. "Let me see that reservation list..."

*****

The cameras flashed as Gherring exited the limousine. He held out his hand to Alicia. She placed her manicured fingers in his palm and rose gracefully from the seat, smiling at the press and waving her

424

unfettered hand. Her dark hair glistened in the streetlights, falling down over a low-backed evening dress with a high side-slit. The black dress, accented with beads and sequins, fell in smooth waves from a ruching on the side opposite the slit. She was striking and sophisticated, and garnered attention seemingly without effort. But effort was involved. Every move and every look was calculated for greatest effect. Her rise in the polls was impressive, due in some part to her recent association with Steven Gherring.

As she took his elbow to saunter into the fundraiser, he felt her soft warmth against his arm. He watched her scan the room as they entered and couldn't help but admire her ability to make an impression. They chatted with the mayor and his wife and other city officials who were seated at their table. While the speaker was discussing federal funding of city projects, Gherring let his mind wander.

He examined Alicia's profile. Her skin was a warm caramel color, and her lips were full. But his mind drifted to another image. Anne's undecorated face, fresh clean skin with a few visible freckles, and two large pink spots that appeared when she blushed. He couldn't help but compare Alicia to Anne, although no two women could be more different. Where Alicia was a master at showmanship, Anne possessed no ability whatsoever to hide her emotions. Every thought and feeling was plainly written on her face. As a single woman of thirty-two, Alicia was an experienced seductress, skilled and accomplished in attracting men. Anne was forty-five years of age, a widow, and a mother of two. Yet she had an aura of innocence and purity, and appeared to be distinctly unaffected. Alicia knew exactly who Steven Gherring was, and admittedly valued him for his power and influence. But when he'd met Anne, she'd had no inkling of his identity, nor the magnitude of his wealth. Yet she'd been unable to hide the flash of attraction in her eyes.

At least he hoped that was what he'd seen burning in those liquid brown pools. He could still picture her as she turned to glare at him in anger. How her soft lips opened in surprise when their eyes met, producing an instant magnetism. How her breathing became shallow and her skin flushed with heat. If only she hadn't been so nervous, so innocent, so unworldly, he would have pulled her into his arms and kissed her senseless. The desire had been almost overwhelming. No one had affected him so strongly in years. Or had anyone ever affected him like that?

Two weeks, and she would be in New York. Living in his apartment building. Working with him every day. But he would have to court her carefully. She seemed fragile. Not her personality, for she was strong and confident. In fact, she might be a bit too confident. He chuckled at the memory of her outbursts. But he could tell she was frightened by her attraction for him.

Then an alarming thought came to his mind. What if he was wrong? What if he'd misinterpreted her reactions? What if she was trembling with repulsion instead of passion? Perhaps he was too aggressive for her.

No... No, he was certain he'd been correct. She'd felt the same attraction he had. But he was sure she'd deny it, hide it, and tamp it down. Yes, he would have to play the game carefully, but he was confident he would win. He always won.

"What are you smiling about?" Alicia asked him.

With a start, he realized the speech was over. "I'm sorry. What did you say?"

"I asked what you were smiling about. You were staring at me." She leaned in close to him, intentionally allowing him a closer view of her décolletage. "I'm hoping you were thinking about what might come after dinner tonight." She smiled suggestively. "I'm still rising in the polls, and I feel like celebrating."

"I'm afraid I'm going to have to call it an evening early tonight. I have a really long training run planned for tomorrow morning."

She let her lower lip push outward. "But surely you could do that later in the day. Besides, I think I could give you a real workout. You might not need that run in the morning."

"Alicia. It's an enticing offer. But—"

"You're not interested, are you? You're not interested at all!" Her eyebrows flew up. "Something's changed since last Saturday. Who is she?"

"What? Nobody—there's no one else."

"I don't believe you. Last week you were beginning to warm up to the idea. Either someone has told you some lie about me, or you've met someone."

"No, really. Nothing's changed. I'm just tired."

"Just tired? Really?" Her voice was full of doubt. "Then we're on for next weekend?"

"Uhmm... No. I think I'll go back to being single. You can play it however you want to the press."

"I think I'll just tell them the truth," she said.

"What's that?" he asked, warily.

"That I couldn't stay with you when I knew you were in love with someone else."

"I'm not in *love* with her. I only just met her."

"Ahhh," Alicia said, smiling smugly. "I knew it."

He covered his face with his hands, groaning at his indiscretion, but Alicia laughed.

"Don't worry, Steven. Your secret's safe with me. I owe you one. I got a free boost in my ratings, even though you did a number on my ego."

"Seriously, Alicia. Any man would be crazy to turn you down."

She chuckled as she rose from her chair. "I'm just teasing. My ego's fine." She bent to kiss him on the cheek—a gentle, sisterly kiss. Then she moved her lips to whisper in his ear.

"I'll be around in case she turns you down."

And she was gone.

As Steven walked alone to his waiting limousine, the cameras flashed and a reporter stuck a microphone in his face.

"Mr. Gherring. You arrived with Alicia Esparza tonight. But now you're leaving without her. Does that mean the two of you are no longer dating?"

"That's correct. We're not dating." He started to duck into the door of his car, but the reporter pressed him further.

"Mr. Gherring. It's going to be quite a contest. Who do you think will win the race?"

He imagined the upcoming arrival of his new personal executive assistant, and couldn't suppress a grin.

"I will!"

About the Author

Tamie lives with her very romantic husband of thirty-one years. Although their daughters are grown and married, they've never had an empty nest. The house is constantly full of young people. Some are temporary residents. Some come to share meals or swim. Some just come to hang out. But the constant flow of young folks in and out of the house brings joy and excitement to the home, and inspiration to the writer.

Tamie loves all things creative: music, composing, painting, and writing. And she hates all things having to do with cleaning the house. She loves to hear from her readers.

Sign up for new release announcements and monthly gift card giveaways at *http://TamieDearen.com/Newsletters*

Follow on Facebook: Tamie Dearen Author

Follow on Twitter: @TamieDearen

Printed in Great Britain
by Amazon